BONEYARD RIDGE

BY
PAULA GRAVES

MILLS & BOON

Published in Great Britain 2014
by Mills & Boon, an imprint of Harlequin (UK) Limited,
Eton House, 18-24 Paradise Road, Richmond, Surrey, TW9 1SR

© 2014 Paula Graves

ISBN: 978-0-263-91377-4

46-1114

Harlequin (UK) Limited's policy is to use papers that are natural, renewable and recyclable products and made from wood grown in sustainable forests. The logging and manufacturing processes conform to the legal environmental regulations of the country of origin.

Printed and bound in Spain
by CPI, Barcelona

Alabama native **Paula Graves** wrote her first book, a mystery starring herself and her neighborhood friends, at the age of six. A voracious reader, Paula loves books that pair tantalizing mystery with compelling romance. When she's not reading or writing, she works as a creative director for a Birmingham advertising agency and spends time with her family and friends. She is a member of Southern Magic Romance Writers, Heart of Dixie Romance Writers and Romance Writers of America. Paula invites readers to visit her website, www.paulagraves.com.

For all the wounded warriors who put their
lives and their bodies on the line every day
to make the world a safer place.
God bless you, and thank you for all you do.

Prologue

Smoky Joe's Saloon had never pretended to be anything more than a hillbilly honky-tonk, a hole in the wall on Old Purgatory Road that served cold beer, peanuts roasted in the shell and a prodigious selection of Merle Haggard hits on the ancient jukebox in the corner.

At the moment, "The Fightin' Side of Me" blasted through the jukebox's tinny speakers, an apt sound track for the bar brawl brewing around the pool table in the corner.

Two men circled the table like a pair of wary Pit Bulls, eyes locked in silent combat. The older of the two was also the drunker, a heavyset man with bloodshot eyes and a misshapen nose, mottled by red spider veins. He seemed to be the aggressor, from Alexander Quinn's vantage point at a table in the corner of the small bar, but the younger, leaner man had shown no signs of trying to de-escalate the tension.

On the contrary, an almost frantic light gleamed in his green eyes, a feral hunger for conflict that Quinn had noticed the first time he'd ever laid eyes on the man.

His name was Hunter Bragg, and he'd finally found the trouble he'd been looking for all night.

"Come on, Toby, you know he's going to beat the hell out of you the second you take a swing. Then I'm going to have to call the police and you've already got a couple of D and Ds on your record this year, don't you?" The reasonable question, uttered in a tone that wavered somewhere between sympathy and annoyance, came from the bartender, a burly man in his early sixties with shoulder-length salt-and-pepper hair and a gray-streaked beard. He was dressed like most of the patrons, in jeans and a camouflage jacket over a T-shirt that had been through the wash a few times, dulling its original navy color to a smoky slate blue.

He was the "Joe" of Smoky Joe's Saloon, Joe Breslin, an Army vet who'd opened the bar with his savings after deciding not to re-up decades earlier when the trouble in Panama was starting to heat up. He'd packed on a few pounds and lost a few steps since his military days, but Quinn had seen him in action a few nights earlier when another loudmouthed drunk had taken the angry young man's bait and lived to regret it.

"He's askin' for an ass-kickin', Joe!" the man named Toby complained, shooting a baleful look at Hunter Bragg. "I don't care if he *is* a damn war hero."

"I'm no hero," Bragg growled, the feral grin never faltering.

"Bragg, I don't want to kick you out of my bar, I really don't," Joe said. "But if you don't shut your damn trap and stop picking fights, I'm gonna. You think your sister needs any more trouble?"

Bragg's gaze snapped toward the bartender at the mention of his sister. "Shut up."

Breslin held up his hands. "Just sayin'. She's already got enough on her plate, don't she?"

"Shut up!" Bragg howled, the sound of a wounded animal. Chill bumps scattered down Alexander Quinn's spine and, on instinct, his hand went to the pistol hidden under his jacket.

Toby took a couple of staggering steps backward until he bumped into the wall, dislodging some darts from the board that hung near the pool table. "You're crazy, man."

Bragg's head snapped back toward Toby, barely leashed violence throbbing in his tight muscles. Quinn wasn't sure if the man had come to the bar armed or not; Joe Breslin wasn't the sort of proprietor who made people check their weapons at the door. And so far, Bragg had never used anything but his fists in a fight.

But things could turn disastrous in a heartbeat, Quinn knew. He'd seen it happen too many times.

He crossed the room with quiet speed, inserting himself into the arena of conflict. As he'd hoped, his mere presence put a big dent in the tension, as both men turned their wary gazes toward him.

"Gentlemen," he said with a polite nod. "Are you still using this table?"

Toby stared at him as if he were crazy, but Bragg's eyes narrowed, his head tilting a notch to one side.

"I know you," he said.

Quinn nodded. "We've met."

"In Afghanistan?"

Quinn shook his head. "At Landstuhl."

Bragg's face blanched visibly at the mention of the military hospital in Germany where combat-injured American troops were treated until they were stable enough to return to the States for further treatment.

Bragg had spent over a week there after an improvised explosive device, or IED, had obliterated his troop transport vehicle, killing everyone else in the Humvee and leaving Bragg with a mangled leg and a head injury. Surgeons had saved the leg, though when Quinn had seen the man in the hospital in Germany, there had been some question as to whether he'd have much use of the limb again.

Now, it seemed, it was the head injury that should have caused the doctors more concern. Bragg's limp was barely noticeable these days. But he was no longer the good-natured practical joker his fellow soldiers had nicknamed the Tennessee Tornado.

"You brass?" Bragg asked warily.

"Civilian," Quinn answered.

The green eyes narrowed further, little more than slits in his stormy face. "Spook?"

Quinn just smiled.

Bragg's eyebrows rose slightly, opening his eyes enough that Quinn could read the sudden recognition in the younger man's gaze. "You're the guy who runs that new PI joint over in Purgatory."

Quinn removed his hand from his jacket pocket, producing a simple, cream-colored business card. "The Gates," he said, holding out the card.

Hesitantly, Bragg took the card from Quinn's outstretched hand. "I'm not in the market for a private eye."

"I'm in the market for employees."

Bragg handed the card back. "I've got a job."

"You sweep floors at the Piggly Wiggly."

"It's honest work."

"So's this." Quinn held up the card.

"I'm not looking for excitement."

Quinn merely lifted one eyebrow, shooting a look toward Toby, who stood next to the dartboard, watching Quinn and Bragg with a confused expression on his whiskey-slackened face.

Putting the card on the green felt surface of the pool

table, Quinn looked back at Bragg. "If you change your mind."

He left the bar without looking back to see if Bragg picked up the card. He couldn't make the decision for the man. He could only offer an option that might channel his anger in a more productive direction.

He wasn't in the business of saving people from themselves, no matter what the good folks of Purgatory seemed to think.

Chapter One

"Damn it!" Susannah Marsh looked with dismay at the jagged chip in her French-manicured thumbnail and mentally calculated whether or not she could work in a trip to the salon over the next seventy-two hours.

Nope. Not a hope in hell.

"What's the matter?" Marcus Lemonde looked up from his desk in the corner of the small office, the expression on his narrow face suggesting the query was more about politeness than interest.

"Broke a nail, and I won't have time between now and the conference to get it fixed."

"Can't you just file it down or something?" Even his feigned attempt at interest disappeared, swallowed by mild annoyance.

She sighed, knowing she'd be just as annoyed in his position. It hadn't been that long ago she'd have rolled her eyes at a manicure mishap herself. "Yeah. I'll do that." Because a perfect French manicure was so easy to achieve, especially when one nail was now considerably shorter than the rest.

How on earth had she managed to choose a career where things like manicures and stiletto-heeled shoes practically came with the job description? Lord, if the kids she used to run around with back on Boneyard Ridge could see her now…

She dug through her purse for the manicure kit she always kept with her, but it wasn't there. Had she left it in another purse? No, she distinctly remembered getting it out of yesterday's bag that morning.

And leaving it on the breakfast bar in her apartment. Damn it, damn it, *damn it!*

The resort had a gift shop at the far end of the hotel that carried things like nail files and other items hotel guests might have forgotten to pack. But she barely had time to get to her meeting with the Tri-State Law Enforcement Society's representatives, who were meeting with her and hotel security to go over last-minute plans for the conference that would start on Friday.

With a glance at Marcus to make sure he wasn't watching, she dipped her hand into her purse and grabbed the slightly bulky Swiss Army knife she also kept with her at all times. Its attached file was a bit rough for a good manicure, but it would do for the meeting. Then she could run down to the gift shop for a nail kit to do the job right.

Flipping open the nail file as she hurried down the corridor, she bit back a laugh. All this drama for a broken nail!

For the first sixteen years of her life, she'd chewed her nails to stubs and never thought twice about it. She'd owned one purse at a time, which she carried only when absolutely necessary. Skirts were the bane of her existence, baring as they did the scars of a lifetime of scratches and scrapes, and high heels were so far off her radar she'd had to spend a whole week of secret practice sessions with her cousin from Raleigh before she could navigate her way across the room in a pair.

How had she turned into such a girl?

The obvious answer was leaving Boneyard Ridge, making a new life for herself in a world where little redneck tomboys from the hills could easily find themselves chewed up and spit out before they could blink twice.

She wasn't going to let her grandmother down, the way everyone else always figured she'd do.

As she waited for the elevator to the third floor, where Ken Dailey, head of Highland Hotel and Resort's security team, would be waiting for her with three of the law-enforcement society's event organizers, she ran the coarse file across her nail, wincing as it snagged heavily on the broken edge. The friction, she saw with dismay, was doing horrible things to the French tip polish. Giving up on the nail-file attachment, she flipped open the scissors and snipped off the whole tip of the broken nail.

The elevator dinged and the doors swept smoothly open just as she snapped the scissors back into the knife handle. She quickly dropped the knife into the pocket of her jacket and pasted on a smile to greet whoever might be inside the elevator car.

There was only one other occupant, a scruffy-looking man wearing a maintenance-crew jumpsuit. His green eyes lifted in surprise as he pulled up to keep from running straight into her.

"Sorry," he said in a voice as deep as a mountain cavern. He stepped back into the elevator to let her in.

"You aren't getting out?" she asked.

"I pushed the button for the wrong floor." His gaze dropping, he reached out and started to push the button for the third floor, then looked sheepish when he realized it was already lit up.

He was a rangy man in his early thirties, with shaggy dark hair that fell into his darting eyes, making him appear to be looking at her from under a hood. He would probably be nice-looking if he didn't come across as such a sad sack, Susannah thought, torn between pity for his obvious discomfort and irritation that he wouldn't lift his head and look her in the eye.

He had spoken in a strong hill-country twang, reminiscent of the harsh mountain accent she'd ruthlessly subdued since leaving Boneyard Ridge.

"Grubby little tomboys from here don't get to live out their dreams, Susie," her grandmother had told her as she handed Susannah $400 in cash and a bus ticket to Raleigh. "You gotta learn how to make it out there in the real world."

The maintenance man let her off the elevator first when they reached the third floor. She moved ahead, trying to ignore the prickle on the back of her neck as he brought up the rear. He didn't overtake her, despite his longer legs. When she stopped to straighten her clothes before entering Meeting Room C, she spared a quick glance his way.

He kept his head down, apparently determined not to meet her gaze as he passed behind her. He walked with a strangely deliberate gait, as if each step were a decision he had to make before he committed himself to the next one. A couple of steps later, she figured out why. He had a limp.

She couldn't remember ever seeing him around the hotel before, but maintenance workers and hospitality staffers had a pretty high turnover rate. Plus, while she wasn't someone who saw the people who pushed mops and brooms as interchangeable drones, the stress and speed of her job as the resort's head events coordinator meant she didn't have the time or opportunity to get to know many people outside of her own office.

For that matter, she thought as she pasted on her best

go-getter smile and opened the door to the meeting room, she barely knew the staff in her own office, including Marcus, her right-hand man. They rarely had time for chitchat and she wasn't one to socialize with her coworkers off the clock. Or anyone else, for that matter.

She couldn't afford friends.

Four men awaited her in the meeting room, Ken Dailey with hotel security and three others. They stood in a cluster near the large picture window that offered a spectacular view of the mist-shrouded Smoky Mountains to the east.

She looked with envy at their cups of coffee but knew she didn't have time to get a cup of her own. They had business to discuss, and she was running out of daylight.

"Gentlemen, sorry I'm late," she said, even though she knew full well she was at least five minutes early to the meeting. "We have a lot to cover, so shall we get to work?"

HUNTER BRAGG STOPPED at the end of the hallway and turned back toward the meeting rooms clustered in the center of this wing of the hotel. The door closed shut behind her, and he started to relax, shoving his hair out of his face and straightening his back.

She hadn't recognized him from the news reports. He hadn't really feared she would, given how different he looked from the clean-cut Army sergeant whose abduction had been a weeklong sensation until something new came along to take over the news cycle.

Of course, he'd recognized her easily from the photo Billy Dawson had shown him and the men he'd selected for the job a few days earlier. "Her name is Susannah Marsh. She's in our way. Y'all are gonna take her out."

In that photograph, taken by a telephoto lens from the

woods that hemmed in the resort's employee parking lot, Susannah Marsh had given off a definite aura of money and sophistication. Her well-tailored suit, the shimmery green of a mallard's head, and shiny black high heels had offered an intoxicating blend of power and sexuality that had sent the other militia members privy to the plan into flights of lustful fancy.

All Hunter had been able to think about was the fact that Billy and the others—men he'd spent the last three months befriending—wanted him to take part in killing a woman just because she was in the way of their plans.

They seemed so ordinary on the outside. Billy Dawson fixed cars out of his garage for a living. Morris Bell drove a Ridge County school bus. Delbert Yarnell worked at the hardware store in Barrowville. They had wives and kids.

And a festering hatred of authority.

Down the hall, the elevator dinged and the doors swished open. A well-dressed man in a silk suit and shiny wingtips stepped out and started to turn away from the end of the hall where Hunter stood, but his gaze snapped back in his direction and he changed course, his long strides eating up the distance between them.

"What are you doing up here?" he asked, frowning.

The question caught Hunter by surprise. He didn't know this man, though he looked vaguely familiar. They'd probably passed each other in the halls at some point in the last week.

But why was this man challenging him?

The other man's nostrils flared. "You can't afford to make her suspicious of you."

Hunter blinked. This man was part of Dawson's crew, too?

"Don't worry," he assured the other man aloud. "She sees me as part of the wallpaper."

"We're making our move tonight."

Hunter's gut clenched. Tonight? Nothing was supposed to go down until tomorrow. What had happened? And why hadn't Billy Dawson warned him of the change in plans?

"I know," he bluffed. "What's the plan?"

The other man narrowed his eyes. "Billy didn't tell me to share it with you."

"I thought we were on the same side."

"Are we?"

Hunter returned the other man's skeptical gaze with a cold, hard stare of his own. "Think I'd be cleaning toilets in this place if we weren't?"

The other man straightened his tie, a nervous habit, obviously, since his tie was already immaculately straight. "Just don't screw this up."

"Wouldn't dream of it."

Without another word, the man in the suit turned and strode away from Hunter as quickly as he'd approached.

Releasing tension in a quiet sigh, Hunter turned the corner and headed for the stairs. Once he was safely out of sight, he pulled his phone from his pocket and hit "one" on his speed dial.

When the voice on the other end answered, he said, "They're moving up the hit."

"To when?"

"Tonight, as soon as she leaves the office." Muscles in Hunter's gut quivered as he tried not to panic. "It's too soon."

There was a brief moment of thick silence before the other man asked, "Any idea when she'll leave the office?"

"Going by her usual schedule, no earlier than six. Probably closer to seven."

"Any idea what they're planning to do?"

"No. I didn't quite make it into the inner circle before this all went down. I've been trying to piece things together, but—" He bit back a frustrated sigh. "I don't know what they're planning. Or where."

"I can try to get some backup into place for you by tonight, but I'm not sure I can swing it before then. I'll see how many people I can move into place by tonight, but you know we're stretched pretty thin at the moment, until I can bring in more new hires."

"I know," Hunter answered tersely. He knew exactly how understaffed The Gates was, if Quinn had resorted to hiring an ex-soldier with a bum leg and anger-management issues.

"You may have to handle this alone for a little while." Another brief pause, then, "Can you?"

"I guess I'll have to, won't I?" Hunter answered, unable to conceal a touch of bitterness in his voice.

SHE NEEDED A PET, Susannah decided as she crossed the darkened employee parking lot. A pet would give her an excuse to leave the office at a reasonable hour instead of finding just one more thing to take care of before she locked the door for the day.

Not a dog. Dogs needed room to run and someone home to let them out for potty breaks. A cat, maybe. Cats were independent. She'd always liked cats. She'd cried for weeks when she'd had to leave her marmalade tabby Poco behind when she left Boneyard Ridge.

She'd left a lot of things behind in Boneyard Ridge. Things she'd never get back again.

She'd parked at the far end of the parking lot when she'd arrived at work that morning, on the premise that the long walk across the blacktop to her office would be almost as good as working out.

Almost. Pulling out her phone, she hit the record button. "Look into joining a gym."

"You don't look like you need one."

The masculine drawl came out of the darkness, sending her bones rattling with surprise. The lamp at this end of the parking lot was out, she realized as she turned in a circle, trying to spot the speaker.

A darker shadow loomed out of the gloom surrounding her car. She instantly regretted not shelling out a few more bucks to get an alarm system with a remote. She peered toward the approaching figure, taking a couple of defensive steps backward.

"I'm not going to hurt you," the man's voice assured her.

She didn't believe him.

Sliding her hand into the pocket of her purse, she closed her fingers around the small canister of pepper spray she made a point of carrying.

"Don't do that," the man warned, a hint of steel in his deep voice. "We don't have time."

Even as the words rumbled from the gathering gloom, Susannah heard the growl of a car engine starting nearby. She saw the shadowy figure shift attention toward the sound, and she took the opening, kicking off her high heels and running toward the lights of the hotel behind her.

She didn't get three steps before he grabbed her from behind, wrapping her upper body in a firm grip and lifting her off her feet so quickly she didn't even have time to scream before his hand clapped over her mouth.

She tried to pull the pepper spray from her purse, but his hold on her was unshakable. She could barely flex her fingers.

The roar of the engine grew closer, and she started

kicking backward against her captor's legs. Her only reward was pain in her own heels as they slammed against what felt like solid rock.

"For God's sake, stop fighting me!" He was running with her, ignoring her attempts to get away as he loped across the parking lot toward the woods beyond. "I'm on your side."

The sheer audacity of his growling assurance spurred her fury, and she clamped down on his hand with her teeth.

A stream of curses rewarded her effort, but the man didn't let her go. He just kept running, an oddly hitching stride that tugged at her memory until she realized where she'd heard that low, cavernous voice before.

The sad-sack maintenance man.

It's always the quiet ones....

Suddenly, a loud stuttering sound seemed to fill the air around them, and her captor shoved her to the ground and threw himself over her body, pinning her in place. Her purse went flying, pepper spray and all.

The least of her worries, she realized as her rattled mind finally identified the sound. Gunfire. Her pulse started whooshing like thunder in her ears as she held her breath for the sound of more shots.

The engine noise she'd heard before faded, followed by the unmistakable squeal of tire on pavement. They were turning around and coming back for another go, she realized, her breath freezing in her lungs.

The man on top of her pushed himself off her, giving her a brief chance to flee his grasp. But she was too paralyzed with shock to make a move, and then the moment had passed. He grabbed her arm, dragging her to her feet, and started running.

As she stumbled behind him, she realized she had

only two stark options—run with him or put up a fight that would give whoever had just tried to gun her down another chance to finish the job.

Her heart hammering wildly in her chest, she ran.

Chapter Two

Night had leached all the warmth from the hills, leaving behind a bitter, damp cold that bit all the way to the marrow. The collection of bone fragments, steel plates and screws holding his left leg together joined forces in a cacophony of pain, but Hunter ignored the aches and kept moving.

He wasn't sure what the men with the guns would do once they realized he'd spirited their target away, but he knew whatever punishment they chose would be brutal and deadly.

Not getting caught was the only option.

A hiss of pain escaped Susannah's lips, but he couldn't let her stop running. Not yet. He could hear the sound of pursuers crashing through the woods behind them, a stark reminder of the consequences of being captured.

"Please," she groaned, tugging at his hand until he slowed the pace, sparing a second to look at her.

In the faint moon glow slanting through the canopy of trees overhead, Susannah's dark eyes gazed up at him in pain and fear. "My feet," she whispered.

He looked down and saw she was barefoot. Blood stained her toes, and he thought about the hard, rocky trail they'd just crossed.

Damn it.

Scanning the woods around them, he spotted a rocky outcropping due east. "Get on my back," he said.

She stared back at him, her mouth trembling open. "What?"

"You either run on those feet or you get on my back. Or you stay here and let those guys back there catch up with you."

Her jaw squared. "Who are they? Who are you?"

He tried not to lose his patience, even though the sound of the chasers behind them seemed closer than ever. "They're the people shooting at you. I'm the guy who's offering to be your damn mule if you'll just shut up and get on my back."

Her mouth flattened to a thin line of anger, but she limped toward him as he bent at the knees, grimacing at the strain on his bad leg, and let her climb onto his back. He grabbed her thighs to hold her in place, surprised and annoyed at how the feel of her firm flesh beneath his fingers sent a sharp, undeniable arrow of lust straight to his groin,

Not the time, Bragg. Really not the time.

She wasn't a featherweight, but running with a heavy load on his back wasn't exactly a new thing to Hunter after two tours of duty in the Army. He'd been looking for a test of his reconstructed leg, hadn't he? Here it was.

It was lucky the rock outcropping was only a half mile distant, he reflected once they reached it and he put her down to rest for a few seconds while he searched the granite wall for any sign of a nook or alcove in the rock face. He found it seconds before he decided to give up and started back toward where he'd left Susannah, only to find that she was a few feet behind, her eyes wide and haunted.

"What are we doing?" she asked in a hushed tone.

"Hiding," he answered succinctly, sweeping her up into his arms.

She made a soft hiss of surprise but didn't resist as he carried her through the dark opening into a cold, black abyss.

NO LIGHT. No sound but that of air flowing in and out of their lungs, fast and harsh in the deep, endless void. After a few seconds, even that sound settled into the faintest of whispers, easily eclipsed by the roar of Susannah's pulse in her ears.

A sliver of deep gray relieved the darkness after a few moments, as her eyes adjusted. The narrow mouth of the cavern, she realized. The only way out. Or in.

If she weren't so bloody terrified, she might find a spot of bleak humor in the idea of being curled up in the hard-muscled arms of a man she knew only as "the sad-sack maintenance man," her bare feet bruised and bleeding, while they hid in a cave from unidentified gunmen.

It was like one of those movies her grandmother liked to watch on cable, the ones where the women were all beautiful, noble victims who inexplicably spent years being treated like garbage by the men in their lives before they finally found their backbones and fought back.

To hell with being a victim, she thought. "What's your name?" she whispered. Because he clearly wasn't the sad sack she'd thought. And if he was just a maintenance man, she was the Queen of England.

"Hunter," he answered after a moment.

"Susannah," she whispered back. "I guess you know that already, though."

"Yeah." His grip on her tightened convulsively, as if he was about to drop her. She grabbed his shoulders in reaction, her fingers digging into an impressive set of muscles.

"Sorry," he whispered.

"You can put me down."

He eased her down until she stood upright, her sore feet flattening on the cold rock floor of the cave. "What happened to your shoes?"

"I kicked them off to run from you. I thought I'd be crossing nice flat concrete, not rocky soil."

"Sorry," he repeated.

He sounded as if he really was sorry, she realized. Of course, maybe that's what he wanted her to think. Maybe he was trying to lull her into being a docile captive.

But two could play that game. If he thought she had decided to go along agreeably, he might drop his guard sooner, giving her a chance to make a break for it.

"You really don't know who those people out there are?" she asked, not believing it for a second.

He didn't answer. Now that she was on her feet, he'd moved slightly away, although she could still feel the furnacelike heat of his body close by, helping cut the biting cold of the cave.

A few seconds later, when it became clear he had no intention of answering her previous question, she asked, "How long before they give up?"

"They don't," he replied.

She'd been afraid of that. "Then how do we get out of here?"

He didn't answer right away, and she felt more than saw him move toward the cave entrance.

She followed, noting with some dismay that while the pain in her feet had lessened, it was mainly because the cold had begun to render them numb. He edged over, giving her an opening to look outside with him, and she slid into the narrow space, her arm brushing his. He really was very muscular, she thought as she peered into the misty gloom.

Scudding clouds gathered overhead, blotting out most of the moonlight filtering through the trees. The darkness outside loomed like a physical entity, threatening and impenetrable.

"Rain's comin'," Hunter whispered, his drawl pronounced. Definitely a mountain native, she thought.

"Is that good or bad?" she asked.

He gave a little shrug, his shoulder sliding against hers. Heat slithered down her arm into her fingertips, catching her off guard.

Good God, woman, she scolded herself silently, inching her arm away from his. *He's your captor. And not in a good way.*

"I don't see anyone out there," he whispered after a few minutes. "I think if we go a little deeper into this cave, we might risk a light."

"A light?"

"Flashlight," he said softly, tugging her with him away from the cave entrance. She stepped gingerly after him, less from pain than from the fear that her numb feet wouldn't know it even if she were walking across a field of broken glass.

A few seconds later, a beam of light slanted across the damp cave walls, illuminating the tight space they occupied. The cave was narrow but surprisingly long, twisting out of sight into the rock wall. Hunter swept the light across the visible space, as if reassuring himself they were alone.

"No bears?" she whispered, quelling a shudder.

"Not at the moment." He flashed an unexpected smile, baring straight white teeth and a surprising pair of dimples high on each cheek. A flutter of raw female awareness vibrated low in her belly, and she jerked her gaze away, appalled by her reaction.

His hand brushed lightly down one arm, scattering goose bumps where he touched her. He closed his fingers around her wrist, his grip solid but gentle. "Let's take a quick look at your feet." He tugged her with him toward a shelflike slab of rock jutting out from the cave wall. "Sit."

She complied, wincing as the coldness of the rock blasted right through her skirt and underwear to chill her backside.

"Sorry. Didn't bring a seat warmer."

But he had brought supplies, she saw with growing alarm, as he reached into the pocket of his jacket and withdrew a soft-sided zippered bag that contained a compact stash of first-aid supplies.

Had he known beforehand that he was going to need to treat a wound?

He ripped open a packet and the sharp tang of rubbing alcohol cut through the musty odor of the cave. "This is gonna sting," he warned a split second before he wiped the alcohol swab across one of the jagged scrapes on the bottom of her foot.

"Son of a—" She clamped her teeth shut and gripped the edge of the outcropping doubling as her seat.

"Sorry." Once again, he sounded sincere, making her feel off balance.

He worked quickly, efficiently, as if he was used to offering aid. Hell, maybe he was. Maybe he was some sort of psychotic cross between Dr. McDreamy and Hannibal Lecter. Emphasis on the McDreamy, she added silently as she watched the muscles of his back flex visibly beneath the thick leather jacket he wore.

He couldn't conjure up a new pair of shoes from his little first-aid kit, but he did wrap her feet in a liberal amount of gauze. As footwear, the gauze didn't have a chance of lasting through another wild hike through the woods, but for the moment, the gauze was bringing her numb feet back to tingling, aching life.

She was beginning to wish they were still numb.

With her feet safely bandaged, Hunter turned off the flashlight, plunging them back into icy blackness. The shocking change from light to dark sent another hard shiver through Susannah's chilled body.

Then warmth washed over her as Hunter settled on the rocky seat next to her, his hip pressed firmly against hers. She felt his arm wrap around her shoulder, and even though she wanted to pull away from his touch, the sheer relief his vibrant heat offered her shivering body was too much of a comfort to rebuff.

With a silent promise to grow a backbone as soon as she could feel her fingers and toes again, she nestled closer to his heat.

HE'D LOST HIS cell phone. In the greater scheme of his present troubles, it wasn't the worst thing that could have happened to him out there in the woods, but it was bad. How was he supposed to call in the cavalry—assuming Quinn could assemble one—if he didn't have his phone?

Beside him, Susannah Marsh had finally stopped shivering, her soft curves molding themselves to the hard planes of his own body. He'd felt her tighten up when he'd first slipped his arm around her, but she was a sensible woman. Even if she thought he was a crazy kidnapper—and really, she'd be an idiot not to—she surely saw the wisdom of letting him keep her from sinking into hypothermia.

"I'm not a crazy kidnapper," he whispered, feeling foolish but unable to stop the words from slipping between his lips.

She stiffened beside him. "What proof can you offer in your defense?"

"I wasn't the one with the guns?" Well, technically he did have a gun, a subcompact Glock 26 tucked in an ankle holster. But if he told her that—

"No, you're the one who accosted me in the parking lot, dragged me barefoot through the woods and told me I had to run or die."

"Those were the only choices at the moment."

She sat up, away from his grasp, and cold air slithered into the space between them. Only a whisper of ambient light seeped into the small cavern from outside, so all he could make out of her expression was the faint glimmer of her eyes as she turned to look at him.

He knew she couldn't see him in the dark, but he wondered what she'd seen earlier, at the hotel, when she'd looked at him. He'd let his hair grow in the year since he left the Army. Or maybe the better term was, he'd let it go. Like he'd let a lot of things go—his self-respect, his control over his temper, his once-upon-a-time ambitions. Even before taking on the role of the life-battered maintenance man, shuffling his way around the Highland Hotel and Resort, he'd been slacking off the simple disciplines of life, like shaving daily and trying to find a job that paid more than minimum wage.

Mostly, he'd wallowed. In self-pity. In anger. In a crushing amount of guilt for everything that had gone wrong for him since Afghanistan.

It had served his purposes to come across as a loser at the hotel. But if she could see him now, with the play-acting role sloughed off, would she see anything different?

He'd hoped this job with The Gates would give him back a sense of purpose. So far, all it had given him was a queasy sense of impending doom, a coming juggernaut of danger and disaster that left him feeling helpless and overwhelmed.

"Can I go?" Susannah asked quietly.

His gut tensed at the very thought. If she left this cave, she wasn't likely to reach civilization again without running into people who wanted her dead. She was a city girl, a pampered, polished princess who might know her way around a mall but had no chance getting out of these woods alive.

Nevertheless, he couldn't hold her captive. Not even for her own good. He'd been a prisoner once, and it had damn near destroyed him.

"Yes," he said quietly. "But I wouldn't, if I were you."

Her voice tightened. "Because there are people trying to kill me?"

"Yes."

"And how did you know they'd be there in the parking lot?"

He could hardly tell her that he was working with the people trying to kill her, but anything else was a lie or a secret he wasn't prepared to tell.

When he didn't answer immediately, her voice sharpened to a diamond edge. "Are you one of them?"

"You're still alive, aren't you?"

"That's not an answer."

"It's all you're gettin'." For now, at least, until they could reach someplace safe and contact Alexander Quinn.

She settled back into silence again, but she'd shifted far enough away from him that he knew any attempt to pull her back into the shelter of his arm would be seen as an assault, not an offer of comfort.

"It's raining," he said as the drumbeat of raindrops hitting the rocky ground outside filtered into the cave. "We're not going anywhere for the next little while, so why don't you try to grab a nap?"

Her voice rose. "You've got to be kidding me."

"Shh!" He slanted a quick look toward the cave entrance. Outside, the steady beat of rain masked almost all other noises. It would certainly cover any movement outside, which meant they were not only cornered with nowhere to run but also vulnerable to a sneak attack.

He'd tried to plan on the fly, once he'd learned the hit on Susannah Marsh had been moved up by twenty-four hours, but even faking illness to leave work early that afternoon had afforded him only a couple of hours to get his supplies together. He'd barely reached the parking lot in time to pull her pretty little bacon out of the fire.

"How do I even know there's anyone out there?" she asked, not bothering to lower her voice. "How do I know that wasn't just a car backfiring?"

She knew better. He could tell by the tension in her voice, the little tremble as her tone rose at the end of the question. She knew she was in danger, though he doubted she had any idea why. But she was also determined not to trust him one whit.

And he couldn't really blame her for that, could he, when he didn't even trust himself?

"You know it wasn't."

"I didn't get hit. They must have been lousy shots."

Fortunately, he was pretty sure they were. For one thing, they'd deliberately chosen to make the hit with pistols fired from a moving car, a piss-poor choice if you were serious about actually hitting your target. A critical thinker with any skills would have set up on the hill overlooking the parking lot with a Remington 700 or an AR-15 with a suppressor to keep down the noise.

Lucky for Susannah Marsh—and for him—they weren't dealing with critical thinkers.

But that didn't mean the men who were undoubtedly out there in the woods trying to track down their prey weren't dangerous as hell.

"There are a lot of them and only one of you," he said. "At close quarters, it won't matter if they're lousy shots."

"Who says they'll get close?" The volume of her voice dropped to a hiss of a whisper.

He almost laughed, trying to picture her out there in the woods, barefoot, dressed in a straight skirt that might make her legs look outstanding but wasn't ideal for hiking. The woman normally looked like a catalog model, all sparkling clean and perfectly groomed. He wouldn't be surprised if he turned on the flashlight right now to find that she'd somehow managed to finger-comb her hair back to its normal glossy state.

"So, you're not just a brilliant event planner but you're also an expert outdoorswoman?"

"You know nothing about me." She somehow made a whisper sound haughty.

He schooled the grin playing at the corners of his mouth. "I'll give you that."

A sharp noise outside sent animal awareness crackling along his nerves. He felt Susannah's instant tension snap across the space between them, as electric as lightning.

He reached out to touch her, to silently urge her to be quiet, and felt her skin ripple wildly beneath his touch. But she held her tongue as they waited in breathless agony for another noise.

The sound of footsteps barely registered above the

hammering downpour of rain. Giving Susannah's arm a quick, reassuring squeeze, Hunter rose from the stone bench and moved toward the cave entrance, ignoring the protest of pain that clawed its way through his bum leg.

Keeping to the shadows just inside the cave, he looked out on the rain-drenched scene, letting his gaze relax. Movement would be easier to pinpoint if he wasn't actively looking for it.

There. He spotted a man dressed in dark camouflage moving slowly through the woods about twenty yards away. He held a pistol in one hand, a satellite phone in the other. It was hard to make out anything more about him through the heavy curtain of rain and mist, but from his general shape and size, Hunter guessed that the man outside the cave was probably Myron Abernathy, one of the handful of men Billy Dawson had directed to take down Susannah Marsh.

Myron had been one of the ones most enamored of her candid photo, Hunter remembered with a grimace. If he were to get her alone—

"Do you know him?" Susannah's taut whisper sent a shock wave rippling down his spine.

Taking a swift breath through his nose, he hissed, "Do you ever stay put when asked?"

"You didn't ask," she whispered back.

The urge to give her a shake was damn near overpowering. He allowed himself a quick glance in her direction, wishing there were more moonlight outside so he could get a better look at her expression.

But he didn't need moonlight to see that her eyes had widened and her perfectly shaped lips had trembled open with shock.

Following her gaze, he sucked in another sharp breath.

It was Myron Abernathy all right. No doubt about it.
Because he was ten yards closer and moving straight
toward them.

Chapter Three

Oh God, oh God, oh G—

Hunter's hand closed over Susannah's mouth as a low, keening noise filled the tight confines of the cave. It took a second for her to realize the noise was coming from her own aching throat.

She swallowed the rest of the sound and moved backward with him, deeper into the shadows of the cave.

Outside, she could still hear the swishing noise of the man with the big gun moving through the thick underbrush and dead autumn leaves that carpeted the forest floor outside the cave. A few more steps and he'd—

A harsh bark of static made her jump. Hunter's arms tightened around her, as if he was trying to keep her from flying completely apart.

"Billy says regroup at the camp." A tinny voice, barely audible through the rain, floated into the cave.

Hunter's grip tightened like a spasm. Then she heard the unmistakable sounds of the man outside retreating, moving steadily away from the mouth of the cave.

Hunter let her go, and she pulled away from him with a jerk, waiting until she could no longer hear the sound of movement outside before she asked in a low growl, "Who the hell is Billy?"

Hunter didn't answer. She hadn't expected he would.

She was beginning to understand that silence meant he knew things he had no intention of telling her.

Like how he'd happened to be waiting in the parking lot at just the right time to play hero for her when the shooting started. Or how he happened to have an emergency kit packed and tucked away in his jacket, as if he wanted to be ready for whatever might go down tonight.

Or why there had been something hard poking into her ankle where his right leg had braced her when he pulled her back into his grasp.

He was armed. Ankle holster, which was why she hadn't spotted it before. Did that explain the limp? If he wasn't used to ankle-carry, he might not realize that unless he balanced the weapon with a counterweight on the other leg, like extra ammo strapped to the opposite ankle, it could seriously mess up his walking gait.

Except he limped with his left leg, didn't he? Not the leg with the weapon.

Before she had a chance to puzzle it out, Hunter snapped on the flashlight, slanting the beam across her face. She squinted, turning her face away from the painful glare. "Do you mind?"

"I do," he said, still speaking softly. "We got damn lucky just now. But you have got to learn to listen when I ask you to do something."

"You don't ask. You order," she muttered, kicking herself for saying anything at all. One of these days, her grandmother had always promised her, her smart mouth was going to get her into trouble.

As if it hadn't a million times already.

But fear made her angry, and abject terror made her furious *and* verbal about it. If Mr. Enigmatic Maintenance Man with the hidden gun and a hidden agenda couldn't handle a little pushback from her when he started barking orders, this night was about to go downhill at blazing speed.

"Look." He was struggling with some anger of his own. She could tell by the way his jaw was working, as if he had a mouth full of chew and no spit cup. "I know you're confused and scared. And I wish I could tell you there wasn't any reason to be, but we both know there is."

"I don't need you to candy-coat anything," she said flatly. "I just want to know all the facts. Why is somebody trying to kill me? And how did you know about it?" She swallowed the final question she wanted to ask, about the gun strapped to his ankle. It might be in her best interest to keep that knowledge to herself for the moment.

He gave her a long, considering look before he turned his gaze away, eyeing the narrow stone outcropping they'd used as a bench earlier. "I meant what I said about getting some sleep. It's cold and it's wet out there, and that gauze wouldn't last long if we started trekking through the woods tonight."

"It'll get torn up just as badly tomorrow."

"If you'll promise to sit tight and wait, I may have a way to fix that problem." He waved the flashlight beam toward the stone bench. "Get some sleep. I've got to go somewhere."

She stared at him, not believing what she was hearing. "You're going to leave me here? Alone?"

"They're convening somewhere else for the night. You should be safe enough." He didn't say it, but she could see the rest of what he was thinking in his hooded eyes. Even if he was here, there wouldn't be much they could do to hold off a whole crew of armed men looking to take her down. She wouldn't be much safer with him than stuck here shoeless with the damp, bitter cold and the rugged mountain terrain between her and safety.

"What are you going to do out there?"

He looked down at her bandaged feet. "Well, first of all, I'm going to get you some shoes." He lifted the flashlight upward again, handing it over to her. "You keep the light. I won't need it out there."

She closed her hand over the flashlight handle. It was warm where he'd gripped it, transferring welcome heat to her numb fingers.

But almost as soon as he slipped out into the rainy night, she extinguished the beam, preferring the comforting obscurity of the darkness to the stark reality the light revealed.

She was trapped and hunted. She was stuck with a man she didn't know, for reasons she wasn't sure she understood, in a place that might as well be the far side of the moon, for all the chance she had of finding her way out of these woods barefoot in the pouring rain.

Who was this man named Hunter? And why did his name seem to ring a bell with her, as if she'd heard it recently but couldn't quite place where? She'd certainly never seen him before, as far as she could remember, but there was still something about him that seemed familiar.

She made herself turn the light back on, aiming the beam around the small cave to get her bearings. Hunter hadn't told her where he was going, so she didn't know how long he might be away.

Bottom line, she did not need to spend the night in this cave with a man she didn't trust. If that meant wrapping her feet in every inch of gauze she could find in that first-aid kit he'd so kindly left with her, then that's what she had to do.

She had to get out of here before he got back, get to a safe place and start figuring out who those men with the guns really were.

Because if they were somehow connected to the Brad-burys, then her life was about to get a thousand times more dangerous.

HUNTER DIDN'T THINK it was likely that Myron and the other boys had stumbled upon his hiding place while they'd been scouring the woods for any sign of Susan-nah Marsh. He'd stashed the large rucksack filled with emergency supplies in a hard-to-access area of the woods, where fallen trees and some rocky granite outcroppings created a natural nook perfect for hiding and sheltering something the size of the rucksack.

It was only slightly damp when he pulled it from its hiding place, and the water-resistant canvas lining would almost certainly have protected anything inside from the elements.

Not that he supposed Susannah Marsh would quibble about wet shoes; they'd certainly be a big improvement on the bloody gauze wrap currently protecting her bat-tered feet.

He'd purchased a pair of hiking boots and another pair of tennis shoes he hoped would be comfortable for walking, though he wasn't exactly an expert on women's shoes. She had narrow, delicate-looking feet, although the hard calf and thigh muscles he'd seen—and felt—while carrying her through the woods on his back had suggested she wasn't nearly as soft and ornamental a woman as she looked.

That was good. She'd need to pull her weight over the next few days, until he could figure out what to do next.

He couldn't be sure Myron or the others had recog-nized him, but it was likely they had. So his undercover assignment was officially over, as far as he was con-cerned. While he suspected his boss might wish him to take a chance and try to get back inside the cell, he wasn't stupid enough to risk it. He'd already come damn close to pushing up daisies twice in his life.

No hurry to do that again anytime soon, right?

Hiking back to the cave with the backpack strapped to his shoulders reminded him of the frantic run through the woods with Susannah Marsh clinging to his back like a leech. A leech with long, well-toned legs and pert little breasts that had somehow managed to feel both soft and firm against his shoulder blades.

Plus, she'd smelled like freshly cut tart apples. How could she possibly have managed such a thing after a long day in the office and a headlong run for her life?

He tried to follow the path he and Susannah had taken earlier that night in hopes of tracking down his missing cell phone, but he'd seen no sign of the phone by the time he reached the cave entrance. He had to assume it was now in the custody of one of the Blue Ridge Infantry foot soldiers Billy Dawson had sent to kill Susannah Marsh.

The phone was a burner, and he took care not to leave any incriminating evidence for Dawson or the others to find. Even his calls to his handler, as he'd come to think of the wily old ex-spy who had hired him for this operation, were calls to another burner phone that would be next to impossible for Dawson and his crew to trace.

Alexander Quinn had made sure of that. After all, the Blue Ridge Infantry might be a crew of authority-hating rednecks with a mean streak, but not long ago, they'd aligned themselves with a band of tech-savvy anarchists as well as a hodgepodge of downright entrepreneurial drug cookers that had once formed the standing army for a criminal named Wayne Cortland.

Cortland had died a couple of years ago, and the

authorities had largely dismantled the organization in a series of raids not long afterwards.

But the remaining remnants now had a blueprint for success. A business model, if you wanted to put it in those terms. When the local cops, already dealing with more than their share of crime, had moved on to other cases, Alexander Quinn had apparently decided to take up the slack. He seemed to be making the job of cleaning up the post-Cortland mess a personal project.

Overhead, a break in the rain clouds offered a brief glow of moonlight, just enough to reveal the rain-slick face of the rocky overhang that hid the small cave where Susannah Marsh was waiting. He slowed his approach, trying to prepare himself for telling her the truth about why he'd confronted her in the parking lot earlier that evening—and just what he had planned for them for the next few days.

She wasn't going to like it. That much he knew for sure. If Susannah Marsh was known for anything around the Highlands Hotel and Resort, it was her polished, professional look. Men and women alike commented on it when she wasn't in earshot, and not all of the talk was kind, but Hunter chalked the negative talk up to envy.

Susannah Marsh was damn near flawless. She dressed with meticulous style, her clothing a compromise between fashion and function. Never inappropriate, but always sleek and attractive. Perfectly groomed, perfectly competent, perfectly lovely.

But what he had in mind for the next few days, he was pretty sure she'd find perfectly appalling.

He had been sticking with a stealthy approach to the cave to this point, but he didn't want to sneak up on her and scare her, so as he reached the mouth of the cave, he made sure to make a little noise to give her notice of his arrival. "Susannah?" No answer.

Peering into the gloom, he tried to make out any signs of movement. But the cave interior was cold and still.

Pulling his keys from his pocket, he winced at the jingle of metal on metal as he located the small penlight he kept on his key chain. With a flick of his finger, the penlight beam came on, and he ran the light across the width of the cave.

The first-aid kit was still there, lying on the stone outcropping where they'd sat a little while earlier. Even the flashlight was there, snugged up next to the first-aid kit.

But Susannah Marsh was nowhere in sight.

The flashlight beam caught a glimmer of white on the cave floor beneath the stone bench. Crouching with a grimace of pain, he shined the light on the floor, taking in several half-moon-shaped white slivers. It took a second to realize what he was seeing.

Nail clippings. She'd cut off her nails.

He picked up the first-aid kit to put it in his pocket and stopped as he realized it was considerably lighter than when he'd used it to bandage her feet earlier. When he checked inside, he found that all of the gauze that had been packed within was gone.

What the hell was the woman up to?

WAS SHE CRAZY to be doing this?

When Susannah had left the cave, she'd been certain that the worst possible choice she could make was to stay there and wait for Hunter to get back. No matter how attractive he might seem, especially when he was standing between her and a bunch of men with guns, he wasn't her friend. He wasn't even an acquaintance. He was just a guy she'd seen for the first time in an elevator earlier that very day. For all she knew, he'd been lying when he told her he'd hit the button for the wrong floor.

Maybe he'd been looking for her the whole time.

But now that she was out in the woods, shivering from the cold and biting her lip to keep from moaning over the pain in her injured feet, she was beginning to second-guess her decision to strike out on her own.

Yes, she knew a little something about getting around in the mountains. And yes, she'd done a pretty damn good job of fashioning shoes out of gauze, tape and a couple of slabs of wood she'd used her Swiss Army knife to shave off a fallen tree limb she'd found near the mouth of the cave.

But the makeshift shoes were already starting to fall apart, no match for the wet, tangled underbrush and rocky soil. The temperature had to have dropped another five or ten degrees since sunset, and her coat was made for getting from the office to the car, not for traipsing around in the woods on a cold, damp October night.

And worst of all, she had a bad feeling she was lost.

She usually could find her way around anywhere, but in her panic to get away from men shooting at her, she'd lost track of what direction they'd gone. She'd never learned to navigate by the stars, having grown up in the middle of the Smoky Mountains, a long way from the sea. And the heavens had opened up again, anyway, mountain fog and driving rain obscuring everything outside a fifty-yard radius.

She might as well be in the middle of a big, tree-strewn void for all the good her surroundings were doing her at the moment.

Stubbornly quelling the panic starting to hurtle up from her trembling gut, she made herself stop and take a long, deep breath. *Look around. What do you see?*

Trees. Fog.

Someone moving through the woods ahead.

Shock zapped through her, compelling her to run. She clamped down on the instinct, knowing that movement was the worst possible thing at the moment. Standing very still, several yards from the dark silhouettes she could barely make out moving through the mist about thirty yards away, she had a chance to escape their notice. Her coat was a dark olive-green trench that covered her from neck to knee, and the underbrush covered her legs from toes to knees. Only her face and hands would be visible in the damp gloom, and they might be mistaken for the patchy white trunk of a birch tree.

As long as she stayed very, very still.

Nearby, something rustled in the underbrush. She held her position, ruthlessly suppressing the urge to turn her head and see what was moving around so close by.

Ahead, the two dark-clad figures walking through the trees kept moving. Apparently they'd heard nothing, or if they had, they'd chalked it up to an animal wandering around in the rain.

The pounding rush of her pulse in her ears was so loud it almost eclipsed the staccato beat of the rain, which had risen to a torrent. Even the thick evergreen boughs overhead weren't enough to keep her from becoming thoroughly drenched. But she didn't move, not even to wipe the rain out of her stinging eyes.

The dark figures kept moving, gliding with terrifying silence through the fog until they disappeared from her sight.

She ignored her body's urge to crumple into a boneless heap and stayed still a few moments longer until she was sure the prowling men were no longer in earshot.

She heard the rustling noise again. Closer this time.

Her patience and control left in a snap, and she started running headlong through the woods, heedless of the noise she was making or the painful slap of her unraveling gauze-and-tape footwear against her battered feet. All she could think about was the chill-inducing menace of the men she'd seen gliding through the misty woods like vengeful ghosts.

The tape on her right foot tore away completely, and she went sprawling, barely catching herself from landing face-first on the rocky ground. She hit hard, the impact driving the air from her lungs and leaving her gasping and heaving for breath.

For a few terrifying seconds, the world around her seemed to go completely black as her oxygen-starved lungs struggled to refill. And in that frightening void, Susannah heard her grandmother's voice, sharp and clear.

"Get yourself together, girl. Ain't nobody gonna fix your troubles 'cept you."

Air seeped into her lungs, easing the blackness. Cold, damp air replaced the burning pain in her chest, and slowly her pulse descended from the stratosphere to a fast but steady cadence.

Get yourself together, girl, she repeated silently, gathering up the remains of her ersatz shoe and examining it to see if there was any hope of making a repair.

Nope. It was a goner.

Allowing herself only a second or two of despair, she rose to her feet and shoved the bundle of tattered gauze and tape in the pocket of her flimsy jacket. Gingerly putting her injured foot on the ground, she gauged the discomfort level and, while it hurt like hell, she thought she could bear it, at least a little while longer.

She took a careful step forward. The ground was rough, wet and hard, but she could take it.

The flurry of movement behind her came out of thick silence, like a whirlwind born from dead calm. She had time to suck in a quick breath and take a stumbling step forward before she was jerked back against a wall of hard heat. A large hand clamped over her mouth and a low drawl rumbled in her ear.

"Don't make a sound."

Chapter Four

He could feel her heartbeat against his chest, fluttering like a frantic bird. Not daring to unclamp his hand from her mouth, he whispered in her ear, "It's Hunter. I know you saw those men out there. You need to stop making so damn much noise."

He felt her body tense up, her muscles knotting as she strained against his grip. He tightened his hold and added, "If I let you go, will you promise not to scream?"

Slowly, she nodded.

He eased his grip, watching for any sign that she wasn't going to keep her promise. She jerked free of his grasp and whirled around to look at him, her eyes blazing in the watery glint of moonlight peeking through the storm clouds overhead. "Who were they?" Her words came out so softly, he saw more than heard the question.

He put one finger over his lips and turned away from her, reaching both hands over his shoulders toward her. With a soft exhalation, she caught his hands and he hauled her onto his back, releasing her hands once she had a firm grip on his shoulders and wrapping his arms around her legs to hold her safely in place.

"This is humiliating, you know," she whispered in his ear, her breath stirring his hair and sending a shudder of raw masculine need scudding down his spine. He closed his eyes, took a long, slow breath and let it out in a ten count. Then he started back through the woods the way he'd come, hoping the rainfall would obscure their trail before anyone came back out here to start looking for them again.

He'd stashed his supplies between a couple of large boulders, hidden under a dun-colored rain tarp, in case someone discovered the cave before he got back. Carrying them in his backpack had made sense when he thought they'd have time for a more leisurely escape. But it was a whole other thing to chase an escapee through the woods while dodging unidentified strangers carrying a heavy pack on his back.

He stopped by the pair of boulders and set her down.

"Why are we stopping?" she whispered.

"For this." He tugged the tarpaulin from over the large rucksack, folding it neatly and handing it to her.

She stared at the large olive-drab backpack first, then at him. "How long were you planning this?" Even though she still spoke in a whisper, her inflection rose, and he could see in the widening of her eyes that she found his foresight alarming.

"This particular set of circumstances?" he answered quietly, slinging one strap of the pack over his shoulder. "About three hours."

She eyed him nervously as he held out his free arm. "You knew there were going to be people gunning for me tonight, didn't you?"

He didn't see the point of dissembling. "Yes."

"How?"

"Let's get back in the cave and see how much damage you did to my handiwork." He didn't wait for her to make a move. He just wrapped his arm around her, lifting her half off her feet, and started walking toward the cave.

He hadn't given her much choice but to stumble along beside him. Considering the flaring anger he could practically see swirling around her like a big red cloud, he was grateful she didn't show any signs of fighting him as he hauled her into the cave.

He should have known he wasn't going to get away with the caveman act for long. The second he let her go and turned to set the rucksack down on the floor of the cave, she sucker punched him right in the kidney.

Pain exploded through his side, shooting off shrapnel of pure agony to tear through his gut and groin. Doubling over, he wheeled to fend off her next blow, but it never came. When the stars cleared from his vision, he found himself staring into her crumpled face.

The damn woman was crying.

Before he could process the unexpected sight, she'd regained control, her expression returning to a cool, neutral mask as she dashed away the tears from her eyes as if they were mere raindrops that had slithered down from her damp hair.

"Think you could answer a question directly now?" she asked in a regal tone that sent ice flooding his veins.

There was the princess he knew.

"You gonna sucker punch me again if I don't?"

Her mask slipped, just a bit, a hint of a wry smile hovering over the corners of her lips. The rain had washed away her carefully applied makeup, leaving her bedraggled and natural, but she still looked utterly royal and in control. "If necessary."

He rubbed his back over the site of her blow. The skin was tender, but the worst of the pain had ebbed to a dull ache. "You went for the kidney."

"Shameful of me." She didn't sound particularly regretful, but he'd seen that moment of breakdown, no matter how quickly she'd managed to don the icy mask again.

"I was working with them. But I wasn't one of them." He hadn't meant to tell her even that much, but the second he opened his mouth, the words had spilled in a rush.

Her eyes narrowing, she nodded toward the backpack he'd dropped when she hit him. "Did you put the flashlight in there?"

"Yeah."

She bent to pick up the pack, grunting a little as she encountered the unexpected weight. "How long did you pack for?"

"A few days. More if we can get to a place where we can do some laundry."

She located the flashlight he'd tucked in one of the pack's outer pockets and flicked on the switch. Light knifed through the darkness, piercing Hunter right in the eyes.

"You planned to kidnap me." It wasn't a question, and her tone was oddly neutral, as if she were merely a disinterested observer trying to make sense of a situation she'd stumbled upon.

"I knew I'd have to get you away from that parking lot, yes."

"Because of the gunmen."

He hadn't really been sure exactly how they planned to kill her. Guns had seemed a reasonable option, since most of the men in the cell owned them. A whole carload of them shooting off their guns and making a lot of noise hadn't exactly been what he'd been expecting, though. The concept of stealth apparently didn't factor into how the BRI conducted their business.

Calling themselves an "infantry," he thought with a

grimace. They weren't fit to lick the boots of the real warriors they claimed to emulate.

She must have seen the grimace. "You weren't expecting the gunmen?"

"I wasn't sure what to expect. I only knew that whatever they had planned was happening this evening, and I had to get you out of there."

She looked at him for a long, silent moment, then walked slowly over to the stone bench and sat. It was a little high and narrow to make a proper bench, forcing her to perch more than sit. She looked bone-tired and disheartened, and one of her feet, the one that had lost whatever crazy bandage she'd put on them for her trek through the woods, was bleeding again.

At least he could help her out with that.

He picked up the pack she'd set down on the cave floor and unzipped the main compartment. The beam of the flashlight slanted toward him, and he made a show of letting her see what he was doing. "I packed some shoes for you. I figured you'd be in heels, and they're not exactly made for wandering around the woods."

"You don't know my size."

She'd be surprised what he knew. Like the fact that she kept a pair of tennis shoes in her desk drawer in case she wanted to do a power walk during her lunch hour. Or her secret addiction to dark-chocolate drops. It was remarkable how many secrets a maintenance man could uncover if he was interested enough to snoop around while doing his work.

She kept her desk and belongings more neat and inscrutable than most, but he'd been able to get her foot size from the running shoes. He'd have preferred to sneak out her actual shoes, but there'd been no chance to slip into the office that afternoon before the trouble started going down. He'd had to make a run into Barrowville to do some shopping at the thrift store in town.

Deciding on the tennis shoes over the hiking boots, he tossed them to the cave floor in front of her and kept digging for the sweater and jeans he'd bought at the same thrift store. The sweater would fit, even if it was a little big. The jeans looked as if they'd fit as well, although he might have to come up with something to use as a belt.

Susannah picked up the shoes and looked inside at the size. Her gaze snapped up to meet his, her lips tight with dismay. "Have you been stalking me? Is that what this is really about?"

He almost laughed at the thought. If she only knew how much he wished he was pretty much anywhere else but here at the moment—

"Don't suppose you have a phone stashed in there?" she asked a moment later when he didn't reply.

"Sorry. No." He found the sweater and jeans and carried them over to her. She looked at the garments through narrow, suspicious eyes. "They're warmer," he said bluntly.

"How long do you plan to keep me out here?" She didn't reach for the clothes.

With a shrug, he set the clothes on the stone bench beside her. "At least forty-eight more hours."

She turned her gaze from the clothes to him. "Why forty-eight hours?"

He waited for her to figure it out.

Her eyes snapped open wider. "This is about the conference this weekend?"

He pulled one last item from the pack, a corduroy jacket. It wouldn't be heavy enough if the temperature really dropped over the next few days, but it should be enough, with the sweater and jeans, to ward off hypothermia during their hike out of this part of the mountain.

He set it on top of the other clothes. "I'm going outside for a few minutes to scout around, see if there's any sign of those other men we saw a little while ago. Go ahead and get dressed. We don't have a lot of time."

"Don't have a lot of time for what?" she asked, not making a move toward the clothes.

He tried not to lose his patience, knowing it was a lot to ask of her to wait for events to unfold when she was cold, injured and probably scared out of her pretty wits. "We need to leave this cave and go somewhere safer and warmer."

"Like a police station?"

He didn't even roll his eyes that time. Improvement.

But he didn't bother to answer her question before he walked out into the rainy night.

HE MIGHT BE a frustrating cipher, but the man knew how to pick warm and comfortable clothes, Susannah had to concede a few minutes later as she tugged a thick corduroy jacket over the fuzzy sweater. He'd chosen clothing a little larger than her size, but his spot-on choice of footwear suggested he'd opted for the larger size deliberately, figuring it would be easier to get around in roomy clothing than a tighter fit. The jeans were a notch too large, but not so big that she needed a belt, thanks to her stress-induced chocolate binge over the past week.

He was waiting outside the cave, his sharp green eyes scanning the misty woods. He seemed to take his sentry duty very seriously, making her wonder what, exactly, he used to do for a living before taking a job as a hotel maintenance worker.

Clearly there was more to the man than she'd assumed.

His earlier show of shy deference was long gone, replaced by a stubborn implacability that was somehow both un-nerving and comforting.

"Any sign of intruders?" she asked quietly.

He answered without looking at her. "No. But we can't assume they're not out there."

"So we hike out of here, anyway?"

"Something like that."

She shifted from one foot to the other, testing the feel of the shoes on her injured feet. He'd included a pair of thick, fluffy socks that padded her wounds well enough, but they made the shoes a tighter fit than she might have liked.

On the other hand, the tight fit offered good arch sup-port, which she'd probably appreciate if they were plan-ning to hike their way out of these woods.

Unfortunately, she realized a half hour later, leaving the woods didn't seem to be part of the plan. They were headed into deeper forest, on a winding but unmistakable upward climb. The mist thickened, but the air thinned. They were heading higher into the mountains, which meant they were going east.

She might not be a geographer, but she knew that Barrowville and civilization lay to the west. "We're not heading out of the woods, are we?"

He didn't look at her. It seemed to be a habit with him. "I have a cabin about two miles from here. Not much, but it's warm and there's food and water there."

"You want us to hike two more miles tonight?"

"If we wait until morning, there'll be cops and search-ers swarming this area looking for you."

"You're not exactly providing me a good reason to go with you."

"Well, how about this? I know there's at least one cop

on the take in Barrowville, which has jurisdiction in this area. I just don't know who he is. Or what he looks like."

"And I have to take your word for that?" she countered sharply. "Because you've given me such a good reason to trust you up to this point."

"I saved you from being mowed down in the hotel parking lot." His voice was razor-edged. "I brought you clothes to warm you up and shoes to protect your feet. Hell, I carried you piggyback. Twice. And let me tell you, princess, you may not be an Amazon, but you're not exactly dainty, either."

She faltered to a stop, shooting him a dark look. "Clearly, you're not looking to impress me with your gentlemanly charms, either."

He laughed, turning to look at her for the first time since they'd left the cave. "I'm a lot of things, darlin', but a gentleman ain't one of them."

As he started hiking forward again, she caught up and asked, "Does the cabin have indoor plumbing?"

She saw the slight curve of his lips but he didn't answer her question, pushing forward at a surprising clip, given his obvious limp.

Gritting her teeth against the pain of her injured feet, she hurried up the mountain after him.

THE CABIN WAS, to put it mildly, rustic. It had running water and electricity, but that was the extent of luxuries his little bolt-hole could offer, and during the winter, when the snows fell, electricity wasn't a given.

He had a woodstove for the long, cold nights when the power failed, and a rainwater cistern if a pipe burst from the occasional deep freeze. Canned goods in the pantry could be opened by hand and heated over the woodstove.

It wasn't Highland Hotel and Resort, and he doubted

Susannah Marsh would find much to please her refined tastes, but she wouldn't freeze and she wouldn't starve. Considering how close she'd come to bleeding out in the hotel employees' parking lot, she'd have to make do, at least until he figured out what to do next.

Contacting Quinn directly was out, at least for the moment, even though he had another burner phone stashed in the cabin. His second call to his boss that afternoon had gone straight to voice mail, a preordained signal that Quinn suspected their line of communication might be compromised.

Hunter didn't know what constituted "compromised communication," but he knew better than to doubt the instincts of his wily boss. Quinn might be borderline paranoid, but he'd managed to survive some of the most hair-raising covert ops in history. Survival skills like those meant something, even to a former Army infantry grunt like Hunter, who'd never cared much for the spooks who'd haunted the perimeters of the battlefield during major military ops.

He might not ever really like Quinn, but he trusted the man's finely honed sense of caution.

They veered off the barely visible path as they neared the hidden cabin. Behind him, Susannah was still struggling to keep up with his long strides, though she walked with less noise than he'd expected. It was taking sheer determination on his own part to maintain as much stealth as possible, because his old war wounds were hurting like hell.

The clearing appeared almost without warning, with no discernible path to announce its existence. A ring of firs, pines and hemlocks stood sentinel around the tiny homestead, protecting the cabin from view even in the winter, when hardwood trees would shed their leaves for the season. The evergreens had been planted there nearly a half century earlier by his grandfather, who'd preferred seclusion to the increasingly dangerous world outside.

Catching up as Hunter slowed his gait, Susannah sucked in a small gasp of air, and he wondered idly what she thought of the place.

The cabin wasn't much to look at from the outside, a low-slung edifice built from rough-hewn logs. The porch extended along the whole front of the cabin, but it wasn't very wide because the cabin wasn't large.

Two steps up and they were at the front door.

Because of its seclusion, there had never been any reason to put in a lock, and for decades, the door had remained unlocked and the cabin undisturbed. But Hunter didn't see the point of taking chances, not after how easily he'd been ambushed and abducted several months ago. He'd installed a sturdy padlock on both the front and back doors of the cabin, and new latches on all the windows.

He saw Susannah eyeing those latches as he led her into the cabin and turned the dead bolt behind them. Probably thought he was keeping her prisoner, and he didn't hurry to disabuse her of the idea. If a little healthy fear would keep her from doing something foolish, like trying to sneak off on her own again, then he'd use it.

"Nice place," she said. Her tone wasn't obviously sarcastic, but he assumed she meant the comment that way.

He knew the place wasn't much, but it offered him a sense of security in an increasingly insane world. It was one of the few things he owned that he hadn't sold to raise his sister's bail money.

"I know it doesn't look very big, but there's a good-size bedroom. You can have it, of course. I'll take the couch."

He saw her eye the old sofa with skepticism, and

he couldn't really blame her. He'd bought the battered piece of furniture at the thrift store in Barrowville a few months earlier, but for all its shabby appearance, the springs were sturdy enough and the cushions comfortable, even though his legs hung off a bit when he slept there.

He'd stayed in the cabin several times since returning home from Afghanistan, when his guilt about his sister's legal troubles had gotten to be too much for him to cope with back at her place. He'd bunked down here on the sofa more often than not, finding its rougher embrace easier to deal with than the civilized softness of the bed.

"How can you be sure I won't sneak out while you're asleep?" she asked quietly as he dropped the rucksack on the low coffee table and began to unpack supplies.

He slanted a look toward her. "You're not my prisoner."

"Forgive me if I feel that way."

He waved his hand toward the door. "You know how dead bolts work. Feel free to let yourself out."

She actually took a couple of steps toward the door before she stopped, her chin dipping to her chest. Not looking at him, she asked, "Why were they trying to kill me?"

There was a strange undertone to her question that piqued his curiosity, as if she already knew the answer but needed him to say the words aloud.

So he did. "You're in the way of their plan."

Her gaze flickered up to meet his, confusion glittering in her eyes. He saw with a jolt of surprise that one of her brown eyes had gone light gray with a touch of hazel around the pupil. He blinked a couple of times before he was sure what he was seeing.

"What?" she asked, noticing his reaction.

"You wear brown contacts."

Her brow furrowing, she blinked a couple of times herself. "Damn."

"Why would you want to hide your eye color?" he blurted.

She looked down. "I like variety."

She was lying.

"You didn't finish answering my question," she continued, her gaze stubbornly averted. "I'm in the way of what plan?"

He might as well tell her, he supposed. If anyone had a right to know what was going on, it was the woman who'd damn near given up her life for what the BRI had planned.

"A militia group called the Blue Ridge Infantry is planning to sabotage the law enforcement convention being held at the hotel this weekend."

Chapter Five

"Why?"

The question spilled from Susannah's lips before she had time to formulate a rational thought. If she had, she might have asked a more important question, such as how he knew these things and how the attack was supposed to take place.

But she supposed "why" was a good start.

Especially since her cousin McKenna was going to be one of the attendees.

Another question popped into her head. Could the Bradburys have made the connection between Susannah and her cousin? Had they targeted the upcoming conference knowing McKenna was going to be there?

Wouldn't that be ironic? Targeting the conference because of McKenna, never realizing that Susannah herself was right there in the thick of it all.

But the Bradburys had never been connected to any militia groups, had they? They'd always been freakishly clannish, prone to trusting nobody but family, however vile and revolting those kinsmen might be.

Hunter's growl of a voice interrupted her musings. "Two hundred top cops from three states in one hotel? Hell of a temptation to a bunch of people who loathe authority." He waved toward the sofa, a tacit invitation to have a seat.

She limped to the sofa and sat on one end, surprised to find the piece of furniture sturdier and more comfortable than it looked. She glanced up at him, putting aside the thoughts of her cousin and any possible connection to the Bradburys of Boneyard Ridge. Sometimes coincidences were just coincidences.

"And you're part of the plan?" she asked.

"I was what you'd call a forward scout, I suppose." He answered with his back to her, crossing to the fireplace that took up half the near wall. But instead of logs, a large space heater filled the width of the fireplace. He plugged it in to the wall socket and a few seconds later, the unit hissed to life, giving off blessed heat and ambient light.

"What do you do for heat when the power's out?" she asked.

He glanced at her. "There's a woodstove in the bedroom and another one in the kitchen. But the lines to this place were laid underground, so there aren't as many outages as you might expect from a place this far up the mountain."

"How did you ever find this place?"

"My grandfather built it. Let's just say, he lived through the early years of the Cold War and prepared for any eventuality." He smiled, but behind the humor, she saw a hint of admiration as well. He seemed to be a man who appreciated the benefits of having a good contingency plan.

Military, she thought after a moment's consideration, remembering the rucksack full of necessary supplies. Not one of those desk-jockey rear-echelon types, either. She tried to picture his hair, currently collar-length and wavy, cut in a crisp, military style. What did they call it, high and tight?

She could see it, she decided, her gaze narrowing as it skimmed the hard angle of his jaw. Could explain the bum leg as well.

Something flitted in the back of her mind, tantalizingly out of reach. Something to do with a wounded warrior—

"No more questions?" he asked, jerking her attention back to her present situation.

"Why me?"

"I told you. You were in the way."

"Of what? I'm not in security."

His gaze flicked her way. "Yeah, I know."

"What was your role? Following me around? Is that why you stayed on the elevator earlier today instead of getting off?"

His lips curved slightly at the corners, carving shallow dimples in his lean cheeks. "No, that was my own bit of freelancing."

"I suppose you're going to tell me you're really on my side."

The dimples deepened, though there wasn't much in the way of mirth shining from his green eyes. "I suppose you wouldn't believe me if I did."

"I don't know," she admitted, then immediately wished she'd just kept her mouth shut. She was in a very vulnerable situation at the moment, and showing any sign of weakness in front of this man was just asking for trouble.

If her grandmother had taught her anything during the long, hard years of her childhood, it was to never show weakness. Displays of weakness made you look like a tasty morsel for the big, bad wolves of the world, and in the neck of the woods where she'd grown up, there were a whole hell of a lot of nasty wolves roaming those hills and hollows.

She knew from personal experience.

"I don't want anyone hurt. But whatever they're planning for the conference is only the opening act. And I'm not sure what they have in mind for the main event."

Though she wasn't a hundred percent confident that he was telling her the truth about where his loyalties lay, he clearly wanted her to believe he was one of the good guys. So for now, she'd play into that conceit, she decided. What she needed most at the moment was more information, and she'd get it more easily with cooperation than conflict. "What you did for me blew your cover, didn't it?"

He released a long, gusty breath. "I'm not sure."

"They were pretty close when they started shooting."

"They consider me a loser. It's why they didn't let me in on all their plans." He turned to look at her. "You almost didn't recognize me out there yourself, did you? And you were a hell of a lot closer."

She hadn't, she realized. Not at first. Of course, she didn't exactly know him well. "I take it you like for them to think you're not much of a threat."

"It served my purposes," he agreed. "If there's one way they're akin to a real military unit, it's that the people in charge like to make sure there are plenty of warm bodies out there as cannon fodder while they plot world domination from the rear."

Yup, she thought, former military. And not a big fan of authority himself. She filed that thought away and turned her gaze toward the glow of the space heater. Her feet felt as if they'd swollen to twice their normal size, and she didn't look forward to putting her weight on them anytime soon, but the lure of heat proved too powerful. Nibbling her lip to keep from whimpering, she hobbled over to the fireplace and outstretched her hands toward the heater.

Hunter stepped out of her view, and it took all her willpower not to turn and watch where he went. But the whole point of this cooperative captive thing was to convince him it was safe to let down his guard.

She heard the scrape of wood against wood, and then Hunter's big, warm hand flattened against her spine, sending shock waves rippling through her flesh. Clenching her jaw to control her body's helpless reaction, she turned and found him eyeing her, his expression wary. He gestured with his free hand toward the ladder-back kitchen chair he'd retrieved for her. "Sit down. Let me take a better look at your feet."

She sat as he asked, curling her fingers around the edge of the chair seat when he picked up one foot and propped it on his knee.

"May I?" He met her narrowed gaze before nodding toward her foot.

She nodded briskly, and he untied her shoelaces, easing the sneaker from her foot. Her feet had definitely swelled a bit, if the painfully tight fit of the shoe was anything to go by. The socks he'd provided were stained in places, sticking to her foot here and there where blood had dried. But she barely felt any pain, her nerve endings focused entirely on the light rasp of his work-roughened fingers against her bare skin.

He winced a little as he tugged the fabric away from a particularly large scrape. "Sorry."

She took the chance to tug her feet away. "I can take it from here."

He left the front room, disappearing somewhere into the darkened back of the cabin and returning a short time later with a wet washcloth. He handed it over, and she gasped a little at the coldness of the water.

"Sorry. It takes a bit for the water heater to kick in, and I didn't want to make you wait. Warm it a minute in front of the heater if it's too cold."

She didn't wait, welcoming the sharp bite of the cold cloth on her skin as a necessary distraction from her body's troubling response to his touch. The last thing she needed to do was get sucked into some stupid Stockholm-syndrome crush on the man who was, for all intents and purposes, her captor.

No matter how sexy he looked when he watched her with those smoldering green eyes.

He passed her a tube of antibiotic ointment when she'd finished washing the scrapes and cuts on her feet. "Want me to make sure you got all the dirt out of those wounds?"

She shook her head quickly and took the ointment. "I'm good." She slathered the ointment over the abrasions, rebandaged her feet and took the clean pair of socks he offered. "Thanks."

He settled back on his haunches, looking up at her through narrowed eyes the color of the Atlantic in winter, somewhere between green and gray. "I know you're scared," he said in a low, gravelly tone that scattered goose bumps along her arms. "I won't let anyone find you here. I promise."

Pretend you trust him. Get him to drop his guard.

She forced a smile. "Thank you."

He gazed at her for a long, unnerving moment before his lips curved at the corners and those incongruous dimples appeared in his lean, hard face. "I'll go get the heater in the bedroom cranked up so you'll be nice and toasty. Sit here a while longer and thaw out."

She watched him until he disappeared through the door that led somewhere in the back of the small cabin. Releasing a gusty breath, she looked into the glowing wires of the heater and willed her trembling limbs to stillness. She wanted to believe him, she realized with alarm. She wanted the warmth and kindness she'd heard in his voice to be real.

But it couldn't be. Even if he was telling her the truth, he had his own agenda and it had nothing to do with her. She'd be a fool to trust her life to him or anyone else.

If she'd learned anything in the last twelve years, it was that the only person she could depend on was herself.

SHE WAS GOING to run again. Hunter didn't think it would be tonight, not after her close call in the woods. She might even bide her time here for a day or two, let her battered feet mend a bit more. Learn a little about the lay of the land, take time to formulate an actual plan, rather than act on impulse.

But she was going to make a break for it, sooner or later.

She wasn't the pampered princess he'd thought she was. That much was certain.

But what, exactly, was she? Why was she hiding those gorgeous hazel-tipped gray eyes behind contacts? Why had he spotted in her dusky hair hints of blond roots gleaming like gold in the firelight?

And those scars he'd spotted, barely visible on her smooth, shapely legs, weren't razor nicks. They were evidence of a hard-knock childhood spent doing things like climbing trees and skinning her knees and shins on rocks and roots.

So, a tomboy. And a mountain girl, too. Her accent

was almost neutral, her vocabulary sophisticated, but he'd caught a hint here and there of her Appalachian roots.

And if he retained any capacity for reading people, the woman was hiding something. Something big. Important.

Life-threatening?

He wished he could get in touch with Quinn, but until he received some sort of all-clear signal, he had to assume that his available lines of communication were compromised. Ever since Quinn had involved himself in the currently dormant investigation of the Blue Ridge Infantry, the former spook had become downright paranoid about infiltration.

A few weeks on the ground with the BRI had convinced Hunter that his boss was probably giving the ragtag band of soldier wannabes and washed-out former grunts a lot more credit for cohesion and strategic planning than they deserved.

But maybe Quinn knew something Hunter didn't. Hunter had been in the Army long enough to realize that sometimes in a war, the soldiers on the ground could see only part of a larger strategy playing out across a wide and varied battlefield.

Maybe Billy Dawson and his crew weren't the tip of the BRI spear.

Maybe they were the distraction.

The hiss of the space heater near the bed wasn't loud enough to mask the sounds of movement coming from the front room. For a second, his gut tightened as he feared he'd miscalculated the strength of her desire to get away from him, and he was halfway out of the room before he recognized what he was hearing.

She was turning on the lamps in the front room. He could hear the soft clicks of the power knobs turning.

Even from here, he could see the glow of the lamp bulbs as they flicked on, one after another.

He supposed she'd had about all the darkness this evening she could stand.

He had, too, he thought, reaching for the bedroom light switch and flicking on the light.

He looked the room over with a critical eye. He hadn't had time to do more than neaten the place up before he'd had to head back to the hotel in hopes of getting her out of harm's way before Billy's men struck.

He heard footsteps approaching down the hallway, and he steeled himself for her appearance as he turned toward the doorway.

She stopped in the portal, looking past him briefly to take in the particulars of the room before turning her sharp eyes to him. She'd removed the other brown contact lens, he saw, receiving the full impact of those cool gray-hazel eyes.

He blurted the first thing that came to mind. "Fresh sheets."

Her lips curved slightly. "Good to know."

Well, now he felt like an idiot.

"Where's the bathroom?"

"The door you passed to get here."

"Thanks."

"I guess I'll go, then."

She gave a little nod and watched him all the way in as he closed the distance between them, edging around her in the tight space between the bed and the door. Her body radiated heat and the lingering green-apple scent that had haunted him all afternoon, ever since he'd shared the elevator with her earlier.

Everything about this whole damn mission had gone belly-up, he thought as he rode a wave of frustration and testosterone into the cabin's small front room. And he had no idea how to fix it.

But he'd better figure it out, and soon. Because this cabin might be well-hidden and reasonably well-fortified, but if the authorities weren't already searching these woods for the pretty young event planner who'd just gone missing, they'd be crawling these hills by morning.

And they were the lesser of the two evils who'd be looking for them.

Settling on the sofa, he reached into his battered rucksack and pulled a slim leather wallet from a pocket hidden deep inside the pack. Flipping it open, he gazed at the photo tucked inside the first clear plastic sleeve. It had been taken almost a decade ago, just before his first tour of duty. His sister, Janet, and her husband, Dale, had driven to Georgia to see him off, and Dale had snapped a picture of Hunter and his older sister, all three of them aware it might be the last day they'd ever spend together.

They'd been right. But it hadn't been Hunter who'd left the others behind. It had been his brother-in-law, who'd passed away from a burst aneurysm a year into Hunter's two-year tour of duty, leaving Janet alone to pick up the pieces of her shattered life.

Hunter could have left the Army when his enlistment ended, but he hadn't. By then, Janet had seemed to be recovering from her loss, working a new job in the county prosecutor's office.

And Hunter had liked the Army, liked the camaraderie and the discipline, things he and his sister had lacked growing up with a good-hearted but soft-willed mother who'd been little more than a child herself. Hunter had never known his father, and even Janet had only fuzzy memories of the man who'd left when she was just four years old. And their mother had died in a car accident shortly after his sixteenth birthday.

For a long time, it had been just the two of them. She'd been part sister, part mother to him for most of his life, but when she'd needed him most, he'd let her down.

He had to figure out some way to make things up to her. He'd hoped his work with The Gates was going to be an answer, but he'd already blown his first assignment. What were the odds Alexander Quinn would ask him back for a second?

Footsteps on the hardwood floor behind him gave him a brief warning. He closed the wallet and turned to look at Susannah Marsh standing in the doorway.

"Is there anything to eat around here?" she asked.

He pushed to his feet. "Of course. Yes."

He had to pass her to get to the kitchen situated at the very back of the cabin. It was one of the cabin's roomier areas, large enough to accommodate a table near the back door and an old gas stove and oven. The refrigerator was small but still kept things cold and the freezer unit kept things frozen. He wasn't sure how much longer all the original appliances would stay useful, but for now, they served the purpose.

"Want something hot?"

"Soup would be fine," she said with a smile he didn't quite buy.

He'd stocked the pantry a while back, long before he'd known he'd be working for The Gates. He'd figured on using the cabin as a place to get away sometimes, to hide from a world that had become alien to him in so many ways. The cabin had belonged to Janet, who'd inherited it from their mother when she died. Janet had handed over the keys to Hunter when he returned home after his injury.

He supposed she'd known that he'd need a place to hunker down sometimes. To lick his wounds in private.

He doubted she'd ever thought he'd be using it to practically keep a woman prisoner.

"I wish I could let you contact your family," he said.

"Let me?" She shot him a look that stung.

"Bad choice of words," he conceded. "I wish it was safe."

"It doesn't matter. Nobody to contact, anyway."

He frowned. "Nobody will notice you've gone missing? I don't believe that."

"No family to contact," she said with a shrug, looking through the freestanding pantry. "People at work will notice, of course. Especially this close to the upcoming conference...." Her voice trailed off, and her gaze rose toward the ceiling. "Do you hear that?"

Hunter listened. At first, he heard only the sound of wind whistling around the cabin's eaves, and the faint whisper of rain drizzle. But slowly, the deep, rhythmic *whump-whump* sound of spinning rotors filtered through the ambient noise.

"Helicopter," he said quietly, his gut tightening.

"Looking for me?"

"I don't know." He reached over and turned off the kitchen light, then headed through the house and extinguished the rest.

"They'll find this place eventually." Susannah's voice was so close behind him he could feel her breath on his neck. "Won't they?"

"Probably," he admitted.

But he couldn't let it happen tonight.

Chapter Six

The only light in the cabin came from the glowing red
wires of the space heater, but it was enough to reveal the
tense set of Hunter's jaw and the dangerous glitter of his
eyes as he peered between the drawn curtains over the
front window. The helicopter had passed nearly a half
hour earlier, but he was still on high alert, his ramrod
posture and spare, deliberate movements convincing her
all over again that he had spent at least some of his life
in uniform.

"They're gone," she murmured.

His gaze cut toward her. "They could come back."

"Meanwhile, we starve to death in the dark?"

For a second, she thought he was going to bark at her
like a drill sergeant and tell her to shut up and fall in
line. But then he visibly relaxed, a hint of a smile con-
juring up one of those rare dimples she was starting to
covet. "No. I think we can manage dinner without exposing our position."

"It's not going to be an MRE or anything, is it?" she
asked. She'd tried one of those military dried-food pack-
ets once, the so-called "Meals Ready to Eat." She hadn't
exactly been impressed.

He slanted a curious look her way. "Why would you
ask that?"

"Well, clearly you're former military."

That statement earned her a double dose of dimples. "What makes you think that?"

She ticked off the clues. "You've approached this whole thing with the planning of a field general. You carry a military-issue rucksack. And use it to carry a field kit of necessary supplies. You know your way around triage first aid. And you have the posture of a bloody soldier."

"I *was* a bloody soldier," he admitted. "A lifetime ago."

"How long a lifetime?"

He sighed as he nudged her toward the back of the house. "A little over a year."

The elusive half memory that had flitted through her mind earlier made another brief appearance before dancing beyond her reach once more. "That long, huh?"

He stopped in the middle of the kitchen and turned to look at her. "Like I said, a lifetime."

Sore spot, she thought, her gaze dropping to the leg he favored. Encased in jeans, there was nothing obviously wrong with the limb, except the limp he couldn't hide, not even here in the cabin, where the floor was level and there were no obstacles to navigate except for the occasional chair or table.

She'd never been the kind of woman who could resist poking at a sore spot. "War injury?" She nodded toward his bad leg.

The glare he shot her way would have scared a lesser woman. But Susannah had stared down her share of monsters over the span of her twenty-eight years. She didn't even flinch.

He looked away and crossed to the pantry. "Yeah."

She crowded him a little, earning another dark glare. "I should know you, shouldn't I?"

"What makes you think that?" He pulled a can of chicken and dumplings from the pantry and made a show of looking at the expiration date printed on the can in the faint orange glow of the kitchen heater.

"Well, for one thing, I keep thinking I've heard your name somewhere. Hunter's not that common a first name."

"You don't know it *is* my first name." He held the can in front of her. "Dinner?"

She nodded impatiently. "Whatever. Hunter is your first name. And you're a former soldier. And there's something—"

"Don't blow a gasket in there." He tapped her head lightly with his forefinger. "There are a couple of bowls in the cabinet over the sink, and a saucepan in the next cabinet to the right. Grab them while I get the stove going."

She fetched the stoneware bowls and a battered but clean two-quart saucepan while he lit one of the gas burners. Blue flames hissed to life, adding soft light to the warm kitchen. "Where's the can opener?" she asked, scanning the bare counter.

He pulled open a drawer and handed her a manual can opener.

"Oh, we're going old-school."

"No, old-school would be an awl and a hammer." He slanted her an amused look. "You've been away from the hills too long, Ms. Marsh."

"What makes you think I was ever in the hills?"

He turned to look at her, a hint of payback glittering in his light eyes. "Scars on your legs, the kind you get from shinning up trees and climbing rocky hills. Your nails are—were—perfectly manicured, but you can't hide the scars on your knuckles or that rope-burn scar on your palm. You've worked with those hands. Used them for more than typing." He was ticking off the clues in the same way she'd added up her conclusions about his time in the military, she noted with a mix of irritation and grudging appreciation.

"And no matter how high-priced an accent you've adopted, you still slip into a mountain twang now and then."

She closed her eyes to shut out the sight of him, wishing she could make him disappear as easily. All her hard work to completely erase her former life, and he'd seen through her in hours. "I don't know what you're talking about."

"Right." He took the can opener out of her nerveless fingers and opened the can of chicken and dumplings.

But her appetite had fled. "I think I'm too tired to eat," she said quietly, already moving out of the kitchen.

His hand closed around her wrist, pulling her to a halt. "A minute ago you were hungry enough to eat this stuff, can and all."

"Let me go."

He released her wrist. "Are you in some kind of trouble?"

Damn him, she thought. "I just spent three hours running from men with guns who want me dead. I'm being held captive in a backwoods cabin by a former soldier who won't tell me his last name. What kind of trouble could I possibly be in?"

His lips thinned to a flat line. "You should eat something. You'll sleep better."

He was right. She knew he was right. Even though her appetite was gone, her body still needed fuel, especially after her adrenaline-fed mountain hike. Relenting, she sat in one of the kitchen chairs and rested her chin on her hand, watching as he turned his attention to heating the soup.

When he was done, he poured the chicken and dumplings into the two bowls and carried them to the table where she sat, sliding one in front of her. He took a couple of spoons from a nearby drawer and handed her one. "Careful. It's hot."

She stirred the creamy soup before dipping up a spoonful and blowing to cool it. She noticed he wasn't eating any of his own soup. "Not hungry?"

He dropped his spoon back in the bowl. "No."

She threw his own words back at him. "You should eat something. You'll sleep better."

He leaned back in the chair, his chin dropping to his chest as he eyed her through a fringe of dark lashes. He looked tired. Despondent. And for the first time since he'd dragged her into the woods that night, she was beginning to believe his story.

Nobody could feign the kind of misery she saw in those green eyes.

THE RAIN ENDED OVERNIGHT, and a watery dawn seeped its way through the thicket of evergreens surrounding the cabin and slanted across Hunter's face, tugging him out of a light sleep.

He hadn't thought he'd sleep at all, given his hyperalertness when he'd finally tried to lie down and doze the night before. But after a while, even his Army training had been no match for the bone-deep weariness that had come from so much exertion after so many months of relative inactivity.

For the past couple of months, he'd been spending as much time as he could in the gym Quinn had set up in what had once been the root cellar of the old Victorian mansion that housed The Gates. The dirt floor and walls had been reinforced with concrete and softened by a springy gym floor and, in places, spongy mats where one of the agents, Sutton Calhoun, put the agents through a series of hand-to-hand combat drills to keep their skills honed to a razor edge.

Calhoun was a former Marine, another mountain boy, hailing from one of the roughest parts of the county, Smoky Ridge. The place where dreams not only went to die but to die in a spectacularly bloody and painful fashion, as Calhoun had put it one afternoon during a no-holds-barred combat drill.

"Stop feeling sorry for yourself, soldier," Calhoun had barked in his best drill-sergeant tone, throwing Hunter back to the floor and daring him to get back up.

Rubbing the ache in his shoulders, where the heavy rucksack had taken a toll, Hunter wished he could go another round with Calhoun again. His time undercover with the BRI hadn't done much for his stamina. For all their military posturing, the BRI was a militia in name only. They had some tough and very dangerous members, but those men dealt in guns, knives and bombs, not hand-to-hand combat.

He pushed himself up from the sofa and padded barefoot down the short hallway to the bathroom, listening for sounds from the nearby bedroom. The door was closed, the house silent except for the hum of electricity coursing through the walls and the sound of his bare feet on the hardwood floor. He winced a little as the bathroom door creaked while closing behind him, hoping it wouldn't disturb Susannah's sleep.

If she'd managed to get any sleep at all.

She might not be the spoiled little city girl he'd assumed, but it wasn't likely she'd ever found herself on this end of a manhunt before.

As he stepped out of the bathroom a few moments

later, the bedroom door opened as well and Susannah stepped out into the hallway, turning to face him. She was dressed in the jeans and sweater he'd provided the night before, though her hair was freshly brushed and pulled back into a sleek ponytail. "I borrowed a rubber band from your dresser drawer."

"Welcome to it." He stepped out of her way, nodding toward the bathroom. "All yours."

"I used it earlier." Her eyes were winter-gray this morning, the dim light of the hallway dilating her pupils until only a fleck of hazel showed in her pale irises. "You have any eggs in the fridge? I could whip up an omelet."

He wasn't sure he trusted her sudden easy friendliness. She'd been downright combative most of the previous evening, and he doubted a night in a strange place, spent under the constant fear of discovery, would have altered her mood so completely.

So she was up to something.

But what?

"No eggs. I wasn't sure when I'd be back here, so I didn't stock any perishables."

Her dark eyebrows ticked upward, and he could tell by the flicker of her eyelids that she was processing the meaning behind his words. He could almost hear her thoughts, the complex calculations winnowed down to the basics: he planned ahead, but not far. And this bolthole, while well-equipped for the purpose of lying low, hadn't been his first choice.

He hadn't thought he'd need a place to hide her, if she wanted to know the truth. He'd planned to stop the plot without her ever having to know that she was on the BRI's target list.

This cabin had been a different sort of hiding place.

Not from specific threats like Billy Dawson and his rag-tag crew of soldier wannabes but from the world in general.

But from a life that had stopped making sense over a year ago on a dust-dry road in the Helmand Province of Afghanistan.

"So, no milk for cereal, either?"

"Sorry."

"Peanut butter and a spoon?" She punctuated the question with a toothy smile that sucker punched him straight in the gut with a lust so acute, so raw that he almost doubled over from the impact.

He nearly took a step toward her, nearly closed the narrow gap between their bodies before he had a chance to think past the pounding drumbeat of desire rattling his bones and fogging his brain.

"Yeah," he managed, turning away before he did something stupid. "There's peanut butter. And you know what? I think there may be a loaf of bread in the freezer. You could toast it." He waved her toward the kitchen while he crossed the room in three limping strides and made a show of looking through the drapes that covered the four glass panes of the back door, even though he expected to see nothing more than morning sunlight dappling the fallen leaves that littered the tiny clearing around the cabin.

"Want some?" She was making busy noises at the counter behind him.

"Sure."

"Got any jelly?"

"Check the fridge." Frost covered the leaves and grass outside, a grim reminder of how close they'd come to spending the night in a cave instead of this cozy, heated cabin. If she'd succeeded in running away from him, he couldn't have given up the hunt. Not when she was out there somewhere, barefoot and running for her life.

"Mmm, peach preserves."

He glanced over his shoulder and found Susannah watching him with sharp eyes. Her gaze softened immediately when she saw him looking, but not before he caught the feral wariness in her expression.

No, she hadn't dropped her guard a bit. But clearly she wanted him to think she had.

Why? So he'd drop his?

"This is home-canned, isn't it?" she asked brightly, giving the Mason jar lid a strong twist.

"I think so." Janet had helped stock the place, overruling his protest by assuring him that staying busy helping him get situated was a much better use of her time than sitting home worrying about what a Ridge County judge was going to decide about her fate.

Susannah looked around the kitchen, her gaze settling first on the brightly colored pot holders hanging from a hook on the wall, then at the sunny yellow curtains hanging on the windows and the door. "Girlfriend?"

His gaze snapped up to meet hers. "Sister."

"Oh." She gave a slight nod, then turned as the first pair of bread slices popped up from the toaster. "So, no girlfriend?"

"No," he answered, trying to figure out if she was really curious or if the question was another attempt to set him at ease. If so, she'd picked the wrong topic.

"Boyfriend?"

Wary or not, he couldn't stop a grin at that question. "No."

She shrugged and turned back to the counter to put two more slices of bread in the toaster. "You never know."

He stepped up behind her, noting how her body stiffened slightly as she felt his body heat wash over her. But she didn't flinch, didn't show any other sign of awareness, save for the slightest tremble of her fingers when she picked up a butter knife from the counter and dipped it into the open jar of peanut butter.

"What about you?" he asked in a low tone, bending close enough that his breath stirred the tawny hair curling in front of her ear. Definitely a natural blonde, he thought as a glint of morning sunlight stole through the narrow gap of the kitchen curtains to glimmer like gold in the pale hair closest to her scalp.

She turned around suddenly, catching him off guard. He grabbed the counter to keep from stumbling backward, and the move drew him even closer to her, so close that his hips brushed against hers.

Her lips trembled apart, but she didn't drop her gaze, staring up at him with fire in those winter-pale eyes.

"What do you really want?" she asked.

A thousand answers flooded his brain, most of them so intimate, so unsayable that for a moment, he felt as if he'd been struck dumb.

But the fog cleared almost as quickly as it had arisen, and with an almost preternatural clarity, he knew that only one answer would suffice.

The truth.

"Absolution," he said in a voice as raw as a wound.

Chapter Seven

There was no nuance to the word. No hint that Hunter was yanking her chain or making a joke. Just a ragged-edged openness that burrowed like an ache in the center of her chest.

She fought the terrifying urge to cry and plastered on a mask of a smile. "Fresh out of absolution, sugar."

He withdrew his comforting heat from her, and the morning chill swept in to take its place. "I'd like to hike over to Bitterwood and see if I can pick up any news about your disappearance, but I don't like leaving you alone here."

"Afraid someone will find me while you're gone?"

Keeping his careful distance from her, he glanced over his shoulder and met the challenge of her gaze. "Afraid you'll bug out while I'm gone."

"I thought I wasn't a prisoner."

"You're not. That doesn't mean I want you to leave. At least, not until I can figure out what the BRI are planning to do next."

"How're you going to do that?" Alarm fluttered in her belly. "You're not thinking you're going to just walk into the next planning meeting and pretend you had nothing to do with what happened last night, are you?"

"I'm not sure anyone saw me well enough to recognize me."

She took a couple of steps toward him before she realized what she was doing. She drew her hand back, but not before her fingertips brushed his bare forearm.

He gave her a look so scorching she felt something inside catch flame and spread until her skin felt hot and tight beneath his gaze. She made herself look away from him, but the fire didn't die. It just continued to smolder low in her belly.

She didn't trust him. Didn't particularly like him.

But apparently, she wouldn't mind wrapping herself around him and riding him like a cowboy on a wild mustang, as her grandmother used to say when she didn't know Susannah was listening.

Well, hell.

She somehow managed to find her voice and the unraveling threads of their conversation. "You can't chance it. If they did see you last night, they're as likely to shoot you dead before you open your mouth as not, right?"

"Probably," he conceded. He took care not to look at her this time, and she supposed he didn't care for all this sexual electricity zipping and zapping around them any more than she did. "I wasn't going to go stick my head in the lion's den or anything. Just thought I could try to touch base with my boss and see if he's heard anything about what happened last night."

He kept talking about his boss. What boss? Was he seriously still trying to convince her he was working some undercover angle and was actually on her side?

What kind of idiot did he think she was?

She decided to play along, for now, however. No need to antagonize the man who had her held captive, for all intents and purposes. "Do you think it's possible nobody heard the gunshots?"

He shook his head. "They weren't using sound suppressors. The noise would have carried to the hotel."

"But there were only night staff on duty. And the employee parking lot is some distance from the hotel." The more she thought about it, the more possible it seemed that the incident had passed without anyone heading down to the parking lot to see what was going on. "The woods are close, and people do go hunting out here at night, sometimes. I've heard the security guys complain about it, but they're not conservation officers, so they don't actually go out to look for the perpetrators. Most of the time they don't even report the gunfire—"

"They'll look into it when you don't show up for work this morning," he said with grim certainty.

"So, maybe I should show up for work."

His gaze snapped up to meet hers. "No."

"It would throw your merry band of domestic terrorists for a loop, wouldn't it? If I showed up for work like nothing was wrong?"

"And give them a second chance to kill you?" He closed the distance between them swiftly, all semblance of restraint gone. He caught her upper arms in his first tight grip, drawing her gaze to his. His eyes blazed with intensity, plucking her taut nerves until her whole body vibrated from the cacophony.

"You said I'm not your prisoner."

"I never said I was going to let you go back there to be killed." His grip on her arms tightened to the edge of pain. "Listen to me. I nearly didn't get to you in time. So many things could have gone very, very wrong last night and we're damn lucky they didn't. You're safe here.

We've bought time to figure out what to do next. You can't throw it all away by being pigheaded and stupid."

She jerked her arms from his grasp. "Pigheaded and stupid?"

He scraped his hand through his hair, his fingers tangling in the dark mass of waves. For a second, he seemed comically surprised by the snag, confirming for Susannah her theory that he'd worn his hair military short not so very long ago.

He met her gaze again, but in a sidelong way, like a puppy who'd been caught chewing up a pair of $800 Jimmy Choos. "Strong-willed and recklessly brave?"

"Better," she relented, trying not to smile. If she smiled, she'd have to consider the notion that she liked him as well as found him smoking hot, and, well, here be monsters, matey.

"Will you stay here and stay put if I hike over the hill to Bitterwood?" he asked after a long, tense moment of silence.

"What do you plan to do there?"

"Just drop in at the diner in town, put my ear to the ground and see what shakes loose."

"What if someone recognizes you?"

"Not too many people in Bitterwood know who I am anymore," he said in a vague tone that suggested he wasn't really sure he was telling the truth.

"But they did once?"

His gaze slithered away. "Not really."

She took a deep breath and let it out slowly. "Okay. I'll stay put. Just don't be long. And don't get caught."

"I'll do my best." He nodded at the toast that had grown cold and hard while they talked. "Meanwhile, you can eat your cold toast and think of me and a plate full of Maisey Ledbetter's hot buttered biscuits and gravy."

"You're such a tool." She picked up one of the pieces of toast and threw it at him as he ducked out of the kitchen, heading for the front of the house.

The second pair of bread slices popped up out of the toaster, and she snagged them before they could cool down, telling herself as she munched the peanut butter-and-jelly-slathered toast that she didn't envy Hunter's oh-so-fattening biscuit-and-gravy breakfast one little bit.

Then she cleaned up quickly, mentally calculated how long she thought Hunter might be gone on his morning trip to Bitterwood, and got to work.

If she was right, he'd be gone no less than an hour, no more than two and a half. He'd taken his rucksack with him, she found as she looked around the front room, checking the small closet close to the fireplace as well as the big footlocker chest that doubled as a coffee table.

The closet was empty. The footlocker, on the other hand, was full. On top of the pile were a couple of spare pillows and a thermal blanket he'd probably used last night to ward off the chill while he slept on the sofa.

Below that, however, she hit pay dirt.

The first item she encountered was a set of dog tags. Bragg, Hunter M. His blood type—A positive—and a nine-digit Social Security number, no spaces or dashes. U.S. Army. Sounded right.

An Army soldier named Hunter Bragg. Why did that seem so familiar?

When the memory hit, it hit hard, spreading a hard chill through her limbs. She sank to the sofa in front of the open footlocker, clutching the dog tags so tightly they dug into her palms.

He'd been kidnapped by elements of the BRI a little over a year ago, taken captive as leverage against his sister. They'd used Hunter to blackmail the woman into drugging her boss, a prosecutor, so that the BRI could kidnap a little boy the prosecutor had been keeping under his protection.

The pictures in the newspaper had been gut-wrenching—the wounded warrior, home after a harrowing near-death experience overseas, now brutalized by homegrown thugs who'd left him battered beyond recognition. The photo of his bloodied, swollen face had won regional photography awards, if she remembered correctly, but it hadn't been the injuries that had caught the judges' imaginations.

It had been the expression on Hunter Bragg's face that had elevated the snapshot to journalistic art. The photo had shown the expected pain and rage in the man's face, of course, but beneath those obvious emotions had roiled a vortex of humiliation and disillusion. So much raw human suffering captured in the blink of a camera lens—Susannah hadn't been able to look at the photo for long before she averted her eyes.

A creak on the wooden porch outside gave her no time to react, but as the front door opened, she reached into the footlocker and grabbed the scabbard that lay half-hidden beneath an olive-drab canteen. In a heartbeat, she'd closed her hand around the knife handle and swept it neatly from the scabbard. Light pouring through the opening door glittered on the shiny steel edge, bouncing a splash of light across Hunter's scowling face as he slammed the door behind him.

"What the hell are you doing?"

With shaking hands, she eased the knife back into the scabbard and dropped it atop the spare blanket. "Snooping," she admitted.

His expression hardening, he crossed to where she sat and closed the footlocker firmly. "There are people out in the woods not too far from here. Looks like they're gathering for a search party."

"You're Hunter Bragg."

He didn't look at her, but in his darkened expression, she saw a hint of that same humiliation and disillusion that had so struck her in his photo. "There's a place to hide in the cellar. In case anyone stumbles on this place and wants a look around."

"Did you infiltrate the BRI for revenge?"

His eyes closed briefly, then opened slowly. He finally looked up, meeting her gaze. "Revenge rarely works the way you think it will. I prefer to think of what I'm doing as seeking justice."

She nodded, understanding the distinction even though she wasn't really sure there was much difference between a thirst for revenge and the willing assumption of dangerous risk Hunter was taking with the BRI.

"How did you ever talk them into letting you join? They took you hostage—"

"That's how," he answered. "I went to Billy Dawson and told him they could have saved themselves the trouble if they'd just come to me first. I would have gladly contributed my services to the group if they'd just let me know what they were up to."

"And they believed you?"

"People believe what they want to. I convinced them I could be an asset. The group has been reeling ever since their leader got captured. They're looking for a resurgence. I made them see I could be a vital part of it."

"As a disgruntled ex-soldier?"

"Why not? They like to fashion themselves as patriots." He shrugged. "I don't think those searchers out there will find this place right away. They'll probably stick to the beaten path, at least at first, and there's supposed to be rain this afternoon, which will probably cut the search short."

"But they'll be back."

"They will," he agreed. "Somebody probably found your car in the lot at the hotel. There may have been bullet holes."

"They'll think someone took me and dragged me into the woods." She couldn't quite stop a wry smile from quirking her lips, since that was pretty much what had happened.

"I know." He dropped onto the sofa beside her, resting his elbows on his knees. His head dipped until his chin almost reached his chest. "We need a plan."

"You don't have one?" she asked, alarmed. As crazy as the past several hours of her life had been, she'd assumed that Hunter had taken her here to this cabin for some purpose. But he was apparently no more certain as to what to do next than she was. "Did you think you'd just snatch me from the parking lot and wing it?"

He turned his head, slanting a dark look her way. "My goal was to get you out of there without any bullet holes in you. Get you somewhere we could hunker down for a little while and figure out the next part."

"So this is where it's time to figure out the next part?" She clamped down firmly on the urge to have a riproaring panic attack, clenching her hands together so tightly in her lap that her fingers began to tingle.

"I can't reach my boss."

That's it. She was over this cryptic garbage. "And who, pray tell, is your boss?"

"The guy who runs that new private investigations agency over in Purgatory. Alexander Quinn." He eyed her, as if he thought she might know the man he was talking about.

But the name meant nothing to her. "Is that unusual? Not being able to reach him?"

"He told me if I ever tried to contact him and couldn't reach him, I had to assume our line of communication had been compromised."

"What does that mean?"

He worried his lower lip with his teeth for a minute, his brow furrowed with thought. "I think we have to assume we're on our own here, at least until Quinn finds a way to contact me."

"And what if he doesn't?"

"Then I have to find some way to get us to Purgatory without being caught. If I can get you to The Gates, we can figure out a plan of attack with a hell of a lot more resources than I have here."

"What about the law-enforcement conference?" she asked, thinking about the two hundred–plus men and women who were supposed to be meeting at the hotel's conference center wing in just about forty-eight hours. Including her cousin. "Getting me out of there, even if I'm alive, served their purposes, didn't it? Someone will have to take my place."

"Who would that be?" he asked.

"I guess Marcus."

"Marcus Lemonde."

She looked up at him. "You already knew the answer to that question before you asked it, didn't you?"

"Call it an educated guess. I knew they were trying to remove you in order to put someone of their own inside the plans for conference security. Apparently they couldn't get anyone inside security itself, so—"

"So they focused on the Events and Conferences office." And Marcus Lemonde had been working with her for a little over a month—had he been in the Blue Ridge

Infantry's pocket the whole time? Or had they offered him enough money to make treachery worthwhile?

"I ran into Lemonde in the hall outside the meeting rooms, not long after you went in there for your meeting with security. I'd seen him around the hotel, but he'd never spoken to me before then."

"What did he say?"

"That they'd moved up their plans. He didn't like that I was up there on the same floor as you. I guess he thought it might make you suspicious, and since they'd decided to make their move last night—"

"I can't believe Marcus of all people—" She wasn't naive; life had taught her some pretty pointed lessons about just how treacherous people could be, even people who seemed as if they could be trusted.

But Marcus Lemonde seemed wholly innocuous, incapable of posing a threat. If he'd met her in that parking lot one on one, even armed, she would have bet she'd have a better-than-even chance of coming out the winner.

"Looks can be deceiving," Hunter said quietly.

She glanced his way, taking in the shaggy, tangled hair, the day's growth of dark beard, the sharp green eyes, and realized that less than twenty-four hours earlier, she'd actually felt pity for him, with his hangdog demeanor and limping gait.

"They can," she agreed. "And now he's going to be completely on the inside of the security plans for the conference."

"Looks that way."

She shook her head, frustration and anger swelling like a runaway tide in the center of her chest. "No way. No way in hell am I letting that slimy little turncoat weasel screw up my conference."

Pushing to her feet, she started toward the front door of the cabin.

He caught her at the door, his grip as strong as steel. She snapped her gaze up to meet his as his grasp tightened enough to hurt. "Get your hands off me."

He loosened his hold but didn't let go completely. "You can't just barge back into the hotel, Susannah. The people who want you out of the way haven't gone away."

"I show up, we thwart the plan. We tell the world what's going on and not even the BRI mole on the Barrowville police force can keep us from stopping the attack on the conference."

As she started to pull away from his grasp, he tightened his grip again. "You can't just rush out there. If that helicopter we heard is the good guys, the bad guys will damn well be out there trying to get to you first. We're a good three miles from anything that resembles civilization."

"Are you suggesting I save myself at the risk of hundreds of cops who have no idea their conference is about to be blown to smithereens or whatever the hell it is your BRI idiots are planning?" she snapped, trying to jerk her arm away from his tight hold.

He cupped her chin with his free hand, forcing her to look at him. His green eyes glittered with a curious mix of determination and fear. "I'm suggesting you stop for a minute and think about your next move. If you go out there now, without a plan or any idea of what you're up against, all you'll be doing is making damn sure that the BRI gets rid of you as planned. And that's not going to help anyone at that conference, is it?"

He was right. She knew he was right, and maybe if the Tri-State Law Enforcement Society gathering was any other conference, attended by any random set of cops, she wouldn't have led with her heart instead of her head.

But it wasn't just any conference. And at least one of the cops who'd be there in forty-eight hours wasn't random at all.

McKenna Rigsby and her parents had taken Susannah under their protection after everything had gone wrong in Boneyard Ridge, hiding her from the Bradburys until she was able to change her name, her appearance and almost everything about her that would tie her to the tow-headed tomboy she'd been when she fled the mountains.

"My cousin is one of the cops who'll be at the conference," she said. "I owe her more than I could ever explain."

The sharp look of sympathy in his evergreen eyes stung. She looked down at his hand on her arm, watched his fingers loosen and fall away.

"Okay," he said after a stretch of silence filled only by the thud of her pulse in her ears. "We'll figure out a way to stop this thing. But we have to have a plan. Agreed?"

She made herself open her eyes, taking in the determined set of his square jaw and the fire of conviction in his gaze. The heat of that fire swept over her, driving away the morning chill and sparking delicious blazes low in her belly.

Joining forces with a man like Hunter Bragg might be the most dangerous thing she'd ever done. And she'd done some very dangerous things in her life.

But she took a deep breath, sketched a quick nod and said, "Agreed."

Chapter Eight

"Wow. You got all of this put together in the short time you worked at the hotel?"

Hunter looked up from the spread of papers and maps on the kitchen table and found Susannah looking at him through narrowed eyes, as if she was already regretting her decision to play this thing his way. But somewhere in the glittering gray depth of those hazel-tipped eyes, he also saw a hint of grudging admiration that sent an alarming amount of pleasure zinging along his nerve endings.

Once her initial agitation had settled down to a simmer, she'd taken a quick shower and changed into a fresh pair of jeans and another one of the sweaters he'd purchased in Barrowville, this time a jewel green, snugfitting V-neck that hugged her curves like a Ferrari on a mountain switchback and brought out hints of misty green in her soft gray eyes.

Everything about her was softer today, as if she'd shrugged off a coat of armor when she'd tossed the bedraggled remains of her business suit into the trash can in the bedroom. Her hair, free of whatever products she used to achieve that perfect, unshakable updo she wore when she was working, hung in soft, still-damp waves around her face and shoulders. Without makeup, she was a different sort of beautiful than he was used to, all dewy pink skin and a hint of tiny freckles across the bridge of her straight nose. She'd shed nearly a decade in the process, looking not much older than some of the fresh-faced baby recruits he'd known in the Army.

"It was a little longer than that," he answered her question, dragging his gaze from her with way too much reluctance. Clearly, he should have given some thought to the logistics of holing up in a cabin with a beautiful woman. Between combat, his injuries and his sister's legal troubles, his sexual needs hadn't exactly been a priority.

As soon as he could get through this mission, he would take time to think about what came next, including his sex life. But he couldn't let himself be derailed by lust when so much was on the line.

Besides, so what if Susannah Marsh had a soft side? It didn't make her any less trouble, and the last thing he needed was more trouble.

"How long has— What's your agency? The Gates?"

He nodded.

"How long has The Gates been looking into the Blue Ridge Infantry?"

"For a while, though not in conjunction with the conference." The conference connection information had dropped into their laps by way of a confidential informant Quinn worked with. Hunter didn't know who the C.I. was, but Quinn thought his source was reliable, and Hunter supposed he would know. "They were part of a multistate crime organization that several of the local law enforcement agencies have been trying to roll up and put away for a couple of years now."

"The last I heard, they'd accomplished that goal. Something about a bunch of files that was practically a road map of the entire organization?" She sent him a sidelong look, and the wariness he saw in those sharp eyes made him wonder if she was just humoring him with her cooperation, looking for a chance to make her break. "I've never read or heard anything different."

"They're like cockroaches. No matter how many you step on, there are always more."

"Didn't your boss inform the cops that there might be a problem with the conference?"

"He did. Nothing came of it. That's how we became pretty sure that there's someone in the Barrowville PD. who's on the take. Or hell, maybe even a true believer."

"What, exactly, would constitute a true believer in the BRI?" She sounded genuinely curious. "You said earlier they think of themselves as patriots."

"They'd like to believe that. Mostly, though, their idea of patriotism is a loathing for authority, I guess." At least, that was how he'd played it when he'd wormed his way into the local cell after Quinn had given him the name of someone The Gates suspected might be a BRI member. "All I had to do was make some noise about how the Pentagon had screwed me over after my injury, and now the government was railroading my sister, and it didn't take long for someone to buy my load of garbage."

"You must have sold it well."

He shrugged. "Wasn't that hard. There have been days when I half believed it myself. There's a fine line between authority and despotism. Gets crossed a little too often for my taste, you know?"

She nodded. "I do, actually. And it's not always the government."

"Oh, I know. I've seen how Billy Dawson runs the local BRI cell. Tin-pot dictators have nothing on him."

"Nobody at the Barrowville PD even checked on what

you were saying about the conference?" A hint of her previous skepticism seeped into her question.

"Police forces in this neck of the woods have a serious corruption problem. But even if they didn't, there's the issue of how these local cops see The Gates."

"As interlopers?"

"Something like that. See, Quinn has this thing about hiring people who maybe don't have the best of track records." He couldn't keep the wry tone from his voice.

"Does that include you?"

"Maybe. I was a wild kid, and if you were to go by the way I've been behaving over the past year or so, you wouldn't think I'd changed that much." He'd gotten into his share of bar fights since returning home from overseas. He couldn't even blame it on booze, since he'd been stone-cold sober every time. Drinking hadn't done a thing to stem the pain and anger.

Of course, the fights hadn't done much to make him feel better, either. He'd supposed, at the time, that pure luck had brought Alexander Quinn into Smoky Joe's Saloon a few months ago in time to stop a brewing fight and hand his business card to Hunter with an offer of a job interview.

Now that he'd worked with Quinn for a while, he realized that the man had probably gone to the bar with the express purpose of recruiting him for The Gates. Quinn didn't do anything without a plan.

He just wished he knew what Quinn's plan was at the moment, because sitting around and waiting wasn't his style. But he'd seen too many missions go belly-up when someone down the chain of command decided to change things on the fly without having all the information.

"What are you thinking?" Susannah asked.

Glancing up, he saw her studying him with eyes too

sharp for his liking. The woman was turning out to be nothing like what he'd thought she'd be. He'd figured her for smart, but he hadn't banked on her being so observant and insightful that he'd feel like a bug she'd pinned under a microscope for further study.

"What makes you think I'm thinking anything?"

She reached up suddenly, her fingertips brushing his forehead. "This little line. It appears when you're trying to figure things out."

He tried to relax his face as she dropped her fingers away, but the feel of her cool touch lingered on his brow. "And you know this because we're such old, close friends."

"I know this because I pay attention." She reached out again, this time touching the muscle directly behind his collarbone. "Your trapezius muscle tenses up when you're worried."

"Doesn't everyone's?" He knew a frontal attack when he saw one. Every instinct told him she was trying to unnerve him with her touch. Maybe that was her way of regaining some sense of control over her life.

Problem was, it was working. Even the slightest flutter of her fingertips against his skin had sent heat rushing south to his groin. If she ever put her mind to seducing him…

She dropped her hand away from his shoulder, and it took an effort not to groan in response. Her gaze sharpened as it met his. "I know a lot about that hotel, Hunter. I know how things work, where things are, who does what. I can help you if you'll just let me in on what you're planning."

He wasn't much for trusting other people under the best of circumstances, and his current situation certainly didn't qualify for best of anything. But she had proved to be a lot tougher—and tougher-minded—than he'd expected. And it wasn't like Quinn was going out of his way to get in touch.

He needed an ally. Inaction wasn't in his nature, either, and if he didn't figure out something to do soon, something that might actually make the situation better rather than worse, he was going to go crazy.

"Okay," he said, releasing the word in a resigned sigh. "I'll tell you what I'm thinking. But I don't know if you're going to like it."

HE WAS RIGHT. She didn't like it. Not one bit. "I'm not going to hole up here in this cabin while you sneak back into the hotel."

"You asked to hear my plan. That's it." His chin jutting stubbornly toward her, he folded his arms across his chest, stretching his shirt across his broad shoulders and powerful chest, a visual reminder that, for all her bluster, she would be no match against this man in a fair fight.

Of course, she'd never had any compunction about fighting dirty if necessary.

"Are you going to lock me in here against my will? Because that would add a lovely little felony to your record."

He sighed again, a long, gusty one that showed her just what he thought of her refusal to play by his rules. "You're free to go. And be grabbed by people who want you dead before you ever get close to the edge of these woods."

She wasn't so sure about that. Now that she had shoes, appropriate clothing and access to supplies, she might be better at sneaking out of these woods than he thought. Sure, this wasn't Boneyard Ridge, but her little hometown wasn't that much farther up the Appalachian chain, only a few miles down the highway that connected several small mountain towns in the Smokies.

Close enough to give her a fighting chance at finding her way around. She knew what the terrain was like. She knew how to find her direction using the position of the sun at this time of year in this part of Tennessee.

"If I leave here without you, you really are going to make a run for it, aren't you?"

She didn't answer, but she could tell he saw through her silence. That furrow came back to his brow, and his trapezius muscle looked as hard as a rock.

He turned away abruptly. "Would you stop looking at my shoulders?"

She couldn't stop a soft huff of laughter. "Why are you fighting this so hard? You one of those guys who thinks a woman can't do anything without a man showing her the way?"

He turned so swiftly he almost lost his balance, and she saw a grimace of pain flit across his features as the leg he favored twisted. Putting his weight on the other leg, he swung the injured one straight and resettled his weight on both limbs. "You don't know me. Don't presume to know what I think about anything."

"I can only go by your behavior."

"And I can only go by yours."

Her smile faded. "What the hell is that supposed to mean?"

He reached out and caught her hand, his gaze narrowing a little as he took in the clipped fingernails. "What would you do if you weren't here? You'd go get a manicure." He dropped her hand, but the tingle of his touch seemed to linger. "You had to run barefoot through the woods because you wear four-inch heels to work instead of comfortable shoes."

"Heels can be comfortable," she protested, annoyed that he was practically echoing the internal argument she had with herself nearly every day. She could well imagine exactly what kind of woman he thought she was because it was the facade she'd fought hard to present to the world, the armor she wore against discovery.

"Then why do you hide comfortable shoes in your desk?"

"You went through my desk?" Her mind swept quickly through her desk drawers, wondering what else he might have discovered. She tended to keep her personal life out of the office, but there was her chocolate stash—

"It was part of my job," he said, surprising her by looking a little embarrassed.

"Then I'm sure you know appearances can be deceiving."

"Why do you dye your hair brown? And wear brown contacts?"

"Ever heard any dumb-blonde jokes?"

His eyes narrowed. "Nobody would mistake you for a dumb anything."

"Thanks. I think."

He took a couple of slow, deliberate steps toward her. "I know when someone's hiding something. And you, darlin', are hiding a whole lot of something. Which makes me very nervous."

"I'm not the one who took a job at the hotel under false pretenses." Which was a lie, of course, but he didn't know it was.

He couldn't know, could he?

"Are you connected to the BRI?" His voice was warm velvet, but she could sense the steel beneath.

She almost wilted with relief. He didn't know. He

wasn't even close. "Are you crazy? I thought you said the BRI was trying to kill me."

"They are. But why?"

"To put Marcus Lemonde in charge of the conference. Isn't that what you told me?"

"I did," he admitted, his eyes slightly narrowed. "But you know, you have a few tells of your own." He pushed her hair back from her forehead, touching one rough fingertip to the skin beneath her left eye. "Your eye twitches right here when you feel threatened. I noticed it last night in the cave. Twitching away." His fingertip lingered for a moment, then traced a slow, shiver-inducing trail over the curve of her cheek and down to the side of her neck. "What are you afraid of now? You're safe here, aren't you?"

"Am I?" She hated the weakness of her voice, the sudden hammering of her pulse beneath his touch.

"As safe as you want to be." His gaze dipped to her mouth, and fire arced its way through her belly. The heat of his body, so close to hers, was as powerful as a magnet, tugging her toward him before she realized what she was doing.

His gaze flicked up to meet hers, his eyes dark and deep. He wanted her. She could almost feel the desire coming off him in waves, enveloping her in a maelstrom of heat.

Slowly, as if giving her time to react, he slid his hand around the back of her neck and tugged her even closer, his breath warm against her lips. "How safe do you want to be?"

Safer than this, she thought, taking a step that she meant to propel herself backward. But somehow, she ended up even closer to him, close enough that her hips brushed against his, eliciting a quick gasp of breath between his parted lips.

A faint vibration ran through her where their bodies met. She didn't realize until Hunter growled a soft profanity and took a step away that what she was feeling was his phone buzzing quietly in the pocket of his jeans. "This is Quinn. I have to take this."

She took advantage of the timely pause to expand the distance between them, crossing to one of the cabin windows and gazing out at the sun-dappled side yard. The small clearing where the cabin sat was barely large enough to contain the cabin. What lawn existed was a narrow, browning patch of halfhearted grass swallowed within a few yards by the encroaching woods.

This place was well-hidden, she thought. People who lived within easy walking distance might go a lifetime without realizing this cabin and its enigmatic owner existed at all.

By design, she thought, sparing a glance toward Hunter. He stood near the fireplace heater, his head bent as he listened to the man named Quinn.

"I understand," he said finally, slanting a quick look at Susannah. She turned her head back to the window before their gazes connected. "I'll see if I can make that happen."

She waited to see if the conversation continued, but after several seconds, she realized he'd already hung up the phone. She angled another look his way.

He was still standing by the hearth, one arm propped up on the mantel. His gaze seemed fixed on the stone floor of the hearth, his expression grim.

"What does he want to do?" she asked.

His gaze flicked up and locked with hers. "He wants me to find a way back into the hotel. We're no closer to knowing what they were planning than we were last night when everything went down. And we've lost almost a day's worth of investigation."

Her mind rebelled at the thought. The place would be swarming with cops, and they wouldn't stand still and let him explain why he hadn't shown up to work the morning after the hotel's director of events and conferences had gone missing. "How're you supposed to do that without getting caught?"

One dark eyebrow ticked upward. "Is that concern I hear, Ms. Marsh?"

Annoyed by his flippant tone, she pressed her lips shut and didn't answer.

His shoulders rose and fell on a sigh. "I'll figure something out. I have the map of the hotel layout—"

"Does the map show the secret entrance in the executive parking deck?" she asked.

His eyes darkened. "No, it doesn't. There's a secret entrance?"

"I don't know how secret it is, really—I'm sure that the people who run hotel operations know it's there. But it must be fairly secret, because they don't cover it with security and it's never locked."

"And you know this how?"

"I'm an executive."

"But you park all the way down in the employee parking lot."

"So?"

"And you made a note in your phone about joining a gym." He turned to look at her, his gaze sweeping over her in a quick but thorough assessment. "It's the chocolate stash, right? Gained a pound or two, so you're parking in the lower forty so you have to get some extra exercise?"

"You were right. You're definitely not a gentleman."

"I did warn you." He pushed away from the fireplace and crossed to where she stood by the window, his movements slow and deliberate, as if giving her the chance to flee if she wanted to. But she couldn't seem to move.

The heat of him poured over her again, and she felt the strangest sense of relief, as if she'd been waiting for him to return. He lifted one hand and tucked a strand of hair behind her ear. "And in case it means anything, there's not one damn thing wrong with your body." His lips quirked with a crooked smile. "Chocolate looks good on you."

"Don't jump the gun there, hotshot." She flashed him a cheeky grin, even though her insides were quivering. "It's a little early in our acquaintance for you to be picturing me in chocolate."

The phone he still held in his left hand buzzed again. He closed his eyes, taking a swift breath through his nose. "Really?" he muttered to the phone, frustration keen in his voice.

She turned back to the window, waiting for him to drift away again. But his heat remained, cocooning her as his gravelly voice rumbled close to her ear. "What now?"

She heard the faint, tinny sound of a voice in response, though she couldn't make out any words. But there was no mistaking the crackle of tension that ripped through the room a second before Hunter's arm wrapped around her shoulders and dragged her backward, away from the window.

"What?" she managed, before he pressed his palm against her mouth, silencing her.

Then she heard the footsteps. Heavy thuds on the wooden porch outside, moving closer. A pause as thick as molasses in December, then a nerve-shattering trio of raps on the door.

"Anybody home?" The voice was low, drawling. Unfamiliar.

"Not a word," Hunter whispered in her ear.

Chapter Nine

It was impossible to determine friendlies from enemies from the cockpit of an ordinary commercial helicopter gliding over a thicket of evergreens and leaf-shedding hardwoods at a hundred miles an hour, but Alexander Quinn had decided that anybody approaching the well-hidden cabin where his newest operative had holed up should be considered a potential threat. So when he'd spotted the two men heading toward the cabin during the last pass-by, he called Hunter Bragg's secondary burner phone and gave him a heads-up.

He hadn't bothered with the first phone he'd given Bragg shortly before the man went undercover. He'd already established the line of contact between that phone and his own had most likely been compromised.

But by whom? It infuriated Quinn to think that someone might have gotten past his byzantine security system, even though people had been raising eyebrows at his choices of operatives ever since the doors to The Gates first opened. The son of a con artist had been one of his first hires. An actual con artist had followed. A couple of slightly disgraced FBI agents—disgraced not by dishonor, of course, but by putting honor above the bureau—had joined the motley crew. A former CIA double agent who'd spent time on the FBI's most-wanted list for terrorism in South America. An ex-Marine living under suspicion of an eighteen-year-old murder. A former Diplomatic Security Service agent with a record of fighting the system.

All good agents for The Gates, or so he'd thought.

Had he been wrong?

He heard the sound of three loud raps, then a whisper, barely audible, on the other end of the chopper's satellite phone. "Not a word," Bragg whispered, apparently to the woman.

He heard the faint rustle of movement, the snick of a door opening and closing. Then the line went dead.

He put the satellite phone back in its holder and looked at the other passenger in the chopper. The man across from him raised an eyebrow but didn't bother speaking. The roar of the rotors made dialogue impossible without using headsets, and neither of them was inclined to risk putting anything into the ether that might be intercepted. It wasn't likely the strutting imposters of the so-called Blue Ridge Infantry had the equipment to snag in-air chatter, but Quinn wasn't sure they were working alone.

Someone had changed the plan for Susannah Marsh's murder in the middle of the game, and only a chance meeting with another BRI operative, one neither Quinn nor Bragg had known was in place at the hotel, had allowed Quinn's agent to get the woman to safety in time.

They had to be very careful how they proceeded from here on. He'd keep contact to a minimum and trust Bragg to run the operation on the ground.

The Army vet didn't realize it, but Quinn's decision to tap him as an operative for The Gates hadn't been a fluke or even an act of pity, as Quinn suspected Bragg believed. Before the IED explosion that had nearly taken Bragg's life and ended his Army career, Bragg had been an exceptional warrior, valued by his men and his superiors alike for his quick mind and fearless leadership.

Quinn believed a man's character didn't change just because he'd taken a body blow in combat. Bragg might have been having trouble getting back on his feet after the injury, but the warrior was still there, aching to get out and do what he'd been trained to do.

Quinn could use that warrior in the mission he'd undertaken. He sure as hell hadn't been willing to let Hunter Bragg waste away in a quagmire of guilt and anger without giving him a chance to salvage that part of himself that still had much to offer the world.

Now he'd just have to trust that he hadn't overestimated the man's ability to swim instead of sink.

THE CELLAR BENEATH the cabin was small, taking up only half the length of the house, but beyond the stone walls of the basement room was a narrow tunnel carved in the rocky soil and reinforced with concrete. There was an outside exit, if they were forced to use it, well-hidden fifteen yards past the tree line east of the cabin. He hoped they wouldn't have to use it, but if the person or persons still knocking on the cabin door decided to come in and take a look around, they'd have to make a run for it.

They hadn't turned on any lights that morning, the daylight filtering through the windows the only illumination, but the heaters had run all night. Even though he'd flipped the switch on the heater in the front room, nobody who entered the front room would be fooled that the cabin was uninhabited.

At least there was a dead bolt on the front door. If their unexpected visitor was a civilian searcher, the locked door might be enough to send him on his way.

An unlocked door might have been better, and a cold parlor, but that option wasn't available.

He'd hoped the secluded cabin would be far enough from the hotel or any well-used hiking trail to be a reasonable hiding place.

He'd underestimated the reach of the Ridge County Sheriff's Department.

"Who do you think it is?" Susannah's voice was a faint whisper in the darkened cellar. There was no light here in the cellar at all, though he'd grabbed a flashlight from the kitchen on his way downstairs.

"Probably someone from the search party for you."

"I thought we were far enough from the hotel that they wouldn't come out here."

"So did I. We were apparently wrong."

Her hand closed around his wrist, cool and remarkably steady, given the way she'd trembled beneath his touch earlier as he led her downstairs. "What if it's not someone from the search party?"

"I'm not sure it matters to us either way. We can't risk being found."

"Not even by the cops?"

"Do you know which cops you can trust and which ones will sell you out in a heartbeat?"

She was silent for a long moment. "No."

There was an odd tone to her voice that piqued his curiosity, but he shoved his interest to the back of his mind to consider later. Right now, he had to figure out what to do if he heard someone enter the cabin above.

The floorboards creaked quite audibly when someone was in the cabin overhead. He'd learned that fact when Janet had helped him move his stuff into the place when he first returned from Afghanistan and decided to make it his getaway. It wasn't officially in his name; Janet still held the deed. It wouldn't be the first place Billy Dawson looked for him, since he'd let Billy think he was estranged from Janet, that he'd hated her job with the county prosecutor's office and she'd hated his political views. He'd hoped it would be enough to protect his sister from trouble if his undercover work went belly-up.

God, he wished he could talk to her right now, let her know everything would be okay.

"Either way, whether they come in or not, we can't stay here after this," he murmured. "You realize that, don't you?"

She remained silent, though her fingers tightened around his wrist.

"I know you don't trust me. But I'm asking you to take a chance here. Even if the people knocking at the door go away, we can't risk staying here now that someone knows this place exists. They may go find the cops, get someone who can break in and take a look around. Sooner or later, they'll connect this cabin to me and then they're going to turn it upside down."

"Because you're their primary suspect in my abduction."

He nodded. "I go missing from the hotel the same day you go missing? Hell, yeah, they're going to think the worst."

"Would they be wrong?"

"Technically, I guess not."

They fell silent, the only sound in the small cellar the whisper of their breathing. Overhead, the cabin remained eerily quiet.

"Do you think they went away?" Her whisper broke the stillness a few moments later, plucking his nerves.

"I don't know," he admitted softly. "I need to go up there and check. Can I trust you to stay put?"

"Nowhere to go but up there with you."

He hadn't told her about the outside exit, he realized. He probably should tell her now, but he wasn't sure he could trust her not to make a run for it. She was strong-willed and hardheaded, traits he ordinarily liked in a woman—unless those traits led her to make risky choices.

But leaving her stuck down here, defenseless, if he met with trouble upstairs would be putting her in harm's way. She was a smart woman, and more resourceful in a crisis than he'd thought. She had a right to make her own decisions, either way.

"There's a door hidden behind that old broken armoire in the corner. When you open the armoire, you'll see it's empty and all the shelves have been removed. Just step into it. There's a pressure switch in the bottom that opens the door to a tunnel that leads to a door outside." He put the flashlight in her hand. "If I'm not back in five minutes, you go. It leads to an escape hatch in the woods."

She was silent for a long moment before her fingers closed over the flashlight, brushing his. "Who are you?"

"The better question might be, who was my grandfather?" he murmured. "He worked at the Oak Ridge National Laboratory during the height of the Cold War."

"A scientist?"

"A maintenance man, but he saw and heard enough to be paranoid about nuclear war, so he did what he could, in his limited way, to build himself a shelter in case the Soviets dropped the big one." He couldn't hold back a wry smile, even though she couldn't see it in the dark. "His understanding of nuclear fallout was clearly limited, but you can't fault him for his will to survive."

"Okay. Five minutes."

As he started toward the stairs to the main floor, she grabbed his arm, her fingers tight. He stopped, turning back toward her, and their bodies collided with a light thump, the softness and the steel of her pressing intimately against him. He found it suddenly impossible to breathe.

"Be careful," she whispered, her fingers convulsing briefly around his arm before she let him go and backed away, robbing him of her soft heat.

Sucking air into his burning lungs, he felt his way to the stairs and climbed as silently as he could. The door creaked faintly as he eased it back open, the sound skating down his back on a razor's edge of alarm. Staying very still, he listened.

The knocking sounds had subsided a few minutes earlier. There were no sounds of occupation, save for his own carefully shallow respirations. No creak of the wooden floor. No rustle of clothing. Everything was utterly quiet.

Edging through the narrow opening of the doorway, he eased down the short corridor to the front room. It was empty. His footsteps sounded like thunder as he crossed quickly to the front window and peered through the narrow gap in the curtains with one eye.

Two men walked away from the cabin slowly, with no attempt at stealth or any show of distress or alarm. One of the men was speaking into a phone. Calling in a report of their attempt to enter the cabin to look for the missing woman?

They'd be back. There was no way the county sheriff's department would leave a cabin in the woods unexamined as long as Susannah Marsh was missing.

They'd bought some time, but not much.

He crossed back to the cellar door and called softly. "They're gone. You can come back up."

For a long, tense moment, there was no sound from

below. Then he heard her footsteps on the wood stairs and his heart started beating again.

"Did you see them?" she asked as she emerged from the stairwell.

"Just their backs. Looks like a couple of search-and-rescue volunteers. One of them was on the phone."

"Reporting the existence of the cabin?"

He nodded grimly. "I'm sorry. I was hoping we'd have a little more time here."

She gave him a considering look before her expression softened and she gave a slight shrug of her shoulders. "What good is it doing us to hole up here, anyway? It's not going to stop whatever your buddies have planned for the conference."

"Yeah. And they're not my buddies."

She gave him another one of her laser-sharp looks. He could almost feel the heat of her scrutiny, as if she'd somehow burrowed her way inside his brain and started sifting around to see what was there. He was both intrigued and unnerved, and it took most of his self-control not to look away.

"Remember I was telling you that I had access to the executive parking deck at the hotel?" she said just before his control snapped.

He nodded. "Yeah, you didn't finish your thought earlier." A flood of heat poured through him as he remembered why.

Her eyes darkened. "Well, what I was going to tell you is that since the door has no security system, I can get us into the hotel without anyone knowing about it."

"But how are we going to get into the executive parking deck without a vehicle that has an access sticker or whatever it is that lets you in?"

"That's the thing," she said with a grin so cheeky

and appealing he almost kissed her right then and there. "Half the battle of any security system is putting up a stern front. But it's mostly show. There are all kinds of holes in the security system at the hotel. Not for the guest rooms of course—management takes guest security and privacy really seriously. And they're careful about cash handling and all that. But for getting in and out of the place? Really not that hard."

He gave her a considering look of his own. "You sound like a thief."

Her eyes narrowed slightly. "Not me. I'm honest as the day is long."

SUSANNAH WASN'T LYING. She wasn't a thief. But her daddy could have written a book on the topic, and he'd taught her just about everything he knew about parting people from their hard-earned cash.

Her grandmother had plucked her out of that situation fast enough, once she realized her daughter had run off and left Susannah and her brother, Jimmy, with their shiftless daddy. Jimmy had run away from their grandmother's place and gone back home to be his father's little sticky-handed apprentice, but Susannah had fought to stay with her grandmother.

Her grandmother hadn't been soft, sweet or maternal, which probably explained Susannah's own mother's desperate need for love and attention. But her grandmother had loved Susannah in her own way, in a pragmatic and fierce way. And that kind of love was better than the selfish claptrap her father tossed around and called affection.

Susannah supposed she was very much like her grandmother where the heart was concerned. Feelings were no substitute for good sense. Feelings would steer you wrong every time. Good sense always carried the day.

"What aren't you telling me?" Hunter asked softly.

She ignored his question. "We've got to get out of here fast, right?"

"Pretty fast. They might not get back here in the next couple of hours, but they'll be back to take a look around."

"So let's not waste any more time talking. Do you have an extra backpack around here for me? That way we could take double the supplies."

"You sure you want extra weight? Where I'm taking you is a two-mile hike up the mountain."

She stifled a groan at the thought. Working a desk job had taken a toll on her endurance, but she was young and mostly fit. Her feet would probably hurt like hell, but there was nothing structurally wrong with her feet, and pain alone wouldn't kill her.

She lifted her chin and met his gaze. "I can handle it."

He gave her another one of those long, thoughtful looks he'd been tossing her way over the past twenty-four hours, as if he were assessing her. She had a feeling his initial impression of her had changed quite a bit since he dragged her out of that parking lot into the woods, with good reason. The woman he knew was Susannah Marsh, a sophisticated, polished professional.

But the woman standing here in jeans and sneakers was all Susan McKenzie, except for the brunette dye job. She wore no makeup, her gray eyes were back to their normal color, and she even carried herself differently, her shoulders squared to challenge an unforgiving world.

She was her grandmother's granddaughter, after all.

"Okay," Hunter said finally with a brief nod. "I'll get the pack."

"I'll see what we can take with us from the pantry."

As she started to pass him, he reached out and touched

her hand. A brief flick of his fingers against hers, but it was enough to send tremors darting down her spine. She looked up, not feeling nearly as fierce as she had just a moment earlier, and the heat that poured into her belly at the look in his eyes only made her feel weak-kneed and vulnerable.

"I know you don't trust me," he said quietly. "I know you have no reason to. But I take protecting you very seriously. I don't want you to be afraid of me."

"I'm not." She forced her chin up, even though she was feeling anything but strong.

"Good." His fingers brushed hers one more time, the lightest of caresses, and fell away.

Somehow, she managed to make it to the kitchen without her wobbly knees buckling under her.

Chapter Ten

About four months earlier, shortly after Alexander Quinn had approached him at Smoky Joe's Saloon in Bitterwood, Hunter had decided to see what the CEO of The Gates was really all about. So he'd followed the man one afternoon on a winding ride up Lamentation Rise, a foothill just outside the Great Smoky Mountain National Park. On a clear day, he suspected, a person could probably see most of Ridge County spread out like a postcard, but the day he'd followed Quinn had been rainy and cool for early June. The peak had seemed to be buried in the clouds, the sprawling cabin near the summit a misty apparition in the afternoon gloom.

All this time, Hunter had believed that Quinn hadn't spotted his tail job. He should have known better.

"Meet me at my cabin on Lamentation Rise," Quinn had said tersely into the phone after warning Hunter about the two men heading for his front door. "I know you know where that is."

"How much farther?" Trudging beside Hunter, Susannah sounded weary. She looked weary as well, her brow furrowed and dark circles starting to bruise the skin beneath her winter-gray eyes. They'd been hiking for almost two hours now, rabbiting around in circles for the first mile up to be sure to avoid any searchers out in the woods. Quinn's cabin was far enough up the mountain that it wasn't likely the searchers would get anywhere near it.

But they had to get there without being spotted first.

"Almost there," he told her, hoping he was telling the truth. Quinn had given him quick GPS coordinates before hanging up, but a lot had been going on. He wasn't sure he'd remembered them exactly, and it wouldn't take much to go completely off track.

If he could just find the narrow road he'd traveled up the mountain to reach Quinn's cabin—

"Is that a road?" Susannah asked.

He followed her gaze and saw the dusty gray of a gravel track barely visible through the trees ahead.

"It is," he answered, relief fluttering in his gut. Reaching for her hand and giving it a tug, he set out for the road, giving her little choice but to follow.

The day was clear, the cabin visible almost as soon as they reached the rocky road up the rise. Next to Hunter, Susannah sucked in a quick breath, and he turned to find her grimacing.

The gravel, he realized, watching her take a couple of limping steps forward. The rocky surface must be hell on her injured feet, especially after so much nonstop hiking.

He shrugged his pack from his back and swung it from the crook of one elbow. "Okay. Hop on." He held his free hand out to her.

She looked at him as if he'd lost his mind. "You've got to be kidding."

"You enjoy pain?"

"*Enjoy* might be a strong word. I can endure it, though."

"You don't have to. Come on. Piggyback time."

She stared at him a moment, her lips pressed into a

thin line of annoyance. But he could see the idea of getting off her sore feet appealed to her as well.

"Oh, what the hell." She grabbed his shoulders and jumped onto his back, wrapping her legs around his waist. "Mush!"

Grinning, he hooked his arm around her legs to steady her and carried her forward. The extra weight of the woman and her pack made the last few yards to the cabin downright grueling, but he made it there without any embarrassing stumbles and deposited her on the first step of the cabin's wooden porch.

Before he had a chance to catch his breath, the front door of the cabin opened and Alexander Quinn stepped out onto the porch, greeting them with a silent nod.

Susannah's surprised gaze flicked toward Hunter. "What's going on?"

"Susannah, this is Alexander Quinn. Quinn, this is Susannah Marsh."

Quinn's eyes narrowed slightly at the introduction, but he managed a hint of a smile as he reached out his hand. "Ms. Marsh."

Hunter watched as the princess reappeared, her neck extending regally and her movement graceful as she took Quinn's hand and shook it firmly. "Mr. Quinn."

Quinn's lips quirked at the corners but the smile faded as quickly as it had come. He released Susannah's hand and looked at Hunter. "Any trouble getting here?"

"We had to do some evasive maneuvers on the way up, but no trouble."

Quinn took the pack from Hunter's arm and motioned for Susannah to give him her backpack as well. "Hungry?"

Susannah's eyes lit up before she could school her features to a neutral mask.

"Food would be great," Hunter answered for her, following her and Quinn into the cabin.

While the large cabin was rustic-looking on the outside, inside Quinn had made the most of the space to showcase an exotic display of furniture, fabrics and knickknacks he'd apparently collected during decades of Foreign Service. Hunter supposed the princess, who was looking around the place with great interest, could probably tell him just what it was he was looking at as he scanned the room and drank in the riot of color and textures, but all he could think about was finding the nearest tub and taking a long, hot soak.

His bum leg felt as if it were about to fall right off his body.

"I have to be back at the office in an hour, so we don't have long," Quinn warned as he deposited the backpacks near the large brown leather sofa that took up most of the middle of the large front room. "The fridge is full, so as soon as we have a quick word about tomorrow, you can dig in and see what you like."

"Tomorrow?" Susannah and Hunter asked in unison.

Quinn looked up at them both. "Tomorrow is the start of the conference. And we're going to have to figure out a way to get the two of you back in that hotel."

Hunter was used to his boss's bluntness by now, but he'd have expected Susannah to bristle. Instead, she gave a short nod and said, "I've had a thought about that."

Even more interesting was Quinn's lack of reaction to Susannah's response, as if she'd behaved exactly as he expected. And there'd been that considering look earlier when Hunter had introduced him.

Just what did Quinn know about Susannah that Hunter didn't?

"THERE'S A SKELETON crew after midnight, so if we're going to get into the hotel before the conference starts, tonight's our best bet." Susannah peered at the hotel floor plans that Quinn had produced when they gathered around the small round table in the kitchen. The cabin was deliciously warm—central heating rather than wall units—and on her way from the front room to the kitchen, she'd glimpsed a large bathroom she couldn't wait to try out.

But first things first.

"The entrance from the executive parking garage leads into the basement level, which is maintenance and storage." She pointed to the floor plans. "There's an elevator here, but it's noisy when it reaches a floor and opens, so we'd lose any advantage of stealth. Plus, it's like being stuck in a cage—if there's someone waiting at the floor we exit, we're busted. I think our best bet is to bypass the elevators and take the stairs."

Across the table from her, Hunter grimaced. He'd been favoring his left leg since they'd arrived at Quinn's cabin, the limp more noticeable. She felt a twinge of guilt about letting him carry her on his back. All she had were some scrapes and bruises on her feet. He probably had bullet shrapnel and God only knew how much surgical hardware in that bad leg of his.

They were going to be quite the cat-burgling pair tonight.

"What's the plan when we get upstairs?" Hunter asked in a lazy drawl that belied the sharpness of his gaze.

"First, I'd like to take a look inside Marcus Lemonde's desk," Susannah replied.

"You think he'd keep something incriminating there?" Quinn asked.

She slanted a look his way. "I don't know. I'll tell you more once I've searched it."

"How're you going to get into the office?" Quinn asked. "Isn't it locked at night?"

And her keys were somewhere with her purse, wherever she'd dropped it during the ambush. "I didn't think of that."

"I did," Hunter said with a grin. "I made a copy of your office key from the master set at the hotel once I realized you were the BRI's target."

"So that's how you got my clothing and shoe sizes." She wasn't sure whether she was impressed by his resourcefulness or a bit creeped out by the fact that he'd gone through her things thoroughly enough to find the change of clothes she kept in the bathroom closet in her office.

"Do you know anything about handling firearms?" Quinn asked Susannah.

"I do," she answered. "I'm best with a Remington 700."

"A bit big for our purposes," Hunter murmured, giving her an odd look.

What's the matter, big guy? You think a girl can't handle a big gun? She shot him a hard look. "I've handled pistols, too. My personal weapon is a Ruger SR40."

Hunter's green eyes glinted amusement. "The princess has teeth."

Princess?

"I have a Glock 27 I think you can use with no problems." Quinn crossed to a large armoire near the fireplace and unlocked it to reveal a gun cabinet. There were rifles, pistols, shotguns, even a couple of high-tech hunting crossbows. From the drawers in the middle of the armoire, he pulled a box of .40-caliber ammunition.

"This should do you for tonight." He handed over the pistol and the ammo.

"I've got my Glock," Hunter said, "and some rounds in the backpack, but if I need more, you have any 9 mm rounds?" The look Quinn gave him made Hunter laugh. "Right. Who do I think I'm talking to?"

"I have to go. Can't be late for this meeting." Quinn was already on his way toward the door. He stopped at the entrance and turned to look at them. "Consider this your place for now. I'll be staying in town. There's a Ford Explorer in the garage out back. I left the keys for you on the dresser in the master bedroom, along with a new burner phone. Call if you need me—my secure number is already listed on the speed dial." His gaze wandered from Hunter to Susannah. "I'll let you two work out the sleeping arrangements."

Then he was gone, the door closing firmly behind him.

"He has a lot of faith in you," Susannah remarked.

"Looks like he has some faith in you as well." Hunter turned to look at her, his eyes narrowed with suspicion. "Do you know each other?"

She shook her head. "Never met him before."

"He seems to know a lot more about you than I do."

Hunter's words set off a flutter of alarm in her belly. She tried to quell it, taking care that her expression showed none of her sudden apprehension. "There's not a lot to know."

"Somehow I doubt that," he murmured.

"Do you mind if I take the bathroom first?" She started moving toward the hall without waiting for him to answer.

Before they'd settled down with the hotel floor plans, Quinn had told her he'd put some clothes for them both in the closet of the master bedroom and had pointed out the door on their way to the kitchen. She detoured to the master bedroom to pick out a change of clothes and stopped short in the doorway.

The room was larger than she'd expected, big enough to accommodate a huge king-size bed, a dresser and chest of drawers, and a sitting area near an enormous wall of windows that overlooked miles of cloud-capped mountains to the east. It was the view that caught her breath, and she made her way to the large-paned windows, wondering just how much Alexander Quinn had paid for a view this amazing.

"I thought you were headed to the bathroom." Hunter's low voice was so close she jumped. He put his hands on her shoulders to steady her, smiling a little as she turned to face him. "Sorry. Didn't mean to startle you."

"This place must have cost a fortune," she said, nodding toward the window. "You don't get a view like that for cheap."

His hands still warm on her shoulders, he followed her gaze. "I guess so. I don't think Quinn's hurting for money."

She wasn't inclined to remind him he was still touching her, since she was in no hurry for him to stop. "I guess The Gates is pretty successful, then?"

He shrugged. "I haven't been working there long. I don't think it's even been in business that long, come to think of it. Maybe it's family money."

"Or whatever alphabet-soup job he had before opening his agency paid better than we thought."

He looked at her then. "Alphabet-soup job?"

"You know, FBI, NSA, CIA, something like that. He has covert operative written all over him, don't you think?" Which might explain why he seemed to know more about her than she liked.

What if he knew exactly who she was? It was possible, she supposed; the situation that had sent her running to her aunt's home in Raleigh had made the papers as far away as Nashville and Chattanooga, she knew. And Alexander Quinn came across as a man who made a point of knowing everything there was to know about anyone who crossed his professional path. Once he knew she was a target, he'd have looked into her past.

How far back had he been able to go?

She'd changed her look in the twelve years since she'd left Boneyard Ridge. Different eye color—at least, until she'd lost the contacts. She had a different hair color and hairstyle. Gone were the faded, sometimes ratty jeans and tees she'd worn most days, now replaced by stylish tailored suits and stratospheric heels. Makeup and polished manners helped her look like a completely different creature, but at her core, she was still Susan McKenzie, a little redneck girl from the hillbilly haven of Boneyard Ridge.

She supposed someone like Alexander Quinn, who'd clearly spent a little time dealing with people who lied for a living, could see through her facade easily enough to know she wasn't who she appeared to be.

But what other secrets had he learned?

Hunter dropped his hands from her shoulders, and she bit back a sigh of disappointment. It wasn't a good idea to get used to having him around. Not good to start thinking about other places he could touch her, either. They would get through this mess tonight, and then she'd have to get serious about coming up with a different name, a different look and a different place to hide.

She'd taken a lot of risks coming here to Barrowville, so close to her hometown just across the county line.

She should have known better.

But she'd missed the mountains, living in the city. In

the flatlands, as she and other hill folks called it. She hadn't been meant to live in the flatlands, especially not in a sprawling, noisy capital city like Raleigh, North Carolina. The job offer at the Highland Hotel and Resort had seemed like a kiss from God himself.

But everything had changed now. Once she was done here, it would be time to move on again.

Hunter wandered over to the closet. "Want to take bets on whether he got our sizes right?" he drawled.

"I'd bet on Quinn." She turned to watch as he pulled out a couple of large suitcases and hauled them up onto the bed.

The CEO of The Gates had done more than select the right sizes. He'd also chosen exactly the clothing she'd have opted for herself in the same situation—sturdy jeans, shirts and sweaters that would easily layer, and a weather-resistant coat that would keep her both warm and dry if she and Hunter were forced to brave the elements again after their hotel caper. Nothing stylish or decorative in the lot. Certainly nothing Susannah Marsh would have chosen for herself.

But Susan McKenzie, on the other hand—

"How'd he do?" Hunter asked, pulling out a pair of boxers, a long-sleeved tee and a pair of jeans from his own clothing stash.

"Not bad," she answered. "How about you?"

"Everything looks like it'll fit." He nodded toward a door next to the closet. "I think that's probably a bathroom, if you'd like a little more privacy. I can take the other bathroom."

She opened the door and found a roomy if utilitarian bathroom behind it, complete with a large tub and a separate shower. "Okay, thanks." She turned to smile at him, but he was already halfway out the door.

Tamping down a sigh, she dug out a fresh change of clothes and headed for the shower.

THE WATER JETS in the whirlpool bath shot warm bursts of water against his aching leg, easing the tension in his muscles and sending little shivers of relief jolting through him. Leaning back against the foot of the tub, Hunter closed his eyes and tried to clear his mind of his escalating list of troubles and concerns. The key to a successful mission, he knew, was laser focus on the ultimate goal.

Tonight's goal wasn't to get in and out of the Highland Hotel and Resort undetected. That was just the means to the end. Nor was the goal to discover exactly what Billy Dawson and his crew were planning for the law-enforcement conference that started the next day, although that was also on their agenda.

No, the goal was to stop the BRI's plan before it ever started. And that meant they were going to have to think like terrorists.

Hunter had some experience with getting into the heads of people who thought nothing of blowing up hundreds or thousands of civilians to achieve their goals. The mind of a terrorist was a bleak, soulless place. He didn't imagine it made much difference what the terrorist's goal might be—anyone who gave no thought to differentiating between innocent civilians and armed troops was a monster. Any deviation was a matter of degree, not intent.

The BRI had already proved their depravity by going after Susannah Marsh. The woman meant nothing to them, other than the impediment she posed to their plans for the conference. She was nothing more than a lock to be broken, moved aside and discarded.

Don't think about her. She's a distraction.

But he could hardly shut her from his mind, could

he? She wasn't merely a target to be protected. She was going to be his partner in this break-in, and if he didn't take hold of his libido when she was around, this mission would go straight to hell.

When the hot water and whirlpool motion finally unknotted his muscles enough to erase the worst of the pain and fatigue in his bum leg, he drained the tub, toweled himself dry and went to look for Susannah.

He found her in the front room, hunched on the sofa in front of the television that hung over the fireplace. She'd dressed in jeans and a dark blue sweater that hugged her lithe body like a lover. But what he saw on her face as she watched the screen quelled any prurient urges he might have indulged.

She looked terrified.

He followed her gaze to the television screen and saw that she was watching a midday news program out of Knoxville. As an attractive blond news anchor spoke, the image on the screen changed to a slightly grainy photo of Susannah. She looked pretty and composed in what must have been her official publicity headshot, a Mona Lisa smile barely hinting at the depths of the woman beneath the placid exterior.

"As authorities widen their search for the missing Barrowville woman, the mystery surrounding her deepens. Who is Susannah Marsh? Authorities aren't willing to discuss anything about her background on the record, but sources close to the investigation admit they're stymied in their attempts to learn more about the missing woman's murky past."

Hunter turned his gaze back to Susannah's stricken face. Her eyes were closed, her lips trembling.

"Who is Susannah Marsh?" he asked softly, crossing to sit on the sturdy coffee table in front of the sofa. She opened her eyes slowly, her eyes dark with fear.

"A lie," she said.

Chapter Eleven

"I was sixteen." The words seemed to squeeze their way from her tight throat, past her reluctant tongue and lips, to spill into the taut silence of Alexander Quinn's cabin. She opened her eyes to find Hunter's green-eyed gaze fixed on her face, serious but somehow comforting, as if he wanted only to understand her.

She wanted to believe there was someone she could trust with the real truth about who she was, because it had been a long, long time since she'd revealed anything true about herself to anyone.

"You were sixteen," he prodded gently when her nerves failed her.

She reached across the space between them, squeezing his hand. "You have to promise me you'll never tell another soul what I'm about to say. Promise me."

His brow furrowed. "Did you kill someone?"

Her whole body went numb, and she jerked her hand away.

He caught her arms in his big, strong hands as she started to rise. "Tell me, Susannah. Tell me what has you so damn scared."

"I can't."

"I won't tell another soul what you tell me. I don't care what it is. I swear it." His fingers cupped her chin, forced her to look at him. His green eyes were solemn. "I won't tell anyone."

"If you do, you might as well put a gun to my head and pull the trigger." She hated how melodramatic those words sounded, how overwrought. But the truth was the truth.

"I told you. Not a word." He dropped his hand away from her face, let go of her arm and sat back, giving her space, as if he understood just how vulnerable she felt at the moment.

She swallowed with difficulty and began again. "My whole life, until I was sixteen, I lived in a place called Boneyard Ridge, just across the county line from here. It's a little nothing of a place, not much more than a road curving over a mountain, a few homes dotting the ridge. Most everybody who had a lick of sense or two pennies to rub together got out as soon as they could, but my grandmother had no intention of going anywhere. 'I was born here, and here I'll meet my Maker,' she always said. I used to think she was crazy. Until I had to leave the place myself."

"Had to leave."

She looked up at him, trying to read his thoughts behind his placid green eyes. "When I was sixteen, a man named Clinton Bradbury decided I was going to be his, and I'd have no say about it. I never gave him any encouragement, no matter what the Bradburys told folks. But he wanted what he wanted, and I don't know why, but he wanted me. I told him no a dozen times, but he thought I could be broken. He threatened my grandmother, which he should've known better than to do."

"What did she do?"

"Ran him off our property with a shotgun and told him never to come back."

"But he did?"

She nodded, unable to meet his gaze. "My grand-mother had fallen down the stairs at the church that morning and they wanted to keep her at the hospital over in Maryville overnight for observation. She didn't want me to stay at the cabin by myself, but I told her I could take care of myself. I was nearly grown up, you know? And Clinton hadn't come around again since the shot-gun incident."

"But he came that night."

"He'd been waitin' for the chance." She heard the way her accent broadened and hardened into the mountain ca-dence she'd spent years trying to erase. She sighed. "He just didn't know I had a shotgun of my own."

Silence fell between them for a long, thick moment before she could find her voice again. "I shot him just the once, but it was close range and true. I guess I hit an artery, 'cause before I knew it, there was an ocean of blood on my bedroom floor."

Hunter reached across the space between them and closed his hand over her arm. Her skin rippled beneath his touch, but she didn't let herself pull away. "I'm sorry," he murmured. "That must have been awful for you."

"I didn't want him dead. I just wanted him to stop. I tried to talk him out of there, but he wouldn't listen. He kept grabbing me. He tore my pajama pants—" She shud-dered at the memory, at the rage and sense of violation that haunted her to this day. "I couldn't let him rape me. I just couldn't. I didn't have a lot in the world, but my body was my own and I hadn't agreed to give it to him."

"The police didn't believe you?"

She looked up quickly. "We'd already talked to the sheriff about the way Clinton had been harassing us.

We'd made reports, played it by the book. Let's just say, they weren't surprised."

"Then why did you have to run?"

"The sheriff isn't the real power in Boneyard Ridge." Her voice lowered with anger. "That would be the Bradburys. And they didn't care what Clinton had done to earn that load of buckshot. They just knew one of their kinfolk was dead, and I'd done it." She could still hear old Abel Bradbury's rough-edged voice. "You don't kill a Bradbury in Boneyard Ridge and get away with it."

"So you had to hide from them."

"If I wanted to live. They damn near killed me once already." She pulled aside the neckline of her sweater and showed him a bullet scar that marred her skin just above her left collarbone.

Hunter muttered a profanity.

"The cops couldn't find the person who took a pot-shot at me right outside my own door. If my grandmother hadn't been there, if she hadn't dragged me inside before they could get off another shot—" She wrapped her arms around herself, even though she no longer felt cold. "The cops never found the rifle that shot me, so they couldn't tie the shooting to the Bradburys."

"A lot of places in the hills to hide your sins."

She nodded. "But I knew who shot me. Besides my grandmother, nobody else in Boneyard Ridge gave a damn about me one way or another. Nobody but the Bradburys, and they just wanted me dead."

Hunter touched her cheek. She tried not to flinch, but it was too soon, her emotions too raw, to handle the feel of his fingers on her flesh. He dropped his hand away. "I'm sorry."

She shook her head. "It's not you. I promise, it's nothing to do with you. It's just—" She stopped short, her gaze sliding toward the now muted television, where the news had ended and a judge show had begun. She reached for the remote on the table beside Hunter and turned off the television. "I look different now. I do. I dyed my hair brown and started wearing it long, and I wore those brown contacts. I changed the way I talk, the way I walk, the way I hold my head, the way I think. I changed my name, legally. I've kept to myself, made no close friendships, never let myself get involved with a man who might want to know more about my past. And for twelve years now, I've managed to avoid detection by the Bradburys."

"But hiding in a crowd is one thing. Hiding when your face has been splashed on the news—"

"I look different," she repeated. "Just not different enough."

"You're going to have to run again."

She nodded. "They'll know the name I'm going by now. They can find out where I was living. I can't go back there now, can't get any of my things. I have to leave everything behind. My savings, what few keepsakes I've allowed myself." She bit her lower lip until it hurt, but she managed to keep the tears at bay. "Good thing I never got that cat I've been wanting, huh?"

He reached toward her again, his hand stilling midair before dropping back to his lap. "Maybe you don't have to keep running."

She stared at him. "Didn't you hear anything I just said?"

"You're alone. So you run."

"Yes."

"What if you weren't alone?"

"But I *am* alone. I have to be alone."

This time, he did touch her, his big, rough hand closing over hers. "No. You don't."

The conviction in his voice sliced into her heart like a razor. "Hunter, no. There's nothing you or anyone else can do."

"I was a soldier, remember? Protecting people is what I did. It's still what I do. It's what I'm doing right now."

"You can't protect me 24/7. You have a life. A job."

"So I make you my job."

"That sounds terrible."

One corner of his lip quirked. "For you or for me?"

She turned her hand over, pressing her palm to his. "For you. And for me. I can't live my life in a cage or wrapped up in cotton batting like a piece of china stored in a drawer. And I could never ask you to make my safety your priority."

"You didn't ask. I offered."

"Because you're a soldier with nobody to protect." She felt a surge of emotion at the thought, equal parts admiration and pity. "You don't know how to be anything else, do you?"

His green eyes darkened, and he looked away. "You don't know me."

"I don't. And I don't reckon you know me, either. And that's why I could never ask you to put your life on hold to protect mine."

He slid his hand from her grasp. "It's not right that you have to run. You did nothing to deserve it."

"I killed a man."

"Who was trying to rape you."

"Be that as it may, I killed him. It's on my soul, whether he deserved it or not." She tried to push aside the memory of Clinton Bradbury's body bleeding out on her bedroom floor. "I'm not willing to give my life as penance, no. But I'm sure as hell not willing to give anyone else's life, either."

"Well," he said, lifting his gaze to meet hers, "what happened to you years ago changes nothing about tonight, does it? We still have a job to do, and if we get caught by the wrong people while we're doing it, what the Bradburys want to do to you may not matter, anyway."

He was right about that much. The Bradburys, while a threat hanging over her head for over a decade, weren't her most pressing concern.

The Blue Ridge Infantry and their plans for the conference tomorrow were. And instead of sitting here feeling sorry for herself, she should be focusing her attention on how they were going to get inside the hotel without being caught—and what they were going to do once they were inside.

She and Hunter rose at the same time, their bodies gliding into each other and tangling for a long, breathless moment. She reached out to steady herself, her palm flattening against the solid, hot wall of his chest. Beneath her fingers, his heartbeat stuttered and began to gallop, as if racing to catch up with the sudden acceleration of her own pulse. His arm roped around her waist, tugging her closer, and in the glimmer of his green eyes she saw fierce, feral intent that should have frightened her. But it didn't.

It thrilled her.

His thighs pressed against hers, driving her back toward the sofa. She wrapped one arm around his shoulders to keep from falling, drawing him even closer. His breath heated her cheeks, his grip tightening as he held her in place.

She should pull away from him. Put distance between them, between what he was offering and what she could afford to have.

But as his gaze dipped to her lips, and he tugged her

body flat against his, she couldn't move. Couldn't think about anything at all but how strongly, how desperately she needed to know what it was like to kiss him.

She imagined his kiss would be fierce and demanding, as strong and relentless as she knew from experience he could be. But what she hadn't reckoned on, what shocked her lips apart and sent her heart rate hurtling toward oblivion as his lips claimed hers, was the tenderness that trembled beneath all that tightly leashed passion.

He might not know her, but he knew exactly what she needed, as if he'd looked deep down in her well-buried heart and saw all the secret longings that writhed there, desperate for discovery.

His fingers threaded through her hair, holding her still as he slanted his head to deepen the kiss. His tongue swept over hers, setting off fireworks behind her closed eyelids, and she dug her fingers into the stone-hard muscles of his chest just to keep from tumbling off balance. When he dragged his lips from hers, she couldn't seem to breathe for a long, shivering moment.

"We have to focus." His voice came out in a raspy growl as he edged clear of her, retreating to a spot near the windows.

She groped for the arm of the sofa and perched there before her trembling knees gave out from under her. "Right."

He was breathing hard, as if they'd just hiked up Lamentation Rise again. As if he'd carried her on his back the whole way. But after a few seconds, the harsh sounds subsided, and as she watched, he visibly composed himself, a soldier packing his kit until it was pin-neat.

"I've got something I need to do," he told her. "Can you start packing our rucksacks? We need food for three days, in case we have to run for it and can't get back here. Lightweight as you can make it."

She nodded. "What's the one more thing you have to do?"

He flashed her a brief, mysterious smile. "You'll see soon enough." He headed down the hall and disappeared into the bathroom.

"It's her, isn't it?"

Asa Bradbury turned his attention from the television screen hanging over the bar and looked at his cousin Ricky. He should be feeling triumph, he supposed, at having found her after more than a decade of searching, but there wasn't really much pleasure in finally tracking down the girl. None of it would bring Clinton back. And, if Asa was honest with himself, he hadn't missed the trouble that seemed to follow Clinton around like a viperous pet, leaving nothing but havoc in his wake.

But family honor was family honor, and the girl had killed one of his kinsmen. Letting her go unpunished was neither wise nor proper, not if he wanted the Bradbury name to mean anything in these hills.

"What are we going to do about it?" Ricky asked.

Asa slanted a gaze at the younger man, disappointed that he'd even felt the need to ask the question. "We're going to find her, of course."

There was no other option.

It had been a year and three months since he'd worn his hair high and tight. Since he'd been completely clean-shaven and spit-polished. His so-called comrades in the Blue Ridge Infantry had never seen him looking like anything more than the down-on-his-luck, chip-on-his-shoulder Army washout he'd presented to them.

The man in the mirror was achingly familiar, a face he'd seen thousands of times in the past twelve years. A man of honor and purpose.

But somehow, the face staring back at him remained a stranger, far removed from who he'd become since his world blew up around him in a valley in Afghanistan.

Fraud, he thought, staring back at the familiar stranger. *Poser.*

He looked away, squaring his shoulders and lifting his smooth-shaven chin toward the bathroom door. He could afford to be neither, not when there was a woman out there with the soul of a warrior who needed him to watch her back. He had to figure out how to be a soldier again, at least for a few more days.

He could do that, couldn't he?

He found Susannah in the kitchen, packing what looked like protein bars, small tins of meat and bottles of water into the backpacks. She glanced up as he entered, did a double take that made him smile, then turned fully toward him, her head cocked and her lips quirked in a bemused half smile.

"Well, hello, soldier," she murmured.

"That's Army First Sergeant Bragg to you, ma'am," he shot back with a grin he almost felt.

Leaving the rucksacks on the table, she made a slow circle around him, observing his new look from all angles. "I think I approve."

"I was holding my breath."

The grin she flashed his way felt like a shot of adrenaline blazing straight to his gut. He felt his spine straighten to attention, along with a quickening somewhere south of his backbone.

Bringing himself back under control with the speed

of the well-trained warrior he used to be, he nodded at the packs. "Anything else we need?"

She showed him what she'd included—food, lightweight tools, more first-aid supplies, even a folded map of Tennessee. "In case we need to make a run for it, at least we'll have some idea where we are when we get there."

"Good thinking." He zipped up one of the sacks and slung it over one shoulder. "How are your feet?"

She looked down at the tennis shoes she wore. "They hurt. But I'll deal. How's your leg?"

"Still held together with nuts and bolts. I'll deal, too."

Cocking her head, she let her gaze fall to his left leg, her scrutiny intense and disconcerting. "What's under there, exactly?"

He considered and rejected a salacious retort, knowing that such an obvious attempt at distraction would only make her more curious. "Some missing muscle tissue. A lot of scarring."

"Can I see it?" Almost as soon as the words slipped from her mouth, her gaze snapped up to meet his, a flush of pink color darkening her face. "I'm sorry. I did not just ask you that."

"I think you did," he answered, stunned by the fact that he was actually standing here in the middle of Alexander Quinn's kitchen, seriously considering dropping trou so she could see his bum leg.

All because she'd asked him to do it.

"I just—" She pressed her lips to a thin line, her brow furrowing. "I don't know why, but I want to know—"

"What it looks like?"

She shook her head, still frowning. "It's not curiosity. It's—" She blew out a long breath. "Never mind. Forget I said anything."

Perversely, her change of heart only made him want to

show her what his jeans were hiding. It wasn't pretty. It might even be shocking—there were still days, even now, when he looked at his scarred leg and cringed at the sight.

But it would be honest. As honest as the moment when she'd looked up at him with those big gray eyes and confessed she'd killed a man with a shotgun.

Before he lost his nerve, he unzipped his jeans and pulled them down, baring his bad leg to her searching eyes.

Chapter Twelve

Susannah's gaze flicked down toward the road map of scars that circled his leg from thigh to ankle. Her mouth dropped open and she released a shaky gasp.

Hunter followed her gaze, trying to remember what it had been like to get that first look at his injury. It had been so much worse then, of course, the edges of torn skin raw and discolored and barely held together with hundreds of sutures.

Even now, with the wounds long healed, the contours of the leg were misshapen in places where the blast had destroyed muscle tissue. There was one particularly large patch of skin on his calf where doctors had used skin grafts to repair the damage from a large piece of flaming debris. And the scars were still purple and angry-looking, potent reminders of the horrors of that day in the Helmand Province.

"Oh," she said. The word came out long and slow, like a lament.

He reached for his jeans and started to pull them back up, but in the span of a heartbeat, she was at his side, her fingers brushing over the long scar on his thigh with exquisite delicacy.

"Does it hurt?" she asked softly, her gaze lingering on the scar.

"No," he lied. It hurt, horribly, but not the way she meant.

And even worse, her fingers on his flesh felt as good as anything he'd experienced in a long, long time. So good that every inch of his skin, even the broken patches that were still partly numb, seemed to burst into flames at her touch.

"I can't believe I let you haul me around on your back."

He pulled away from her pity, dragging his jeans back into place and zipping the fly with trembling fingers.

"I didn't mean—" She broke off midsentence, frustration evident in her pale eyes. "I'm sorry. I shouldn't have—"

"No. I shouldn't have." He scraped his hand through his hair, shocked by how effortlessly it ran across the short spikes of his newly shaved cut.

"You don't think it makes you less—" Once again, she stopped short.

He made himself look at her and saw her gazing back at him with a look so full of misery that he felt like a heel.

"Less what? Less virile? Less of a man?"

"Do you?"

He didn't know how to answer that question. The injury certainly hadn't done a damn thing to quell his sex drive, if his current state of arousal was any indication.

But he hadn't had sex since the injury. Never even really considered it seriously, not to this day.

And he was pretty sure the mangled condition of his leg figured into that equation somewhere.

"I know guys aren't as sensitive as women about their looks," she said quietly. She still stood close to him, close enough to touch. Close enough to catch fire if the flames surging inside him broke loose of his faltering control.

"Probably not," he admitted. "I'm not ashamed of my scars."

He was ashamed of what had led to them, however. If he was being perfectly honest with himself, a circumstance he mostly avoided these days. Honesty was painful, and he was tired of hurting.

"You shouldn't be."

He wanted to argue with her, the urge to spill the whole ugly tale so powerful it felt like poison in his gut. His leg was bad. It couldn't do the same things he'd once asked of it. But he was stronger now than he had been in the middle of that burning hell.

He'd never known that level of utter helplessness before in his life. He prayed to God he'd never know it again.

He willed Susannah to step back from him, to take away her soft warmth, her sweet scent, her gentle, disarming gaze.

Of course, being Susannah, she stepped closer, her hands lifting to his cheeks, ensnaring him. "I have no idea what to say to you," she said, her voice a whisper. "I don't know what you need."

You, he thought with growing dismay. *I just need you.*

When she leaned in, he thought she was going to kiss him. But then her face turned, her cheek glided like silk against his, and she pulled him into an embrace that threatened to deconstruct him completely.

He tried not to return the embrace, tried not to let his arms wrap around her slim waist and tug her closer, tried not to bury his face in the curve of her neck. Tried not to need her so desperately.

He did not succeed.

Time seemed to slow to nothing, and still she didn't move away from him. They settled there, his hips pressed back into the kitchen counter, her legs tangled with his as she settled her body against his. Despite his arousal, he felt no burning need to change anything, no desire to break away from her grasp nor to take control and push the closeness between them to a different place.

Slowly, the tension in his body eased, and even desire ebbed to a slow, sweet burn low in his belly. He felt her fingers brush through the crisp stubble of his buzz cut, exploring lightly, like a curious child.

A bubble of humor rose unexpectedly in his chest. "The ladies always love the buzz cut," he murmured against her throat.

She laughed in his ear, but he felt it rumble through him everywhere their bodies touched. "It's hypnotic."

He eased her away from him, but not too far, still holding on to her waist to keep her close. "In case you're wondering, my virility is just fine."

She flashed him a sly grin. "Yeah, I can tell."

She crossed back to the table, picked up her own pack and slipped her arms through the straps, adjusting them until they fit. By the time she put the backpack down and turned to face him again, she'd donned a mask of cool professionalism, as if the warm, sweet woman who'd just hugged him out of his bad mood had disappeared.

He felt the loss more keenly than he'd expected.

"I think we're going to have to risk leaving the packs somewhere off the hotel property," she said. "If we take them with us, we'll stick out like sore thumbs, and I don't like the idea of leaving them in the SUV, in case we can't get back to the parking garage."

"Good thinking." He flashed her a grin. "Sure you didn't spend some time in the Army?"

She smiled, but there was careful distance in her expression. "I'm sure. But I think my grandmother may have spent some time as a boot-camp drill sergeant."

There was a thread of sadness in her voice, underlying the composure. It had sharp edges, pricking his conscience. He'd spent so much of the last few months with his head stuck in the middle of his own problems, it hadn't even occurred to him that she had spent over a decade isolated from everyone she'd loved. "Do you ever get to see your grandmother?"

She looked away, her profile sharp with regret. "She died two years ago." She turned her winter-bleak eyes to meet his gaze. "We made a deal before I left, you see. That she would take out a classified ad in the online Knoxville newspaper once a week, just to let me know everything was okay. Then, one month, it wasn't there. And I knew. I checked the obituaries for the month and there it was. She died peacefully in her sleep at the age of eighty-nine."

Despite the distance she'd deliberately put between them, he couldn't have stopped himself from touching her again if he'd tried. Cradling her face between his hands, he bent and kissed her forehead. "I'm sorry. I would hate to find out about my sister's death that way."

She covered his hands with hers, gently easing them away from her face and stepping back. But she kept her fingers entwined with his. "Does your sister know? What you're doing? Where you are?"

Her question was as good as a bucket of ice water in the face. Janet knew he'd joined the BRI. But she didn't know he was working undercover. Quinn had convinced him he couldn't let her know the truth.

Now he wished he'd listened to his own instincts. But he couldn't dwell on what he couldn't change.

Avoiding the question, he let go of her fingers and nodded toward the back door. The garage that held their transportation was through that door. "Let's get everything packed in the SUV for tonight. Then we should probably try to get some sleep. It's going to be a long night."

Without waiting for her, he headed out the cabin's back door.

SHE SHOULD BE feeling anxious, Susannah thought. Jittery. But somehow the mere act of doing something besides running and hiding had a calming effect on her nerves, so that by the time they pulled up to the ticket gate of the executive parking garage, she rattled off the employee access code without even having to think about it, though it had been months since she'd parked there.

"Will hotel security be able to identify you by the code?" Hunter asked a moment later as the metal gate rose and they drove into the belly of the concrete garage.

"No. It's a universal code. They do change it whenever an executive leaves or is fired, but there's not a lot of turnover here. The company treats executives well, and it's hard to beat the view from our offices."

"I didn't spot a camera, but I assume there is one?"

"I honestly don't know. Like I said, security expenditures tend to lean heavily on the guest-protection side of the equation. If there is a camera, it's probably not great quality." She glanced at him, taking in his pin-neat appearance. "And trust me when I say, even up close, you look nothing like the maintenance man I ran into in the elevator the other day."

The corner of his lip crooked. "Should I say thanks?"

She grinned back at him. "Entirely up to you."

He picked out a parking spot halfway between the exit

and the basement entrance, close enough that they had a chance of winning a footrace to the SUV but not so close that they'd have to drive the whole curving length of the garage to reach freedom.

They'd stashed their rucksacks behind a fallen tree about a quarter mile up the winding two-lane road that led to the Highland Hotel and Resort. If they managed to ditch pursuers by the time they reached that spot in the road, they could pull off down a dirt road about two hundred yards past the hiding place, hide the SUV in the trees and circle back to get their supplies.

For the hotel invasion, they'd agreed to take a minimum of tools. Their weapons, of course—Hunter's Glock still safely hidden in his ankle holster, hers tucked into a pancake holster at the small of her back, the bulge covered by her loose-fitting rain jacket. Susannah's multi-blade Swiss Army knife was tucked in the pocket of her jeans. She'd packed another pocketknife she'd found at Quinn's place in Hunter's backpack, but she'd forgotten to grab it when they stashed the packs. It probably didn't matter—she assumed former First Sergeant Hunter Bragg was probably carrying something even more useful, and deadly. And they both carried small pen-size flashlights, in case they needed to provide their own light.

They entered the hotel through the basement door and stopped just inside a narrow corridor that ended at a simple steel door about ten yards away. "Tell me that door isn't locked," Hunter said quietly.

She had no idea whether it would be, she realized with dismay. She hadn't even remembered there was a second door into the maintenance area. "Only one way to find out." Bracing herself, she strode forward and turned the door handle.

It gave easily, the door swinging open with the faintest of creaks. A shiver of relief washed through her and she edged inside the larger maintenance area.

The mysterious, humming source of the hotel's electricity, air-conditioning and heat wasn't visible from this part of the basement, hidden behind a row of doors that lined the left side of a wider corridor leading from the garage to the service elevators located near the center of the room. Susannah bypassed the elevators and went to a large steel door just beyond. EMERGENCY EXIT was written in bright red letters on a sign just over the doorframe.

The door opened into a roomy stairwell. Once she and Hunter made it inside the relative safety of the enclosed area, Susannah let out a gusty sigh of relief.

"On the service elevators, this is marked *P* for Parking. I think the stairway doors to the floor levels should be marked the same way—lobby will be one, second floor two, etc." She realized he was looking at her with a faint smile on his face. "Oh, right. You worked maintenance here. You probably already knew that."

He shrugged. "I did. And you're right. That's how they're marked. So where do you want to go first?"

"My office," she said. "I want to see if Marcus Lemonde is hiding anything in his desk that we need to know about."

As they reached the lobby level, she reached for the door, but Hunter caught her wrist before she could push the handle. "Let's go up another flight. If I'm remembering the floor plans correctly, this door comes out in view of the lobby desk. We go up to second, we can go down the hall, come back down from the other side and none of the night staff is likely to see us."

"Good thinking," she conceded, following him up one more flight of stairs to the second floor. So far, her healing feet weren't giving her too much trouble, thanks to the excellent fit of the tennis shoes Hunter had purchased at the thrift store and the last-minute bandaging job he'd done before they left Quinn's cabin.

"How're you holding up?" he asked as they opened the door that led into the second-floor corridor.

"I'm good. How's your leg?"

He slanted a narrow-eyed look her way. "It's fine."

Okay, then. Not a profitable topic of conversation.

"It hurts," he said a moment later as they edged out into the hallway after a quick look around. "Some days worse than others. Like I said before, lots of bolts and pins in there."

The hallway was deserted, the lights set on emergency lighting. There had been a few times Susannah had pulled an all-nighter preparing for a big event at the hotel, so she was used to the look of the place after hours.

But apparently Hunter hadn't worked any evening or night shifts during his short stint in the hospitality industry. "Is it always this dark at night?"

"Saves power, which saves money. Because it's occupied, they don't cut out the lights, even in the business section of the hotel. But after six, they go to what they call the evening protocol, cutting out all but essential exit lighting."

"So if we turn on the light in your office, someone's likely to spot it from outside."

"If they're looking."

"I think we have to assume they will be."

Susannah stopped with her hand on the door of the stairwell at the far end of the corridor. "You really think they'll be watching my office?"

"I honestly don't know. I just think we have to go on the assumption that they're watching. Safer that way."

He closed his hand over hers, pushing the door to the stairwell open.

She slipped inside, trying to ignore the little shudder of awareness that rippled through her as his body pressed close against her back. He placed his hand over her arm, stilling her forward movement, as the door clicked shut behind them.

In the echo chamber of the stairwell, his whisper sounded impossibly loud. "Speaking of assuming the worst, what if there's already someone in your office when we get there?"

"You mean Marcus?"

"If he's up to his eyes in this plot, he might be here, finalizing things," Hunter said.

"We're armed. We take him down, tie him up and make him tell us what they have planned." She was only half joking, she realized.

Hunter looked at her through narrowed eyes. "Bloodthirsty."

"Just tired of sleeping in strange beds." She shot him an apologetic glance. "Not that your bed wasn't perfectly nice. And really quite warm." As warm as the air in the stairwell had become since they'd been standing there, pressed intimately close. She edged away from him before she did something reckless, like stand on her tiptoes and kiss him. "There's a window in the door of my office. It's not very large, but it should allow us to take a look inside to see if anyone's moving about."

The first-floor corridor was empty when they eased through the stairwell door into the hall. Handing over the office key, Hunter scouted ahead a few yards, stopping just long enough to glance through the window in the office door. "All clear," he said softly, moving up the hall to make sure they were still alone as she scooted toward her office.

She unlocked the door and slipped into the darkened room, her heart knocking in rapid thuds against her sternum. Crazy, she thought, that two days ago, this office was as familiar and comfortable to her as her own apartment. Now it felt like an alien place, full of shadows and threat.

The door handle rattled behind her, and she whipped around, her hand already closing on the Glock tucked behind her back.

Hunter held up his hands. "I come in peace."

She dropped her hand to her side, squeezing her trembling fingers into a fist. "All quiet?"

He nodded, moving past her to the windows, where the wooden blinds were currently levered open. One by one, he eased the blinds closed, then turned back to look at her. She could barely see him in the faint light seeping in through the window in the door, the dimmed hall lights offering little in the way of illumination.

Pulling his penlight from his pocket, he nodded toward her desk. "The cops have probably already searched your desk—was there anything in there that would reveal your real identity?"

"No," she said firmly.

"Does such a thing exist?" he asked curiously as he flicked on the penlight and aimed the narrow beam on Marcus's desk. "Anywhere?"

"Not anymore." After her grandmother's death, with nothing else to connect her to her old life but a blood vendetta she'd spent over a decade desperate to elude, she'd destroyed the handful of keepsakes she'd held on to for memory's sake.

Her grandmother had never been sentimental, and

she'd managed to strip most sentiment from Susannah, as well. There hadn't been a lot to hold on to, anyway. Just memories of a foolish mother, a venal father and a weak brother who could have made a better choice for his life but chose to follow in his father's shiftless footsteps instead.

And her grandmother, who never sat for a photo in her life besides her driver's license photo.

She crossed to where he crouched, looking under Marcus's desk. "I used to have a piece of an old driver's license that belonged to my grandmother. The photo part." It had been one of the keepsakes she'd finally destroyed after her grandmother's death, the grainy photo almost a decade old. Her grandmother had cut up the license when she'd received a new one shortly before the shooting that had sent Susannah out of town.

Hunter looked up at her. "Just the photo part?"

"She'd cut it up when she got her new license in the mail," Susannah explained, tugging at the top right-hand door of the desk. "This is locked."

Hunter pulled a small wallet from his jeans pocket. "I was prepared for that possibility." He flipped open the slim leather wallet to reveal something that brought back a few old, unpleasant memories for Susannah.

"You have a lock-pick kit?"

He glanced at her again. "You know what a lock-pick kit looks like?"

"Did I mention my daddy was a thief?" She watched as he wielded the thin pieces of metal to pop open the lock on the drawer. "Explains why I was living with my grandmother, huh?"

"What happened to the picture of your grandmother?" he asked as his penlight flicked across a collection of perfectly ordinary office-desk minutiae—a small box of staples, a few loose rubber bands, several paper clips in a variety of sizes. Nothing that screamed "domestic terrorist."

"I burned it after she died." The memory stung. "She would have wanted me to. In fact, she'd have been furious if she'd known I'd kept the picture. She was so adamant about changing everything about my life, including my past."

"She was probably right. If the wrong person had seen it—"

"I didn't keep it on me. I bought this old locket at an antique store in Raleigh. A cheap piece of junk jewelry, but I kept my grandmother's driver's-license photo inside that locket. I never wore it or anything. Just kept it around so I could open it when I was feeling lonely."

Hunter put his hand on her arm, his touch gentle and deliciously warm. "I'm sorry you've had to live that way."

"As long as there's a Bradbury in these hills, I'll be living that way. I guess it's time to stop wishing for something else."

Hunter closed his other hand around her arm, penlight and all. "Don't stop wishing for something else. When you stop wishing, you start dying."

"Why does that sound like the voice of experience?" she murmured, her heart hurting a little at the sight of his bleak expression, barely visible in the gloom.

"Because it is." He gave her arms a squeeze and let go, turning back to the desk.

With the lock picks, he unlatched the rest of the drawers. In the top left drawer, the beam of the penlight flickered across what looked like loose tea leaves scattered along the right edge of the drawer.

"Hmm," Susannah said.

"What?"

She waved at the dried leaves. "I never figured Marcus as a tea drinker. In fact, I don't think I've ever seen him drink anything but coffee before."

"Well, I don't think he's going to wipe out a cop conference with a bunch of rogue tea leaves, so maybe we should look elsewhere." Hunter closed the desk drawer and looked around the office. "Is there anything you can remember about Lemonde that might lead you to believe he's not what he seems?"

"Honestly? We don't really interact that much. He tends to do his job without talking much, which is fine by me."

"Antisocial much?"

She arched an eyebrow. "Pot…kettle…"

He grinned at her retort before his expression grew serious again. "Where would his personnel records be kept?"

"Actually," she said, moving toward the file cabinets behind her desk, "I should have a copy in here somewhere." Flicking on her penlight, she aimed the beam toward the top drawer of the cabinet on the left and pulled it open, grimacing as some dark powder came off on her fingers. "Ugh, is that fingerprint powder?"

Pausing at the edge of her desk, Hunter pulled a couple of tissues from the box by her phone. "Here."

"Thanks." She wiped her fingers on the tissue, then used it to pull the drawer open wider so she could get to the file tucked in the back. She pulled it out and carried it over to her desk. "He had pretty good references from his last job."

"Which was?"

"Public relations at a construction company. The hotel wanted someone who'd worked in the real estate and construction industry because we're interested in bringing in more manufacturing events." She scanned the résumé that sat on top of the other papers in his file. "Hmm."

"What?" Hunter leaned closer, his chest brushing against her shoulder. A flood of heat swamped her, making her light-headed for a second.

She gripped the edge of the desk and pointed her pen-light toward the third entry under "Employment" in his résumé. "He worked for Gibraltar Mining."

"As a PR person?"

She shook her head, alarms clanging in her head. "As an explosives expert."

Hunter closed his hand over her arm, his grip painfully tight. Suddenly he was moving, bundling her along in front of him, heading for the door of the small bathroom behind her desk. He pushed her inside and half closed the door behind them. Within a second, he had his Glock out of the ankle holster and in his hand.

"What—" she managed to get out before he pressed his fingers to her lips, silencing her.

Then she heard the rattle of a key in the office door.

Hunter wrapped his arms around her as she started to shiver, his head bending low until his lips just brushed her ear. "Don't make a sound." The words came out on a soft breath.

Outside the bathroom, a light came on, almost blinding her. Squinting she peered through the narrow gap between the door and the frame and bit back a gasp as she spotted Marcus Lemonde walking slowly across the office.

Heading straight for the bathroom door.

Chapter Thirteen

Susannah's fingers tightened over Hunter's hand and gave a sharp tug, pulling him backward. For a second, he resisted, but she yanked harder and he gave in, backing deeper into the shadows of the bathroom. He heard the faintest of snicks, the tiniest of rattles, and then she was pulling him with her through the narrow doorway of the bathroom closet.

She pulled the door closed behind them, not quite engaging the latch, and even the ambient light from the hallway that had managed to seep into the bathroom disappeared into inky nothingness.

Susannah's breath was warm against the back of his neck, sending animal awareness prickling through his flesh. She kept her death grip on his hand, her fingers flexing and loosening in a frantic rhythm.

He tucked the Glock into his waistband and reached behind him to catch her other hand, bringing both of her arms around his waist until her body pressed flat against his. The heat of her, the rapid thud of her heartbeat against his spine, felt like a tonic, filling his flagging soul with purpose. With confidence and focus.

He could do this. He could handle whatever happened next, because he had to.

She needed him to.

Footsteps clicked on the tile floor of the office bathroom, and the light came on, sending a narrow sliver of illumination through the crack between the door and the frame. Behind Hunter, Susannah pressed her face against his shoulder. He ran his thumbs soothingly over hers, then released her hands and withdrew the Glock from his waistband.

He felt her moving as well, quick, economical movements that made her body brush his in the tight confines of the bathroom closet. Outside in the bathroom, the water came on, and Susannah leaned closer. "I'm armed now, too." He felt her words more than heard them, the faintest whisper of breath in his ear.

Until today, the idea that the sleek, sophisticated businesswoman he'd been following around for the past three weeks would wield anything more lethal than a letter opener had seemed ludicrous.

But he'd seen her loading the borrowed Glock that afternoon, her movements quick and confident. She knew her way around a weapon. She'd already proved she was tough enough to brave a mountain hike on wounded feet. And she had enough courage to come here tonight, knowing that her life was in danger on multiple levels, because she had inside information that Hunter needed to complete his mission.

She was a far more amazing woman than he'd given her credit for.

Far too amazing for the likes of him.

The water turned off, followed by retreating footsteps. The light in the bathroom extinguished, plunging them once again into darkness.

A moment later, they heard a click. The door to the office closing?

"We should follow him," he whispered. "See why he's here so late."

"We'd be spotted in a heartbeat," she disagreed. "There's nowhere to hide." She caught his arm and gave a tug, turning him toward her. As he started to speak, she stopped him with her mouth, hot and hard against his. Her tongue swept over his, fiercely demanding, and his heart seemed to bolt like a frightened horse, galloping wildly to keep pace with the frantic rhythm of her pulse against his chest.

She released him almost as suddenly as she'd grabbed him, leaving him feeling off balance.

"Thanks," she whispered. "I needed that."

His eyes had adjusted just enough to the ambient light leaking through the door crack to see the flash of her white teeth as she grinned.

Forget amazing, he thought. The woman was bloody magnificent.

Gathering what wits he had left, he edged out of the closet and into the bathroom, leading with the Glock, while Susannah trailed behind him, one hand on his back, tethering them together. They eased out of the bathroom and into the main office, Hunter sweeping his penlight and weapon together across the room, looking for a trap.

There was no one else there.

He clicked off the penlight. "I don't suppose there's an alternate exit from this office. Besides the main door, I mean."

"Not that I know of."

He sighed, considering their options. If Marcus Lemonde had any suspicion at all that someone had broken into the office, he might be waiting outside to ambush them as they left.

"I'm going to risk it," he said, already moving toward the door.

Her hand closed over his arm, her grip strong, stopping him in his tracks. "You, as in, you alone?"

He turned toward her, saw the anger in her eyes and braced himself. "Yes. Me. Alone."

"And I just stay here and wait for the big, brave man to play hero and then come back and rescue me when it's all over?"

"I wouldn't have put it quite that way. But, yeah."

"I realize we only met a day or two ago, so that might explain why you would think that ordering me to stay here like a good little girl is a smart idea. But it's really, really not." She let go of his wrist.

"Two of us will be more conspicuous."

"It's a hotel corridor. Unless you're the size of a spider, there's nowhere to hide." She shook her head. "Look, I know you're a man of action and all that—"

"And all that?"

"But I think we need to stop, take a breath, let the adrenaline settle down and try to figure out what the BRI has planned for tomorrow before we go running around like a couple of headless chickens."

There was a part of him, a barely leashed part of him, that wanted to tell her she didn't know what the hell she was talking about. He might not be wearing the uniform anymore, but he was still a soldier at his core. A man who took action. Who saw the fight and dived right in.

But Susannah was right. This hotel wasn't his home turf, not really. Marcus Lemonde had been working here a lot longer than he had, and if he was a vital part of whatever the BRI had planned for the conference tomorrow, he had all the advantages.

To win this particular battle, he needed to hunker

down and figure out where the planned strike would happen and how to stake out high ground so he'd have the advantage once the battle was underway.

He forced himself to relax, to let the spike of adrenaline ease back to a manageable level. "Okay. You're right."

"I'm right?" Her look of surprise was so comical, he couldn't stop a laugh.

"Yeah. There must be a reason Marcus is working late, and I don't think it's last-minute preparations for a great conference this weekend."

"It may be last-minute preparations, all right." She looked around the office. "You know what? We shouldn't stay here to discuss it. He might come back."

"What do you have in mind?" he asked as she crossed to the file cabinets again.

"We're pretty sure it's the conference that's the target, right?" She opened the top file cabinet and used a penlight to see inside, coming back a moment later with a large file folder she'd pulled from the drawer. "This is my backup file on the conference. I print out two copies of every file I deal with so that we're never without backups. I'm pretty sure Marcus has the master file but I don't think he even knows about this one."

"And what are we going to find in that file?" he asked as she tucked the folder under one arm and started for the office door.

"Hopefully, answers."

THE MINUTE HAND on her watch clicked past twelve. Two in the morning. They'd been holed up in one of the basement-level maintenance rooms for over an hour, poring over every file, every scrap of paper, every hastily jotted note that Susannah had filed away over the past few months in preparation for the Tri-State Law Enforcement Society's annual conference.

"I keep going back to Marcus's experience with explosives," she said, stifling a yawn as she looked up from yet another voucher. "If the BRI wanted to make a big splash, blowing up that conference would be one way to do it."

"It wouldn't be easy to get their hands on the amount of explosives necessary to make a really big splash," Hunter disagreed. "Anything really high-grade is very hard to procure. That's why people go for things like ANFO—ammonium nitrate and fuel oil."

"I know what ANFO is."

He slanted a look at her. "I'm trying very hard not to ask why you do."

She flashed him a grin. "I'm from the hills, remember? We know how to explode all sorts of things around here."

"Well, it takes a pretty big stash of ANFO or something like it to blow up a big building the size of this hotel. Or even a big section of it. At the Murrah Building in Oklahoma City, they had barrels of the stuff to do the kind of damage that bomb did."

"Maybe they're not going for anything quite that big."

"Billy Dawson seemed pretty sure what he had planned would rival Oklahoma City in scope." He looked down at the file folder on the worktable in front of him, one hand flexing over his left knee. "I was really, really hoping it wasn't going to be explosives, though."

Of course, she thought. The last thing he'd want to deal with would be another explosion.

"Hunter—"

His gaze snapped up to meet hers. "Don't do that."

"Do what?"

"Don't pity me."

She *had* pitied him, once. Before she'd seen his scars and realized just how close he must have been to death after the explosion—and how far he'd come in such a short time.

Pity was the last thing she felt for him.

"I wouldn't dare." She touched his arm. "I just wondered if you think we should call in reinforcements now, while there's still time."

"You mean call Quinn."

"We have nothing to offer the police in the way of evidence, but maybe Quinn has some ideas."

"If he did, he'd have given them to us."

Susannah wasn't so sure. She hadn't spent much time with Alexander Quinn before he'd left them alone in his cabin, but what interaction they'd shared convinced her he was the sort of man who always had an agenda. Did he want them to find out what was going on here at the Highland Hotel and Resort? Absolutely. Did he want them to put a stop to it? She thought so.

But there was a reason he'd assigned Hunter Bragg to this particular job, and Susannah was beginning to suspect Quinn's motives were more about getting something from Bragg than stopping the threat to the conference. Or, at the very least, the two goals were of equal importance to Quinn.

But what was it that he wanted from Hunter?

"Why did Quinn assign this job to you?" she asked as he bent his head back over the hotel floor plans once again, his brow furrowed as he looked for something, anything, they hadn't yet discovered.

"I was a disgruntled vet with a chip on my shoulder," he said with a grimace, his gaze not moving from the floor plans. "Prime militia bait."

"Disgruntled?"

He sighed and turned to look at her. "Not about combat. I mean, yeah, I supposed I'm as frustrated as the next grunt about how wars are all about politics these days, but I'm not out to blow up the Pentagon."

"You just wanted the BRI to think so."

He nodded. "I've been pretty angry since I got back stateside. About this." He pressed the heel of his hand against his bad leg. "About what happened to my sister because of me. At myself for letting it happen."

"You didn't let it happen."

"You don't know that. You weren't there."

"So tell me. What happened?"

He lowered his head. "Let's just concentrate on the job at hand."

"We've been staring at these files for an hour as if we could magically conjure up the answer if we just looked hard enough. My eyes are starting to cross. Let's take a break for a minute." She touched his arm, felt his skin ripple beneath her touch. "I won't ask any more questions if you don't want me to."

His lips flattened to a thin line. "Good."

Silence fell between them, marred only by the soft sounds of their breathing and the hum of the hotel's power plant close by. The small maintenance break room where they'd holed up to do their research was almost as small as her office bathroom, or felt that way, at least, with the large square table in the middle of the cramped space and the long countertop nearby, holding a coffeemaker and a couple of big cans of ground coffee. A tiny refrigerator stood in the corner, its soft hum of electricity swallowed by the noise from the hotel's heating system.

Hardly a place conducive to figuring out how to save the world. Or, for that matter, to save the Tri-State Law

Enforcement Society's annual conference from going up in smoke.

Frustration boiling in her gut, she pushed her chair back with a scrape and started to rise, but Hunter grabbed her arm, holding her in place.

"I woke up in the middle of the night and couldn't move. At first, I thought it was a nightmare. I'd been having my share of those." He passed his hand over his jaw, his palm making a whispery sound as it rasped against the beginning of beard stubble. "Then I realized there were hands holding me down. On my legs and my arms. On my head. However they'd gotten into my sister's place, they'd done it without waking me up."

"Where was your sister?"

"She'd gone to a concert in Knoxville with a couple of women from the prosecutor's office. That's where she worked at the time. They made a night of it, booked a room in a hotel near the concert venue." He shook his head. "I don't know how they knew she'd be gone. Or maybe they didn't know. Maybe the plan had been to take me and terrorize her at the same time."

"I know you must have fought back."

His eyes narrowed, his gaze unfocused, as if watching the past play out in his mind. "I think I did. I think I must have. They put something on my face—a cloth drenched in something. Maybe chloroform, maybe something else. All I know is, my mind went to a complete fog and the next time I could think clearly, I was cuffed to a water pipe in a cabin in the middle of nowhere. And there I stayed until the cops showed up to rescue me. Way too late to be any help to Janet."

"You think that constitutes letting it happen to you?"

He grimaced as if in pain. "I should have figured out

something. Gotten loose somehow. Or, hell, if I hadn't gotten myself blown up in Afghanistan—"

"I suppose that was your fault, too?" She couldn't quite keep the dry sarcasm out of her voice.

He snapped his gaze up to hers, his eyes blazing with anger. "Getting blown up might not have been my fault, but—"

When he didn't continue, she looked down at his leg, watching his fingers as they massaged his thigh. "But something was?"

His lips parted and a shaky breath escaped his lips. His fingers clenched around his leg, so tightly that she knew it must hurt.

She released a gusty little sigh. "Forget it. I shouldn't push—"

His gaze locked with hers, raw-eyed and fierce. "It was an early morning patrol, about two years ago. Helmand Province. Predawn."

She eased back into her chair, her heart pounding. She'd wanted details, but now that he was talking, her chest tightened with dread.

"We weren't really fighting anymore by then. Just trying to keep a lid on the tension. Taliban, warlords battling it out for turf in the opium trade—wild, wild West kind of stuff. If we weren't there, they'd have been happy enough to slaughter each other. But we gave them a target they could all agree on." His hand slid away from her arm, but she caught it in hers, needing the connection.

His gaze tangled with hers for a moment before he looked away. But he held on to her hand, his grip tightening.

"It was October, and the summer heat had finally passed. The whole place seemed like a dust bowl to us most of the time, so I can't really call it beautiful, but the milder weather had us all feeling like we could breathe again." A smile flirted with his lips but didn't linger. It never touched his haunted eyes. "Maybe we dropped our guard. I don't know. I've been over and over that morning, trying to figure out how we let ourselves get surrounded."

She frowned. "Surrounded?"

He bumped gazes with her again before looking away, his eyes angled forward, toward the blank wall across from them, as if he were watching something playing out on the flat surface, something she couldn't picture. Didn't want to picture.

"Sometimes that was the point of the IEDs," he said softly. "To make the troops vulnerable to attack. Blow up the vehicle and prey on the survivors."

Susannah's gut roiled. "Did they—"

"Prey on me?" His mouth twisted in a grotesque parody of a smile. "No, not me. I was lucky. The blast sent me flying into a small ravine. They didn't know I was there, so they didn't—"

Her fingers flexed, tightening on his.

He turned to look at her again, his gaze holding this time. "This isn't something anyone needs to hear."

"But maybe it's something you need to say."

His gaze held hers a moment longer, then he closed his eyes and leaned toward her until his forehead rested against hers. "I could hear them attacking—" He swallowed hard, his breath releasing in a soft, guttural growl as he pulled away from her. "I could hear them brutalizing the handful of survivors. I could hear it, but I couldn't drag myself up that ravine to lay down any cover fire for them. I've gone over it and over it a million times since that day—if I'd tried a little harder, could I have made it up that rock wall? My leg was a mess, yes, but only one leg. Not the rest of me. Why couldn't I make it up that wall?"

"Stop," she said, fighting a surge of anger as she reached up and cradled his face between her palms, making him look at her. "You nearly lost your leg. You were probably losing blood by the buckets, right? You think you could have saved anyone even if you'd gotten up that wall?"

"I don't know." He lifted his hands, covering hers, pulling her hands away from his face. But he didn't let them go. "I don't know. I just know I wasn't any kind of war hero for being the sole survivor."

She didn't agree. She thought he was a hero just for putting his life on the line there in the first place. But that wasn't what he needed to hear, so she swallowed her protest and simply squeezed his hands. "I'm sorry. I'm sorry it happened to you and your team. I'm sorry they didn't survive."

"Me, too." He released her hands and picked up the folder she'd brought with them. "There's got to be something in here that tells us what they're up to. Some vulnerability we're missing."

"I don't think it's a bomb." She forced her voice past the lump in her throat. "I've looked over and over these floor plans, and I don't see how they could plant a bomb close enough to the conference rooms that would do the damage they're looking to inflict, do you? The best bet would be to pack a large truck or something similar with ANFO or another kind of explosive and set it off with a timer, but there's nowhere to park anything at all on the side of the hotel where the conference is taking place. Those rooms were built specifically for the view of the mountains out the picture windows, and they overlook a bluff. There's no parking area on that side of the building. And unless they were able to set explosives that would bring the whole structure down, like a controlled demolition—"

"We've already looked around for something like that. It's just not here," he said.

"So how else would you try to do damage at a conference if you couldn't blow it up?"

"Radiation poisoning," he suggested.

"God forbid."

"I think we can rule out any sort of armed ambush," he said thoughtfully. He still looked haunted, but some of the tension in his shoulders and neck eased as he applied his mind to their current problem, leaving the past behind. "Assuming the hotel is allowing all those cops to carry weapons. Are they?"

"There was some debate on the topic," she admitted, "but I convinced the naysayers that you can't expect a bunch of cops to agree to hand over their weapons just because they're at a conference."

"So, no armed siege. No bomb. Probably not a suitcase nuke."

She shuddered at the thought. "Unless someone worked down at Oak Ridge and could get their hands on—"

"Not going to happen. Suitcase nukes are more fiction than fact, and if anyone ever successfully pulled it off, the fissile materials would almost certainly come from somewhere overseas." His brow furrowed. "I wonder, though…"

"You wonder?" she prodded when he didn't say anything more.

"I was thinking about the rash of polonium poisonings in Europe a while back. Remember those?"

"Vaguely. Didn't everybody think that the current

incarnation of what used to be the KGB did it? Eliminating enemies of the state or something?"

"Or something," he agreed. "And polonium wouldn't be easy to get your hands on, especially for the BRI. But poisoning a food source isn't that hard if you have access to the catering kitchen. All kinds of ways to do it, I'd think. Who's catering the deal?"

"Ballard's," she answered. "It's a large catering outfit in Maryville." Her stomach dropped. "Oh, my God. Of course."

"What?"

"Marcus is the one who hired them. He'd been handling the whole thing until about three weeks ago, when I found out he was dating one of the chefs. I couldn't exactly change caterers so close to the event, but I did relieve him of his liaison duties and took them over myself. I didn't want there to be any whiff of a conflict of interest."

"Three weeks ago is when Billy Dawson called me and the others in to discuss ways to get you out of the way." He reached across the space between them and brushed her hair away from her temple, letting his fingertips linger on her cheek. "They're going to poison the conference luncheon."

Chapter Fourteen

"The caterer is bringing their own cooking pans and utensils, but they'll be using the conference-hall kitchen." Susannah was pacing the small break room in agitated strides, circling the table where Hunter sat as she spoke. "The conference dining hall is on the second floor."

"I know."

"The kitchen is just off the main hall," she added as if he hadn't spoken. Her gaze was angled forward, but he knew she wasn't really seeing the drab break-room walls, with the out-of-date wall calendar displaying Miss August in tight jeans and a crop top, wrench in one hand and toolbox in the other. Instead, he knew, she was picturing the second-floor layout, from the large banquet hall in the center to the compact kitchen in the next suite over.

"Do they police access to the kitchens?"

She looked at him that time, her gaze shifting into focus. "Not really. Not unless we're asked to."

"Did the top cops ask you to?"

"No."

"Okay." He reached out and caught her hand as she wandered past, pulling her off course. She almost stumbled into his lap before catching herself with one hand on his shoulder.

Her gaze darkened as he dropped his other hand to

the curve of her hip, holding her in place. "Do you know anything about poisons?"

She shook her head. "Nothing that didn't come from true-crime TV."

"I don't know much, myself," he admitted, leaving his hand in place. He liked the soft heat of her body beneath his fingers, liked the way the sensation spread up his arm and into his chest like a river of warmth. "My expertise tends to be chemical weapons, thanks to my training."

"I don't think it can be anything fast-acting," she said thoughtfully. She seemed to be leaning into his touch, so he let go of her wrist and laid his hand on her other hip, gently drawing her closer. She took a couple of steps forward, settling between his knees. She wrapped one hand around the back of his neck, her other hand toying with the collar of his shirt. "If it was fast, someone would figure it out before everyone was affected. So what poisons would that eliminate? Cyanide?"

"Cyanide's definitely fast-acting." He leaned toward her, drawn by the heat of her body. So tempting and comforting at the same time. "What's the menu?"

"The usual. Mixed-green salad. Baked chicken and asparagus in a cream sauce for meat-eaters, and grilled portabello mushrooms with wild rice and asparagus in a basil sauce for vegetarians."

"Poisonous mushrooms?"

"I don't know. The caterers are supplying all the main ingredients. I'm wondering if it's something that has to be added here rather than at the caterer's. Since Marcus is here so late. Maybe he's switching out something the caterers brought early, like condiments or something that doesn't have to be brought here fresh?"

"Maybe herbs or spices?"

"Oh, my God," she said, remembering the leaves

they'd seen in Marcus's desk drawer. "What if those weren't tea leaves in his desk?"

"I think we'd better figure out a way into that kitchen."

"SHE'S SOMEWHERE INSIDE that hotel." Kenny Bradbury's voice had risen a half octave since Asa's arrival, his dark brown eyes glowing with a chaotic mix of excitement and anxiety.

"You're absolutely sure?"

"We had a rifle scope camera on the office windows, like you suggested. How'd you know she'd go back there?"

Because that was the kind of girl Susan McKenzie had always been, even at sixteen. A tough little hillbilly girl who never gave up on a fight.

He knew that the Blue Ridge Infantry was up to something at the hotel. He wasn't a member himself, but in his business, it was impossible to avoid rubbing elbows with people who were part of that ridiculous mock army. Not the sort of people he could trust with his business, of course, but they were sometimes useful as informants or, occasionally, cannon fodder.

"Did you get a shot of her?" Asa asked Kenny.

Kenny pulled out the rifle scope camera and showed him the image on the display. The lighting wasn't great—she and the man with her were using small, low-power flashlights, and the narrow beams barely provided enough light to make out their features.

But the shape of the face was right. The slight upward curve of her nose. Those full lips that Clinton had been downright obsessed with, obsessed enough to risk everything to have her, even though she didn't want any part of him.

Stupid fool.

"It's definitely her, right?" Kenny asked, his earlier confidence beginning to flag in the wake of Asa's continued silence.

He sighed and let his cousin off the hook. "It's her. You have the exits covered so she can't get away?"

"Every one of them."

Asa made a note to confirm that fact for himself. It had been years since he'd been anywhere near this close to finding little Susan McKenzie and bringing her to justice.

It was way past time to get the whole mess over with.

THERE'S A DUMBWAITER," Susannah said suddenly, tapping her fingers on the piece of paper in front of her with a jolt of excitement.

Hunter leaned toward her to look at the paper, his hard-muscled shoulder pressed to hers, distracting tingles racing along her flesh where they touched. "Where?"

"In the conference-room kitchen." She pointed to the notation on a copy of the security department's correspondence with the caterer. "The caterer asked if we had parking-level access to the conference-room kitchen by way of a dumbwaiter, and security says yes."

"It's not on the floor plans."

"Maybe it was added after the plans were drawn." She reached for the hotel floor plans, locating the conference-room kitchen. "Okay, the kitchen is about twenty yards east of the central elevators." She rose and walked to the break-room door, edged her head out the door and looked toward the elevators. "All clear. Shall we go hunting?"

Hunter stayed close as they crossed to the central bank of elevators and looked east. About twenty yards down the narrow hallway was a door located close to the exit that led to the parking garage. "That must be it," he said.

"It's the room where the main breaker and fuse boxes are. I'm not sure I've ever actually been in there."

"Me, either." They tried the door, found it locked. Hunter pulled out the keys he'd grabbed from the maintenance office and unlocked the door.

The room was larger than he'd expected, covered nearly wall to wall with a variety of electrical boxes and numerous switches and levers. "Careful," he warned as she moved past him into the room, toward the only place the dumbwaiter could possibly be located: a narrow door in the wall between the main breaker and a small gray fuse box.

"Please be unlocked," she murmured as she twisted the doorknob.

The door opened with ease, revealing what looked like a small closet with a square metal cage filling most of the upper half of the space. A sturdy cable hung on a pulley to one side of the dumbwaiter.

"Bingo," Susannah murmured, flashing him a grin.

"It's too small for me," he said, his voice dark with frustration.

"But not for me."

His gaze clashed with hers. "No, Susannah."

"Yes, Hunter."

"We came here together, and I plan for us to leave together. And the only way to ensure that is if we stay together."

"We need to get into the kitchen. There are only two ways for that to happen—either I take that elevator up to the second floor and risk being seen in the hallway, or I sneak into the kitchen in this dumbwaiter. I know which option I'd rather choose."

"What if you get up there and Marcus Lemonde is waiting on the other side?"

"I'm armed."

"He may be, too."

"I'm not afraid of Marcus." She'd faced down much tougher enemies. "Look, I know you're only trying to protect me. But I'm not helpless. When I was sixteen, I killed a man trying to rape me. And then I left home a few weeks later after that man's family tried to kill me in retaliation. I've lived isolated from everything and everyone who ever meant a damn thing to me because that's the only way I knew to survive. Now, I have a chance to stop an attack on a group of people who are out there, day in and day out, trying to keep people like you and me safe from harm."

"Susannah—"

"Susan," she snapped. "My name is Susan. Susan Elizabeth McKenzie. I'll probably never get to use it again, but I just want one person to know who I really am."

Hunter touched her cheek, his thumb sliding over her trembling bottom lip. "Nice to meet you, Susan Elizabeth McKenzie."

"One of the people who'll be eating at that conference luncheon is my cousin, whose family took me in when I had literally nowhere else to turn." She pulled away from his grasp, afraid she couldn't stay strong while he was touching her. "I have to find out what the BRI has planned for the conference. And I have to put a stop to it."

Tension crackled between them in the thick silence. Then Hunter gave a short, barely-there nod and looked away from her.

"What are the odds that this thing doesn't creak like a rusty hinge?" Wincing in anticipation, she climbed into the steel cage. There was a faint rasp of metal on metal, but the dumbwaiter seemed sturdy enough.

"You don't have to do this." Hunter's voice was a growly whisper. He didn't meet her eyes, his gaze focused on the rope-and-pulley system designed to move the dumbwaiter up and down the chute between floors. "We can figure out another option."

"We could be running out of time," she replied, reaching across the space between them to curl her fingers over his arm.

He looked at her then, his green eyes blazing a maelstrom of emotions her way. Anger was there. Fear. And something else, something that rang through her like a newly struck bell, true and resonant.

"When you reach the top, tug three times on the rope to let me know you're there and you're okay. And be careful. Don't take chances you don't have to." He bent in a rush, slanting his mouth over hers in a fierce kiss. His lips softened within a second, caressing hers with such tenderness she felt her heart contract.

He pulled away as quickly as he'd moved toward her, reaching for the rope. He gave a tug, the pulley turned and the dumbwaiter began to rise.

She hadn't counted on the darkness. Once she was inside the chute, the dumbwaiter blocked out almost all light from above or below, plunging her into a lurching void of darkness and jerky motion. Steeling herself against a rush of panic, she concentrated on breathing in slow, steady rhythm with the pulse in her ears. One breath for every four heartbeats. In and out.

With a jarring clunk, the dumbwaiter jolted to a stop. Playing her penlight on the surface in front of her, she saw she had reached another door.

She tugged three times on the rope, knowing Hunter would be able to feel the vibrations on his end. Then, holding her breath and lifting a quick, fervent prayer, she opened the door.

Beyond was more darkness.

SOLDIERS WERE NO bloody good at waiting. They were men and women of action. The point of the spear. Hunter felt useless standing there holding a dumbwaiter rope and waiting for someone else to take all the risks.

When his cell phone vibrated against his chest, it felt as jolting as a bolt of electricity. He shoved his hand into the jacket's inside chest pocket and withdrew his phone. An unfamiliar number on the display threw him for a second, until he remembered Quinn had a new burner phone.

He answered with the "all clear" code phrase Quinn had given him at the cabin before he left. "Baker Electric twenty-four-hour hotline."

"My garbage disposal has a short," Quinn answered.

Hunter relaxed marginally at the sound of the "situation normal" response code.

"Anything new?" Quinn asked after a brief pause.

"We have an idea how the BRI plans to target the conference." Hunter told Quinn about Marcus Lemonde's connection to the catering company and their theory about how he planned to sabotage the luncheon. "Depending on what kind of poison they go with, the results could range from mild sickness to mass murder."

"You've been inside the BRI for three months," Quinn said. "What's your gut feeling? How far are they willing to go?"

"At one point, I thought they might be blowing this place up," he answered grimly. "I don't think they'd balk at mass murder."

"The question is, do they have a bigger agenda?" Quinn fell silent on his end of the line for a few seconds, causing Hunter to wonder if he'd lost the phone connection. But a second later, Quinn added, "What are you doing now?"

"Holding a rope," Hunter answered, not hiding his frustration.

THE DARK SPACE beyond the door turned out to be the conference-room kitchen, as they'd hoped. Painting the dark space with the narrow beam of the penlight, Susannah mapped the long narrow room in her mind, then shut off the small light and navigated in the darkness.

There was a large, stainless-steel refrigerator in one corner. She eased the door open, the automatic light inside the refrigerator casting a glow across the immediate area. It gave her enough illumination to make out the rest of the long, narrow room—large commercial cooking ranges, double ovens, a pair of high-powered microwave ovens and what looked to be a large double-door pantry barely visible from this end of the kitchen.

After a quick look in the refrigerator revealed it to be empty, she closed the door and flicked her penlight on again, crossing to take a look inside the pantry.

Unlike the refrigerator, the pantry seemed to be stocked with basic cooking staples. Cans of chicken, beef and vegetable broth sat on one shelf, along with canned evaporated milk and several cans of tomato paste. Standard herbs and spices took up space on the shelf below. The bottom two shelves were occupied by flour, sugar and cornmeal in carefully labeled canisters.

Susannah scanned the pantry contents again, trying to think logically. The canned items seemed to be unlikely potential sources of a poisoning, sealed as they were. The spices might be better bets, but it would probably take a lab days to work out what the ingredients of those bottles really were.

Being quick about it, she looked into the canisters and confirmed that the contents did seem to be sugar, flour and cornmeal. There was also a large cylindrical carton of basic table salt and, near that, three pepper mills containing three different colors of peppercorns.

In other words, she was looking at a fairly standard kitchen pantry. With any number of herbs and spices that might look like those leaves in Marcus's desk.

If those leaves had anything to do with the plot at all.

Focus. If Marcus wanted to poison the food, how would he go about it?

Marcus was dating the woman from the catering company, but removing him from acting as a liaison with the caterer had seemed to be a sufficient change to waylay any possible questions of ethics.

Little had she known just how bloody unethical Marcus Lemonde could be when he put his mind to it.

Based on her discussions with the catering company, and the notes she'd made in her files, Ballard's Catering was supplying all of the primary ingredients for the dishes they were preparing, but they had asked for the hotel to supply the cooking facility and basic staples. Susannah imagined they'd probably include salt and pepper as basic staples. What about other herbs? Could Marcus have tainted the herbs in the pantry in some way? Maybe with those leaves they'd found in his desk?

She looked over the possibilities. If those leaves were a plant poison, such as belladonna or maybe hemlock, he could pretty easily mix them into aromatics like oregano or basil, couldn't he? She grabbed those spice bottles as well as the ground thyme and the small bottle of bay leaves. Maybe Alexander Quinn could test these herbs for toxins before the conference started tomorrow—

As she turned away from the pantry shelves, she heard a quiet click, followed by a slow, steady cadence of tapping, moving inexorably closer. Footsteps, she realized, shoving down a sudden spike of panic.

Padding across the narrow kitchen floor as quietly as possible, she hurried back to the dumbwaiter and folded herself inside, wincing as the heel of one foot caught the edge of the steel cage, making a soft thunking noise. Closing the door behind her, she gave the pulley rope four sharp tugs. The dumbwaiter lurched briefly and began a shuddering descent.

It was making too much noise, she thought, her heart rate climbing until her pulse seemed to hammer in her head like a piston.

Suddenly, the dumbwaiter seemed to drop precipitously, stopping with a loud clang that made her teeth crack together. It didn't move again.

"Hunter?" Keeping her voice to a whisper, she extended her hand in the dark, expecting to find the cool steel of the dumbwaiter chute. Instead, she felt solid wood.

It was the door in the basement. But why wasn't it open?

"Hunter?" she whispered again, sliding her hand to the right in search of the doorknob.

There. She gave it a turn, suddenly terrified she would find it locked, trapping her in the dark. But the knob turned easily enough, and she shoved the door open, already halfway out of the dumbwaiter by the time she realized it wasn't Hunter standing on the other side of the door.

"Hello, Susan. Nice to see you again after such a long time."

Ice flooding her veins, Susannah stared into the feral smile of Asa Bradbury.

Chapter Fifteen

Hunter had never lost consciousness, only the ability to move with any coordination until the thumping pain in his head subsided to a dull throb. But those few seconds had been enough time for the four men who'd ambushed him to strip away his Glock and the folding knife he kept in his jeans pocket.

Unarmed and outnumbered, he had few options. Better to let them think he was unconscious. It wasn't as if he'd be able to do much to thwart them with his head pounding and his limbs currently feeling like wet noodles.

But he had to keep his mind alert. Because whoever these guys were, they weren't Billy Dawson's BRI thugs. Which meant—

He heard the door of the dumbwaiter open, the scrambling sound of someone—Susannah—crawling out. Her footsteps faltered, and for a second, the whole room seemed to grow utterly still.

Then one of the men who'd wrestled him to the floor spoke in a hill country drawl. "Hello, Susan. Nice to see you again after such a long time."

Panic clawed at Hunter's gut, clanged along his nerves and pushed through the misty half fog in his brain. Lying perfectly still while his mind was whirling like a tornado took every ounce of control he had.

"Asa Bradbury." Susannah's voice was low and remarkably calm, considering she was apparently facing the man who'd driven her into exile nearly a decade ago. "It saddens me to see you here. I really thought you were the rare Bradbury who had a lick of sense."

"I'm chock-full of sense, sugar." From the tone of the man's voice, Hunter suspected he was smiling. "Primarily a sense of justice."

"Justice. Really."

The man she'd called Asa sighed. "You killed a kinsman, Susie. You know it's not something a Bradbury can just let go."

"Even though your kinsman was trying to rape a sixteen-year-old girl in her own bedroom?"

"Sadly, even then."

"And so, what? Summary execution? Shall we just get it over with right here and now?"

Hunter's pulse stuttered in his ears, escalating the ache in his head. He sneaked a look at the scene through his eyelashes, taking in the four men circling Susannah, guns drawn. Her gaze slanted toward him, and for an electric second, he thought she could see through his ruse.

But she looked back at the tallest of the four men, the one she'd called Asa. "What's it going to be, Asa?"

"There will be a tribunal tomorrow morning at ten. Your crimes against our family will be aired, and you can defend yourself." Asa Bradbury's tone was almost formal, as if he really did believe he was behaving according to some code of honor, however twisted.

"And if my defense is found wanting?" Her voice was deep and raspy.

"An eye for an eye," Asa answered. He nodded his head toward the others, and they moved even closer to Susannah.

"Wait," she said, her gaze slanting toward Hunter again. He closed his eyes, in case anyone followed her gaze. "Is he—"

"He's alive. He isn't our concern."

"What did you do to him?"

"Incapacitated him so that he couldn't try to keep us from doing what we came here to do." Asa's tone was dismissive, as if Hunter was no more significant to him than a door that had had to be unlocked to reach Susannah.

"I have to leave something for him," Susannah said.

Hunter heard the shuffle of feet and risked a quick peek through his eyelashes. She was trying to move past the three men who'd surrounded her, but they held her in place. "Please, Asa. I get that you're going to take me out of here no matter what I have to say about it, but we were trying to stop a mass murder from taking place. That's why he and I are here."

Asa glanced toward Hunter, forcing him to close his eyes again. "Also not our concern."

"I never realized you were a monster, Asa."

"I'm not."

"Then let me give him these."

Hunter heard more shuffling noises, but he didn't dare open his eyes.

"What are these?" Asa asked.

"Herbs. We think someone's planning to poison people at a conference tomorrow, and Hunter will need to get these herbs tested. Time is essential. Please let me leave these for him."

For a long moment, there was no sound at all beyond the soft whisper of breathing. Then Hunter heard footsteps moving toward him. Heavy footsteps, so definitely not Susannah's. He heard the soft click of something hard thudding against the floor near his head.

"I need to leave a note," Susannah said, her voice still a few feet away.

"Unnecessary. I'm sure your friend will figure it out." Asa's voice moved away from Hunter as the man joined his companions where they held Susannah captive. "It's time for us to go."

"I don't know why you pretend this is going to be justice, Asa," Susannah said as he and the other three men pushed her toward the exit door. "There's nobody on Laurel Bald who'll choose my word over yours. You know that. Why not just get this over with here and now?"

What was she doing, trying to goad them into killing her right now? Had she lost her mind?

Then, as the door closed behind them, he realized what she'd said.

Laurel Bald.

Brilliant, beautiful woman. She'd just given him somewhere to start looking for her.

HE'D BEEN CONSCIOUS, hadn't he? All Susannah had seen was the slightest flicker of his eyelids, but there had been a tension in his stillness that convinced her Hunter had been conscious, at least for the last few minutes of her confrontation with the Bradburys.

But had he picked up on the clue she'd given him?

"I know you think this is unfair." Beside her, Asa Bradbury shifted in his seat, the movement tugging the handcuffs that chained her to Asa's wrist.

"How on earth did you figure that out?" she responded in a tone as dry as desert sand.

"Do you think I'm unaware of my brother's more venal pursuits?" Asa asked softly, his head turned to look at her.

She made herself meet his gaze, unsurprised to find a hint of sympathy in the man's dark eyes. She hadn't been lying when she'd said she'd always thought Asa had more sense than most of the Bradburys. He hadn't been part of the family's meth business, at least not back when she'd still been living in Boneyard Ridge.

But she supposed things might have changed.

"Our family is in a battle for its life," Asa added more quietly. He sounded genuinely regretful, and Susannah supposed he might be, at that. Being the titular head of a mountain crime family had to be stressful for a man like Asa, who'd once dreamed about leaving the mountains to see the world outside. He'd wanted to go to college, maybe come back with a business degree and the chance to build a different sort of reputation for the Bradbury name.

But most of the other Bradburys had liked their name just the way it was. Synonymous with brute power and fast, dirty money.

"What happened to you, Asa?" she asked softly. "You had such plans for your life."

He didn't answer, but the tense set of his profile suggested she'd found a sore spot.

"You could let me go. Just end this madness here, once and for all. You know I didn't do anything that wasn't my God-given right. I had a right to protect myself from Clinton. I had a right to choose what to do with my own body."

"I can't stop them," he said quietly. "I can barely control them as it is, and if I were to show any sign of softness—"

"They'd destroy you," she finished for him, overwhelmed with hopelessness.

"I *am* sorry." Asa looked at her then, his brown eyes surprisingly sympathetic. "I always liked you, Susie McKenzie. You had fire."

She looked away, her gaze settling on the back of Kenny Bradbury's shaggy head where he sat in the driver's seat of the panel van carrying her inexorably toward her fate.

Please, she thought, *please let Hunter have been conscious. Please let him figure out what I was trying to tell him.*

"THESE NEED TO be tested for toxins," Hunter said without preamble, handing Alexander Quinn the four bottles of herbs Susannah had taken from the hotel kitchen before she'd been ambushed by the Bradburys. Quinn had met him on the road at the place where Hunter and Susannah had stashed their extra supplies. "And if there's anything in them, the cops need to get a warrant for Marcus Lemonde's desk in the Event Planning office."

Hunter bent to pick up both packs and slung them over one shoulder, already headed back to the borrowed SUV.

Quinn followed at a brisk pace. "Where are you going?"

"Boneyard Ridge. There's a place there called Laurel Bald. That's where they're taking her."

"The Bradburys?" Quinn asked.

Hunter stopped midstep, turning to look at his boss. "You knew about the Bradburys?" All he'd told Quinn on the phone was that their plans had gone sideways and now Susannah had been kidnapped. He hadn't mentioned the Bradburys. Of that, he was certain.

"I know her real name is Susan McKenzie and that she killed a man named Clinton Bradbury when she was sixteen years old."

Hunter stared at Quinn in silence before he breathed out a stream of profanities. "Of course you knew. You know every damn thing there is to know about everybody, don't you? You probably even knew that if you assigned me to watch her, I'd end up willing to take a bullet for her. Because I'm that sort of guy, aren't I?"

"Yes, you are. I just didn't have any idea you'd be willing to do it because you'd fallen in love with her."

Hunter started to protest, but the words never got past the back of his throat. What was the point of arguing? If he wasn't already in love with her, he was awfully close, wasn't he? Even now, the thought that he might not reach her in time to stop the Bradburys from doing whatever they planned to do to her was enough to make him feel weak-kneed and sick.

But it was also enough to make him ignore the pain still throbbing in his head, because he didn't have time to worry about whether or not he had a concussion. He couldn't afford to wait for a CAT scan or to get checked out by the paramedics.

Susannah needed him. And she'd given him a way to find her.

"You're going after her." It wasn't a question.

"I am," Hunter said, already moving toward the SUV again.

"You'll need backup."

"I probably will," he conceded, opening the driver's-side door.

"I'll get these samples to a lab. And I'll put some agents on call. Will six be enough? They can be in Boneyard Ridge in half an hour. Siege protocol?"

Hunter thought about it. He wasn't sure how many Bradburys there were in Boneyard Ridge, but unless they were all commando-trained warriors, they wouldn't be any match for seven well-trained agents from The Gates.

"Six should do it. Siege protocol," he agreed as he slid behind the steering wheel and put the keys in the ignition. "If there aren't toxins in those herbs, then get back to that hotel and figure out what Billy Dawson's up to, even if you have to call in a fake bomb threat to get the cops involved. Because I've got something else to do."

Hunter put the SUV in Drive and pulled away from Quinn, heading north toward Boneyard Ridge.

DAWN WAS STILL several hours away when the panel van carrying Susannah and her captors chugged its way up the winding mountain road to Laurel Bald near the top of Boneyard Ridge. Next to her, Asa Bradbury released an audible sigh, as if reaching his home territory came as a physical relief.

She herself felt nothing but sheer, gut-twisting panic. No matter how much she'd once loved this place, Boneyard Ridge had long since become a place of fear and loathing. Her grandmother was gone from this place, leaving only a mixed bag of memories and the ever-present threat of violence and retribution.

Retribution she was about to face, after so many years trying to run from the inevitable.

"Where do you plan to keep me?" she asked, trying not to let her fear show.

She could tell from the look in Asa's eyes that she hadn't been successful. "Jennalyn's cabin. She's made you up a place to rest in the cellar. It'll be a mite cold, so I asked her to make sure you had extra blankets."

"You're keeping me prisoner in a root cellar. In October."

"Did you expect a comfortable guest suite?" he asked in a flat tone, slanting another look her way. "You killed my brother."

"In self-defense."

"So you say."

"You know it was self-defense. You as much as admitted it."

"You'll have your say at the tribunal."

"Will I be provided with legal counsel?" she countered, deciding to play the game by Asa's rules. If he wanted to pretend he was seeking justice, then she would humor him. But on her own terms.

"You can serve as your own counsel, just as we'll serve as Clinton's."

"And the judge?"

"Three of our elders."

"Names?"

He was silent for a long moment. "Colton Bradbury, Mary Partlain and Brantley Bradbury."

She tried to place their positions in the Bradbury family. Asa's parents were both dead, but Asa's father had had two brothers, if she remembered correctly. "Colton's your uncle, right? And Mary Partlain?"

"My father's cousin. And Brantley is my uncle Bevill's eldest son."

"And in what possible way is this a fair tribunal?"

"You'll have your say. It's more than you gave Clinton."

"Oh, he had his say." Anger eclipsed fear as the images from that terrible night flooded her brain, driving out everything but rage at what Clinton Bradbury had forced her to do to defend herself. "He said a lot of profane and wicked things to me before he tried to pin me to my bed, strip off my clothes and violate my body against my will."

"You're wasting your breath on me, Susan. I am not the one you'll need to convince." Even as he spoke, the van pulled to a stop.

Kenny Bradbury cut the engine and turned around to look at Asa. "We're here."

Asa rose to his feet and reached across to open the panel van's side door. Attached to him by the handcuff, Susannah had no choice but to rise as well, following him out of the van into the cold night air. Her ragged breath condensed as it hit the cold air, mingling with the misty swirls of Asa's slower, calmer exhalations.

In silence, he led her to an angled door, well-hidden by high-growing grass, about ten yards from the small, silent cabin that slumbered in the clearing. Surrounded by towering evergreens and autumn-hued hardwoods already starting to shed their leaves for the winter, the clearing was overgrown and littered with fallen leaves that crunched beneath Susannah's boots as she stumbled after him, tugged along by the handcuff and the sheer strength of Asa Bradbury's determination.

He waited for Kenny to unlock the padlock holding the cellar door closed, then nudged Susannah down a set of cinder-block stairs descending into the dark belly of the root cellar. With a tug of a chain, he turned on the only light in the room, a bald bulb screwed into a fixture attached to an exposed wooden beam in the cellar's unfinished ceiling.

He gave her a prod toward an old, battered sofa someone had pushed up against one of the cellar's dirt walls. "Sit."

She did as he ordered, gauging her chances at making a run for her life. Not good, she decided as he deftly removed the cuff around his wrist and slid it through one link of a chain hanging from a hook in the ceiling. "You should have enough chain to reach the toilet if you need it," he said, waving his hand toward a portable toilet chair standing nearby. "And you should be comfortable enough sleeping. I suggest you try to rest. There's not a lot of night left."

Without saying anything more to her, he headed back up the steps and disappeared through the door, closing it behind him. She heard the rattle of the padlock being reengaged.

Then there was nothing but silence, broken only by the thunderous cadence of her own pulse in her ears.

She checked her watch. Only four hours had passed since she and Hunter had left Quinn's cabin for their mission at the hotel.

Hunter, she thought, her heart sinking. What if she'd been wrong? What if he'd really been unconscious, or worse? She'd seen him breathing—she'd been able to reassure herself of that much, at least. But he might have sustained a closed head injury. His brain might be swelling right now, deadly pressure building in his skull.

Why hadn't she made them let her check on him?

How could she have left him behind that way?

She had to get out of here. Yes, the cellar door was padlocked, and yes, she was handcuffed to a chain, but there were ways of getting out of handcuffs, right? All she had to do was find the right tool.

The cellar was mostly bare—probably cleaned out specifically to make sure she wouldn't find anything to aid in her escape. But after a few minutes of searching, and stretching the chain to its limit, she found an old mesh bag of what looked to be desiccated, rotted potatoes. The blackened lumps only vaguely resembled their original state, and the smell rising from the bag was less than pleasant. But the bag itself was tied at one end by a metal twist tie. Susannah unwound the tie from the bag and stripped away the paper coating to reveal a thin, flexible wire.

"That'll do," she murmured with satisfaction, returning to the sofa and bending the wire in an L-shape. Before her grandmother had pulled her out of her father's home, she'd learned a few lessons in, well, less-than-legal arts. One of those things had been how to pick a handcuff lock.

The wire her father had used to teach her had been a twisted paper clip, which was considerably stiffer and less flexible than the twist tie she was currently applying to the handcuff lock. But with some finesse and, she had to admit, a whole lot of luck, she managed to get the wire in just the right position to spring the lock. The cuff fell open and she pulled her hand free, elated.

But her elation seeped away almost immediately. She'd won only the first battle, she knew, her gaze sliding toward the closed cellar doors at the top of the cinder-block stairs. The next part of the war would be the hardest. She had to figure out a way to get rid of the padlock trapping her in place.

From the inside, without a single tool at her disposal.

Chapter Sixteen

Hunter parked near the top of the ridge and consulted the map application on the burner phone Quinn had provided. Based on a few calculations and some extrapolation of information he'd found online, he figured that Laurel Bald should be dead ahead as the crow flew.

He lifted the binoculars he'd packed and peered through the predawn gloom. The night was mostly clear, but cold and damp enough for mists to settle into the coves and valleys between the rounded mountain peaks, partially obscuring his view.

After a few moments, however, his eyes adjusted to the darkness and a faint paleness began to separate itself from the gloom. A mostly treeless summit, dun-colored due to autumn die-off—a bald, as it was known in this part of the Appalachians.

That had to be Laurel Bald, didn't it?

He scanned the mountain beneath the bald, looking for signs of habitation. Most of the homes in Boneyard Ridge were scattered along the main road that wound its way around the mountain, denser in the lower elevations but growing more scattered where the road began to climb more steeply as it reached the summit.

There were a couple of houses located near the bald. He couldn't make out any lights from within the cabin walls, but slender fingers of smoke rose from stone chimneys to mingle with the mountain mists.

He punched in the number of Quinn's latest burner phone.

His boss answered on the first ring. "Still alive?"

"So far. Don't suppose you've had any luck analyzing those herbs?"

"This soon? No. I'm going to make some calls come daylight, though. See if we can't get the cop conference put on hold. I know some people high up in that law enforcement society—they'll listen to me."

"Why didn't you just do that in the first place?"

"I wanted to see what you could come up with first. It's a hell of a lot easier to go to them with all the information you and Ms. Marsh managed to put together than to go in there with nothing concrete to offer."

There was a lot Quinn wasn't saying, but Hunter didn't have time to sort through his boss's half-truths and lies of omission. "Any chance you could give me some insight on the Bradburys before I go running in there halfcocked?"

"I was hoping you'd put the brakes on long enough to ask a pertinent question or two," Quinn said, grim amusement tinting his voice. "There are three main branches of the family, but only one you really need to worry about—Asa Bradbury, the younger of Aaron Bradbury's two sons and the head of the family now that the old man and Clinton are gone. Old Aaron had two brothers, Colton and Bevill, but Bevill had a stroke several years ago and he's disabled. His son Brantley has taken over for his father in the family business but he's not that interested in getting his hands dirty. And Colton's getting old now, so his son Kenny's doing a lot of the work of transporting drugs and keeping their dealers from getting any ideas about branching out on their own. He's more brawn than brains."

"Asa must have been the one doing all the talking tonight." Hunter pushed his hand through his short-cropped hair, wincing as his fingertips brushed over the painful lump at the back of his head. "He mentioned a tribunal tomorrow at ten. They're actually pretending to put her on trial?"

"Some of these old hill families see themselves as the law in their own little enclaves. You ought to know that, growing up in Bitterwood."

"So we have until ten in the morning to get her out of there."

"You ready for that backup I offered?"

He thought about it. "I'd like them in position. I'm parked at an overlook right now that could work as a staging area. It's far enough from Laurel Bald that I think they'd be safe gathering here. I need to go in alone, see if I can get her out of there without raising a big ruckus, but it would be real nice to have backup close enough that they can help us get out of there if things go bad before we can get to safety."

"Give me the coordinates and I'll get everyone in position. You're going in now, I presume?"

"Yeah. I've spotted a turnoff about a quarter mile from the bald that should give me a place to leave the SUV and strike out on foot."

"You up to that? You took a hell of a knock to the head. I saw the lump. That wasn't a love tap."

"I'm fine," Hunter answered. It was mostly the truth. His head hurt, yes, but primarily on the outside. He wasn't dizzy or confused. The past few days of hiking had actually built up his stamina, rather than reduced it.

And even if none of that had been true, he would still be heading up the mountain after Susannah.

"Backup's on the way. You have Sutton Calhoun's cell number memorized?"

"I do."

"He'll be the point man, then. Call him and he'll take care of getting the backup crew where you need them." Quinn hung up without another word.

Pocketing the phone, Hunter started the SUV engine and pulled out of the overlook parking area and back onto the two-lane mountain road.

WHAT SHE NEEDED was an ax. She could chop through the weathered wood of the cellar door without worrying about the padlock if she just had an ax. Unfortunately, Asa Bradbury hadn't seen fit to leave such a tool at her disposal. Nor could she have tried unscrewing the hinges—not that she had a screwdriver—because the hinges were on the outside of the door.

No ax. No screwdriver. No hope.

She backed down the cinder-block stairs and settled on the musty old sofa, tears of despair pricking her eyes. She fought against them, both the tears and the despair, determined not to be paralyzed just because she hadn't yet found an easy solution.

A quick glance at her watch told her she still had several hours left before the tribunal. Part of her, the bleary-headed, gritty-eyed part, wanted to spend that time asleep. Surely the only thing worse than running out of time was spending what was left of her time on earth futilely beating her head against a cinder-block wall she had no hope of tearing down.

But what if Hunter needed her? What if he was still lying on the floor in the hotel basement, his brain swelling past the point of no return? What if she could save him if she could just find her way out of here and reach a phone?

A soft, swishing sound coming from outside the cellar door drew her attention back to her current problem. The sound grew closer, then stopped. For a long moment, there was no sound at all except for the thudding of her pulse in her ears.

Then she heard the faint rattle of metal against metal.

Someone had just moved the padlock.

Panic setting in, she reached for the handcuff dangling from the chain and slipped it around her wrist, stopping just short of clicking it shut. If her visitor outside was Asa or one of the other Bradburys, maybe they wouldn't look too closely at the cuff.

As she waited, breathless, the furtive metal-on-metal noises continued, barely there, and she realized whoever might be working on the padlock outside, it wasn't anyone who had a key.

Which meant it wasn't one of the Bradburys.

Slipping the cuff from her wrist, she quietly crossed to the stairs and climbed until she could put her eye against the narrow slit between the double cellar doors. She could see almost nothing through the narrow space, the darkness outside nearly complete.

But she could hear someone breathing, a soft whisper of respiration that seemed so familiar she almost thought she was imagining it.

Was she hearing what she wanted to hear? Panic could play terrible tricks with a person's mind, and she was about as scared as she'd ever been in her whole life.

But she had to take a chance. If she was imagining things, if there was nobody out there at all, what could it hurt?

"Help me," she said, her voice little more than a whisper.

For a second, the world around her went thick with silence again. Then she heard a whisper in return. "Susannah?"

Her knees wobbled, forcing her to grab the inside handle of the door to keep from tumbling backward down the cinder-block stairs. "Hunter?"

"It's me, baby. I found you. I just—I don't have anything to pick this lock. Your friends took my gun and my knife, and stupidly, I didn't pack another one."

"I did," she whispered back to him. "I found one at Quinn's place, and I didn't have room in my pack, so I stuck it in yours. But I forgot to get it before we hiked to the hotel. It's in one of the inner pockets."

She heard a rustling noise and then a soft murmur of excitement. "You wonderful, wonderful woman."

"Don't try picking the lock. Use the screwdriver blade and just unscrew the door hinges." Tamping down the flood of excitement that threatened to swamp her senses completely, she added, "But be careful. The Bradburys may be on the lookout for an escape attempt."

"I'm keeping an eye out. And I'm not alone. There are six other agents from The Gates out here in the woods behind me. I called in backup."

She heard a new rasping sound, coming from the right side of the door. He must be attacking the hinges now. She settled on the steps, listening to the sounds of his handiwork, and realized she'd been wrong about miracles.

Being snatched from the hotel parking lot and hauled off into the woods by this maddening, marvelous man had been one of the most miraculous things that had ever happened to her.

Considering how slowly time had been passing since Asa Bradbury had dumped her in this cellar, it seemed only a few seconds later that Hunter whispered through the door, "Let's give it a go."

She turned to watch as Hunter eased the door away from the hinge. The padlock didn't allow the door to move much, but the narrow opening provided enough space for Susannah to slide through and scramble onto the grass outside.

Before she had a chance to say a word, Hunter had scooped her up and started running with her. A heart-beat later, the sharp bark of a pistol explained his sudden flight.

Someone was shooting at them.

ASA BRADBURY HAD been eighteen years old when his brother Clinton broke into Myra Stokes's neat little cabin with the intention of claiming Myra's granddaughter for himself. Asa had had one foot out of town, a hardship scholarship to Tennessee in his pocket and visions of a life outside the claustrophobic rock bluffs of Boneyard Ridge when his mother had walked into the bedroom he shared with his older brother and informed him that Clinton was dead.

"You're the head of the family now," she'd said, her voice like steel beneath her tears. "You know what you have to do."

Oh, he'd known. But he hadn't liked it.

Still didn't.

But that's what came from being trapped in a life he didn't want. His choices had been stripped away that cold November night. Just as he had no choice now but to go after the McKenzie girl and the man who'd stolen her away.

He didn't waste time wondering what would happen if he called off the pursuit. He might be the alpha dog in this pack, but there were hungry young curs circling his position, waiting for any sign of weakness.

There was no walking away from the life he'd inherited. No different path available to him, the way it had been available so briefly, a tantalizing prize just out of his reach, until Clinton's death.

Murder, he thought. He should call it murder. That's how the family still spoke of Clinton's death, as if it had been an act of evil perpetrated by a selfish, venal, young temptress.

But Asa drew the line at lying to himself. He knew what Clinton had been like. The impulse-control problems. The colossal sense of entitlement that had come with inheriting control of the Bradbury family business long before he was ready for it.

Asa hadn't been ready for it, either. But at least he'd been smart enough to do whatever it took to learn how to be a ruthless mountain drug lord before the circling wolves could take him out.

One of those lessons was about the folly of mercy. Mercy was a sign of weakness. There was no place for mercy in the world in which Asa and his family lived. So the girl had to face the tribunal. And her protector had to be eliminated.

That was the law of the hills. The law of the Bradburys.

Swallowing a sigh of frustration, Asa reloaded his Winchester .700 and followed his kinsmen into the woods.

A BULLET WHIPPED past Hunter's ear and hit the tree beside him, sending wood and bark shrapnel flying. A splinter grazed his forehead but he kept running, pushing Susannah ahead of him as they scrambled through the underbrush, heading deeper into the forest.

The straighter path to the place where he'd left the SUV would have been to head right over the bald, but the dearth of trees would have made them easy targets for whoever was behind them taking potshots. They were lucky to have gotten a head start; if the person snapping off rounds at them were better with that rifle he was wielding, they might both be dead already.

"Left!" Susannah threw the word over her shoulder, letting the cold morning breeze carry the word back to Hunter as she jogged left, into a dense thicket of mountain laurel bushes. He had to fight his way through, with no time for stealth or hiding their trail. He wasn't sure there was any way to sneak out of these woods without the Bradburys following them.

But apparently Susannah had a different idea. Almost as soon as they'd reached the middle of the mountain laurel thicket, she stopped, tugging him to the ground with her. They crouched there, trying to slow their breathing and listen for any sign of their pursuers.

After a long spell of silence, Susannah reached for his hand, closing her fingers tightly around his. In the pale light of predawn, her eyes reflected the first faint rose hues of sunrise, dark with emotion. "I was so scared," she whispered.

He cupped her cheek with one hand. "I know. I'm sorry I let them take you, but—"

"But you came after me." She slid her hand over his, holding it in place. "I thought I saw your eyelids move, when you were lying there, but I wasn't sure. I started to second-guess myself. I was so afraid you were really hurt, and I'd left you there to die—"

He touched his forehead to hers. "I've got a hard head."

She fell silent for a few moments, just letting him hold her. Finally, however, she pulled her head away from his, drawing a deep breath. "They're out there. I can't hear them, but I can feel them."

"I know." He felt them, too, like a gathering storm.

"You said you have backup?"

"They're on the way. I called them in as soon as I spotted the cabins."

"How did you know where to look for me?"

"Honestly? I didn't." He'd never felt more helpless in his life than he'd felt as he crouched there on the edge of the clearing, wondering how on earth he was supposed to find Susannah and get her away from the Bradburys without getting both of them killed. "I was sneaking around the cabin, trying to see if I could find any sign that you were even there, when I almost stumbled over the root cellar doors hidden in the high grass. The door itself was faded and weathered, but the padlock holding it shut looked shiny and new. Got me to wondering."

She flashed him a quick smile. "Smart man."

God, he wanted to kiss her. It was the worst possible time for sentimentality, but he was so damn glad to see her still alive and well.

"I think we're going to have to make a run for it. Before they have time to surround us," he said.

"What if we're already too late?"

He brushed her jaw with his fingertips. "It's a chance we have to take. Ready?"

She stared at him, her eyes wide and scared. But her jaw jutted forward, her expression made of solid mountain granite. She gave a short nod. "Ready."

He pushed to his feet, tugging her up with him.

And six rifles cocked in a stutter of metallic clicks, their long barrels surrounding Hunter and Susannah on all sides.

Chapter Seventeen

"Take her back to the cabin." Asa Bradbury spoke in a low, bored tone that sent a hard, racking chill down Susannah's spine. "I'll take care of her friend."

"No!" She took a rushing step toward Asa, but Hunter's hand closed around her arm, pulling her back.

"Go with them," he said quietly.

"No!" She wrapped her arms around him tightly, trying to surround him completely with her body. "If they're going to kill us both, then they can damn well kill us together."

"Very touching," Asa drawled, as tonelessly as if he were remarking on the weather on a mild day.

She shot a look at him over her shoulder, hating him in a way she never had before. She'd been running and hiding from Asa and his kin for years, but she'd never hated him the way she'd hated Clinton. She'd always seen Asa as collateral damage, the Bradbury who'd gotten sucked into this blood vendetta against his will.

But looking at him now, seeing how little he cared about her life, one way or another, she finally understood what the philosopher Hannah Arendt had meant when she wrote of the banality of evil. Under any other circumstances, Asa Bradbury might have been an ordinary man, living an ordinary life, not hurting anyone and maybe contributing something meaningful to the world.

But he'd taken the path of least resistance and let his family's corruption swallow him whole. He wasn't driven by greed or hate or any emotion that might make sense of his determination to see her dead.

He was driven by inertia. And that's what made him truly frightening.

Hunter's arms tightened around her suddenly, pulling her closer. He pressed his lips to her temple and let them slide lightly down her cheek to her ear. "Duck," he whispered, and pushed her down to the ground.

"Drop your weapons!" The voice, hard and commanding, boomed through the woods around them, amplified by a bullhorn.

Hunter rolled over on top of her, pressing her to the ground beneath his body as chaos erupted around them. She heard a cacophony of shouts and curses, punctuated by a couple of gunshots, close by. Hunter tucked her even more firmly beneath him, whispering reassurances in her ear that she felt more than heard.

Over the bullhorn, the deep voice rang again. "You're surrounded. Put down your weapons and no one has to die today."

The chaos subsided into a strange, uneasy silence. Then she heard the sound of grass swishing, bushes rustling, and within her limited range of vision, she saw Kenny Bradbury bend and drop his Winchester to the ground.

A minute later, the voice she'd heard over the bullhorn spoke again, without amplification and so close her nerves jerked. "Situation contained, Bragg. You injured?"

Hunter rolled away from her and pushed to his knees. He helped her into a kneeling position as well, not answering his colleague as he looked her over with an anxious gaze. "You okay? Anything hurt?"

She shook her head, finding speech beyond her capacity at the moment.

The man who'd spoken earlier crouched beside her, flashing her a brief smile that displayed a set of dimples nearly as disarming as Hunter's. "We're going to have a talk with these folks, okay?" He waved one of the other agents from The Gates over, a slim brunette woman dressed in the same woodland camouflage pattern worn by the rest of the agents who were gathering discarded rifles and herding the Bradburys toward their cabins.

"I'm Ava," the brunette introduced herself. She glanced warily at Hunter, as if she expected him to protest. When he remained silent, she ventured a smile at Susannah. "Let's get you out of here."

Hunter might not have resisted, but Susannah did. "Hunter—"

"Ava will take care of you. I need to stay here, just for a bit."

She lowered her voice. "What are y'all going to do?"

A feral light gleamed in Hunter's green eyes. "We're going to let the Bradburys know just how things are going to go from now on."

"It's my fight. Don't trundle me off like I'm the girl."

"You *are* the girl." He touched her face, his lips curving. "My girl."

"Don't make me go all Gloria Steinem on you—"

"If she wants in on this, let her in." The man still holding the bullhorn shrugged. "She's right. It's her fight, too."

Hunter shot the other man a frown that might have alarmed a weaker man, but the man with the bullhorn didn't even react.

Signaling his surrender with a deep sigh, Hunter threaded his fingers through hers and nodded toward the line of agents still pushing the Bradburys through the woods ahead of them. "Come on, let's get this over with. I'd like to get back to the hotel in time to watch your buddy Marcus get what's coming to him."

"THIS IS HOW it's going to go." Hunter stood in front of the group of disarmed Bradbury kinsmen, scanning the room carefully for any sign of impending insurrection before he settled his gaze on the Bradbury in charge.

Asa Bradbury looked for all the world like a slightly shabby accountant, all lean angles and a nebbish sort of averageness. His brown eyes were sharp but mostly devoid of emotion as he held Hunter's gaze without speaking. There wasn't even a hint of the sullen anger he saw in the faces of Bradbury's kinsmen, only a tepid sort of resignation.

"Susan McKenzie is dead. She no longer exists. Your blood vendetta is over as of now." Hunter paced slowly in front of the subdued group of Bradburys who now sat facing him, but his gaze never left Asa's face. "Any attempt to cause any problem whatsoever for the woman named Susannah Marsh will be met with any and all force necessary to make you and yours wish you'd never been born. She's under the protection of The Gates now. You do not want to test our resolve."

Asa Bradbury's gaze didn't waver. He said just one word. "Understood."

Hunter finally released his gaze and looked at Susannah, who stood next to Ava Trent a couple of feet away. Susannah's winter-sky eyes glittered with an emotion that did more to make his knees quiver than anything that had happened to this point.

His fellow agent Sutton Calhoun stepped forward, still holding the bullhorn dangling from one hand. "Your weapons have been emptied of ammunition and left in the root cellar where you were keeping Susannah Marsh. Please don't do anything foolish that might necessitate our returning here in the future." He nodded toward Hunter.

Hunter crossed to Susannah and took her hand. "Let's go."

Flanked by Sutton and Ava, they left the Bradbury cabin and started the long walk back to the staging area.

SUSANNAH HAD NEVER felt more tired in her life than she felt at the moment, slumped in the executive chair in front of her desk in the office she'd called her home away from home for the past two years. The small clock on her desk blotter read 7:00 a.m.

Marcus Lemonde should be walking through the door any minute.

"You don't have to be here. I'm not really sure you should." Perched on the edge of her desk, Hunter slanted a worried look in her direction.

"Wouldn't miss it for the world," she assured him.

Alexander Quinn was seated at Marcus's desk, his posture relaxed. He was conversing quietly with the fourth person occupying the office, Ridge County Sheriff's Department lieutenant Hale Borden, a tall, lean man in his early forties, with thinning flax-colored hair and sharp blue eyes. He was in civilian clothes, but there was no missing the bulge of his service pistol tucked in a holster at his hip, ill-concealed beneath his suit jacket.

Quinn had called in a favor from the Ridge County sheriff himself, using the county's crime lab to rush the testing of the spice jars Hunter had handed over. "There were several ounces of belladonna leaves in the basil and the oregano that was slotted for the wine reduction the caterer was going to use for both the chicken and mushroom dishes," Quinn had told them as soon as they drove up to the hotel. "Enough to make everyone extremely sick—or worse. They executed a search of his desk a few minutes ago and found what looks like more belladonna leaves. I think we've got him."

There were four deputies, also dressed as civilians, waiting for Marcus Lemonde's arrival. They would follow him to the office to make sure he didn't give Lt. Borden any trouble.

Across the office, Borden's cell phone hummed. He checked the display screen and nodded at Quinn. "Showtime."

A couple of minutes later, the office door opened and Marcus Lemonde entered, his gaze lowered, focusing on the cell phone in his hand.

The look of dismayed shock on his face as he took in his four unexpected visitors was everything Susannah had hoped for.

"Marcus Lemonde, you're under arrest for conspiracy to commit murder," Lt. Borden informed him cheerfully.

Marcus turned to run but the four trailing deputies blocked his exit, pushing him back into the office.

Wild-eyed, Marcus looked back at Susannah, then noticed Hunter sitting on the edge of her desk. His eyes widened with surprise.

"Hi again," Hunter said with a satisfied smile. "Remember me?"

"ARE THE CHARGES going to stick?" Susannah's voice was thick with weariness.

She'd been silent for most of the drive to Quinn's

cabin, so her sleepy question came as a jolt to Hunter's nervous system. He glanced at her, taking in her heavy-lidded gaze. "Quinn thinks so. The lab didn't get any prints off the bottles, but the search of Marcus's desk yielded more belladonna leaves. Since the police didn't use our testimony of finding the leaves in the drawer to get the warrant to search the desk, it should stand up to legal scrutiny."

"Do you think the BRI will target you for your part in the sting?"

"Spoken like a woman who's spent the past twelve years running from a blood vendetta."

Her lips curved slightly. "Well, if you need me to go all commando on the BRI for you, you know where to find me."

"Will I?" he asked, almost afraid to hear her answer.

She turned her gaze toward him slowly. "You think I'm planning to go to ground again? Change my name, cut my hair, find a new place to live?"

"Wouldn't be the first time."

"No, it wouldn't." She leaned her head back against the seat. "But I like it here in Ridge County. I missed the hills when I was gone, and I'm getting too old and too settled in my ways to keep running."

"Are you worried about the Bradburys?"

She shook her head. "Asa's heart was never really in it, you know. And I think you and your pals at The Gates made your point."

Quinn's cabin came into view, and Hunter fell silent the rest of the way, pondering how to bring up the next question he wanted to ask. Getting her to agree to stick around Ridge County had been easier than he'd antici-pated, given her past. He wouldn't have blamed her if she'd wanted a fresh start.

Hell, he might have offered to go with her.

She staggered a little as she started up the porch steps. Hunter caught her before she fell, closing his hands over her elbows as he walked her to the door. He still had Quinn's key in his pocket—the Bradburys hadn't bothered to take it from him when they patted him down. He unlocked the door and nudged her inside ahead of him.

She made it as far as the sofa before she slumped onto the plush cushions and gazed up at him, bleary-eyed. "I could sleep for a week."

He settled next to her, nudging her shoulder with his own. "Before you drift off, Sleeping Beauty, there's something I need to ask you."

Rolling her head onto his shoulder, she looked up at him. "I hope it's not an overly complex question."

"It might be," he admitted, nuzzling his nose against her forehead. "It's about the future. Specifically, your future. And mine."

She sat up and looked at him, her eyes sharpening. "Is this a question or a proposition?"

He couldn't quell a grin. "Possibly both."

Her lips curved slowly in response. "Well, the proposition part might need to be tabled until I get some sleep."

"I think we have something between us. Something good." He grimaced, feeling inarticulate. "I think maybe I'm in love with you."

The curve of her lips deepened, and her soft gray eyes flashed a hint of fire. "Maybe?"

"Probably."

"That's marginally better."

"Most likely?"

She bent toward him, brushing her smiling lips against his. "Getting warmer."

Definitely, he thought as her kiss sparked a thousand little fires along his nervous system.

Her fingers playing at the back of his neck, she tugged him closer, her lips parting to deepen the kiss. Her tongue tangled with his before she slowly pulled away to gaze up at him with desire-drunk eyes.

"Lucky for you, I'm most likely falling in love with you, too." She plucked lightly at the top button of his shirt, stopping tantalizingly short of pulling it out of the buttonhole. "And I will definitely prove it to you soon."

"After you sleep for a week?" he murmured against her temple.

"See?" She smoothed her fingers over his chest, making his heart pound. "It's like we can read each other's minds."

She settled in the curve of his arm, warm and sleepy and perfect. After a few minutes, her breathing slowed and deepened as she drifted to sleep.

Relaxing deeper into the sofa cushions, Hunter let himself watch her for a few moments before he eased from beneath her and stretched her out on the sofa, covering her with the fuzzy brown blanket draped over the arm. She made a soft grumbling noise but curled up under the blanket and went back to sleep.

Hunter walked quietly into the kitchen and pulled out the burner phone Quinn had given him back at the hotel before he and Susannah had left for the cabin. "I think there's a call you need to make. Don't you?" Quinn had asked.

Settling in one of the kitchen chairs, Hunter punched in the number and made himself push SEND. A couple of rings later, he heard the familiar timbre of his sister Janet's voice. "Hello?"

"Hey, Jannie," he said. "It's me."

"My God, Hunter! I've been so worried about you! Are you okay?"

Tears pricking his eyes, he smiled at the warm autumn sunlight drifting through the kitchen windows. "I'm fine," he answered. "Just fine."

"Where are you? What have you been doing?"

He couldn't hold back a watery laugh. "That's a long, interesting story, Jannie. You got a minute to hear it?"

"Are you kidding? Of course I do."

In her voice, he heard a hint of worry and a lot of curiosity, but not a single ounce of censure, even though he had been out of touch for far too long and, as far as she knew, doing something she hated. Her love for him was unconditional, and most of the time he felt entirely unworthy of it.

As he thumbed away the tears that escaped his eyes, he heard soft footsteps behind him. Turning, he saw Susannah standing in the kitchen doorway, looking sleep-tousled and irresistible. Her shapely eyebrows lifted in a question, and he stretched his hand toward her.

She crossed to the table and put her hand in his, letting him tug her down to his lap. Curling her arms around his shoulders, she nestled into his embrace, her head tucked in the curve of his neck.

"Hunter?" Janet's voice buzzed in his ear.

Leaning his head against Susannah's, he let go of his tension in a soft sigh. "Ever heard of a private investigation firm called The Gates?"

* * * * *

"Why the hell has your witchy face been in my head for the past fifteen years?"

McVey didn't expect an answer. He wasn't even sure why he'd asked the question. True, she looked very much like the woman in his recurring dream, but the longer he stared at her—couldn't help that part, unfortunately—the more the differences added up.

On closer inspection, Amara's hair really was more brown than red. Her features were also significantly finer than…whoever. Her gray eyes verged on charcoal, her slim curves were much better toned and her legs were the longest he'd seen on any woman anywhere.

He might have lingered on the last thing if she hadn't slapped a hand to his chest, narrowed those beautiful eyes to slits and seared him with a glare.

"What the hell kind of question is that?"

NIGHT OF
THE RAVEN

BY
JENNA RYAN

Published in Great Britain 2014
by Mills & Boon, an imprint of Harlequin (UK) Limited,
Eton House, 18-24 Paradise Road, Richmond, Surrey, TW9 1SR

© 2014 Jacqueline Goff

ISBN: 978-0-263-91377-4

46-1114

Harlequin (UK) Limited's policy is to use papers that are natural, renewable and recyclable products and made from wood grown in sustainable forests. The logging and manufacturing processes conform to the legal environmental regulations of the country of origin.

Printed and bound in Spain
by CPI, Barcelona

Jenna Ryan started making up stories before she could read or write. As she grew up, romance always had a strong appeal, but romantic suspense was the perfect fit. She tried out a number of different careers, including modeling, interior design and travel, but writing has always been her one true love. That and her longtime partner, Rod.

Inspired from book to book by her sister Kathy, she lives in a rural setting fifteen minutes from the city of Victoria, British Columbia. It's taken a lot of years, but she's finally slowed the frantic pace and adopted a West Coast mind-set. Stay active, stay healthy, keep it simple. Enjoy the ride, enjoy the read. All of that works for her, but what she continues to enjoy most is writing stories she loves. She also loves reader feedback. E-mail her at jacquigoff@shaw.ca or visit Jenna Ryan on Facebook.

To Anne Stuart, who got the writing ball rolling for me.
Thank you, Anne, for all the great books.

Chapter One

Los Angeles, California
15 years ago

The scene felt so real, McVey figured this time it might not be unfolding in his head. His totally messed-up head, which wasn't improving thanks to the dream that had haunted him every night for the past two weeks.

The moment he fell asleep, he found himself trapped in an attic room that smelled like old wood, wet dirt and something far more pungent than boiled cabbage. The air was muggy and strangely alive. Thunder crashed every few seconds and tongues of lightning flickered through a curtain of fetid gray smoke.

He knew he was hiding, hunkered down in some shadowy corner where the two people he watched—barely visible within the smoke—couldn't see him.

The man's fingers clenched and unclenched. The woman circled a small fire and muttered unintelligible words.

Two violent thunderbolts later, only the woman and the smoke remained. The man had vanished.

Okay, that couldn't be good. McVey searched frantically for a way out of wherever he was before whoever *she* was saw him and made him eat the same black dripping thing she'd given the now-gone man.

With her eyes closed and her hair and clothes askew, she mumbled and swayed and breathed in choking fumes. Then suddenly she froze. In the next flash of lightning her head began to turn. Slowly, creepily, like a rusty weather vane in a bad horror film.

Her eyes locked on McVey's hiding place. He heard the black thing in her hand plop to the floor. She raised a dripping finger and pointed it straight at him.

"You," she accused in a voice that made him think of rusty nails soaked in whiskey. "You saw what passed between me and the one she would have you call Father."

Whoa, McVey thought on an unnatural spurt of fear. That was a whole lot, what she'd just said. A whole lot of nothing he understood, or wanted to.

"You have no business here, child." She started toward him. "Don't you know I'm mad?"

Right. Mad. So why the hell couldn't he move his—? He stopped the question abruptly, backpedaled and latched on to the other word. Child?

Shock, slick and icy, rolled through him when he looked down and saw his feet encased in tiny, shin-high boots.

Thunder rattled the house. His head shot up when he heard a low creak. Watching her smile, he realized with a horrified jolt that she was beautiful. He also realized he knew her, or at least he recognized her.

When she pointed at him again, the spell broke and he reached for his gun on the nightstand. Except there was no nightstand, and the next streak of lightning revealed a hand that wasn't his. Couldn't be. It was too small, too pale and far too delicate.

"Don't be afraid, child." Her voice became a silky croon. Her ugly clothes and hair melted into a watery blur of color. "I won't harm you. I'll only make what you think you've seen go away."

McVey wanted to tell her that he had no idea what he'd seen and the only thought in his head right then was to get out of there before her finger—still dripping with something disgusting—touched him.

He edged sideways in the dark. He could escape if the lightning would give him a break.

Of course it didn't, and her eyes, gray and familiar, continued to track his every move.

"There's no way out," she warned. With an impatient sound she grabbed his wrists. "I don't want to hurt you. You know I never have."

No, he really didn't know that, but wherever he was, he had no gun. Or strength, apparently, to free himself from her grasp.

She laughed when he fought her. "Foolish child. You forget I'm older than you. I'm also more powerful, and much, much meaner than your mother."

His mother?

She dragged him out of the corner. "Come with me."

When she hauled him upright, he stumbled. Looking down, he saw the hem of the long dress he'd stepped on.

"Why am I…?" But when he heard the high, unfamiliar voice that emerged from his throat, he choked the question off.

The woman crouched to offer a grim little smile. "Believe me when I tell you, Annalee, what I will do to you this night is for your own good…."

McVey SHOT FROM the nightmare on the next peal of thunder. The dark hair that fell over his eyes made him think he'd gone blind. A gust of wind rattled the shade above his nightstand and he spotted the stuttering neon sign outside. It wasn't until he saw his own hand reaching over to check his gun that he let himself fall back onto the mattress and worked on loosening the knots in his stomach.

That they remained there, slippery yet stubbornly tight, was only partly due to the recurring nightmare. The larger part stemmed from a more tangible source.

It was time to do what he'd known he would do for the past two weeks, ever since his nineteenth birthday. Ever since his old man had pried a deathbed promise from his only son.

He would set aside the disturbing fact that every time he fell asleep these days he turned into a young girl who wore long dresses and old-fashioned boots. He'd forget about the woman he thought he should know who wanted to give him amnesia. He'd focus strictly on keeping the promise he'd made to his father. If that meant turning his back on the people he'd worked with since…well, not all that long actually, so nothing lost there. He was going to walk away now, tonight, keep his promise and change the course of his life.

Maybe if he did that, the nightmare would stay where it belonged. Buried deep in the past of the person he feared he'd once been.

Chapter Two

New Orleans, Louisiana
Present Day

"Make no mistake about it…"

Moments after the sentence had been passed, the raspy-voiced man with the stooped shoulders and the tic in his left eye had looked straight at Amara Bellam and whispered just loud enough for her and the two men beside her to hear.

"Those who brought about my imprisonment will pay. My family will see to it."

Although her eyewitness testimony had played a large part in his conviction, at the time Jimmy Sparks had uttered his threat, Amara had thought his reaction was nothing more than knee-jerk. After all, life in prison for someone of his dubious health surely meant he wouldn't see the free light of day ever again.

But the word *family* crept into her head more and more often as the weeks following his incarceration crept by. It took root when Lieutenant Michaels of the New Orleans Police Department contacted her with the news that one of her two fellow witnesses, Harry Benedict, was dead.

"Now, don't panic." Michaels patted the air in front of her. "Remember, Harry had close to two decades on Jimmy."

"Lieutenant, Jimmy Sparks is the two-pack-a-day head of a large criminal family. He has a dozen relatives to do his legwork. Harry was a hale and hearty seventy-nine-year-old athlete who hiked across Maryland just last year."

"Which is very likely why he died of a massive coronary just last night." The detective made another useless patting motion. "Really, you don't need to panic over this."

"I'm not panicking."

"No, you're not." His hand dropped. "Well, that makes one of you. Chad, our overstressed third witness, knocked back two glasses of bourbon while I was explaining the situation."

"Chad dived off the temperance wagon right after Jimmy Sparks whispered his threat to us." She rubbed her arms. "Are you sure Harry died of natural causes?"

"The path lab said it was heart failure, pure and simple. The man had a history, Amara. Two significant attacks in the past five years."

Hale and hearty, though, she recalled after Michaels left.

For the next few weeks she fought her jitters with an overload of work. Even so, fear continued to curl in Amara's stomach. She had thought she might be starting to get past it when the harried lieutenant appeared on her doorstep once again.

"Chad's dead." She saw it in his dog-tired expression. "Damn."

The lieutenant spread his fingers. "I'm sorry, Amara. And before you ask, the official cause, as determined by the coroner's office, is accidental suicide."

"This is not happening." A shiver of pure terror snaked through her system. When the detective spoke her name, she raised both hands. "Please don't try to convince me that suicides can't be arranged."

"Of course they can, but Chad Weaver was surrounded by eleven friends when he collapsed—in his home, at a party arranged by him and to which he invited every person in attendance. No one crashed the event, and the drugs and alcohol he ingested were his own."

She swung around to stare. "Chad took drugs?"

"Like the booze, he got into them after Jimmy Sparks's trial. As witnesses, you all had—er, have—impeccable credentials."

"Right. Credentials." Feeling her world had tilted radically, Amara headed for her Garden District balcony and some much needed night air. "Mind's really spinning here, Lieutenant. What kinds of drugs did Chad take?"

The cop rubbed his brow. "Ecstasy, mostly. A little coke. Might've smoked some weed earlier in the day."

She made a negating motion. "No chance that any of those substances could've been tampered with prepurchase, huh?"

"Amara…"

Her sarcastic tone didn't quite mask the anger beginning to churn inside her. "It's a fair question, Lieutenant. We're talking about street dealers, people who aren't exactly pillars of the community. Are you saying that, given the right inducement, not one of them could or would have slipped a little extra something into the goody bags Chad bought?"

"The coroner is convinced it was—"

"Yes, I heard that part. Accidental death."

"Suicide."

It cost her a great deal to work up a smile. "I guess we'll find out, won't we?" She struggled to maintain her composure. "I can read your face, Michaels. You're going to tell me there's nothing you can do in terms of police protection. I mean, on the off chance the coroner is mistaken."

The detective regarded the toes of his scuffed shoes.

"Massive coronary for Harry. Private party for Chad. No one except the three of you and me heard Jimmy's threat. The media would love to jump all over this, but they won't, because the powers that be are well aware of Jimmy Sparks's many and varied connections. Sure, the odd question is bound to surface, but they'll die as quickly as they're born. After all, there's no evidence of wrongdoing in either case."

"I suppose not. Well, then." Amara took a deep breath. "At the risk of sounding paranoid, do you have any suggestions as to how I can avoid a date with the forensic team?"

When he raised his head, the steely look in his eyes said it all. "You need to disappear," he told her. "Get out of the city and go someplace safe."

"Safe. Great." She pressed firm fingers into her temples. "Where?"

Tossing a worried look onto the street below, Michaels pulled her away from the wrought iron railing. "Your parents are in South America, aren't they?"

"Central America. They're doing medical relief work, have been for the past two years. Mostly with children, Lieutenant. I'm not taking this nightmare to them."

"You have relatives in Maine, don't you?"

"What? Yes—no."

"We'll go with the first answer." When the lights bobbed, he closed the French doors and pulled the curtains. "Let's do it this way. You pack, make whatever calls you need to, and I'll drive you to the airport." He managed a feeble grin. "If there's one thing I'm good at, it's shaking criminal tails."

Amara's mind swam. "Surely Jimmy Sparks's family will have the airport covered."

"Not in Jackson, Mississippi. I know this guy, Amara. It won't be a group hunt so much as a single-person stalk."

"As in one person sent to make sure I choke to death on a bite of crawfish or drop dead on the sidewalk from a nonexistent blood clot that'll dissolve before… God, what am I saying? No, wait, what am I doing?" She turned to face him. "I can't endanger the lives of my family members. You know I can't."

"You can, and you should. Most of those family members live in a spooky little town in a remote and densely wooded section of coastal Maine. Raven's Cove is your best and safest option right now."

She stared at him for five long seconds before countering with a flat "It's Raven's Hollow, and I will call my grandmother. I'll explain the situation. But if she's the least bit hesitant, I'm choosing another destination."

"Deal." He ran his gaze over the ceiling when the lights bobbed again. "Pack only what you need."

What she needed, Amara reflected, was a time machine. Unfortunately all she had was her iPhone, her grandmother's number and a waning glimmer of hope that she'd ever see anyone in or out of Raven's Hollow, Maine, again.

Chapter Three

"I've already broken up two bar fights tonight, Chief, and the crowd here's spoiling for more." Jake Blume's tone, surly at the best of times, soured. "It's gonna be a free-for-all by the time this two-town party—which ain't no kind of party, in my opinion—plays out. Still three days to go and the hooligans on both sides are making their feelings known with their fists." His voice dropped to a growl. "What do you want me to do about tonight's ruckus?"

McVey heard about half of what his griping deputy related. More important to him than a minor barroom scuffle was the TV across the room where the Chicago Cubs were cheerfully mopping up Wrigley Field with his beloved Dodgers.

"Run," he told the slow-motion hitter who'd just slugged the ball to the fence.

"From a bar fight?" Jake gave a contemptuous snort. "This town ain't turned me into a girl yet, McVey."

"Talking to the television, Deputy." Disgusted by yet another out, McVey took a long drink of beer and muted the sound. "Okay, which bar and what kind of damage are we talking about?"

"It's the Red Eye in the Hollow—a town I'm still trying to understand why we're working our butts off to cover so its police chief can sun his sorry ass in Florida for the next couple weeks."

"Man's on his honeymoon, Jake." Amusement glimmered. "The novelty'll wear off soon enough."

His deputy gave another snort. "Said one confirmed bachelor to another."

"I was never confirmed—and that was a ball," he told the onscreen umpire.

"Look, if I'm interrupting…"

"You're not." McVey dangled the beer bottle between his knees and rubbed a tired eye. "I assume the damage at the Red Eye is minimal."

"As bar fights go in these parts."

"Then give whoever threw the first punch a warning, make the participants pay up and remind everyone involved that it's you who's on duty tonight, not me."

"Meaning?"

"You've got a shorter fuse, zero tolerance and, between the towns, six empty jail cells just begging to be filled."

"Good point." Jake cheered up instantly. "Can I threaten to cuff 'em?"

"Your discretion, Deputy. After you're done, head back to the Cove. I'll be in at first light to relieve you."

When he glanced over and saw his team had eked out two hits, McVey gave his head a long, slow roll and sat back to think.

In the fourteen months since he'd arrived in Raven's Cove, he'd only had the dream five times, which was a hell and gone better average than he'd had during his six years with the Chicago Police Department or the nearly eight he'd put in in New York. At least once a month in both places, he'd found himself up in a smoke-filled attic while a woman he still couldn't place told him she was going to screw up his memories. Not that he'd given up city life over anything as nebulous as a dream. His reasons had run a whole lot deeper.... And was that a floorboard he'd just heard creak upstairs?

With the bottle poised halfway to his mouth, he listened, heard nothing and, taking another long swallow, switched his attention back to the TV.

A third run by the Dodgers gave him hope. A screech of hinges from an interior door had him raising his eyes to the ceiling yet again.

Okay, so not alone. And wasn't that a timely thing, considering he'd received two emails lately warning him that a man with secrets should watch the shadows around him very, very closely?

Standing, he shoved his gun into the waistband of his jeans, killed the light and started up the rear stairs.

The wind that had been blowing at near-gale force all day howled around the single-paned windows. Even so, he caught a second creak. He decided his intruder could use a little stealth training. Then he stepped on a sagging tread, heard the loud protest and swore.

The intruder must have heard it, too. The upstairs door that had been squeaking open immediately stopped moving.

Drawing his weapon, McVey gave his eyes another moment to adjust and finished the climb. He placed the intruder in the kitchen. Meaning the guy had the option of slinking out the way he'd entered—through the back door—or holding position to see what developed. Whatever the case, McVey had the advantage in that he'd been living in the house for more than two weeks and had committed the odd layout to memory.

Another door gave a short creak and he pictured the intruder circling.

The anticipation that kindled felt good. Sleepy coastal

towns worked for him on several levels these days. Unfortunately, as action went, they tended to be…well, frankly, dead. Unless you counted the increasing number of bar fights and the sniping of two local factions, each of which had its own legend, and neither of which was willing to admit that both legends had probably been created by an ancient—and presumably bored—Edgar Allan Poe wannabe.

Another blast of wind rattled the panes and sent a damp breeze over McVey's face. It surprised him to see a light burning in the mudroom. Apparently his intruder was extremely stupid, poorly equipped or unaware that he'd broken into the police chief's current residence. The last idea appealed most, but as it also seemed the least likely, McVey continued to ease through the house.

He spotted the shadow just as the wind—he assumed wind—slammed the kitchen door shut. The bang echoed beneath a wicked gust that buffeted the east wall and caused the rafters to moan.

Shoving the gun into his jeans, he went for a low tackle. If the person hadn't swung around and allowed a weak beam of light to trickle through from the mudroom, he would have taken them both hard to the floor. But his brain clicked in just fast enough that he was able to alter his trajectory, snag the intruder by the waist and twist them both around so only he landed on the pine planking.

His head struck the table, his shoulder the edge of a very solid chair. To make matters worse, his trapped quarry rammed an elbow into his ribs, wriggled around and clawed his left cheek.

He caught the raised hand before it could do any serious damage and, using his body weight, reversed their positions. "Knock it—" was all he got out before his instincts kicked in and he blocked the knee that was heading for his groin.

Jesus, enough!

Teeth gnashed and with pain shooting through his skull, he brought his eyes into focus on the stunning and furious face of the woman from his nightmare.

FEAR STREAKED THROUGH Amara's mind, not for her own safety, but for that of her grandmother who'd lived in this house for close to seventy years.

Although she was currently pinned to the floor with her hands over her head and her wrists tightly cuffed, she attempted to knee him again. When that failed, she bucked her hips up into his. If she could loosen his iron grip, she might be able to sink her teeth into his forearm.

"I'll kill you if you've hurt her," she panted. "This is about me, not my family. You of all people should understand that."

He offset another blow. "Lady, the only thing I understand is that you broke into a house that doesn't belong to you."

"Or you," she fired back. "You have no right to be here. Where's my grandmother?"

"I have every right to be here, and how the hell should I know?"

Her heart tripped. "Is she—dead?"

"What? No. Look, I live here, okay?"

Unable to move, Amara glared at him. "You're lying. I spoke to Nana last night. There was no mention of a man either visiting or living in her home."

He lowered his head just far enough for her to see the smile that grazed his lips. "Maybe your granny doesn't tell you everything, angel."

"That's disgusting." She refused to tremble. "Have you hurt her?"

"I haven't done anything to her. I don't eat elderly women, then take to their beds in order to get the jump on their beautiful granddaughters."

"That's not exactly reassuring."

"Yeah, it really is, Red."

When her eyes flashed, he sighed. "Red… Red Riding Hood. Now, why don't you calm down, we'll back up a few steps and try to sort this out? My name's Ethan McVey and I—"

"Have no business being in my grandmother's house."

"You're gonna have to get past that one, I'm afraid. Truth is I have all kinds of business here." He shifted position when she almost liberated her other knee. "As far as I know, your grandmother's somewhere in the Caribbean with two of her friends and one very old man who's sliding down the slippery slope toward his hundred and second birthday."

His words startled a disbelieving laugh out of her. "Nana took old Rooney Blume to the Caribbean?"

"That's the story I got. No idea if it's true. Her private life's not my concern. You, on the other hand, are very much my concern, seeing as you're lying on my kitchen floor behaving like a wildcat."

"Nana's kitchen floor."

"Rent's paid, floor's mine. So's the badge you probably failed to notice on the table above us."

Doubt crept in. "Badge, as in cop?"

"Badge as in chief of police. Raven's Cove," he added before she could ask.

The red haze clouding Amara's vision began to dissolve. "You said *rent*. If you're a cop, why are you renting my grandmother's house?"

"Because the first place she rented to me developed serious plumbing and electrical issues, both of which are in the process of being rectified."

Why a laugh should tickle her throat was beyond her. "Would that first place be Black Rock Cottage, rebuilt from a ruin fifty years ago by my grandfather and renovated last year by Wrecking Ball Buck Blume?"

"That'd be it."

"Then I'm sorry I scratched you."

"Does that mean you're done trying to turn me into a eunuch?"

"Maybe."

"As reassurances go, I'm not feeling it, Red."

"Put yourself in my position. My grandmother didn't mention a Caribbean vacation when I spoke to her yesterday."

"So, thinking she was here, you opted to break and enter your grandmother's home rather than knock on the door."

"I knocked. No one answered. Nana keeps an extra key taped to a flowerpot on her back stoop. And before you tell me how careless that is, mine's bigger."

To her relief, he let go of her wrists and pushed himself to his knees. He was still straddling her, but at least his far too appealing face wasn't quite so close. "Your what?"

"Omission. Nana didn't mention an extra key to you, and she didn't mention you to me." She squirmed a little, then immediately wished she hadn't. "Uh, do you mind? Thanks," she murmured when he got to his feet.

"I'd say no problem if the damn room would stop spinning."

Still wary, Amara accepted the hand he held down to her. "Would you like me to look at your head?"

"Why?"

"Because you might have a concussion."

"That's a given, Red. I meant why you? Are you a doctor?"

"I'm a reconstructive surgeon."

"Seriously?" Laughing, he started for the back door. "You do face and butt lifts for a living?"

What had come perilously close to going hot and squishy inside her hardened. Her lips quirked into a cool smile. "There you go. Whatever pays the bills."

"If you say so."

She maintained her pleasant expression. "Returning to the omission thing… Can you think of any reason why Nana would neglect to mention you were living here when we talked?"

"You had a bad connection?"

Or more likely insufficient time to relate many details, thanks to Lieutenant Michaels, who'd done everything in his power, short of tearing the phone from her hand and tossing her into the backseat of his car, to hasten their departure. Amara glanced up as a gust of wind whistled through the rafters. "My mother would call this an omen and say I shouldn't have come."

"Yeah?" The cop—he'd said McVey, hadn't he?—picked up and tapped his iPhone as he wandered past the island. "She into the woo-woo stuff, too?"

"If by that you mean does she believe in some of the local legends? Absolutely."

He glanced at her. "There're more than two?"

"There are more than two hundred, but most of them are offshoots of the interconnected original pair. The Blumes are very big on their ancestor Hezekiah's transformation into a raven."

"I've noticed."

"That transformation is largely blamed on the Bellam witches."

"The Bellams being your ancestors."

"My grandmother's surname gave it away, huh?"

"Among other things. Setting the bulk of them aside and assuming you're Amara, your gran sent me a very short, very cryptic text message last night."

"You're just opening a text from last night now?"

"Give me a break, Red. It's my day off, this is my personal phone and the windstorm out there dislodged four shutters that I've spent the better part of the past twelve hours repairing and reattaching." He turned his iPhone so she could see the screen. "According to Grandma Bellam, you're in a whack of trouble from the crime lord you helped convict."

Amara read the message, then returned her gaze to his unfathomable and strangely compelling eyes. "*Whack* being the operative word. Look, it's late, and I'm intruding— apparently. I'm sure one of my aunts, uncles or cousins will put me up for the night." Wanting some distance between them, she started for the door. "I left my rental car at the foot of the driveway. It's pointed toward Raven's Hollow. As luck would have it, that's where my less antagonistic relatives live. So I'll leave you to whatever you were doing before we met and go break into one of their houses." She rummaged through her shoulder bag and produced the back door key. "I'll put this back under the flowerpot. Nana locks herself out at least three times a year."

Setting his phone on the island, McVey moved toward her. "Forget the key, Amara. Talk to me about this 'whack of trouble.'"

"It's a—sticky story."

"I'm a cop. I'm used to sticky. I'm also fine with 'sounds crazy,' if that helps."

It didn't. Neither did the fact that he'd ventured far enough into the light that she could see her initial assessment of him had been dead-on. The man was…well, gorgeous worked as well as any other word.

Long dark hair swept away from a pair of riveting brown eyes, and what female alive wouldn't kill for those cheekbones? Then there was the lean, rangy body. She wouldn't mind having that on top of her again…. And, God help her, where had that thought come from? She seriously needed to get her hormones under control, because no way should the idea of—okay, admit it—sex with an überhot man send her thoughts careening off to fantasyland.

Jimmy Sparks, vicious head of a family chock full of homicidal relatives, wanted her dead. She couldn't go back to New Orleans or her job, and she couldn't reasonably expect Lieutenant Michaels to do any more than he'd already done to help her. Her grandmother wasn't in Raven's Hollow, and Amara figured she'd probably alienated the Cove cop who was to the point where he might actually consider turning her over to Jimmy's kith and kin simply to be rid of her.

"I really am sorry about all of this." She backed toward the mudroom. "I wasn't expecting to find…"

"A wolf in Grandma's cottage?" He continued to advance. "Still waiting for the story, Red. If the trouble part's too big a leap, start with the 'less antagonistic relatives' reference."

"First off, I'd rather you called me Amara. You can see for yourself, my hair's more brown than red. Which, when you get right down to it, is the story of my relatives in an extremely simplified nutshell."

"Gonna need a bit more than that, I'm afraid. So far all I've got is that you're the descendant of a Bellam witch."

"Yes, but the question is which witch? Most Bellams

can trace the roots of their family tree back to Nola. There are only a handful of us who have her lesser-known sister Sarah's blood."

Finally, thankfully, he stopped moving. "If Nola and Sarah were sisters, what's the difference blood-wise?"

"Nola Bellam was married to Hezekiah Blume. At least she was, until Hezekiah went on a killing spree. According to the Blume legend, he repented. However, all those deaths got him turned into a clairvoyant raven. There wasn't a large window of opportunity for Nola to get pregnant. Unless you add in the unpleasant fact that Hezekiah's brother Ezekiel raped her, accused her of being a witch, then hunted her down and tried to destroy her. Thus, Hezekiah's killing spree."

"Complicated stuff."

"Isn't it? It gets worse, too, because, as luck would have it, sister Sarah had a thing for Ezekiel."

"And that 'thing' resulted in a child?"

"You catch on quick. Sarah had a daughter, who had a daughter and so on. So did Nola, of course, but not with Hezekiah. Even in legend, humans and ravens can't mate. Long story short, and rape notwithstanding, Nola never gave birth to a Blume baby. Sarah did." Amara shrugged. "I'm sure you know by now that Blumes and Bellams have been at odds for…well, ever. Raven's Cove versus Raven's Hollow in all things legendary and logical. So where does a Bellam with Blume blood in her background fit in? Does she cast spells or fall victim to them? And which town does she claim for her own? You can imagine the genetic dilemma."

McVey cocked his head. "You're not going to go all weird and spooky on me, are you?"

"Haven't got time for that, unfortunately."

"Knowing Jimmy Sparks, I tend to agree."

Her fingers froze on the doorknob. "You know him?"

"We've met once or twice." McVey sent her a casual smile. "Well, I say *met,* but it was really more a case of I shot at him."

"You fired bullets at Jimmy King-of-Grudges Sparks and lived to tell about it?"

"Put the living-to-tell part down to pure, dumb luck. I was painfully green at the time, but I was also a better shot than my partner, who took it upon himself through me to try to blow Sparks's tires out after we witnessed an illegal late-night exchange."

"And?"

"I hit two tires before someone inside the vehicle fired back. The shooter winged my partner. He got me in the shoulder, then got off when our report of the incident mysteriously disappeared. Before the night was done, we'd been ordered to forget the whole thing."

"Lucky Jimmy."

"Is that censure I hear in your voice, Red?"

"On the off chance that you actually do have a concussion, let's call it curiosity."

"Let's call it not your business, and move on to why one of this country's least-favorite sons is giving you, the descendant of a Maine witch, grief."

"I helped send him to prison. Seems my testimony pissed him off."

"Thereby landing you in a whack of trouble and leaving me with one last burning question." Without appearing to move, he closed the gap between them, wrapped his fingers and thumb lightly around her jaw and tipped her head back to stare down at her. "Why the hell has your witchy face been in my head for the past fifteen years?"

Chapter Four

He didn't expect an answer. He wasn't even sure why he'd asked the question. True, she looked very much like the woman in his recurring dream, but the longer he stared at her—couldn't help that part, unfortunately—the more the differences added up.

On closer inspection, Amara's hair really was more brown than red. Her features were also significantly finer than…whomever. Her gray eyes verged on charcoal, her slim curves were much better toned and her legs were the longest he'd seen on any woman anywhere.

He might have lingered on the last thing if she hadn't slapped a hand to his chest, narrowed those beautiful charcoal eyes to slits and seared him with a glare.

"What do you mean my face has been in your head for fifteen years? What the hell kind of question is that?"

A faint smile touched his lips. "Given my potentially concussed state, call it curiosity and forget I asked."

The suspicion returned. "Are you sure my grandmother's in the Caribbean and not locked in a closet upstairs?"

"This might not be the best time to be giving me ideas." With his eyes still on hers, he pulled a beeping iPhone from his pocket and pressed the speaker button. "What is it, Jake?"

"Got a problem here, Chief."

His deputy sounded stoked, which was never a good sign. But it was the background noises—the thumps, shouts and crashes—that told the story.

"Bar fight got out of hand, huh?"

"Wasn't my fault." Jake had to yell above the sound of shattering glass. "All I did was tell the witch people to mount their broomsticks and fly off home."

"You know you're in Raven's Hollow, right? Raven's Hollow, Bellam territory."

"Can I help it if folks in this town are touchy about their ancestors?"

"This night is deteriorating faster by the minute," McVey muttered.

Jake made a guttural sound as a fist struck someone's face. "Raven's Cove was settled first, and that's a fact. Why're you sticking up for a bunch of interlopers who can't hold their liquor and are proud of the fact that one of their stupid witch women made it so my great-great-whatever-granddaddy got turned into a bird?"

Were they actually having this conversation? McVey regarded Amara, who'd heard every word, and, holding her gaze, said calmly, "I'll be there in fifteen."

He could see she was trying not to laugh as he pocketed his phone and bent to retrieve the gun he'd lost during their scuffle.

"Sorry, but I did warn you, McVey."

"No, you didn't. You said your Raven's Hollow relatives represented the less antagonistic side of the family. That's not how Jake Blume's telling it."

"Twenty bucks says Jake started it."

Since that was entirely possible, McVey stuffed his weapon. "What can I say? He came with the job."

"The job's a powder keg, Chief, a fact that whoever

talked you into it obviously neglected to mention. Raven's Cove goes through police chiefs—"

"Like wolves go through grandmothers?" In a move intended to unsettle, he blocked her flight path. "Gonna need your keys, Red."

Unfazed, she ran her index finger over his chest. "Are you telling me, Chief McVey, that a deputy came with the job, but a vehicle didn't? Sounds like someone suckered you big time."

"I'm beginning to agree." And, damn it, get hot. "Keys are in case your car's closing my truck in. Knowing Jake as I do, we need to leave now."

"We?"

"You're coming with me."

"Excuse me?"

"Whack of trouble," he reminded her, and was relieved when she ground her teeth.

Their banter was getting way out of hand. Given the situation, a distraction like that that could turn into something bad very quickly.

He caught her shoulders before she could object, turned and nudged her through the mudroom. "As much as I'd love to argue this out, my instincts tell me you have a functioning brain and no particular desire to wait here alone for whatever family member Jimmy Sparks chooses to sic on you."

"I wasn't planning to wait anywhere."

"Right. You want to search for a place to flop in Raven's Hollow. At night, in a windstorm, with no idea how many of your relatives are home and how many are participating in the destruction of a Blume-owned bar at Harrow and Main in the Hollow."

"The Red Eye?" She laughed as he reached back to snag his badge from the table. "That's gonna piss Uncle Lazarus right off—assuming he still holds the lease on the place, which he will, seeing as he's notorious for acquiring properties and never selling them. Never selling anything, except possibly, like his ancestor Hezekiah, his soul."

"I'm getting that you don't like your uncle."

"It's not a question of like or dislike really. Uncle Lazarus is a miser and a misery of a man. He's also quite reclusive. Even so, your paths must have crossed a time or two since you arrived."

"More than a time or two, only once that mattered."

Wind whipped strands of long hair up into her face the moment they stepped onto the back porch. "What did you do, fine him for jaywalking?"

"Nope." McVey held the key ring in his mouth while he clipped the badge to his belt and checked his gun. "I arrested him for being drunk and disorderly."

Amara clawed the hair from her face. "I'm sorry. I thought you said he was drunk."

"He was hammered."

"And disorderly."

"He lurched into a dockside bar in Raven's Cove, staggered across the floor and slugged a delivery driver in the stomach." He pointed left. "My truck's that way."

"I see it. I'm waiting for the punch line."

"No line, just two punches. The second was a right uppercut to the driver's jaw. He's lucky the guy didn't file assault charges. I'd guess your uncle did a little boxing in his day."

"He did a lot of things in his day. But burst into Two Toes Joe's bar drunk? Not a chance." She hesitated. "Did he say why he did it?"

"Driver was a courier. He'd delivered a large padded envelope to your uncle's home in the north woods earlier that afternoon. Four hours later the guy's eyes were roll-

ing back in his head. Lazarus pumped a fist, laughed like
a lunatic and fell facedown on the floor."

"After which, you locked him in a jail cell."

"Yep."

"You put Lazarus Blume in jail and you're still in the
Cove? Still chief of…? Hey, wait a minute." Already standing on the Ram truck's running board, she turned to jab a
finger into his chest. "That is seriously not fair. I knew—
I just knew he'd let a male get away with more than a female."

"What?"

"You heard me. You arrest him and nothing. No reper-
cussions, no threats, no embellishing the whole suddenly
sordid affair to your grandmother."

Okay, he was lost—and beginning to question her san-
ity. "What suddenly sordid affair?"

She poked him again. "I snuck out of my grandmother's house once, just once, so my friend and I could spy on
her older sister's date with the local hottie, and wouldn't
you know it, Uncle Lazarus spotted me. He dragged me
back to Nana's and informed me I'd be mucking out his
stable for the rest of the summer. Yet here you stand, still
employed and without a speck of manure on your hands."
She indicated herself, then him. "I'm a female, you're a
male. It's not fair." Huffing out a breath, she sat, yanked
the door closed and flopped back in her seat, arms folded.
"I should have put two curses on him."

McVey climbed in beside her. "You put a— What did
you do to him?"

She gave her fingers a casual flick. "What any self-
respecting Bellam in my position would have done. I put
a spell on the midnight snack Nana told me he always ate
before going to bed. He had severe stomach cramps for
the next three days. Some of my relatives swear they heard

him laughing hysterically while the doctor was examining him. Other than cleaning his stables, I didn't hear or see him again for the rest of the summer. He'd always been a loner, but Nana told me he became even more of a phantom after his...spell of indigestion. I don't know if that's true or not. I was fourteen when it happened, and except for a mutual relative's funeral, our paths haven't crossed again."

McVey's lips quirked as he started the engine. "Note to self. Grudges run in your family."

She sent him a smoldering look. "Not a problem in your case, seeing as Uncle Lazarus's grudges don't appear to extend to men."

"I was referring to you, Red." The quirk of his lips became a full-fledged grin. "I'm not overly fond of stomach cramps."

On the heels of that remark, wind swooped down to batter the side of his truck. McVey heard a loud crack among the trees crowding the house and glanced upward.

"Stomach cramps will be the least of your problems if one of those evergreens destroys Nana's roof." As Amara spoke, the porch light went out then stuttered back on. "That's not good."

"Tell me something that is."

Overhead, a fierce gust of wind brought two large branches crashing down into the box of his truck.

"Dodgers probably lost by a landslide." He handed Amara his cell phone. "Do me a favor and speed-dial Jake. Tell him I'll need more than fifteen minutes."

"I can help you pull the branches from the—"

That was as far as she got before three shots rang out behind them.

She started to swing around, but McVey shoved her down and dragged the gun from his waistband. Keeping a hand on her neck, he risked a look, saw nothing and swore softly under his breath.

Amara pried his hand free. "Who is it?" she asked with barely a hint of a tremor.

"No idea. One of my backups is in the glove box. It's loaded. Use the keys." He gave the door a kick to open it. "Meanwhile, stay here and stay down. Unless you want to be pushing up daisies next to your Bellam and/or Blume ancestors."

"McVey, wait." She grabbed his arm. "I don't want you taking a bullet for me."

"Don't sweat it, Red." He risked a second look into the woods. "Chances are only fifty-fifty that those shots were fired by someone in Jimmy Sparks's family."

HE DISAPPEARED SO QUICKLY, Amara had no chance to ask what he meant. Or to wonder if she'd heard him correctly.

For a moment she simply stared after him and thought that somewhere along the line she must have fallen down a rabbit hole into a parallel universe where police chiefs looked like hot rock stars and any vestige of reality had long since been stripped away by a raging northeaster. Who was this stranger with the wicked sexy body and dark hypnotic eyes?

"More to the point," she said to her absent grandmother, "why didn't you mention him when I called you last night?"

Knowing she needed to think, Amara tucked the question away. Three bullets had just been fired at close range. A glance through the rear window revealed nothing except the moon, a scattering of stars and no flashlight beam. Actually—had McVey even taken a flashlight?

"I need you to step on it, Chief." Jake Blume's unexpected shout sent Amara's heart into her throat and almost caused her to drop the phone she'd speed-dialed without thinking. "You there, McVey?" the deputy yelled again. "Come on, what's taking you?"

"McVey's busy." As she spoke she pulled the key out of the ignition. "My name's Amara. We're still at Shirley Bellam's place."

"You fooling around with my superior officer out on the edge of the north woods ain't exactly my idea of help, sweetheart. Now, I don't give a rat's ass why you're in possession of McVey's phone. I just need you to put him on it." He waited a beat before adding a reluctant, "Please."

Amara tried one of the smaller keys in the glove box lock. "What you call fooling around, I call dodging bullets while your superior officer goes all Rambo and takes on an unidentified shooter in the woods. Trust me, his plate has more on it than yours does at the moment."

"Wanna bet?" The deputy's tight-lipped response gave way to a resounding punch. "You said Amara, right?" Another punch. "You wouldn't be that little witch bitch who used to come here in the summer, would you? Because if you are, you scared the bejesus out of my kid brother by telling him you could talk to ravens."

"Does it matter if I'm her?"

"Makes us cousins is all."

Since he practically spit the words out, Amara assumed the idea didn't sit well with him.

Behind her, three more shots rang out. She shoved another key into the lock—and breathed out in relief when the compartment popped open to reveal a 9 mm automatic. "Thank God."

"Depends on your point of view," Jake muttered. "As I recall, your last name's Bellam."

Irritated, she regarded the phone. "Did I mention someone's firing a rifle out here? I've counted six shots so far."

"Rifle shot, huh? Could be Owen thinking the sky's fixing to fall on his cabin. Old Owen ain't been right for years."

Parallel world, Amara reminded herself. "Will 'Old Owen' know the difference between McVey and a piece of falling sky?"

"I said it could be Owen," Jake countered. "It could just as easily be one of your backwoods cousins looking to shoot himself something feathered for the upcoming street barbecue."

Now she frowned at the phone. "You people are deranged."

She heard a grunt and a punch. "This from a raven whisperer?"

"I can't talk to—" She spun in place as three more shots sounded. "The whole world's deranged. Later, Deputy."

Tossing the phone aside, she firmed up her grip on McVey's gun and slid cautiously from the truck.

The wind blew in wild circles and made pinpointing the shooter's location next to impossible.

Amara searched the dark woods. Would Jimmy Sparks abandon all discretion this way? She didn't think so, but then, what did she know about the man's psyche? Maybe he'd sent a hothead after her.

Heart pounding, she worked her way along the side of the truck. She hissed in a breath when the tips of a broken branch snagged her hair like claws. She had to stop and untangle herself before she could continue.

Continue where, though, and do what when she got there? Her grandmother had taught her how to shoot clay pigeons, but she doubted the owner of the rifle would move in a high, wide arc for her.

"What the hell are you doing?"

The question came from close behind her. Snapping the

gun up, Amara spun on one knee and almost—almost—squeezed the trigger.

When she saw who it was, her vision hazed and she lowered her arms. "Jesus, McVey."

"Have you gone mad?"

"Don't you dare glare at me. I counted nine shots, none of which came from a handgun. For all I know, you could've been dead or bleeding to death in the woods."

"I also could've shot you in the back. You want to protect yourself, you use the best cover you've got. Case in point, my truck."

"I'll remember that next time someone decides to fire a rifle in the middle of nowhere, during a windstorm, while a cop with a much bigger weapon than the one he left behind disregards his own advice and takes off in pursuit." Pushing aside the hand he held out to her, she stood and dusted off her jeans. "I talked to your deputy while you were gone. He seems to think the rifleman might be someone called Owen, worried that the sky's falling."

McVey ran his gaze around the clearing. "It wasn't Owen."

"Figured not. A Bellam bird hunter was his second suggestion. Looking for barbecue night's winged entrée."

"Red, the most common birds in these woods at night are owls, and not even a grill can make a screech owl taste good."

Moving her lips into a smile, Amara dropped the gun into his free hand. "I keep telling myself that at some point this night will end. Whether any part of it makes sense when it does remains to be seen. Moving on, if not Owen or someone who likes to hunt owls, are we back to a member of the Sparks family as the prospective shooter?"

He kept scanning. "Not necessarily."

"Didn't think so."

"Yeah, you did, but think deeper. Sparks wouldn't want you taken out in such an obvious fashion. It's true, Jimmy has moments of blind rage during which he loses all control, but that's the reason he gets people with cooler heads to do his dirty work."

"There's good news. Look, McVey, if you think the shooter's close enough to be watching us, why are we standing here having his discussion?"

"Shooter's gone." He made a final sweep before bringing his eyes back to hers. "If he wasn't, we'd be dead."

Spreading her fingers, she gave a humorless laugh. "I am so out of my element right now. Is there any chance you're going to tell me what you think just happened here?"

"Someone fired a rifle nine times, then took off."

"And you know he's gone because…?"

"I heard his truck."

"Are you—?"

She saw him move, but not in time to avoid the fingers that curled around the nape of her neck.

He stared down at her. "The only thing I'm sure of, Amara, is that we need to get something out of the way before it gets both of us killed."

"What? No." With the truck at her back, she had nowhere to go, no escape. "Don't you dare do this, McVey. I'm messed up enough already without adding sex to the mix."

A dangerous grin appeared. "I wasn't thinking sex quite yet, Red, but I could probably be persuaded."

She planted her palms firmly on his chest. "You're messing with my mind." And tangling everything inside her into a hot ball of… She wasn't sure what, but something that wanted very badly to take things a whole lot deeper a whole lot faster than she should.

"Lady, you've been messing with my mind for fifteen years."

"Don't go there."

"Not planning to." Eyes gleaming, he lowered his head until his mouth hovered a tantalizing inch above hers. "If you really want to stop me, Red, this is your last chance."

"Seriously, McVey. We shouldn't... I'm not..." She exhaled heavily. "I hate you." Casting caution to the still-howling wind, Amara took his face in her hands and yanked his very sexy mouth down onto hers.

LIEUTENANT ARTHUR MICHAELS mopped the back of his neck as he climbed the stairs to his Algiers apartment. He'd taken a roundabout route from Jackson, Mississippi, to New Orleans—by way of Arkansas and an old friend, who'd given him both a bed for the night and a name: Willy Sparks.

Rumor had it Willy could outthink a fox, outmaneuver a weasel and poison an enemy so neatly that the best forensic teams in the country were left scratching their collective heads as to why the corpse they were examining didn't simply get up and walk out of the room.

And speaking of rooms... He saw right away that the door to his apartment was still marked with the tiny paper he'd placed between it and the frame before leaving town. Absurdly relieved, he went inside, shed his jacket and cranked the high windows open.

One of his neighbors was having a party. Boisterous jazz, led by trumpet and saxophone, drifted through the openings. The smell of gumbo made his mouth water and his system long for a cold beer. Being a cautious man, however, he settled for water from the jug in his fridge.

He didn't hear the sound behind him as much as sense it in the light brush of air on his neck.

It only took him a split second to unholster his gun, spin and aim at— Nothing, he realized. Funny, he could have sworn...

Several rapid eyeblinks later, he lowered his arm.

He continued to blink as the edges of the apartment fuzzed. His fingers lost sensation. The gun clattered to the floor.

"Son of a..."

"Ah, ah, ah." One of the long shadows came alive in the form of a wagging finger. "Don't be rude, Lieutenant, or I'll go against orders and add unspeakable pain to your death. It's a well-known fact that Willy Sparks's mother is not what you were just about to call her."

He couldn't move, Michaels realized; not anything except his eyes.

He slumped to the floor. Hands groped his pockets, then rolled him onto this back like a discarded doll. He heard a series of beeps beneath his neighbor's music. When they stopped, a low chuckle floated downward.

"You have a most obliging BlackBerry. Raven's Hollow, Maine. That's very far north, isn't it? But you know, Lieutenant, I've heard the water's much safer to drink up in Maine than it is here in the Big Easy."

The BlackBerry hit the floor. Water gurgled down the drain. The music played on. His apartment door clicked shut. And Lieutenant Arthur Michaels thought of ravens....

Chapter Five

Lock it away, Amara cautioned herself. Bring it out later—because how could she not? But she'd kissed men before and would again, so…not a problem.

Unless she acknowledged the fact that ten minutes after she'd dragged her mouth from his, her senses continued to zap like an electric wire gone wild.

Did McVey feel the same? They were in his truck, driving. She couldn't read his profile, and he hadn't really looked at her or talked to her, so who knew?

There was that other thing, too; the part about her face having been in his head for fifteen years. What was she supposed to do with that weird knowledge?

He finally glanced over as they neared the outskirts of the Hollow. "You're annoyed, aren't you, Red? I can feel the vibes taking bites out of me."

Amara flicked him a similar look. "Don't flatter yourself, McVey. It's been a very bizarre night. I was torn between kissing you and kneeing you. It just so happens I'm a pacifist."

"Is that why I have four gouges in my left cheek?"

"You tackled me in my grandmother's house. Maybe you're renting it at the moment, but I didn't know that going in."

"Breaking in."

Her lips curved. "I'm fairly certain that using a key to enter a property can't be construed as a break-in. However, to answer your question, yes, I'm annoyed, just not for the reason you probably think." Lowering the visor, she regarded the tangled mess of her hair, sighed and began rooting through her shoulder bag for a brush. "I liked it."

"I know."

She heard the amusement in his tone and told herself not to react. "I know you know. That's why I'm annoyed. Tell me—" she worked the brush through the tangles "—do you eat midnight snacks?"

"Not anymore." He swung onto Main Street, made a wide U-turn and stopped in a no-parking zone. "You might want to stay behind me when we go inside. I see two broken windows."

"I see four. I hope whoever broke them likes mucking out stables. Male or female, when it comes to serious property damage, Uncle Lazarus is a tyrant."

"You know your family's a little scary, right?"

"Which side?"

"Take your pick," he said as they approached the front door. "Now, unless your repertoire contains a curse for every occasion, remember to stick close when we go in."

Low lights tinged with red burned throughout the bar. Kiss rocked the jukebox and glass crunched like pebbles underfoot. Oh, yeah, Amara thought, Uncle Lazarus would be plenty pissed.

To the left of the entryway, behind a long line of pool tables, a dozen broken chairs and tables sat in a cock-eyed heap. Groups of customers continued to hurl insults back and forth across the remaining tables. Amara spotted more than a few drops of blood both on the people and on the floor.

"Well, hallelujah, Chief, you made it." A tall man with

receding brown hair, heavy stubble and bean-black eyes pushed through the crowd. He wore a tan T-shirt, a shoulder holster and a frown that became a sneer when he spied his newly arrived Bellam cousin.

"Spit and I'll suspend you," McVey warned, not looking at him. "I assume you two have met."

"I know who she is." A muscle twitched in Jake's jaw. "She don't look much different than she did the night she gave my brother Jimbo the screaming meemies up on Raven's Ridge."

"I imagine that was unintentional, Deputy."

As a wave of people began to enfold him, Amara shrugged. "It wasn't, actually. I meant to scare him, and it worked."

"Jimbo was a year and a half younger than you," Jake accused.

"He was also forty pounds heavier, six inches taller and trying very hard to coax me into jumping off the edge of the cliff."

"You could've said no."

"He said he didn't like that word. *Push,* though...he liked that word a lot."

Jake thrust his chin out. "He was a kid."

"So was I."

"He still half believes one of his spooky Bellam cousins can talk to ravens and make them do her bidding. Frigging witch."

Losing patience, Amara regarded him through her lashes. "Don't tempt me. I'm older now and less...tolerant."

Jake showed his teeth but didn't, she noticed, utter another word.

"Smart man." Through a crowd that was now vying loudly for his attention, McVey indicated the carnage in the corner. "How many arrests have you made?"

Jake dragged his resentful gaze from Amara. "Six. When you didn't show, I called the Hardens in to help out."

"Part-time Hollow deputies," McVey said over his shoulder. "Twins."

"Thick as bricks, the pair of them." Jake snarled at a trio of men who elbowed him aside and began pleading their cases to McVey. "The Hardens are kin to Tyler Blume. No idea why he took the job, but Tyler's the police chief here in the Hollow." He raised his voice. "A town we Cove cops are being forced to watch over while he's off snorkeling with his new Bellam wife."

"That would be my cousin Molly." When McVey shifted his attention from the squabbling men to arch a brow in Amara's direction, she let her eyes sparkle. "It gets complicated very quickly if you start talking relatives around here. Think of me and Nana as the link between two feuding families." Without missing a beat, she offered a placid, "Say *missing link,* Jake, and you'll have hemorrhoids by the end of your shift."

She felt the deputy's glare before he pushed his way to McVey's other side.

A man with a pockmarked face and no neck shouted over Amara's head, "Was a Blume who started it, McVey. Called our beer donkey—er, well, anyway, he accused Yolanda of cutting it."

Amara poked McVey's hip. "Does Yolanda Bellam manage this bar?"

"More or less…. Yeah, Frank, I heard you…. From your expression, I'd speculate you and Yolanda aren't BFFs."

"Put it this way, if I'd known she was here, I'd have taken my chances with the shooter up at Nana's."

On cue, a high female voice sliced through the predominately male grumbles. "Amara? My God, is it really you?"

Her cousin had a little-girl drawl, glossy pink lips and

red-blond curls clipped back at the sides to show off her angelic face.

Yeah, right, angelic, Amara thought, tipping her lips into a smile as a pair of wide blue eyes joined the mix. "Hey, Yolanda. It's been— Well, years."

Her cousin pushed a man out of her path, slung the dish towel she carried over her shoulder and spread her arms in welcome.

"Cousin Ammie's back. And isn't she a living doll? She brought me the best present ever." Those welcoming arms knocked Amara aside and wrapped themselves tightly around McVey's neck. "How's the handsomest lawman on the East Coast tonight?" Her eyes and mouth grew suddenly tragic. "You'll make them pay, won't you, McVey? I tried, but I couldn't get any such promise out of your mean-mouthed deputy."

Amara's opinion of Jake shot up ten full points. She wasn't so sure about McVey.

To his credit, however, he removed her clinging arms, sent Amara a humorous look and headed for the pool tables, where three men with pierced body parts were holding their cues like baseball bats.

Yolanda pouted after him...until someone stepped on her foot and then the pout became a snarl. "You still nipping chins and lifting butts?"

Unruffled, Amara smiled. "Why? Are you looking for a freebie?"

"I wouldn't come to you if I was."

"Only because we apply the word in different ways."

Yolanda's fists balled. "I could blacken both your eyes, you know."

"I'd say the same, except you've already done it yourself."

"I— Damn!" Wiping a finger under her lower lashes,

Yolanda scowled. "Some dumb Blume threw a beer and got me square in the face." She gave her other eye a wipe. "Talk to me, Amara. Why have you come here after fifteen years of not here?"

"I wanted to see Nana."

"In that case, Portland's an hour's drive south and have a nice flight. Nana's in St. Croix. Or maybe it's the Cayman Islands. Anyway, you'll find her if you look hard enough." With the speed of a striking snake, she grabbed Amara's trench coat and yanked her forward to hiss, "He's mine. You got that?"

Amara pried her hand away. "I got it when you turned into a barnacle a minute ago."

Her cousin's eyes flashed. "I can make your life hell."

"You can try." And, she admitted silently, might have succeeded if Jimmy Sparks hadn't beaten her to it. "In an effort to keep the peace, Yolanda, if McVey says he's yours, he's yours. And welcome to you."

A finger jabbed her shoulder. "You can't stay at Nana's house while you're here."

"Yep, figured that one out, too."

"Can't stay with me and Larry, either."

"Your brother, Larry, the nighttime nudist? Uh, no."

The overhead lights surged and faded and caused an icy finger to slide along Amara's spine.

"Stupid wind." But Yolanda observed her more keenly now. "A little raven told me you had some heavy court action going on down south. Saw someone die who wasn't on your operating table when it happened."

She didn't need this, Amara thought, but rather than snap at her cousin, she shrugged it off. "I saw. I testified. It's done." When the lights faded again, she added a quick, "Uh, how's Uncle Lazarus?"

Yolanda sniffed. "Still pays me next to nothing to manage this rude branch of hell, but he's a Blume, so what do you expect?" Her lips quirked. "Word is the man you testified against is the mean and powerful head of a family that's into all sorts of nasty things. Extortion, weapons, drugs—murder."

"My, what big ears you have, Grandma." His pool-player problems apparently dealt with, McVey surprised Amara by dropping an arm over her shoulders. "Some analogies go on forever, don't they, Red?" Before she could answer, he made a head motion at the crowd. "I'm seeing a lot of unfamiliar faces, Yolanda. They drifting in for the Night of the Raven Festival already?"

Amara knew her cheeks went pale. She glanced at a nonexistent watch on her wrist, then at the walls for a calendar. "Is it—? What's today? The date," she clarified, still searching.

"May 10," McVey supplied. "Why?"

"What? Oh, nothing. I forgot...an appointment."

But damn, damn, how on earth had she forgotten about the scores of strangers who drove, bussed, cycled and hitchhiked to Raven's Hollow to take part in the three-day celebration known as the Night of the Raven?

The Night festival was the Hollow's once-a-year answer to the Cove's once-every-three-years Ravenspell. Although the story at the root of the events was the same, it was told from two very different perspectives. Over the years both events—the Cove's in the fall and the Hollow's in the spring—had become a magnet for every curse-loving fanatic in and out of the state.

This was, Amara realized, the worst possible time for her to be in either town.

Her smile nothing short of malicious, Yolanda drew a raven's head in the residue of a spilled beer. "Bet the Cayman Islands are looking better and better about now, huh,

Amara? Say the word and I'll get right on my little computer and book you a flight out of Portland."

When a shrill whistle cut through the crowd noise, she banged her fist on the bar. "I'm not a dog, Jake Blume. What do you want?"

He wagged the receiver of a corded wall phone. "Boss man's on the line and he's in a crappy mood."

"I hate that man," Yolanda breathed. "Both men. Remember the spiders, Amara." With a lethal look for her cousin, she snapped the dish towel from her shoulder and vanished into a sea of bodies.

"She put a jar of them in my bed," Amara said before McVey could ask. "Well, I say *she,* but Yolanda only had the idea. Jake and Larry collected and planted them."

"In your bed."

"Under the covers, at the bottom. She told them to leave the top off so the spiders could crawl around wherever. The things were big. I freaked and refused to sleep in that particular room again."

McVey tugged on a strand of hair to tilt her head back. "Did you tell your grandmother?"

"No need."

"Do I want to know why?"

"Because all three of them, Jake most particularly, are terrified of snakes." She swept an arm around the room. "Is the fighting done?"

"For now." He nodded at a row of dull brass taps that glowed an eerie shade of red under lights that continued to surge and fade. "Do you want a drink before we leave?"

"Poison is a witch's weapon, McVey, and Yolanda's a Bellam. But thanks for the offer."

"Festival slipped your mind, didn't it?"

She ran her hands up and down her arms. "Unfortunately. The prospect of eminent death must have pushed it out. I've only ever been to one Night celebration myself. If it's of any interest to you—and it should be—the Hollow's Night of the Raven isn't quite as civilized as the Cove's Ravenspell."

"Translation, Tyler Blume deliberately planned his honeymoon so he'd miss it."

"If you've met him, you know he did. On the other hand, Jake should be in his element." She glanced up when the lights winked off. "Uh…" Then back on. "Okay, my nerves are getting a way bigger workout than they need."

She heard a familiar double beep beneath wailing Tim McGraw. As she hunted in her shoulder bag for her phone, she saw McVey pluck a mug of beer from a much larger man's hand.

"You're over your limit, Samson. Unless you want to join your buddies in jail, go home."

The man's face reddened. "Gonna get my wife to put a pox on you, you don't give that back, McVey."

"Do it, and I'll get Red here to put one on you."

"My wife's got an aunt who's a Bellam." The man jerked his stubbly chin. "What's she got?"

Staring at her iPhone, Amara felt her brain go cold. What she had was a text message from a man who'd sworn he would only contact her in an emergency.

"Beat it, Samson."

Giving the mug to the bartender, McVey turned her hand with the iPhone and read the name on the screen. A name Amara's terrified mind didn't want to see or to acknowledge. Willy Sparks.

SHE PACED THE back office of the Raven's Hollow police station like a caged tiger, dialing and redialing her cell. At the front desk Jake muttered about the Harden brothers being allowed to go home while he had to ride herd on a bunch of drunks in a town that wasn't his and didn't even supply its officers with a decent coffeemaker.

On his side of things, McVey was seriously wishing he'd never made any kind of deathbed promise to his father. Raising his eyes, he watched Amara pace. Okay, maybe not so much wishing as wondering what the hell he was supposed to do with this mess.

"Come on, McVey, give me one good reason why I can't haul these boozers to the Cove. Cells there are way more comfortable than here."

McVey scrolled through a list of New Orleans police officers. "Paperwork, Jake. Triple the usual amount if we start shuffling prisoners around. And you'll be doing every last bit of it."

The deputy gave his rifle a resentful pump. "I could get me a job in Bangor, you know."

"Any time you want that to happen…" A raven-shaped wall clock told McVey he'd been on his iPhone for more than forty minutes. Out of patience, he took a procedural shortcut to a friend of a friend on the New Orleans force. "Samson's texted me three times since we left the Red Eye," he said absently. "Wants me to pay for the beer he didn't get to drink."

Amara kept pacing. "Sounds as though Samson's spent some time around Uncle Lazarus…. There's still no answer at the lieutenant's apartment, McVey. I've tried his BlackBerry and his landline a dozen times each."

McVey flicked her a look but said nothing. Didn't need to; she knew the score as well as he did.

It took the better part of an hour to connect with someone in a position of sufficient authority to have Michaels's apartment checked out. Another hour and a blistering headache later, the captain from the lieutenant's parish contacted him personally.

"Michaels is dead." The man's tone was lifeless, a condition McVey understood all too well. "Officers found him on his back, staring at the ceiling. He had both hands clamped around his BlackBerry."

"Cause of death?"

"Given the situation, I'd go with some kind of off-the-radar toxin that simulates a stroke. Forensic team's scouring the apartment as we speak. I'll let you know what they turn up."

Amara rubbed her forehead with her own phone after the captain signed off. "Michaels is dead because he helped me get out of New Orleans. This is my fault."

Figuring sympathy wasn't the way to go here, McVey countered with a bland, "You know that's a load of bull, right? And if we all just went with it, Willy Sparks would go on killing cops and civilians ad infinitum."

She shot him a vexed look. "Thanks for the shoulder."

"You don't want a shoulder, Amara. You want to pound your fists. If I tell you it's not your fault, you'll get angry and say it should've been you, because that's who Jimmy Sparks was gunning for."

"He was. He is. And as emotional releases go, angry words are better than furious fists."

"Not always. Back on point, what if Sparks's nephew, godson, second cousin—whatever—had killed you instead of Michaels. Then what? True, he'd get paid, maybe bask on a tropical island for a while, but what he'd really be doing is waiting for Uncle Jimmy to crook his finger again and point it at a new target. The way things stand, this job's not done. In fact, it's a good bet Willy Sparks is either en route to or has already arrived in whatever Raven town the lieutenant entered into his BlackBerry."

Amara frowned at her cell, then at him. "He said he buried the destination and phone number."

"There's buried, and there's buried, Red. The phone wasn't taken, therefore there was no need to take it."

"As in the killer got what he wanted from it before he left." She closed her eyes. "My ex is a geek. He could hack into just about any device."

"Geeks can murder as effectively as anyone, Amara."

"So it seems." She looked around the office. "I need to leave before he gets here."

McVey regarded his iPhone screen, shook his head and pushed off from the windowsill where he'd been leaning. "You're not getting this, are you? Skip past the beating-yourself-up part, Amara, and think."

"I'm not beating myself...well, yes, I am, but that's because I feel responsible."

"Did you kill him?"

"You're joking, right? I'm a doctor, McVey. Psychology doesn't work on me."

"Fine. Here's the reality. You leave town, Willy arrives. He's pissed off to start with. Then he stops and thinks. And being a pro, sees a golden opportunity to draw you back."

"By hurting members of my family."

"Wouldn't you, in his position?"

"Let me think. Uh—no."

"Put your mind in his. We're talking about a killer here." When she didn't respond, McVey held his arms out to the sides. "Look, if it'll help get you past the guilt and make you see reason, you're welcome to take your best physical shot. All I want in return is a handful of Tylenols, a couple hours of sleep and no argument from you about where you'll be spending the night. You have two options. Come with me to your grandmother's place or hang with Jake on a cot in the back room."

"That's quite a choice. Seeing as I know all the hidey-holes at Nana's house and wouldn't trust Jake not to sell me out for cab fare, I'll go with the lesser evil and take you. As for the gut punch, I'll take a rain check."

"Excellent choices," McVey returned.

Although it felt like a betrayal of sorts, he deliberately neglected to tell her about the text message Michaels's captain had sent him less than a minute ago. But it continued to play in his head like a stuck audio disk.

In the captain's opinion, if one of his most experienced detectives could be taken out as easily as Michaels apparently had been, then it was only a matter of time—likely short—before the fourth person on Jimmy Sparks's hit list followed him to the grave.

Chapter Six

If you believed local lore, the wind on Hollow Road was an echo of Sarah Bellam's dying wail. A final protest, Amara supposed, against the unfair hand she believed she'd been dealt.

As a child, Amara had loved hearing stories about Sarah. As an adult—well, suffice it to say the last place she wanted to be was on a twisty, turny, extremely narrow strip of pavement that wound an impossible path to the edge of the north woods, listening to the wind howl like a raging witch.

She glanced out and up as the road forked. The left side made a steep and treacherous climb to the imposing structure that was Bellam Manor. The first time she'd seen it at four years of age, all the Gothic points, tall gables and arrow-slatted windows had struck her as extremely castle-like. Bad castle, not good. This was where Sarah had been born, raised and, most agreed, confined for the final years of her life. The locals of the day had branded her evil, and the description had stuck.

The same description could be applied to Jimmy Sparks. Unfortunately, even in prison, Sparks wielded sufficient power to have people murdered.

The picture of Lieutenant Michaels's face that swam into Amara's head caused pain to spike and spread. Had he died because of her, or had Jimmy Sparks wanted him gone in any case? Would she ever know? Would it make a difference if she did?

"So, Red, is it the wind, Michaels's death or me that's bothering you?"

McVey's question shattered the beginnings of a dreadful memory. Amara pressed on a nerve at the side of her neck. "The death's the worst. But as we get farther and farther from so-called civilization, I am starting to wonder why you've taken such an active interest in my welfare."

A smile grazed his lips. "It's my job to be interested, isn't it?"

"It's not your job to play personal watchdog. You could have fobbed me off to any number of relatives, including Yolanda and her extremely strange brother, Larry."

"The sleepwalking streaker who spends his winters working at a Colorado ski resort?"

"He's part of an avalanche control team. Helps bring the snow down before it gets too deep and dangerous. Nana said he wound up in the hospital with frostbite after one of his naked nighttime walks. I guess he knows his way around plastic explosives. Have you met him?"

"Several times. Four of them at night."

"That's unfortunate. But it doesn't answer my earlier question."

"Yeah, it does. I don't fob people off. And I'm definitely not a sadist."

"You're something, though, aren't you?" Tucking a leg up, Amara turned to study him. "Something not what or who people think you are."

His smile widened and caused a shiver of excitement to dance along her spine. "You're fishing, Red. I'm not biting."

"You don't have to. You gave it away when you told me

there was only a fifty-fifty chance the shots we heard at Nana's were fired by someone in Jimmy Sparks's family. What's the flip side, McVey? What or who represents the other fifty percent?"

"Could be I have an angry ex."

"Could also be Yolanda and I will develop a sisterly affection for each other. But back in the real world, what aren't you telling me about those shots? We heard nine of them, in three groups of three. Is the number significant? Is it connected to the fact that you think my face has been in your head for fifteen years—which, by the way, is exactly how long it's been since the last time I was in the Hollow."

"Yeah?" He glanced at her again.

"Fifteen years this June."

"Huh."

She sighed. "Please don't go all dark and mysterious on me."

He regarded the towering trees through the upper portion of the windshield. "I asked a simple question, Red. Right now I'm just trying to keep my truck on the road."

"And I'm trying to figure out if I'm riding with a man or someone who was hatched from an alien pod. Call me anal, but informing me I have the same face as some woman in your head isn't your usual 'first time we've met' remark. Assuming, of course, this is the first time we've met."

"I did meet a beautiful redhead at the tail end of a wedding reception a few years back. Her features are a bit of a blur at this point, but I remember thinking she was gorgeous. The reception was in Albany. I was the guy playing the air guitar—with a little help from Keith Richards."

She fought back a laugh. "Don't do this, McVey. It's been a very long, very weird night, to say nothing of sad." A picture of Yolanda popped in. "And irritating."

He looked at her for a thoughtful moment. "You're part

of a dream, Amara. A nightmare, actually. One I've had off and on since I was nineteen."

"Ah, well, that clears things right up, doesn't it—seeing as we're total strangers." Her expression grew wary. "You're not a Bellam somewhere in that dark and mysterious past of yours, are you?"

"If I am, it'll be a hard thing to prove. I'm what's called a foundling. Or close enough that the term applies."

Sympathy softened everything inside her. "I'm so sorry, McVey. Were you adopted?"

"In a sense."

"You know that answer's a form of avoidance, don't you?"

"I know it's the best you're going to get right now. As for me seeing your face, I dream what I dream, and believe me when I tell you, I don't enjoy the experience."

"Well, that's me flattered."

"You're a hag in the opening act."

"Better and better."

"You come into my head chanting over a fire in a room filled with smoke. Next thing I know, you've sent a man God knows where and you're telling me you intend to take my memories away. And, hell, maybe you pulled it off, because the dream ends there every damn time I have it."

A pinecone bounced off the windshield, catching Amara's gaze. "I'm sliding very quickly across the line to freaked, McVey. I'm not responsible for your dreams. I don't chant over fires or zap memories from men's minds or—"

"I'm not a man in the dream."

"Boys' minds, then... Whoa!" She braced herself with both hands as a blast of wind punched the truck like a giant fist.

McVey glanced skyward. "If there's anything in your

background that can affect the elements, Red, now would be a really good time to call on it."

"I've never actually... Oh, my God, is that the yellow-ribbon tree?" Shocked, she stared at the huge, uprooted oak that currently lay between her grandmother's house and one of the outbuildings. "It was a hundred and twenty years old."

"It missed the roof by less than five feet." McVey pulled into the driveway. "It also flattened the old well." With his eyes on the exposed roots, he reached for his beeping cell. "What is it, Jake?"

Amara slid from the truck while he talked to his deputy. Some of the branches had scraped the outer wall of the house. Thank God her grandmother hadn't been inside at the time.

Still on his phone, McVey headed over to survey the damage. Amara left him to it and turned for her rental car. She needed at least one of her suitcases and she wanted her medical kit. It might not be smart for her to touch McVey given their earlier wow of a kiss, but as she'd put the scratches on his cheek, she felt she owed it to him to clean them up.

Score settled. Or as settled as it could be with lust doing its best to tie her in knots.

She scooped the hair from her face as she approached the vehicle. "Dozens of so-called witches in Raven's Hollow, yet no one's moved this stupid wind along." She shot a vexed look at the night sky. "I'm sure Bangor could use a good airing out."

The wind shrieked in response and almost caused her to stumble into the driver's-side door.

"I'll take that as a no."

Releasing her hair, Amara reached for the handle. And froze with her fingers mere inches away.

Her throat dried up. "Uh, McVey?"

Of course he couldn't hear her. She could barely hear herself. But she could see. And what she saw was a man. He was slumped over the steering wheel of her rental car. Long blond hair obscured his features, but he wore a sleeveless shirt and, most significant to Amara, he wasn't moving.

"McVey?" She inched closer. Was he breathing?

"McVey!" she called again. When the man failed to stir, she took a bolstering breath and opened the door.

His head came up lightning-fast. His eyes glinted. "Hello, gorgeous." He offered a freakish smile, whipped his right hand around and gave his wrist a double flick. Amara saw the gleam of a knife a split second before she turned and bolted.

Thoughts scrambled in her head. Had there been blood on the blade? On him? Pretty sure she'd seen red streaks on his arms.

Trees and bushes rushed past in a blur. There it was, the lit porch of her grandmother's house, less than fifty feet away. "McVey!"

Suddenly the porch light winked out. Everything around her went dark. Amara stepped on a fallen branch and had to slow down. "Ouch! McVey!"

A man's hands descended on her shoulders from behind.

She didn't think or hesitate. She simply spun, knocked the hands away and brought her knee up hard.

She heard a cursed reaction.

"Are you insane? Amara, it's me."

McVey swung her around so they were back to front, holding her in place with a forearm pressed lightly across her throat. "Have you lost your mind?"

She pointed straight ahead. "Man. In my car. With a

knife." Her fingernails sank into his wrist. "There might be blood."

McVey released her. "Stay here."

"What? No. Now who's insane? He could be anywhere."

"Fine. Stay behind me."

She did. Unfortunately she was so close behind that she collided with his back when he halted.

He said nothing, just passed her a penlight from his pocket and pressed a hand to her stomach to keep her in place. He had his gun out, but as it was aimed at the ground, she understood even before she angled the light at the car.

The man inside had vanished.

"I AM SO done with this night," Amara declared.

McVey followed her around the fallen tree and across the yard to the porch. Thankfully, the generator had kicked in.

"I want to believe the guy I saw was your resident nutball taking refuge from the falling sky, but the Crocodile Dundee knife suggests...well...not." He saw her shoulders hunch. "Do you have any theories?"

"None worth mentioning."

"Figures." When she turned for a last look behind them, he felt her eyes on his cheek. "And then there's this." A sigh escaped. "They're not deep scratches, but I bet they sting." Lifting a hand, she used her index finger to draw a circle. "They should heal fast enough."

"They always do."

Smiling a little, she drew another circle. "Meaning you've been scratched before?"

"I worked in vice in Chicago. Cops get scratched, punched, kicked and shot at on a regular basis."

"I guess the Hollow's a cakewalk by comparison."

"Depends on your definition of the term. I've been scratched, kicked and shot at within the space of five hours tonight."

"Pretty sure Samson was thinking about punching you at the Red Eye." Her eyes danced. "You're four for four, Chief, and the Night of the Raven hasn't even begun."

"Maybe I should have gone to Florida with Tyler and Molly."

"You still can."

He dropped his gaze briefly to her mouth. "No, I really can't." Wouldn't if he could. And, God help him, he had no desire to explore that scary-as-hell thought.

She circled the scratches a third time and then let her hand fall away.

Was it crazy that, for a single blind moment, he wanted to abandon all logic and have wild sex with her on the kitchen floor? His hormones said no. Fortunately for both of them, his brain retained control.

"You should go upstairs," he said before the badly frayed threads of his restraint snapped and he turned into the big bad wolf they'd been playing with all night.

He started to step back. Then blew his good intentions to hell and covered her mouth with his.

For the first time in memory the world around him dissolved, leaving him with nothing except the full-bodied taste of woman and the mildly unnerving sensation that some small part of her was seeping into his bloodstream like a drug. Whether good or bad, he couldn't say. He only knew his control currently teetered on a very ragged edge. Drawing on the dregs of it, he gripped her arms and set her away from him.

"Well, wow." Amara fingered her lips. Her eyes had gone a fascinating shade of silver. "That was...amazing. I don't normally kiss men I've just met like that. Not altogether sure I've kissed any man like that." She bit lightly on her lower lip. "You?"

"I try not to kiss men at all if I can avoid it."

She laughed, and that didn't help a damn thing. "No Irish or Italian in your background, hmm?"

He fixed his gaze on hers. "You want to go upstairs, Amara, now, before it occurs to me that self-restraint's never been my best quality."

A sparkle lit her eyes. Tugging him forward by his shirt, she whispered a teasing "Mine, either."

He let her stroll away. This might be Grandma's house, but he hadn't regressed to a wild-animal state quite yet.

Rifle shots, he reminded himself. Supersize knife. Twisted leer. Oh, yeah, that worked. Anticipation rose. Adrenaline ramped it up.

He gave Amara sixty minutes to settle in—and his libido the same amount of time to settle down. Then he checked his guns, pulled on a dark jacket and made himself part of the night.

Location presented no problem. He'd discovered several spent cartridges earlier in a section of the woods where three giant oak trees stood bent and tortured around a collection of boulders that resembled witches' hats.

A silent approach wasn't necessary. The wind raged on—like a huffing, puffing wolf, if he wanted to keep the fairy tale alive a bit longer.

He reached the clearing within fifteen minutes. Playing his flashlight over the tops of the stone hats, he let a wry smile form. Despite the whirling gusts, he clearly caught the sound of a rifle being primed.

Sticking to the shadows, he called, "You want to shoot me, Westor, do it now. I don't play mind games these days."

"Like hell." The reply came from a patch of darkness some fifty feet to McVey's left. "You've been playing with minds in two freaking—and I gotta say freaky—towns for more than a year. I did some sniffing around tonight, old friend. You've got these people believing you're a man of honor, someone who'll stand up for them should the need arise. But you and me, we know different, don't we? You'd sell your granny, if you had one, for the gold fillings in her teeth. You'd sell me, if you could, for a whole lot less."

"Or I could just keep it simple and arrest you for shooting at my landlady's granddaughter."

"In that case, I might as well kill her and let the chips fall. A little bird told me she's got majorly big problems that'll land her six feet under before long anyway."

"Raven." McVey scanned the darkness. "It's all about big black ravens around here."

"Ravens and witches is how I heard it."

"From your little bird?"

Westor Hall gave his rifle another Jake-like pump. "Tell me why I shouldn't kill you where you stand, McVey. You came to Los Angeles a few months back, and being a cop and a turncoat, decided my sister needed some jail time to straighten her out."

McVey wove a roundabout path through a crop of evergreens. "Why would I do that after fifteen years of silence?"

"I don't know." For the moment Westor sounded uncertain. "I don't, but it doesn't matter." Anger tightened his tone. "Dicks came for her six weeks ago. She rabbited and wound up wrapping her car around a power pole. Took three and a half hours to peel the wreck away so paramedics could pull her out. In the end, they covered her with a sheet and drove her to the morgue."

McVey hadn't known that. But he'd known Westor's sister, and an alcoholic haze had been her answer to most of life's problems, big and small.

"She was all I had, McVey." Loss layered over loathing. "It's not a coincidence. You came to Los Angeles and two days later the cops had a line on my sister."

"I'm sorry she's dead, Westor, but I didn't draw that line. And I sure as hell didn't cross it."

"Well, I say you did, and I've come all the way here to say it to your face."

Lowering to a crouch, McVey sized up a tangle of brush that could hide a dozen large men. He considered drawing his gun, but when the leaves separated slightly and he spied the laser light on Westor's rifle, he opted for hand-to-hand.

"See how you feel when you lose someone who matters." Westor jerked the rifle sideways. "That tasty lady I saw you with tonight, for example."

Although his stomach clenched, McVey saw his opportunity and took it.

If Westor spotted the motion, he didn't swing around fast enough to evade it. McVey's forearm snaked across his throat, cutting off his oxygen and reducing his protest to a wet gurgle as he tried to shake his attacker off. Finally, with his eyes beginning to roll, Westor gave McVey's wrist a limp slap.

"Yeah, as if I'm gonna believe that. Kick the rifle away." McVey tightened his grip when Westor hesitated. "Do it now."

The hesitation became a gagging cough. "Okay, you win." The rifle spun off. "It's gone, and now neither of us can see a frigging thing. Tree could fall and kill us both. Still, it might be worth dying to know I'd be taking you with me."

"Always a possibility," McVey agreed. "But I think you missed your opportunity with the trees."

"Are you kid—?" In the process of tossing his head,

Westor stopped struggling and let his gaze roll skyward. "What happened to the wind?"

"It died."

"Just like that?" Westor made a scoffing sound. "Wind's not alive. It can't die as fast as a person. One of which your tasty lady is."

McVey set his mouth menacingly close to Westor's ear. "I'm only going to say this once, old friend, so you want to listen. If anything—" he cinched Westor's arm for emphasis "—I mean anything at all happens to Amara, I'll find you and I'll kill you."

Westor craned his neck for more air. "That's not fair. Way I heard it, there's a strong chance the lady has a truckload of heavy looking to squash her."

"Yeah? Who's your little bird, Westor?"

"Woman at the bar where the fight went down doesn't like your lady much. Told someone on the phone a nasty dude named Sparks could be looking to do her."

"In that case, you might want to think seriously about leaving town."

"I'll leave when I'm ready, and not before. I didn't come all this way to tip my hat at you, McVey. I want to watch you squirm, knowing I'm here, knowing I know how it used to be, how you used to live and who you stepped on to get out." His teeth gleamed in profile. "It's not as if the tasty lady's hard to look at."

With a warning squeeze, McVey released his prisoner and shoved him forward. "Did the woman in the bar happen to mention that my tasty lady's got the blood of a three-hundred-year-old witch in her veins?"

On his knees and coughing, Westor rubbed his throat. "Come on, man, you don't believe that spooked-up crap, do you?"

McVey slung the rifle over his shoulder. "I believe what

I see. Amara wanted the wind gone and, what do you know, it is. So here's the really intriguing question." His grin fell just short of evil. "What do you think would happen if she wanted you gone, too?"

Chapter Seven

Amara woke to find a raven staring at her from the ledge outside her window. Now, there was an interesting start to her first full day in Maine. On the upside, there'd been no spiders in her bed last night, and ravens, for all the local superstitions about them, had never frightened her.

McVey was another matter. She'd dreamed about him—hot, vivid dreams that had culminated with the two of them having sex in a north woods clearing filled with pointy boulders. The location might have been questionable, but the sex had been spectacular.

She replayed the highlights while she showered and dressed in a pair of faded jeans, black boots and a charcoal sweater the same color as her eyes. As far as Lieutenant Michaels's death, Willy Sparks's mission and the come-and-go man with the big knife and the creep-show leer went, she shut those thoughts away for examination later. That being after she'd poured at least two cups of coffee into her system.

The raven watched while she tidied the room but flew off with a noisy caw when she turned for the door. Very odd.

There was no sign of McVey on the second floor and no sound of him in the kitchen. At 8:15 a.m. on a misty Thursday morning, she imagined he was busy processing the handful of hungover brawlers who'd smashed up her uncle's bar last night.

Better for the brawlers that McVey should mete out the punishment than her uncle. She was chuckling at that thought as she pushed through the swinging door. Two steps in, the chuckle gave way to stunned silence.

"Uncle Lazarus." She made herself smile. "What a… nice surprise." She raised her hands, palms out. "For the record, I didn't throw a single punch at the Red Eye."

"Never crossed my mind you did, niece. Taught you to kick and jab and get your knee up whenever possible. But all punching'll get you is a fistful of swollen knuckles."

"Right." Why was she drawing a blank here? "Would you like some coffee?"

"Coffee is the devil's brew."

Strangely, his unyielding attitude relaxed her. "As I recall, you used to tell Nana I was the devil's spawn. Maybe that's why I can't start my day without caffeine."

"Likely so."

He hadn't taken his raven-black eyes off her, hadn't moved in his seat or altered his expression since she'd come in. Although his stare was designed to intimidate, she held it for five long seconds before skirting the table and reaching for the pot of coffee McVey, bless him, must have brewed earlier.

Lazarus Blume had always been a riveting man, and fifteen years had done nothing to diminish that quality. He might be a little leaner around the cheekbones, but he still made her think of a pilgrim, right down to his plain clothes, his gray-streaked beard and the hair that stuck up in windblown tufts.

Determined to find whatever humor she could in the situation, Amara brought her mug back to where he sat. "There was a raven outside my window this morning,

Uncle. He was watching me exactly the way you are now. If I didn't know better, I'd swear you were him in human form."

"And I'd say you were spouting useless Bellam rhetoric to avoid an unpleasant conversation."

"Which would be an appropriate tactic since I'm a Bellam."

He thrust himself forward. "You're a Blume as well, and don't you forget it."

"My mother—"

"Gave you the surname that was given to her by her mother. I know how the Bellam family works, Amara. I also know that three people with whom you had a courtroom affiliation in New Orleans are dead, and the man around whom the affiliation revolved likely engineered those deaths from his prison cell."

"Very likely. Unfortunately no one can prove it."

"Which is why you've come home to Raven's Hollow." He turned a thumping fist into an accusing finger when she opened her mouth. "Don't you dare say this isn't your home. Your mother grew up and married here, and you spent ten consecutive summers in this house with your grandmother. You're connected, as we all are, to the first settlers who landed on these shores with the intention of forging better lives for themselves."

He'd start reciting the Blume family history if she didn't stop him. So she sat back, let her lips curve and said simply, "I hear you got yourself arrested recently, Uncle. I believe drunk and disorderly was the charge."

He inhaled sharply through his nose. "I had my reasons."

Because it wasn't in Amara's nature to be cruel, she softened her tone. "I'm sure you did. And you of all people know I've done my share of wrong things." Because it *was* in her nature, she let mischief bubble up. "Like spy on a friend's sister's hot date. Or try to."

Lazarus gave an approving nod. "Best damn mucking out of stables I ever saw. And now you're a cosmetic surgeon."

"Reconstructive surgeon." Cupping her mug in her palms, she said, "Why did you come here today, Uncle? I know you don't like me."

"Don't like you," he bellowed, and pounded the table again. "Why, you were the only person, young or old, who ever made me laugh."

"I did? You did?" Amara frowned. "When?"

"The summer of your fourteenth year, when I punished you for sneaking out of this house. Your grandmother said you put a spell on me."

Why did the morning suddenly feel completely surreal to her? "I didn't—well, yes, I did. But I put the spell on your midnight snack, not you."

He nodded again. "Showed initiative. I appreciate that quality."

"I think it showed I had a temper, but in any case, the medical side of my brain says your stomach troubles didn't come from me."

"It was still a feisty counterstrike."

Amara sipped her coffee. "Aunt Maureen believed in the Bellam legend. She encouraged me to memorize a number of rhyming spells from a book she and Nana found in one of the attics at Bellam Manor. We—all of us—wanted Yolanda's brother, Larry, to stop sleepwalking, or at least to wear clothes when he did it. I failed miserably."

Her uncle flapped a hand. "My sister had a streak of ridiculous in her. Had an even bigger stubborn streak. She smoked herself into an early grave. Didn't want a service or even a family gathering. That's not right."

"It was for her. I know you would have preferred a funeral, Uncle, but Aunt Maureen hated sad faces."

"And naked sleepwalkers, it would seem."

Amara glanced up, but his saturnine expression remained intact.

Pushing her chair back, she started to ask if he'd seen McVey, but a beep from her iPhone signaled an incoming message.

"You immerse yourself in the technology craze, too, do you?"

His stoic expression made her grin. "Let me guess. You think technology's only a step below caffeine on the devil's list of temptations."

"Can't tell you that, as I own a similar device. But I set it to vibrate when I'm socializing face-to-face."

"It's probably one of my colleagues in New Orleans. I had to reschedule several surgeries on the drive to…" Her voice trailed off. "Jackson."

She stared unbelieving, first at her phone, then at the counter next to her. If her uncle spoke, and she thought he probably did, she only heard a freakish buzz, and even that was drowned out by the roar of blood in her ears.

She knew, vaguely knew, that the screen door slammed and someone else came into the kitchen.

McVey. Had to be.

He said something and crossed to the counter. Because she was already there, it was easy enough to catch his arm and stop him from reaching for a mug.

"Probably not the best idea," she said, showing him the message she'd just received.

DID YOU DRINK THE COFFEE, AMARA?

WILLY SPARKS SWITCHED off the stolen phone and tossed it into the trees. Time to leave, but hmm…

Uncle Jimmy was far more intrigued by small towns than he was by big cities. He claimed you could live in one your whole life, know everybody by name yet never know for sure who might be doing what to whom.

Maybe he was right. While the quite lovely Amara Bellam was inside her grandmother's edge-of-the-woods house, undoubtedly thinking she'd been poisoned—too bad about the police chief showing up, but not every circumstance could be foreseen—a truly fascinating situation was unfolding a mere fifty yards away.

Perched in the branches of a leafy chestnut tree, Willy spied someone dressed in shades of brown and green. Someone with binoculars and a large hunting rifle, who appeared to be watching the people in the house.

"I'D BE ROYALLY pissed off if I could get my heart to beat normally again." Amara checked the tips of her fingers for any discoloration. "You swear you made this coffee, McVey?"

"Made it and drank two cups before I left."

Her uncle nodded. "I've been sitting here since he left, so I can tell you no one's tampered with it. Unless the tampering was done to the beans themselves. Then you'd both be poisoned."

"More likely we'd be dead," McVey remarked.

"Could be we're all dead," her uncle postulated, "and having this conversation wherever we wound up."

McVey poured some of the brewed coffee into a jar and capped it. "That'd be hell for me."

"Me, as well," Lazarus agreed. "Since I don't drink coffee, though, I must have died some other way. Maybe my heart gave out."

Amara pressed lightly on her temples. "Excuse me, people, but am I the only one here who thinks this so-called conversation is almost as bent as the person who sent the message? Wait a second…" She narrowed accusing eyes at her uncle. "You were here before McVey left?"

"I had business," he said stiffly.

"Business with a man who arrested you and whose butt you should have but didn't put in a sling?" She aimed an I-told-you-so smile at McVey. "See? Males get preferential treatment over females."

"We were talking poison, Red." McVey opened the bag and sniffed the coffee beans, a sight that did nothing to quiet her still-jumping nerves. "We should stay on topic."

"That being someone—undoubtedly Willy Sparks—wants me to know how easy it would be for him to kill me. And a strong dose of psychological terror never hurts, either."

Her uncle stood. "What do you propose to do about this, Chief McVey?"

"What I can." McVey picked up and tapped Amara's phone. "Sparks is a pro. It'll take more than a lucky guess to identify him. No one outside the family has a description, and no one within it will talk. You talk, you suffer. I understand Jimmy has a long-standing policy in that regard."

"The Night of the Raven is coming up fast." Amara paced off her jitters. "People are already arriving for the event."

"I told my late sister's nephew he could reopen Blume House to guests for the duration." The look her uncle shot McVey had *challenge* written all over it. "What will you do about that?"

McVey glanced from the phone to her uncle and back. "I could suggest the name of the place be changed to the Hotel California and hope that that alone would cause the out-of-towners to turn tail. But more realistically, I'll run incoming names and license plates, see what comes up."

"That won't—"

"He can't arrest people for being strangers," Amara interrupted her uncle. "And he can't treat every stranger as if he or she were a criminal."

"Hit man," Lazarus corrected.

"Yes, thank you, I was trying not to use that phrase. The best idea—" she looked at McVey "—is for me to leave."

"Been down that road, Red. Even if you could slip away—unlikely in my opinion—Willy won't be happy, and neither will some of your relatives."

Because he hadn't raised his head to speak, Amara grabbed a handful of his hair and did it for him. "Fine. Give me a viable alternative."

"Joe Blume." He held up her phone. "The message you received was sent from Two Toes Joe's cell."

Amara released him because…well, mostly because his eyes and mouth were even more riveting today than they had been last night, and she really didn't need to be quite as aware of that as she suddenly was.

"So Willy Sparks is a thief as well as a murderer," her uncle said. "Is that your point?"

Amara held McVey's gaze. "I think his point is simply an expansion of what he said before. Not only is Willy Sparks here, but he's already connected some of the dots. If I leave the area, I'll still die. I just won't be the only member of my family to do it."

THEY CLIMBED UP to the attic, where the overview of the north woods tended to be impressive. Although Amara had hoped her uncle wouldn't follow them, he pushed through the trapdoor a few seconds behind her.

He wouldn't have it in him to "feel" the room, she

thought, certainly not the way she'd felt it as a child. Family history books claimed Sarah had come here to hone her craft. Whether she'd done so alone or not had never been determined. Unfortunately much of Sarah's life remained a mystery, even today.

She'd conjured things, Amara knew that much. The air smelled faintly of herbs and even the must of three centuries couldn't erase lingering traces of woodsmoke.

She ran her fingers over a stack of dusty trunks. "Antiques hunters would see this place as a treasure trove."

McVey pushed aside an enormous cobweb on his way to the cupola. "Spiders, mice and birds sure as hell do."

"Spiders, right. Forgot about those." Amara twitched away a shiver. "I was phobic as a kid." She nodded. "Ladder's there, McVey. I'm not sure how much better the view will be, though. And unless he's a complete fool, Willy Sparks won't be hanging around. Why are we doing this?"

"Because I saw a flash downstairs. Possibly light bouncing off glass or metal."

"Great. So Willy Sparks is a fool and he's abandoned the subtle approach."

"Or he has backup."

"An even more cheerful thought."

"It's also possible a raven picked up a piece of glass or metal and dropped it in a tree."

"Whatever the source, I can't just hang around and wait for a hit man to do his job."

"We'll have to believe that McVey will do his job first." Her uncle spoke from the top rung of the ladder stairs. "Meanwhile, Amara, you have excellent medical skills."

She knew what was coming. However, a spider the size of a baby rat crawled out from behind an old chair and caused her muscles to seize. "You want me to help Dr. Whoever at— There's a clinic in the Hollow, right?"

"There's a midwife," he said.

"And for anyone who's not pregnant?"

"There's the Cove."

"Which has?"

McVey hopped from the cupola. "Sorry to say, the best we can boast is a nearsighted former army medic who still hasn't grasped the concept of painkillers. Fog's rolling in. If someone's out there, he won't be able to see us."

Amara leaned over to check on the tarantula-size spider's progress. "What aren't you telling us, McVey?"

"You can't read my mind?"

"Be a terrifying prospect if she could." Her uncle glanced down, pulled a BlackBerry from his pocket and scowled at the screen. "I hate goat's milk," he declared.

"Must be Seth," Amara said while her uncle raised the phone to his ear. "What?" she asked when McVey grinned. Then she got it and blew out a breath. "His nephew, Seth Blume, has a farm in the middle of nowhere, two hundred miles north of the Cove. He raises chickens, pigs and goats, McVey. I don't read minds."

He started toward her. "But you do other things."

"I'm told I bake a mean lasagna."

It occurred to her when she stopped scanning for spiders that she'd let him get too close. Before she could side-step, he wrapped his fingers around the nape of her neck.

"Look at me, Amara."

"It would be hard not to from here."

"What do you see?"

A mouth she was tempted to kiss. But he didn't mean that, so she shifted her gaze to where he wanted it—the cheek she'd scratched last night.

"They weren't gouges. Don't give me more credit than I deserve."

"They're gone."

"I still see marks."

"Yeah?" He lowered his head and, damn it, made her breath stutter. "What would Jake's kid brother see?"

"The same thing as anyone with a brain the size of a snow pea." She refused to break eye contact. "I'm hoping yours is bigger than that."

McVey's lips crooked into a smile. She thought for a moment he was going to kiss her, but her uncle cleared his throat and the moment vanished.

"Seth can't get hold of his mother."

Dragging her eyes from McVey's, Amara searched her mind for a name. Hannah, she thought.

"His mother's your cousin, isn't she, Uncle? People used to call her, uh, your cousin. Does Seth think something's wrong?"

"A squirrel bit her two weeks back. She phoned him last Sunday to say her leg had swelled up like a balloon. Seth's been trying to contact her for three days. He wants me to make sure she's all right, maybe take her some aspirin."

"Because a person with an infected leg must have a headache to go with it. Where does she live?"

He aimed a look up Bellam Mountain. "She moved to the manor six months ago. She wanted solitude. The outer wings are only partly habitable since Molly and Sadie Bellam left. Road that takes you there's bumpier than the stairway to hell."

"Heaven," Amara corrected absently.

McVey gave the yard below a final visual sweep. "I drove up to Bellam Manor last fall, Red. Nothing about that road can be called heavenly."

"Making it a perfect counterpoint to the state of my life." Without looking over, she indicated the dense fog that was beginning to obliterate the upper limbs of the trees. "Coming from the north, right?"

"Yep."

"That's the way to Bellam Manor."

"Know it. You might want to pack a few things. We can pick up any medical supplies you think you'll need in the Hollow. I'll make sure both towns are covered deputy-wise."

Amara brought her eyes calmly to his. "I could tell you I know the way and you don't have to come."

"You could," McVey agreed. "But then I'd have to tell you I went through the kitchen cupboards after you got that text message. There were two bags of coffee inside. I picked up supplies yesterday. I only bought one."

Chapter Eight

"Take whatever you need, Dr. Bellam." The pharmacist poked his Buddy Holly glasses up a little higher. "Just fill out the supply form so I know what to restock." He ticked a finger behind him and whispered, "Bathroom. Gotta go."

Amara selected the antibiotics and anti-inflammatories she required. She added a bottle of hydrogen peroxide, another of rubbing alcohol, a roll of gauze and two candy bars, then hoisted the substantially heavier medical bag onto her left shoulder.

The one and only pharmacy in Raven's Hollow had been retrofitted into the back of an old-fashioned general store. The shelves were high and crowded, every floor plank squeaked and, when running at full capacity, the ancient refrigeration units tended to shimmy away from the walls. A quarter of the lights were either burned out or flickering, and she imagined the thirty-year-old cash register probably still died in the middle of a lengthy transaction.

Some things never changed.

"Excuse me." A woman with huge brown eyes and a noticeable overbite waved a hand. "Do you have this lip-stick in other colors? I'm looking for bubble-gum pink. It's my trademark shade."

"Yours and my cousin Yolanda's. I don't work here." Amara lowered her bag to the floor. "The cashier's at lunch

and the pharmacist's in the back. I just came in to shop-
lift some drugs."

"Cool—and bold. I'm Mina Shell. I'm in town for the…
Oh, there, I see one." She reached over the glass counter
to snag a tube. "Blast O' Pink. Perfect. D'you suppose I
could leave the money with a note? Except I haven't got
any paper. Or a pen."

Amara was tearing a blank sheet from the supply pad
when she heard a creak behind her. Before she could raise
her head, a man gripped her wrist and jerked her around.

"Hey, there, gorgeous. I've been looking for you all over
this freaky bird town." He caught the other woman by the
scruff of her neck and squeezed. "Not so fast, Pretty in
Pink. I got a few things I want to say to Glinda while we're
more or less alone."

The knife Amara had glimpsed the previous night dangled over her shoulder. The man rubbed a thumb across the
blade and offered a lewd smile. "Don't you just love how
some store owners are so trusting? Not a security camera
in sight—if you're wishing and hoping, that is. Okay, so,
brass tacks time, Glin." He leaned in closer. "Is this your
real body or do you fog a man's mind so he only thinks
you're a babe? Shut up," he snapped when Mina squealed.

"You're pinching me."

"Duh, yeah. In case you haven't guessed, I'm not a nice
guy. And speaking of not nice—" he turned to Amara "—I
think it's time you and me—"

It was as far as he got. Amara brought her heel down
on his instep, plowed an elbow into his ribs and, spinning
free, took a swing at his head with the bottle of rubbing
alcohol she'd managed to slip from her medical bag.

She hadn't expected to knock him out, but she had
hoped to stun him. Instead he whipped the knife up and
showed his teeth.

"I am so gonna do you," he growled.

Spotting a movement at the rear of the store, Amara shouted, "Benny, get McVey." She straight-armed the plastic alcohol bottle as if it would shield her from a knife the size of a machete.

Thankfully the man glanced over, saw the pharmacist and, shoving Mina aside, took off through the side exit.

Lowering the bottle, Amara released her fear on a trembling breath. Pale-cheeked and clutching his phone, the pharmacist rushed forward.

"Are you hurt? Did he hurt you? I called the police station. I'm so sorry."

"I broke a heel," Mina told Amara. "And a fingernail." She blinked. "All I wanted was a tube of lipstick and I got pinched, shoved and maybe almost decapitated by the Machete Kid. Not sure I should hang for the Raven thing after all. I mean, that was one humongous knife."

It was also the second time Amara had seen it.

She was returning the rubbing alcohol to her medical bag when Jake burst through the front door, armed and clearly prepared for battle.

"Where's the creep?" he demanded, waving his .38 Special back and forth.

Amara eased the barrel aside with her index finger. "He left by the exit to the alley."

Jake's jaw clenched. "You let him go? Why didn't you…?"

"Hemorrhoids," she reminded him. Then she shrugged. "As long as you insist on believing in the absurd."

"I saw the knife." Mina piped up. "But I was too scared to notice the guy's face. Sorry."

"I saw his face." The pharmacist poked at his glasses. "Saw it here a few minutes ago and through my bedroom window early this morning. The man wearing it came out of the building across the alley, the one with the raven and the witch on the door that kids keep spray painting red. You know the place, Deputy. It's where Yolanda Bellam lives."

PANDEMONIUM REIGNED AT the station house. No fewer than ten voices shouted at the same time. McVey made no attempt to separate one from the other. Instead he tried to keep an eye on Amara, who stood in front of the dispatcher's desk, relating her account of the incident to one of the Harden twins.

"Stop badgering me." Yolanda's shrill whine rose above the din. "Is it my fault some jerk with a knife happened to be sneaking out of a building that has three other apartments in it besides mine at whatever o'clock in the morning? McVey…"

"I said take her statement, Jake, not accuse her of harboring a fugitive."

"He wasn't a fugitive when she harbored him."

"I didn't harbor him." Stepping directly into McVey's line of vision, Yolanda walked the fingers of both hands up his shirt. "My brother wasn't there when I got up this morning, so I can't prove I was alone. Jake thinks I'm lying, but you believe me, don't you?"

What he believed, he thought as he eased her aside, was that he should turn in his badge, hunt Westor Hall down and hang him from one of the tortured oaks by his—

"I hate to interrupt a man who looks as if he wants to put a bullet in someone's head." Amara tapped his arm from the side. "But is there any chance of us ditching this town before the fog that's rolling out to sea gives way to the nasty black clouds that are creeping down from the north? Because the only thing worse than the road to Bellam Manor in a downpour is—well, actually, short of a mudslide, not a whole lot."

McVey indicated the crowd. "How many of these people were in the pharmacy when Wes—the guy with the knife appeared?"

She regarded him for a moment before perusing the room. "The pharmacist and Mina, but she freaked and left when Jake started waving a second gun around."

"Smart woman."

"Benny's your best witness, McVey. And maybe one or two people from the alley. Everyone else is either bored and curious or waiting for the Red Eye to open."

McVey reached around her to intercept Yolanda's curled fingers. "No scratching," he warned.

She glared at Amara. "You stayed at Nana's last night."

Amara glared right back. "Pretty sure you said I couldn't say with you."

"I also said…" She glanced at McVey, then back. "I hate you."

"So no change there."

When Yolanda's hands balled at her sides, McVey got between them. "Lazarus had a call from his nephew, Seth, this morning, Yolanda. He thinks his mother might need medical attention."

She sniffed. "Since when does Seth worry about his mother? If it doesn't cluck or have four legs, he doesn't notice or care about it. That includes Hannah—who's a story unto herself—and why Lazarus gives two hoots about her is beyond me."

Pushing a hefty man aside, Jake joined them. "Seth's only worried his mother'll kick off before Lazarus does. Then, poof, there'll go his chance of worming any inheritance money he might be in line to receive from her." He shrugged an irritable shoulder. "Lazarus can't stand Seth. Or me. Or my brother. Or half the Blumes, or any of the Bellams in either town."

"He likes Nana," Amara pointed out. "He also holds the title on Bellam Manor."

Jake's lips peeled away from his teeth. "Well, hell, Amara, anyone could get past the Bellam name to own a house and land that are worth a fortune. As for actual Bellams, you can't blame the guy for not liking them. The only one I ever dated threatened to turn me into a toad."

McVey pressed on his now-throbbing eyes. "Only threatened?" he asked. "Do your job, Jake. Talk to Benny and anyone who saw anything in the alley. Send the rest of these people home."

Jake's jaw tightened, but he nodded. "What about the guy with the knife? Are we just gonna let him roam around free until whenever?"

"He won't be roaming, Deputy."

"He will if we don't go after him."

"He doesn't need to roam, Jake." Amara glanced toward the north woods. "All he needs to do is follow McVey and me up the mountain to Bellam Manor."

IF WESTOR WAS SANE—and McVey figured he had his moments—he wouldn't attempt to follow them even part-way up the mountain.

By 4:00 p.m., the sky had turned an ominous shade of black. Swollen clouds tinged with purple collided and swirled. Where they did, tiny bolts of electricity shot from one to the other.

"This is fascinating, really." Amara secured her medical bag in the space behind her seat. "The family history books claim that Hezekiah Blume became a raven on a night that started exactly like this."

McVey shoved their backpacks in from the driver's side. "He did."

"Did what?"

"Become a raven during an electrical storm…. And how the hell would I know that?"

"Maybe you're possessed. Don't crush the candy bars, McVey. We'll need the sugar buzz by the time we reach the manor."

"We'll need more than a sugar buzz, and I've got a bottle of it safely stowed." Disinclined to pursue his earlier remark, he climbed in and motioned for Amara to buckle up. "Believe me when I tell you the potholes on the Hollow Road can swallow a large truck if you hit them straight on."

She pulled the shoulder harness across. "You're just full of optimism today, aren't you?"

"My goal is to get us up the mountain and back in one piece."

"I applaud the sentiment, McVey, but I have to tell you, too much secrecy makes me twitchy."

He felt her eyes on his face.

"You know the guy with the Texas-size knife, don't you? Know him personally, I mean."

He could lie, but why bother? So he forced his muscles to relax and draped a hand over the steering wheel. "You're observant, Red, I'll give you that. Jake hasn't figured it out yet."

"Jake wasn't with us last night when you made your one-man foray into the woods. We both know that rifles are more powerful than handguns, and I'm betting the one we heard came equipped with an infrared scope. If the shooter wanted you dead, we'd be digging your grave right now."

Answer or evade? McVey opted for middle ground with a leading edge of truth.

"I recognized the shot pattern, Amara. Three times three. It's a signal we used to use. It also had the benefit of making enough noise that anyone in the vicinity who shouldn't be there got the hell out fast."

"Where exactly were they getting the hell out of?"

"A potentially dangerous situation."

"That's not an answer."

"Yes, it is. Or it's as much of one as I'm going to give you right now. Let's leave it at…I wasn't always a cop, and even after I became one, not every cop I met lived by the same code."

He felt more than saw her exasperation.

"Are you ever not cryptic—" She broke off to swing around in her seat. "I saw a light. Did you see a light?"

"Three streaking overhead and a more substantial one behind us. The one behind could be a local heading for the north woods. I'm told there are a number of pocket communities scattered around. I've also heard about, but haven't crossed paths with yet, a group of nomads who live off the grid in a collection of campers, trailers and caravans."

"The raven tamers." She strained to see farther back. "Mostly Blumes. They teach ravens to do tricks and create mechanical ones that can do what the real ravens won't. The tamers are bound to come into the Hollow for the Night. They'll put on shows, sell their amazing raven crafts, then disappear back into the woods with tons of orders for what they do best."

"Which is?"

"Brewing and bottling raven's blood—wine, not actual blood—and their signature 'gonna knock you out for two whole days if you're not extremely careful' whiskey."

He knew he shouldn't be amused, but his lips quirked even so. "Why haven't I heard about these people?"

Her grin was a punch of lust straight to his groin. "You're joking, right—Police Chief McVey?"

"Amara, in the past fourteen months, I've unearthed half a dozen stills. Unless I see some kind of trouble directly related to one of them, I'm willing to turn a blind eye."

"Ty isn't."

"I'm not Ty."

"I got that right off, but gaining the raven tamers' trust will take a bit longer."

"Have you met any of them?"

"Only Brigham, and only because I bumped into him on the single occasion I visited Bellam Manor. It was a family thing. A funeral. A really old Bellam uncle wanted to be buried in the really old cemetery behind the house. It was the spookiest experience I've ever..." She pivoted in her seat. "I saw another beam. I'm sure it was a headlight."

He nodded, glanced in the mirror. The road, such as it was, had already become a serpentine river of rain and mud. And, as he recalled, there was worse to come.

Thunder began to rumble overhead as the grade increased. Amara kept her gaze fixed behind them. "Do you think it's the knife guy or Willy Sparks?"

"I'd go with Willy."

"I knew you'd say that." She craned her neck for a better view. "So when was the last time you had a report on the bridge? Obviously it was passable when Sadie and Molly lived at the manor, but it's been a few years since Sadie got married and moved to New York and Molly left to live with Ty."

McVey ground his teeth as his left rear tire slammed through a pothole. "Road's a lot worse than it was last fall. As for the bridge, we'll see when we get there."

If they got there. An extended peal of thunder shuddered through the mountainside and up into his truck. The only positive he could see here was that whoever was behind them would need to navigate the same minefield to reach the manor.

Assuming the goal was to reach the manor and not run them over the edge.

"You're looking in that rearview mirror entirely too much, McVey. Do you think he's going to ram your truck?"

"Odds are. This road's got *death trap* written all over it. We shoot off and go for a roll, there'll be no way to prove it was a deliberate act." He glanced at her, his expression mildly humorous. "Wishing you'd said no to your uncle yet?"

More tiny lightning bolts zapped from cloud to cloud. "Maybe. A little. But the truth is, Hannah's ten years up on Uncle Lazarus, and he's old. She used to babysit him when he was a kid."

"Lazarus was a kid? Not sure I can picture that."

"I'll admit it's a stretch imagination-wise. Jake told me people in both towns call her Mother Goose." Amara held up both hands. "Hey, I never met the woman. I'm only repeating." She grabbed the dash when McVey swerved around a jagged cluster of ruts. "Whatever she's called, I think it's time for her to swap the seclusion of Bellam Manor for a more accessible north woods' cabin."

McVey swore as a thin beam of light streaked across the rear windshield at the precise moment the rain, already pounding down, became a veritable waterfall. Where was the damn bridge?

"Half a mile ahead." Amara sent him a quick smile. "Read it in your face, Chief. I don't think he's gaining on us."

"He's not."

"So you see—" She broke off to stare. "My God, those dips in the road look like duck ponds."

"Hang on" was all McVey said.

It took him fifteen long minutes to maneuver through the damaged sections. A dozen potholes and three hairpin turns later, he spotted the bridge.

Amara studied the sagging structure. "I don't see getting across any other way except on foot, do you?"

He reached for his gun on the dash. "On foot and preferably naked. Clothes have weight," he added, then grinned. "Plus the visual gave me a wicked sexual rush."

"I'm flattered, but I'd prefer an assessment from the part of your brain that lives above the waist."

"The bridge is crap, Red. We'll need our rain gear." He opened the glove box. "Can you hit a moving target?"

"If we're lucky, we'll never find out."

Unfortunately, judging by the next slash of light, their pursuer was less than half a mile behind them.

Because he'd dealt with hysteria before, McVey set his hands on her shoulders and checked her eyes. They were dark, determined and striking enough that his train of thought almost slipped away. Did slip away for a moment. And he knew he wouldn't be getting it back in a hurry when the corners of her mouth curved into a teasing smile.

"On the subject of wicked sexual rushes…" she began.

Lightning forked overhead. As it did, her eyes sparkled silver. A second later McVey's hand was in her hair and his mouth was on hers. And somewhere on the hazy fringes of his mind, it occurred to him that the danger in his truck might be much greater than the danger behind them.

Chapter Nine

The taste of him plunged Amara's senses into a whirlpool of desire. A thousand electric volts sparked in her head. She wanted to touch every inch of him with her mouth and with her hands.

She felt his fingers on her face and heard the moan that emerged from her throat. While his tongue explored, she ran her palms over his chest and absorbed the feel of him. Sleek, hard muscles; smooth, firm skin…and heat everywhere she touched.

She nipped his lower lip, bit the corners of his mouth, then moved to the button of his jeans and prepared to enjoy herself.

Miniature lightning bolts snapped the air like whips. Two of them seemed to race along her arms while a third sizzled down her spine. She wished she could block reality and go back to savoring, but something shifted in her brain and she pulled back. She needed to breathe quite badly, needed to think even more.

"McVey, we can't… This is crazy. We're crazy." She struggled to reorient and settle herself. "There's a homicidal nutball on the road behind us and we're playing Spin the Bottle in your truck."

"More like Russian roulette." He kissed her again and made her head swim, before pulling away to stare straight into her eyes. "Okay, here's the deal. You go first. Carefully. We hear shots, you hit the ground. Got it?"

"Shots, ground, got it."

Lunacy, she thought as they tugged on rain gear and loaded up with packs. What rational woman let herself be sidetracked by the prospect of sex—okay, potentially amazing sex—when she knew there was someone who probably wanted her dead close behind?

Since the question had no answer and a premature darkness had begun to steal across the mountain, she let it go. For now.

Bellam Bridge was a blend of deteriorating wood planks and badly rusted iron framework. With regular maintenance, it might have lasted another two decades. Without it, Amara's body weight appeared to tax the entire support system.

McVey followed her onto the shrieking planks, close enough to grab her but with a wide enough gap between them that they were never on the same piece of wood at the same time.

Amara inched forward and told herself that any sponginess she felt was her imagination working overtime. Neither of them was going to plunge to death on the rocks below.

Razor-thin shafts of lightning continued to electrify the sky. If there was another form of light behind them, she could no longer see it.

One step, two, three… Every muscle in her body threatened to seize. She took another step, heard a loud crack and willed the nightmare to end. How long was this stupid bridge anyway?

Her nerves had long since passed the breaking point when she spotted solid ground. Put her foot on solid ground. Considered dropping to her knees and kissing that ground.

Instead she released a shivery breath and shouted, "The manor's a mile away by road, but there's a stone path—really steep—or there used to be, that can get us there much faster."

"Go for it," he shouted back and gave her a nudge. "Eyes forward," he said when she turned to peer past his arm. "I saw headlights behind my truck a few seconds ago."

Being a doctor had definite moments of sucking, Amara reflected.

She was able to locate the old path without the aid of a flashlight. In another ten minutes, however, they'd be relying entirely on the storm and whatever other light sources McVey had thought to bring along.

In areas where the stone steps had crumbled, she was forced to claw her way up. In others, McVey gripped her waist and gave her a boost.

It felt as if they climbed for hours, but it was probably only twenty minutes. Did a thin beam of light bob directly behind them? Did she care when breathing had become an exercise in pain, her knees and elbows were bruised and her palms had been scraped raw?

Drawing on the last of her strength, Amara hauled herself up and over the edge.

Bellam Manor stood like a brooding black fortress against the stormy sky. Rain blurred the peaks and towers, but as she recalled, even on a good day, nothing about the place said welcome.

"The central core of the house splits the wings where my cousins used to live," she shouted when McVey pulled himself up beside her. "We could search all night and not find Hannah. So…" Lowering her pack, she unzipped the top flap and removed her iPhone. "Uncle Lazarus gave me her number. For some weird and wonderful reason, wireless tech works up here."

"Put it down to residual Bellam magic and the fortunate placement of a cell tower." McVey crouched near the edge of the precipice and looked down. "If you get through, tell her to leave the house dark."

Booming thunder caused the rocks under Amara's feet to vibrate. She tried Hannah's number three times with no luck.

"Guess we'll have to search after all." Slipping the phone into her pocket, she peered over McVey's shoulder. "Any sign of pursuit?"

"Not so far."

"That's good, right?"

"Not necessarily."

She sighed. "You'd think I'd learn not to ask." Turning, she regarded the manor. "East or west wing?"

"Anything coming to you?"

"Other than a strong desire to run, no." But she turned her mind as well as her eyes to the house, because…well, why not?

Sensing nothing, she pointed at the ruined central core.

A giant raven's-head knocker on the double front doors echoed louder than the storm. Now, there was an inviting sound, Amara reflected, and twisted the brass entry ring. The right door swung inward on eerily silent hinges.

"How is it possible that hinges not creaking is a thousand times creepier than the other way around?" She set her pack on a floor littered with plaster, glass, dust and wood. "Hannah?"

McVey produced two powerful flashlights and shone his up the once-grand staircase to the remnants of a cob-webbed chandelier.

"It's shaped like a pentagram." Pulling out her phone, Amara tried Hannah's number again. "Do you hear a ring?"

"Are you serious?"

But they listened for several seconds.

After turning a circle in place, Amara ended the call and shook her head. "She's not here, McVey."

He crossed to a narrow window. "Pick a wing, then, Red."

"At the risk of sounding like Sarah, I don't think she's anywhere in the house. No vibes," she added when he glanced at her.

McVey returned to his scan of the ceiling. "That probably shouldn't make me feel better, but it does. She might be in one of the outbuildings. Or the cave."

"There's a cave?"

"In the woods behind the manor."

Exasperation mixed with uncertainty. "You're not on some kind of medication I should know about, are you, McVey? Who told you—?"

With so many dense shadows enfolding them, she didn't see him move, didn't realize he was behind her until his hand covered her mouth and his lips moved against her ear.

"Your uncle told me about it. There's someone outside. He's circling the manor."

Amara's heart shot into her throat. Unable to speak around it, she let him slip his backup gun between her fingers.

Jimmy Sparks's face darted through her head. Teeth gleamed, and Jimmy morphed into the man with the big knife. Not Willy Sparks, her blipping mind recalled. Not if McVey was to be believed.

A little unsure, she flattened herself against the wall while he watched through the window.

"Whoever it is moves quickly and well," he remarked.

"I imagine most assassins would."

"He's heading for the west wing." McVey pushed an extra ammo clip into her free hand. "Don't shoot unless you're certain of your target."

"No, wait, McVey, you can't..."

But he could and did. And left her wishing she really had inherited some of Sarah's power, enough at least to put a binding spell on him.

Lowering to her knees, she braced her wrists on the sill and ordered herself to listen for sounds within the storm.

She spied an arc of light to her right. It slashed across the clearing and for less than a heartbeat of time revealed a figure dressed in shiny black. The person was bent low and appeared to be running away from the manor.

Amara eased up for a clearer look. But the lightning winked out, the person vanished and only the thunder and pelting rain remained.

Two seconds later a gunshot exploded outside.

THE BULLET WAS a rogue, McVey suspected. And it came from a handgun, not a rifle, which tended to be Westor's weapon of choice. So...probably not him.

Lightning raced through the sky in long, skinny bolts. McVey moved between flashes and kept an eye peeled for any motion that didn't involve rain, flying objects or swaying trees.

Fifty feet ahead, a leg disappeared around the west side of the manor. Fixing his mind on the spot and keeping to the shadows as much as possible, he ran.

They'd called it foot pursuit back at the academy. Bad guys bolted; cops gave chase. Sometimes the bad guys got cornered and attacked, but in vast, open areas they didn't tend to launch themselves out of the darkness like human projectiles, roaring and, in the case of this particular projectile, packing upward of two hundred and fifty hairy pounds.

McVey glimpsed the human mass, but not quickly enough to avoid it. The best he could do was duck low to prevent an all-out tackle that would have landed him on a jagged clump of rocks.

As it was, the blow knocked him sideways and slammed his shoulder into the stump of a tree.

Aware that he'd only half struck his target, the man went from his knees to a feral crouch to another roaring attack in a New York second.

Knowing he'd only get one shot, McVey rolled onto his back, double-handed his Glock and, as the man rushed toward him, squeezed off two shots.

It might have been his attacker falling or a particularly violent clap of thunder, but the ground beneath McVey's feet shook. Cursing, the man swung onto his side and would have reared up if McVey hadn't used his gun to slam him in the jaw.

His attacker went down like a felled tree.

Winded, and with his shoulder throbbing, McVey took aim at a bearded face. "Give me a name, pal, and hope like hell it's one I want to hear. Because right now I'm just pissed off enough to forget I took an oath to serve and protect."

A flashlight beam sliced through the murk. As it did, he heard Amara shout, "Don't shoot him, McVey. He's not Willy Sparks. His name's Brigham Blume. He's a raven tamer."

"OUCH, AMARA."

The oversize tamer jerked, but Amara merely went with the motion and finished pumping the contents of her syringe into his tattooed upper arm.

"Both bullets penetrated flesh, Brigham. A few stitches and you'll be good to go."

"Figuratively speaking," McVey put in.

He poured three glasses of whiskey in a kitchen too tidy to have been abandoned for any length of time. When he added in the fact that the place had power—fading in and out, but working for the moment—it appeared they'd found Hannah's home. As for Hannah herself, he'd searched the entire west wing from top to bottom without success.

Brigham picked up one of the drinks, downed it and glared. "Why'd you shoot me?"

McVey tossed his own whiskey back. "Why did you attack me?"

"I thought you were the other guy. Same time I realized you weren't, I saw you had a gun. I figured if you were anything like your dumb-ass deputy, you'd be inclined to shoot first and congratulate yourself on the result."

Okay, that was a lot of information. McVey homed in on the significant point. "What other guy?"

"The one who followed you up the mountain. I noticed he was on your tail after I got on his."

"Where was that?" Amara asked.

"While you were lollygagging across the bridge. I came to collect storm noises. Around the bridge gives a great echo."

"For their amazing animated ravens," Amara informed McVey. "Nana says the raven tamers do a killer show throughout the festival, complete with sound effects."

"Other guy," McVey reminded her.

Brigham slid his glass forward for a refill. "That's all I've got, McVey. Guy followed you, I spotted him. I went up the stone path behind him, behind you. I lost him at the top, but decided to skulk a bit, because even though I shouldn't, I liked Amara when I met her all those years

back, and while you might think we live like our ancestors in the north woods, we stay connected to some of our
relatives in the Cove. We know what's what. Don't always
like to admit we know, but we do." He shrugged his good
shoulder. "I put knowing and seeing together and came
up with someone who wants Amara here to be joining her
fellow witnesses in death."

"Fellow witnesses and the cop who helped her get out
of New Orleans." McVey sent the whiskey bottle sliding
across the table.

"Soda pop's got more of a kick than this stuff," Brigham
scoffed. He jerked again. "I said, ouch, Amara."

"Heard you the first time." She pulled a suture through
his flesh and made McVey's stomach roll. "We should
check the house as well as the outbuildings for Hannah.
I might not be feeling her vibe, but my Bellam senses are
far from infallible."

"I'll help." Brigham poured himself a full six ounces of
whiskey and knocked it back as if it really was soda pop.
"Hannah's kin of a sort. Weird, but kin."

"Pot, kettle," McVey said into his glass. "How much
longer, Red?"

"All done." She tapped Brigham's shoulder. "No pulling, no fiddling. They'll dissolve as you heal. I'll give you
something for the pain."

Brigham gave McVey a hard look. "I've got that covered at home—I hope."

McVey just smiled. "Let's find Hannah."

As Amara washed her hands, she nodded at the full
second sink. "Wherever she went, Hannah left a week's
worth of dirty dishes behind."

Joining her, McVey counted ten plates, six bowls with
food hardened on the bottom and a single coffee-stained
mug that smelled like bio-diesel fuel.

He held the mug out to Brigham, who was shrugging cautiously into his jacket. "Residue of your kick-ass whiskey?"

The big man sniffed the mug. "Well, damn me. And we've been making do with ginger ale. I should've checked out the cupboards when we came in. My mind must've gone south from the pain of having two bullets drilled into my shoulder."

"You want to launch an official complaint, I'll be happy to take your statement while you're showing me around your raven tamer property." McVey picked up a wineglass that was coated red inside. "Raven's blood, I assume?"

Amara took the glass and smiled. "Nana says it's an acquired taste." She rubbed her thumb over a pink smudge on the rim. "If Hannah drank raven's blood and chased it with raven tamer whiskey, it's possible she's passed out somewhere between here and one of the outbuildings. Passed out equals no vibes. Or so the theory goes."

As a fresh round of wind and rain buffeted the manor, McVey rezipped his jacket. "Let's get this done. If Hannah's on the property, we need to find her." He regarded Brigham, who was currently rooting through the pantry. "Do you know if there's power in the other wing?"

"Doubt it." He sent Amara an evil grin. "But I'm willing to bet there're plenty of really big spiders."

BRIGHAM WAS RIGHT about the lack of power. Unfortunately he was also right about the spiders. Amara found evidence of several in each of the rooms she inspected.

"How is it possible," she asked the big raven tamer when he passed her in a dusty second-floor corridor, "that you know so specifically what terrifies me?"

"Could be a little raven told me." But he chuckled when she beamed her light directly into his face. "Okay, McVey told me. He made a sweep while you were digging out your instruments of torture. He made me look under the table. Me, Amara, the guy with two bullet holes in his arm."

"Any time you want to swear out that complaint, Blume." McVey came down the ladder stairs from the attic. "Any luck?"

Amara jerked her hand away from a sticky web. "No. You?"

"I spotted a bunch of small sheds and a larger building that was probably a barn or stable at one time."

"She might have gone to a neighbor's place," Brigham said. "How bad was her leg?"

"Swollen like a balloon according to Uncle Lazarus." Amara fastened her rain jacket and pulled on the Dodgers cap McVey had loaned her.

"You and me, left. Him, right." McVey took her hand and tossed one of the flashlights to Brigham. "Don't assume the person you saw earlier is gone."

"Because he's probably not as considerate as you and won't settle for shooting me in the shoulder."

Amara watched him slog away. "I like Brigham better, but he reminds me of Jake. Which makes sense, I suppose, since they're both Blumes, and he seems to know about your dumb-ass deputy's penchant for firearms."

McVey gave the bill of her cap a tug. "You have a strange group of relatives, Red. Barn's about two hundred feet west. Tuck in close behind me."

The wind had picked up and the rain was falling in buckets now. Mud sucked at Amara's boots and made running impossible. Even if they found Hannah, she couldn't see them getting her back to McVey's truck.

And if they couldn't get back, she thought as they approached the barn, neither could the person who'd apparently followed them. All in all, not a positive prospect for the next several hours.

The barn turned out to be even more derelict than the manor. A full third of the roof and most of the wall that faced the ocean had been torn away. There was no sign of Hannah, only a dozen or so rusty vehicles from another era.

"What now?" Amara asked when they rejoined Brigham in the central core.

McVey shone his flashlight up the staircase again. "Only place we haven't looked is here."

"Not infallible," she reminded him. "Up or down?"

"With a leg like a balloon, I doubt she'd have gone either way. This floor's our best bet."

Brigham took the front of the house, leaving the back to her and McVey.

"Oh, wow, now here's a kitchen only my great-great-many-times-grandmother would recognize." Stepping carefully, Amara beamed her light into a hearth large enough to roast an ox. She ran it over broken counters, cupboards with no doors and appliances so old their purpose eluded her. "Hannah?" Her voice echoed up to the rafters. "Brigham could be right, McVey. She might have made her way to a neighbor's—"

The last word never emerged as McVey gripped her arms and yanked her down below the level of the windowsill.

"Someone's heading into the trees."

A glimmer of lightning revealed a figure, but it could have been a deer for all Amara saw of it. Moving ahead of her, McVey led the way along the line of windows to the door.

"It's as if we crossed Bellam Bridge and stepped into

the worst horror film ever," she whispered. "What if it's another raven tamer, McVey?"

"I'll try not to shoot any vital parts. Stay here, Amara, and be ready. Anyone you don't recognize appears, fire a warning. If he keeps coming, shoot him."

He stood as he spoke and eased the door open.

Amara set a hand on the floor. She would have gone from a crouch to her knees if her fingers hadn't recognized the thing beneath them and gone still where they lay.

"McVey?" Even being a doctor, she didn't want to lower her eyes. "I, uh...could you shine your flashlight this way for a minute?"

"Not now, Red."

"Yes, now." Her throat tightened, threatened to close. Before it did, she made herself look.

McVey angled his light down. The beam bounced off a pair of green eyes. Lifeless eyes, Amara's shocked mind corrected. The lifeless green eyes of her uncle's cousin, Hannah Blume.

Chapter Ten

In Amara's opinion, Hannah had been dead for at least two days. If appearances could be believed, she'd struck her head on one of the broken counters. But given her severely swollen leg, why she'd been in this part of the house was anyone's guess.

"Maybe she was delirious." Brigham watched as McVey gathered what evidence he could without disturbing Hannah's body. "Could've wandered over here not meaning to."

"It's possible" was all McVey said, and he did so absently while taking pictures with his iPhone.

When he was finished, Brigham got a sheet from Hannah's living quarters and Amara draped it over her. Because he'd known her best, she asked Brigham to say a few words.

After a last look around the property, McVey secured the manor and they headed back to Hannah's wing.

"Power's out," he noted halfway across the yard. "All the lights on the lower floor were burning when we left."

"I didn't see a generator in any of the sheds," Brigham shouted forward.

"There was nothing in the barn, either," Amara called back.

Leaning into the house, McVey tried the light switches. When nothing happened, he flipped his jacket collar up and came back out. "With our mystery man still at large, this could turn into a hell of a long night."

"We've got gens." Brigham's surly tone told Amara quite clearly that he didn't want to take them anywhere near the raven tamers' camp. "I'll need some assurances first, though, McVey."

"Only assurance you're getting is that I'm not Ty."

Brigham's teeth appeared, but not in the form of a smile. "Makes two of us. Grab your gear and let's roll. Camp's a fair hike away."

They walked single file with Amara in the middle. Lightning continued to flicker. Thunder rumbled behind it and the rain just kept on falling.

Amara knew she should be worried about Willy Sparks, but all she could think about was Hannah's vacuous expression, her glassy eyes and, of course, the dried blood.

Whether he'd let it show or not, Uncle Lazarus would be upset. She was upset, and she hadn't known the woman.

The north woods went on forever. Although she worked out five days a week at a New Orleans fitness center, negotiating rocky paths that climbed, dipped, tilted and often vanished altogether made Amara's legs feel like rubber bands. Wherever they were going, she figured they would have crossed at least one state border before they arrived.

Gradually a sprinkling of lights came into view. As they descended into an odd-shaped clearing, trailers of various sizes, ages and states of disrepair took shape. If any permanent structures existed, Amara couldn't see them. Prepared for the worst, and with McVey close behind her, she trailed Brigham to an outlying RV.

"Mine," he said, yanking the battered door open. "Go in, stay in. I'll come for you in the morning. Door locks. I'd use it. Your cell phones'll probably work. We pirate three satellite television stations. Best one plays old movies 24/7. There's food in the cupboards. Sorry about Hannah, Amara. Sleep well."

When he was gone, Amara looked around. Man space, she decided. Single man's space, with clothes and dishes scattered, furniture duct taped and every surface dusty, except for a forty-year-old television that still had a channel dial and a chair with raven-wing arms that sat directly in front of it.

"Not bad," McVey remarked over her shoulder. "Good, actually, as it's off the beaten path."

"Way off, McVey, and a lot more beaten than any of the paths we took to get here. The word *dump* springs to mind."

He moved past her. "As long as the word *grateful* is close behind it."

"Oh, I'm grateful. Not entirely sure we'll be allowed to leave, but happy not to be spending the night with no power and the prospect of a run-in with the homicidal hit man who apparently followed us across Bellam Bridge."

"Always good to think positive, Red."

She touched a set of raven wind chimes above the TV and offered him a smile. "Also, I'm related to these people and theoretically safe from harm—on the off chance that the tales about the raven tamers turn out to be true."

McVey stowed their packs next to a lopsided sofa. "I'll have to hope my badge will be enough to get me out in one piece. And the fact that, while I did shoot Brigham, I didn't kill him."

Amara hung their rain gear on a wobbly rack, looked at the kitchen and decided she was hungry enough to check it out.

"How did Hannah die, McVey?"

"I don't think Willy Sparks had anything to do with it,

if that's what you're asking. Beyond that, her death will have to be investigated."

"Along with that second bag of coffee beans you mentioned this morning?"

"I had Jake send both bags and the brewed sample off to the county lab for analysis. Bases covered, Amara."

She opened a cupboard and, standing back, stared in astonishment. "Seriously. Brigham has soup. In cans."

"Why does that surprise you?"

"Well, duh, McVey. Look around—metaphorically speaking. Not a store in sight. I'd expect people living in such a remote area to grow herbs and vegetables, raise chickens—you know, make homemade soups, pickles and other off-the-beaten-path things."

"Maybe they're too busy teaching ravens to do tricks to worry about pickling and preserving. Anyway, I like food that comes in cans."

"That's very sad." She opened the fridge. "Okay, now, this is more what I expected. Self-bottled beer, mason jars with not-sure-what inside, and something that looks like brownies."

"Ones that'll give you a wicked case of the munchies."

Laughing, Amara closed the door and leaned back against it. "When I was a kid, Nana and my aunt—Uncle Lazarus's sister, Maureen—used to encourage me to get in touch with my Bellam side. I don't mean cast spells or brew potions…"

"Although your uncle Lazarus could present a case for the casting of spells."

"I doubt he actually thought I'd bewitched him. He just found the coincidence funny. Anyway, the point is, I got as far as being able to sense things. I'm not sure how to say this so I don't come out sounding crazy, but sometimes I could sense life, or the lack of it, in a place."

"You're talking about Bellam Manor and Hannah, aren't you?"

"There was no life inside the house, McVey. Not anywhere. Spiders don't count. Human-wise, the whole place felt—dead."

He crouched to rummage through a metal container. "You don't have to sell me on your Bellam ancestry, Red. I'm open to a fair number of beliefs. And lifestyles for that matter."

"Right. Because you weren't always a cop."

He met her questioning gaze with an unfathomable one of his own. "Were you always a doctor?"

"No, but I always wanted to be one."

"So you could make people prettier?"

"In a way." Just not the one he thought. "Talk to me about how you knew the knife guy in the days before you were a cop, McVey."

"I knew a lot of people in those days." He pulled a bottle from the container, blew off a layer of dust. "Raven's blood wine?"

"I don't see a label, so probably. How did you know him?"

He met her eyes again. "If I said the truth might shake your faith in me, would you let it go?"

A smile tugged on her lips. Circling around behind him, she set her hands on his shoulders and bent to whisper in his ear, "I'm in an RV that belongs to a raven tamer, McVey. There are stories about raven tamers that would send squeamish people like Jake's brother, Jimbo, under their beds for a week. Brigham's the only tamer I know, and I suspect he's considered affable. Hannah's dead, this storm's not moving on and we all saw someone creeping around the manor. Someone who, like us, could be stranded on this side of Bellam Bridge. There's a better

than excellent chance that person is Willy Sparks. I believe
you can and will deal with him, because dealing with criminals is your job. So, really, short of telling me you used
to be a mass murderer, there's not a whole lot you can say
about your past that'll shake my faith in you."

He turned his head just enough for her to see his expression. She couldn't read it, of course, but that was nothing new.

"I told you I was a foundling, Amara. What I didn't
tell you is that the people who took me in were part of a
smuggling operation."

"Part of a— Really?" She leaned farther around him.
"Are you serious?"

"It was a small business, salvage items and minor arti-
facts from Central America. No drugs or weapons. My father had an antiques shop. My mother was his bookkeeper.
I harangued them into letting me be their go-between. Everything was fine until my mother died. I was seventeen
at the time. Two years later my father's heart gave out. He
knew he wasn't going to make it, so he wrangled a promise from me. He wanted me to give up the life and get out
before the business got out of hand. I told him I would,
and I kept my word."

"You became a cop."

"Yep."

"And then?"

A smile ghosted over his mouth. "Still wearing a badge
here, Red."

"Yes, but it's a Raven's Cove badge."

"What, you want me to quit and let Jake take over?"

And now they were back to evasion.

"At the risk of sounding repetitive, where does the guy
with the knife enter the picture?"

He considered for a moment while lightning flickered

and fading peals of thunder echoed through the woods. "His name's Westor Hall," he said at length. "After my mother died, my father let himself be talked into expanding the business. Stakes got higher, more people got involved. Westor's sister, his father and two uncles were part of the expansion. Westor's sister died a few months ago. He thinks I turned her in. He wants to get even with me."

"So why was he holding a knife on me?"

"He saw us together. He won't hurt you, Amara. He likes to threaten, even role-play to some extent, but he's no killer. All he really wants to do is tell you about my sordid past."

"Ah. So he thinks…?" She moved a finger between them.

"It's how his mind works. You're a beautiful woman, you're with me, you must care."

A laugh tickled her throat. "What an intriguing line of reasoning." Unable to resist, she angled herself toward him. Close up, in a close space, with rain drumming on the metal roof and the windows of the RV steaming up, she suddenly found herself wanting to touch.

Somewhere inside, she knew she'd been struggling with these feelings since he'd tackled her in her grandmother's kitchen. Now here they were, all alone—well, more or less alone—in the mysterious north woods, and that struggle had become an all-out war.

She skimmed a suggestive finger over his jaw. "Tell me, McVey, just how perceptive is Westor?"

He curled the fingers of both hands lightly around her arms. "You don't want to start something with me, Amara. I can handle being a cop, but in every other way that matters, I'm a crappy risk."

The heat inside her cooled a little, but she held on to her smile. "Oh, good. So the wedding's off. Because right at

the top of my to-do list was the task of seducing the new
Raven's Cove police chief. Seduce, have sex, plan a rela-
tionship with, then ensnare for a lifelong commitment.
After all, McVey, we've known each other a whole twenty-
four hours now."

"Amara…"

"I'm not angry." But she was something, and seduction
no longer played into it. She pushed at one of his hands.
"I'm not upset either, or not very, which surprises me because I have a temper. Insulted, though. I'm definitely
that. And I promise you, in about five seconds, if you don't
let go of me, I'll work my way up to slapping your face."

"Look, you've been through a lot…"

"Yes, I have." Now she plucked his hands free one at a
time. "So much so that, using typical male logic, you've
decided I'm scared. Worse, you think I'm on the verge of
throwing myself into your arms, and when I do, you'll
feel obliged to protect me, because…well, hey, helpless
female." Her eyes chilled. "I'm not Yolanda, McVey. And,
yes, I know that sounds catty. It *is* catty, which must mean
I'm more upset than I realized. So my mistake for starting this, and now is really not a good time to touch me."

His expression took on a suspicious edge. "Are you
hysterical?"

She closed her eyes before giving in to a humorless
laugh. "I'd say I have every right to be, but I'm not. I'm—"
she spread her fingers "—no idea, actually. Irritated, I
suppose. Frustrated."

"Mentally, emotionally or sexually?"

Her next laugh was genuine. "Okay, we are not having
this conversation, right? Because, honest to God, it's way
too zigzaggy for me. You say we can't start anything, yet
you want to know if I'm sexually frustrated. If I say yes

or even maybe—square one. So I guess no would be the appropriate— What are you doing?"

"Something I don't often do, Red." He slid the fingers of his right hand from the side around to the back of her neck. Keeping his eyes on hers, he pulled her slowly forward. "I'm changing my mind."

She refused to be tempted. Or amused. But she did meet his eyes and fist the front of his shirt. "What you said before was valid, McVey. This shouldn't happen. I have stuff, too. A past. Baggage. An ex who expected me to fall in line with his plans."

"I don't expect." As he eased in closer, anticipation pulsed through her. "All I want is for you to do the same."

"I never expect." Because his mouth was almost on hers and, hello, this was what she'd wanted all along, Amara relaxed. It was only a kiss after all.

His thumb stroked the sensitive skin below her ear. Then suddenly his hand was in her hair, his mouth was covering hers and everything inside her flipped upside down.

A single word flashed in her head. *Trouble.* It repeated, over and over again, the same word.

And it had nothing to do with Jimmy Sparks's hit man.

McVey HADN'T MEANT to start anything, but now that he had, he couldn't stop. Couldn't think beyond the raging force of his needs.

One taste of her and he was hungry for more. Hell, he was ravenous. One touch and his brain shut down. He hadn't given up this much control since he was sixteen— more than half a lifetime ago. He'd grown jaded with time, cynical with experience—and rock hard in every possible way.

Her lips and hands yanked him right to the edge of his restraint. All he could think about was more. Of her. Of everything.

His tongue ravaged her mouth while his fingers teased the curve of her breasts.

"McVey…" She said his name as his lips slid over her jaw.

"Busy here, Red."

"I hear—music, I think."

He heard blood pounding in his head. And rain. Maybe thunder.

The pounding grew more insistent. From within it came a voice. And finally he heard the music, too.

Grasping her arms, he dragged his mouth free, swore and held them both still. "That's your phone, isn't it?"

"I can't tell. Maybe. Yes." She breathed deeply, in and out. "Yes." And turned to locate her jacket. "Someone's at the door."

He swore again, focused and heard the banging fist.

"McVey! Amara! Answer something! Phone, door, whatever!"

Amara dug out her phone and frowned. "Brigham?"

"Open the damn door!"

The latch jammed. In no mood to finesse the thing, McVey kicked the stuck metal panel until it flew outward. "What?" he demanded.

Brigham stuck a hand in, grabbed McVey's shirt and pointed with his cell. "One of the trailers fell off its blocks. The owner, Rune, went out to level it, and the whole edge of the ravine gave out. It took half the trailer down and trapped Rune underneath. I can't get to him. I'm too big and too heavy to shimmy down with a rope. But someone has to do something fast or he's a dead man."

McVey didn't think. He just took the jacket Amara shoved into his hands, said, "Show me" and went out to do his job.

THAT JOB HAD drawbacks and benefits, and McVey experienced both over the next two hours. It turned out that only Amara had been able to slide between the precariously balanced trailer and the rock wall that formed the outer edge of the ravine.

A chain of men and women had held the rope that had held him while he'd lowered her inch by inch toward the stuck man. She'd managed, after three failed attempts, to loop the end around his chest and pull it snug.

Braced just over the edge, McVey had seen her thumbs-up and pulled. Behind him, Brigham had provided a solid anchor, with everyone else holding him.

Rain had come down in sheets and caused them to slip more than once. But finally, after a grueling tug-of-war, the nightmare had ended. Several backslaps later—and after a stony once-over by a woman who looked like Mother Time—he and Amara found themselves in the well-camouflaged raven tamer barn.

Fires roared in a trio of woodstoves, tarps closed off the entire rear section and the Grateful Dead pumped from an old boom box at ear-splitting volume.

While Amara sat cross-legged on the slatted floor and put twenty stitches into the rescued man's leg, Brigham came over with two jugs of raven's blood and an assortment of mugs. He plunked his makeshift tray on a tree stump, uncorked the jugs with his teeth and poured double handed.

"Marta says you're 'common.' Means you're welcome in."

Chuckling, McVey took the mug Brigham thrust at him. "The logic being, if I'm welcome in, I'm less likely to bust anyone for whatever's behind those tarps. My guess is five or six stills and an illegal winery. Marta's a smart woman."

Brigham sampled the wine. "You don't live as long as she has by being dumb." He raised his voice, "You're common, too, Amara."

"I bet that's a first for a Bellam."

"It's a never-gonna-happen-again-Blume-blood-be-damned, so finish the patch job on Rune's leg and prepare to drink yourself stupid."

She cast an amused look in McVey's direction. "The logic being that on the off chance someone did follow us here, I'll be so ratted I won't care if my head gets blown off."

McVey sampled the bloodred wine—and found it surprisingly good. "Willy Sparks doesn't blow heads off, Amara. He'll toss you into the ravine, or try to. But he'll have to get past me and fifty raven tamers to do it." Raising his mug, and hoping like hell his system was up to the challenge, he grinned. "To being common."

THE BRIDGE WAS a nightmare. Willy made it back over, but shuddered in spasms until the lights of Raven's Hollow came into view.

The bitch was going to die in agony for this. The cop, too, for involving himself and making everything ten times harder than it should have been. Who played white knight in today's world? What kind of person put his or her own life on the line for a complete stranger? Yes, Amara was lovely, but they were talking life and death here. Cops didn't really want to die, did they?

Whether he did or not, McVey would be toast, right behind Amara Bellam. Unfortunately neither death would be taking place tonight. For the moment, they were on opposite sides of the bridge to hell.

So…what to do in Raven's Hollow that might be fun and end with a little consensual sex? When in doubt, the locals said, head to the Red Eye.

Gonna get me some tonight, Willy decided. And if the drink caused anything to slip out that shouldn't, well, more than cops and witnesses could be eliminated. What was it Uncle Jimmy liked to say? Practice made perfect.

Once again, Willy reflected, what better place to start than the Red Eye?

Chapter Eleven

"This isn't your fight, Annalee.…"

The words wound through Amara's head like bright silver threads that tangled into a ball and eventually turned black. She saw a pot—a cauldron?—and smelled coffee, but no way did she plan to drink it.

The scene shifted. Where was she now?

A raven with a pink beak sat in a duct-taped chair, filing its talons.

"You're so naive, Amara," it rasped. "I told you McVey was mine. Why didn't you listen? You never listen. You're headstrong. Just like Uncle Lazarus said." One of the talons snaked out to snare her wrist. "How hard did you make him laugh…?"

Another shift, and in the swirl of thoughts flooding her mind Amara saw a woman covered in black feathers. She had Hannah's waxen features—and her lifeless green eyes. Only her mouth, thin-lipped, chalky and trembling, moved.

"Why am I in this part of the manor? Why didn't I die in my own bed?"

Like a scenery screen yanked sideways on a stage, everything changed again. The black pot that had nothing to do with Hannah popped back in. Thick red liquid bubbled up, spilled over. A woman's hand reached inside, pulled something out, held it up to look.

Amara's breath stalled. Her heart gave a single hard thump.

The hand was hers. So was the face that stared in fascination at the…whatever it was. Some kind of dripping black root.

Lips that were hers, yet not hers, moved. A voice that was definitely not hers emerged.

"Evil spirit, good spirit—no and no. Man becomes raven, yes, but the spirits that bring this transformation about are human, in action and in form. You will remember nothing of this night, Annalee…"

Amara woke with a suppressed hiss and every muscle in her body clenched like a fist. Who the hell was Annalee, and why did the name sound so familiar?

Falling back on Brigham's lumpy mattress, she regarded the dented ceiling and tried to decide if she was feeling the aftereffects of the raven's blood wine she'd consumed last night or reacting to the dream it must have spawned.

"Did you scream?"

The unexpected question had her wincing before she levered up onto her elbow.

Well, hell, her bleary mind sighed. McVey, wearing jeans and nothing else, filled the doorway of what could only be called a bedroom by virtue of the fact that there was a bed in it. One bed, four thin walls and now an überhot cop on the threshold.

"I'm, um…"

She'd seen a half-dressed man before, right? Maybe not one who was quite so sleek and sexy, who wore his hair too long and whose sleepy eyes didn't look entirely awake, but still…

"Did you see something?" he asked. "Someone? A pink elephant?"

Amara wondered vaguely if she was wearing anything. "I think I'm good." She glanced down. Nope, not a stitch. "I had a dream. A very bizarre dream."

"Doesn't everyone who drinks devil's blood?"

"Raven's blood."

"Devil's whiskey, then."

Holding the sheet to her breasts, she regarded him with a blend of surprise and amusement. "You drank their whiskey, too—and you can walk?"

"Not especially well right now, but it'll come back to me." He'd set his hands on the door frame above his head. Whatever his condition, his dark eyes gleamed when he spied the arm banded across her chest. "This is the strangest hangover I've ever lived through, Red. I keep seeing ravens in my head. Beautiful talking ravens."

"That's because we saw talking ravens last night. Preview of coming attractions. Pretty sure they weren't real. I remember them having red eyes." She released a slow breath, rolled her head. "That wine has a wicked kick."

"You could say." McVey's pressed briefly on his eyelids. "If my brain goes south—very likely at this point—remind me when we're back on our side of the bridge to contact Lieutenant Michaels's captain as well as the county lab. If there was poison in Michaels or the coffee, I want to know about it."

"Happy thought. On a brighter note, Brigham says the raven tamers are going to do their Main Street Kickoff-to-the-Night parade on Friday."

"Yeah, I got the memo. Now that I'm 'common,' Marta informs me I'm honor bound not to notice what they'll be selling at the end-of-parade market. Or at what she's calling the preparade teaser on Thursday"

"The tamers will sell what they sell, McVey, with or without your approval. They've never had any trouble getting around Ty. And yes, I know, you're not Ty. Making you 'common' doesn't mean they'll be overt, only that they won't feel the need to post sentries. Anyway, I feel better knowing they're on our side. Now, having said that, can I please get up?"

He dropped his hands, grinned. "If you can't, I'll be more than happy to help you."

A rush of heat, Amara reflected, should not consume her because of a single suggestive remark. In fact, sex should be the furthest thing from her mind. She twirled a finger for him to turn, then stopped and nodded forward. "I believe your jeans are beeping, Chief. One, two, three, pause. One, two, three, pause…"

"You can stop the count, Red." He pulled his phone out and tapped the screen. "It's Westor."

Curious, Amara bundled the sheet around her body and scooted off the bed. "Why's he contacting you?"

"He wants to meet me tonight at the Red Eye."

"Are you sure he's not a killer?"

"He never was." McVey shrugged. "Doesn't mean he can't be bought."

She glanced through the bedroom window at the dissipating morning mist. "Why does this side of Bellam Bridge suddenly seem a lot safer to me than it did last night?"

Capturing her chin with his thumb and forefinger, McVey dropped a light kiss on her lips. "Don't get too comfortable here, Red. My observations at the manor told me that although a blow to the head was in fact responsible for Hannah Blume's death, that blow wasn't inflicted by a fall. Someone hit her."

IT GOT CRAZIER by the minute. Who would want to kill a harmless hermit of a woman?

"I'm going with a Bellam as the perp." Scowling fiercely, Jake strode back and forth at the Raven's Hollow police station. "There are loony bands of them all over the north woods. Tell me you're not thinking the same thing, McVey."

"I'm not thinking anything perp-wise. All I said was that Hannah Blume didn't fall and hit her head."

"Which you know because?" Amara asked.

He glanced up from his computer. "Any way you spin it, Red, the body position was wrong. You said yourself the blow would have killed her instantly. Means she dropped like a stone—in this case parallel to, yet away from, the corner of the counter where we found the dried blood. The facts contradict themselves."

A muscle in Jake's jaw jerked. "This bites, McVey."

Amara paced away from him. "Be glad you don't have to tell Uncle Lazarus. Be equally glad you haven't been forced to cross Bellam Bridge twice in eighteen hours. There must be another way on and off that mountain."

"Why don't you ask your new raven tamer friends?" Jake sneered. "If there's another way, they'll know about it."

She stopped pacing to frown. "Why the hostility? You're related to most of them."

"They tame ravens. That's unnatural. They brew hooch. That's illegal." He planted his hands on the desk across from McVey. "What I want to know is why we're not questioning them about Hannah's death."

"Because." McVey looked past him to Amara. "Coffee's

a negative, Red, and the forensic team on Michaels's case is still testing for toxins."

She pushed on a pressure point in her neck. "You have to figure it won't be an easy find. I need to talk to Uncle Lazarus."

"His nephew who lives with him—R.J., I think—said he was in Bangor and wouldn't be taking calls while he was gone."

"I wasn't planning to tell him about Hannah on the phone, McVey. I'll wait at his place until he gets back."

"R.J. said he might be late."

She faced him, dropped her hands. "You want me to go to the clinic, don't you?"

"It'll keep you busy."

"It'll keep me surrounded with patients."

"Patients and my deputy."

Amara told herself not to laugh at Jake's expression, which was equal parts outrage and horror.

"I've got work, McVey, over in the Cove." Jake's voice lowered. "I don't want to be around a bunch of sick people."

"You're assuming, Jake, that a bunch of sick people will magically discover there's a doctor on the premises and come flooding in."

"Word spreads fast."

"Like measles." McVey turned his attention back to Amara. "Ever since his electrical panel bit the dust six months ago, Lazarus has been living at the old Raven's Nest Motel off the even older inland highway. There's nothing else out that way."

Amara drew a mental map. "Isn't his sister's house out that way?"

"His late sister's abandoned house. The last guest at the motel signed the register back in March. He stayed for two nights and tried to skip without paying."

A nasty smile split Jake's face. "I remember that. We had us a high-speed chase that ended with him sideswiping a tree. Guy was tanked. Kept threatening to sue the tree for damages." He snickered. "As if a 1972 Pacer with bald tires and rust everywhere you looked was worth spit."

Amara rubbed her arms now. "So fond reminiscence aside, and getting back on topic, you're determined that I should hang around town for the rest of the day."

"I'm meeting the county sheriff in ninety minutes," McVey told her. "Meeting'll last at least two hours. Lazarus might or might not be home for dinner, word does spread, and as a reward for clinic duty, Jake'll be happy to hear I want him to spend the better part of his evening shift at the Red Eye."

The deputy's mouth, open to object, closed with a snap. "I guess that'll partly make up for the sickies." He stuck out a warning finger. "But I better not get measles."

Amara's eyes sparkled. "I'll give you a shot, Jake. It'll stop those measles germs in their tracks. Unless your immune system's really weak."

"Well...what if it is?"

McVey came around his desk. "Life holds few guarantees, Deputy, but here's one you can count on. Anything happens to Red between now and the next time I see her, you'll be covered in red spots. And they won't be the kind that go away."

WORD DIDN'T SO much spread as erupt. From early afternoon to early evening, Amara poked, prodded and treated more than twenty-five people, including her second cousin Two Toes Joe, who owned a dockside bar in Raven's Cove and did indeed possess only two toes on his right foot.

"Shot myself," he'd revealed, and wiggled his remaining digits. "Never point a gun at your foot if folks nearby are throwing punches. One bad bump, and *bam*."

Having offered those words of wisdom, he'd dropped his pants and showed her his hernia.

The upside of being overrun was that time passed very quickly. Jake sulked, balked and avoided anyone who so much as coughed, but he did as ordered and stayed put in the waiting room until the last patient left.

"You tell McVey I deserve to be carried out of the Red Eye singing, Amara. Any fights break out on account of the Night or because people are as thick as twenty bricks about Hezekiah and how he came to be cursed, it's for him to handle."

"I'll pass it along."

"I don't know what all the fighting's about anyway," he grumbled. "Story's simple as Owen the Sky is Falling's brain. Nola Bellam should have stayed in the Hollow where she belonged. It wasn't Hezekiah's fault she flirted with Ezekiel and made him want her, too. And it sure as hell wasn't Hezekiah's fault he went a little crazy after Ezekiel raped her."

"So crazy that an evil spirit, who just happened to be in the vicinity, decided to help him out."

"That story's been accepted as true for a lot of years, Amara. Until some glory-seeking Bellam came along and challenged it. Put the power—good and bad—in the hands of a bunch of witches."

She smiled. "As I recall, your brother believes in that power, Jake."

"Because you scared him with your phony stories."

She packed up her instruments, said goodbye to the midwife in charge and exited the clinic ahead of him. "Guess we'll never know whether those stories were phony or the real deal, will we, seeing as Jimbo decided not to shove me off that cliff." She glanced up and around at the fog that had been rolling in for the past hour. "This stuff's getting thicker by the minute."

"It'll be pea soup before I'm done with my second glass of whiskey. Which won't be long, as the first'll be going down in a great big gulp."

"If we were talking raven tamer whiskey, you'd be the one going down, Jake—onto the floor and under the table. Do you know if McVey's back from the sheriff's office yet?"

"He's back." His expression sour, Jake walked beside her toward the noisy bar. "He said for us to meet him inside— Aw, damn, is that Lazarus going through the door?"

Amara laughed. "Oh, come on, Jake. You know Uncle Lazarus wouldn't make the same mistake…" Her denial evaporated as the fog parted to reveal Lazarus Blume's unmistakable profile. "Okay, that's me shocked."

"This night's getting crappier by the minute." Jake yanked the door open. "McVey's over talking to the bartender. I'm gonna find me a nice dark corner and crawl into it with a bottle. Let me know when the old spook of spooks leaves." With that, he vanished into the shadows.

The room was hot, crowded to the point of being barely navigable, and although Amara managed to keep McVey in sight, she lost her uncle in the first few seconds.

McVey met her halfway across the floor. "Where's Jake?" he asked above thundering Steven Earl.

"Far corner, near the washrooms." She grinned as he scouted the room. "He stuck at the clinic all afternoon, McVey, even when a seventysomething woman showed him a collection of truly hideous boils on her inner thigh."

He continued to search, but she saw his lips curve. "I'm

not looking for Jake. I'm trying to find Westor. Could be he'll go with a disguise."

"And now we add in a disguise. Does he have a favorite look?"

"He pulls off a decent old man."

"Maybe he's posing as Uncle Lazarus. Jake and I thought we saw him come in."

"He did. He's got a mad on at Yolanda. Something about cost overruns and breakage. She hightailed it. Your uncle's expression suggested her head was going to roll."

"How could you tell? His expression never changes." Not expecting an answer, Amara lifted the hair from her neck to cool it. "How did it go with the sheriff?"

"We're heading up to Bellam Manor tomorrow with full forensic and medical teams."

"Oh. That's good, I guess." Her forehead creased. "Why do I feel left out?"

"No idea. You're part of the medical team."

"I'm— What?" Mistrust swept the mild sting aside. "McVey, you know I'm not a forensic specialist. You just want me where you can see me."

"See you, feel you, touch you, Red." He draped an arm over her shoulders as the music changed from "Copperhead Road" to "Beast of Burden."

"What say we hijack a corner booth and make out until Westor shows?"

As ideas went, Amara liked it.

Or she did until glass crashed, someone screamed and the whole right side of the bar burst into flames.

WILLY HAD LEARNED from experience never to be surprised. Not by anything or anyone. But this was a shocker, and while it made no sense on the surface, logic said there had to be a reason.

Unless the person across the alley was clinically insane.

It took no more than that second of puzzled immobility for the perpetrator to turn and hesitate as Willy did. To snap an arm up as Willy did.

To shoot as Willy did....

Chapter Twelve

Fire shot from floor to ceiling. People panicked and bolted. Drinks spilled and fed the flames.

McVey knew which direction the stampede would take. He also knew the main door was already fully involved. Shouldn't be, not so rapidly, but was. Meaning this blaze had been carefully planned and executed.

He heard a bang to his right and shoved Amara down. The bartender vaulted out of harm's way as the bottled stock behind him began to crash and burn.

Amara fought the arm that restrained her. "There's an exit at the end of the corridor near the washrooms, and a delivery door in the storeroom behind the bar." She dipped down again as smoke began to blacken the air. "I think I see Uncle Lazarus. I'll get him and as many other people as possible out through the washroom corridor exit."

When a man rushing to escape knocked Lazarus Blume into a table, McVey gave up. Amara wasn't helpless, and he couldn't do it all.

"If you see Jake, tell him about the delivery door." He kissed her once, hard, then ran for the fire extinguisher on the far wall and hoped to God the cylinder was full.

AMARA KNEW SMOKE killed more effectively than fire. She used the sleeve of her jacket to cover her mouth. To reach her uncle, she had to dodge tables and chairs and at the same time try to round up as many terrified people as possible.

It didn't help that a number of them already had several drinks under their belts or that the ones who'd been playing pool were swinging their cues to clear a path through the crowd.

"Uncle Lazarus." She bent to peer at his face. "Are you hurt?"

He was doubled over a chair, gripping the back as if it were a lifeline. "Winded," he wheezed.

She wrapped an arm around his waist. "Come with me." Her voice rose. "Listen, everyone. There's a door this way. We can get out."

Slowed by her uncle's weight, she nevertheless managed to direct at least twenty people toward the little-used exit.

Her legs wanted to buckle. Lazarus Blume was not a small man, and the smoke he'd inhaled was taking its toll.

In the corridor, Yolanda burst out of the women's washroom. Half a dozen expressions raced across her face when she smelled the smoke and heard the commotion. "What's going on? What was that bang?"

"Fire in the front." Amara winced when her uncle stepped on her foot. "Help me with Uncle Lazarus."

"I can manage." Regaining his balance, he took some of his weight back.

Amara was about to release him when the people who'd rushed past them earlier backpedaled in a panic.

"Door's burning," one of the men shouted.

"We're trapped," his companion wailed.

Were they? Amara looked around her uncle at Yolanda. "Are there windows in the washrooms?"

"No—or, yes. But they're really skinny."

"We'll have to squeeze. This way," Amara said, giving

her uncle over to Benny the pharmacist. "Let the smaller people go first in case someone bigger gets stuck."

"I twisted my knee." An inebriated woman in painted-on jeans hobbled along the wall. "I can't climb."

"She goes last," Yolanda decided.

"We go last," Amara countered. "It's our uncle's bar."

"It was." Her cousin waved at the choking smoke. "Tomorrow it'll be ashes. What the hell happened? Did the gas oven blow?"

"Some kind of bomb came through the side window, I think." Amara raised her voice again. "Benny, if it's stuck, break the glass."

A few seconds later a toilet seat crashed through the window.

People climbed, crawled, wedged and wiggled through the narrow opening. When she was sure they'd reached the alley safely, Amara returned to the corridor. No way was McVey going to die because of her.

She spied Jake farther along the hall. He was hunkered down with his hand on a black pack. He surged to his feet when he spotted her—and was immediately engulfed in smoke.

Before she could take another step, Amara found herself flying—through a door and onto a tiled floor. The impact stunned her, but not as badly as the explosion in the hallway outside. The hallway she'd been standing in two seconds earlier.

McVey MADE SURE Amara was unharmed, then, ignoring her protests, lifted her through the bathroom window. After one last foray into the inferno that was the Red Eye, he made his own escape via the smoldering delivery door.

On its own, the fog was a swirling curtain of white.

Add in plumes of black smoke and the scene around the bar went from grim to macabre.

It took several hours for volunteer firefighters to extinguish the flames.

McVey instructed the Harden twins to gather anyone in need of assistance at the clinic. Paramedics came from Bangor to help Amara treat the injured—some who'd been burned, but more, McVey suspected, who'd hurt themselves during their frantic flight.

Once the site had been taped, he posted four deputized guards and, accepting he'd done all he could, joined what Jake sarcastically referred to as "the major players" at Lazarus's Raven's Nest Motel.

They'd agreed to gather there for the simple reason that Lazarus took medication to control an erratic heartbeat and he hadn't brought it with him.

As roadside accommodations went, McVey had seen worse. On his final stakeout in New York, he'd woken up eyeball to eyeball with a rat twice the size of his fist, in a room so badly infested with cockroaches they'd crunched when he'd walked across the sagging floor.

Oh, yeah, Band-Aid-colored walls, brown carpet and a kitchenette straight out of the seventies was paradise compared to Cockroach Central.

While Louis Armstrong rasped out a tinny blues song, Lazarus sat in a straight-backed chair and listened without interruption as Amara told him about Hannah. She didn't use the word *murder,* but McVey knew they'd have to deal with that hard truth, as well. Eventually.

When she walked past him en route to her medical bag, he stopped her. "Is your uncle okay?"

"About Hannah? I can't tell. Probably not." She jabbed his stomach. "You know, you could have shouted instead of tackling me into the men's room at the Red Eye. I have excellent reflexes."

"No time." He repositioned the makeshift ice pack she'd given him when he came in—ice cubes wrapped in a towel—flexed his bruised right arm to make sure he still could and shot Jake a dark look. "I told you not to disturb any suspicious objects."

"Since when's a backpack suspicious?" Jake retorted.

"This particular pack was propped against a door with a wire running between it and the knob. In the cop world, we call that suspicious."

Lazarus batted Amara's hand away when she attempted to unbutton his jacket. "I'm not feeble, niece. I took my heart pill. It's ticking just fine." He narrowed his eyes at McVey. "Are you saying someone planted an explosive device in the rear corridor?"

"In the rear corridor, behind the bar, under one of the pool tables, above the front door. Some were on timers. Others were rigged to blow if moved."

"In other words," Lazarus said, "we're dealing with a mass murderer."

Amara plucked a piece of glass from his collar. "That murderer has a name, Uncle. It's Willy Sparks."

Seated on the floor, knees pulled up, arms tightly folded around them, Yolanda speared Amara with a vicious look. "This is your fault. You brought it here. Danger. Death. Bombs. And now, because we were all shaken and stupid and wanted to get out of town in case the whole main street blew up, we rushed to the back of beyond—no offense, Uncle Lazarus—to try to sort out what most of us already knew but were too rattled to realize until we got here."

"She means we're sitting ducks." Jake flung an angry arm. "And damn it, she's right. Who says this Willy Sparks person you told us about won't decide to come barreling through the front window in a truck loaded with explosives?"

"He does that, he'll be dead right along with us." Lazarus searched his pockets. "I need a pink pill. R.J. knows where all my medications are. Where is he?"

"I sent him up to the roof." McVey watched the fog. "He won't see anything coming, but he might hear it."

"He's a good man." Lazarus patted his inside pockets. "Ex-army. I was sure I brought them with me."

"You take two kinds of heart medication?" Amara asked.

"I take antacid, the pink kind, when I eat shellfish for dinner." His shoulders slumped. "I was fond of Hannah in my way. She amused me with tales about Hezekiah and his transformation when I was young. When I got a little older, she taught me to play chess on the raven board her grandfather carved by hand and passed down to her."

Amara rubbed his arm. "I'll check the medicine cabinet for that antacid."

Unable to see through the fog, McVey followed her to the bathroom.

"Who lives in a motel?" She yanked the mirrored cabinet door over the sink open and almost off its hinges. "Before you answer, McVey, I know his home electrical panel shorted out."

He rested a shoulder on the door frame. "Good electricians are hard to find, Red."

The quick play of emotions on her face fascinated him. It also made him hungry for another taste of her. He bridged the gap between them in half a stride, cupped the back of her head and brought her gaze up to his. "This isn't your fault, Amara."

A hollow smile grazed her lips. "Of course it is. I ran

and hid, or tried to, in a place where people I love live. It wouldn't have been much of a brain strain for Jimmy Sparks to have considered the possibly and send his— whatever Willy is—to Maine to check it out. And wonder of wonders, here I am."

"That's Yolanda talking. And Jake. Yes, word does spread quickly in small towns, but from what I've heard about your day, no one who came to the clinic was worried that he or she would be taking a bullet on your behalf. Story I got was that you were swamped."

"That's just people in need weighing risk against discomfort and deciding that a few minutes of the first are worth a lessening of the second." She wrapped her fingers around his wrist. "Are you sure nobody was killed tonight?"

"Firefighters went through the wreckage, Amara. There were no bodies. You and the paramedics patched up eleven people who were cut by flying glass and three who suffered minor burns. No one showed any serious signs of smoke inhalation, and I've seen more scrapes and bruises after a weekend bar brawl than I did tonight."

"Hmm." Taking his hand from her face, she hunted through the medicine cabinet for antacid tablets. She found them behind two large vials and an old-fashioned shaving brush. Staring at the bristles, she said, "Why would Willy blow up an entire bar, McVey? It's out of character—if he has a character." A breath shuddered out. "I want him to stop."

"I know."

"Do you think that's the point? He's pissed off because he wants the job done and it's not getting done?"

"Maybe." McVey prevented her from leaving by trapping her arms as she tried to pass him. "You're forgetting something, Amara."

"Pretty sure I'm not."

"Hannah." He said it simply and had the satisfaction of seeing her eyes snap to his. "Willy Sparks didn't kill her. The time frame's off and, like the bar fire tonight, so's the M.O."

She let her forehead fall against his shoulder. He thought she probably wanted to bang it there. "I'm so confused. It's as if there's this huge disco ball in my brain where thoughts, ideas, facts, you name it, bounce off the mirrored pieces into the dark. How am I supposed to collect and process all of them?"

He kissed her hair. "Collecting and processing is my job, Red. You treat cuts and burns and make the world a prettier place."

"Is that a crack about the surgeries I perform?"

"Nope, it's an observation." He tipped her head up and kissed her just long enough to make himself hard. Not the brightest thing he could have done. Stepping back, he kissed her one more time and said, "It's way past late. I have a lot of rubble to dig through in the morning and a mountain to scale in the afternoon."

She regarded him through her lashes. "What aren't you telling me, McVey?"

"I can't answer that until I find out what Westor didn't tell me. I'm not holding my breath it'll be worth anything, but you never know. In the meantime, you know the drill."

A reluctant smile appeared. "Bet you wish you'd stayed in New York."

"Trust me, Amara. An unarmed midnight stroll through Central Park would be a piece of cake compared to this mess." He nodded at the bottle in her hand. "Take those to your uncle. It's time we headed back to your grandmother's place. Instincts I've learned to trust, but don't necessarily like, are telling me tomorrow could be a day worse than anything either of your ancestral families ever faced."

IF HIS INSTINCTS were even half-correct, Amara wanted no part of the coming day. Not the postdawn tromp around the blackened shell of her uncle's bar, and definitely not the trip up Bellam Mountain to fetch Hannah Blume's body down to Raven's Cove.

It relieved her that the morning promised good weather. Somewhere between the time they'd left the motel and that lovely moment when she'd toppled facedown onto her bed, the fog had rolled out to sea. It said a great deal about her state of exhaustion, Amara reflected, that she hadn't performed her habitual when-in-Grandma's-house spider check before she fell.

Not trusting the sunny weather to hold, she dressed in snug jeans, comfortable hiking boots, a white tank and a scarlet jacket. Birds and deer got shot in the woods. She didn't intend to.

McVey wisely suggested they buy their morning coffee at a nearby filling station en route to the Hollow. Until they'd taken their first sips, neither of them spoke beyond a grunt. Then reality slithered in.

Pulling herself onto the running board, Amara regarded McVey over the top of his truck. "Am I right in thinking that you're thinking the same person who killed Hannah might have planted those explosives at the Red Eye?"

McVey set his coffee cup on the roof to shrug out of his jacket. "I'm thinking lots of things, Red. That's one of them."

"Score one for the noncop." She waited a beat before asking, "Why?"

"Because, as you said last night, murdering a room

full of innocent people isn't Jimmy Sparks's M.O. He's all about family. His own first and foremost, but word has it, he's very discriminating when it comes to murder. Choose a target, hit a target. Deviate when necessary, but order Willy to blow up a bar filled with people who might or might not be related to you? Not his style."

"Plus, Willy couldn't have been sure I'd be there, and several of those devices must have been planted either before or shortly after the Red Eye opened. Bringing me full circle to totally confused."

"You're not alone." He flipped his sunglasses down, climbed in. "Let's go find some answers."

Amara was fastening her seat belt when she heard the distant report of a rifle.

Hunters was her first thought. But two more blasts followed by a pause, followed by three more blasts and another pause had prickly knots forming in her stomach.

Before the final three shots sounded, McVey had the truck started and the front end pointed back toward her grandmother's house.

When he braked at the edge of the woods, Amara turned to face him. "Don't even think about telling me to stay here."

"Not planning to. I'm guessing those shots came from the tortured oaks. Gun." He pointed to the glove box, then climbed out and, with his Glock shoved in his waistband, removed an AK-47 rifle from the locked box in the back.

Fear skated along Amara's spine. "Okay, so...not taking any chances."

"Not anymore. Stay right on my heels, Amara. Anyone comes up behind you, spin and shoot. Can you do that?"

"It goes against the Hippocratic oath, but yes, I can."

"You've got balls, Red." He used the rifle to gesture. "This way."

They left the main trail almost immediately and forged their own faster path through the trees. At one point, Amara found herself knee-deep in brush on terrain only a goat would deem traversable.

The shots were much closer when they repeated—less than fifty yards to her left.

The tortured oaks, the personification of agonized death, came into sight behind a clump of pines. Nothing and no one stirred in the small clearing. Stray beams of sunlight sliced through the pointed rocks like crossed swords.

McVey went down on one knee. Amara knelt beside him and strained to hear what she couldn't see.

"There's a lot of birdsong," she noted. "Animals scrabbling. Insects chirping." Closing her eyes, she took a deep breath and held it.

She caught a rustle and under it, a barely audible moan. "There." Opening her eyes, she touched McVey's arm. "In the scrub behind the second oak."

He didn't question, merely reached for his Glock and used it to draw an invisible arc from their current position to the tree.

Birds tweeting for mates masked their footsteps. Amara willed her heart to stop its frantic thudding. Hyperventilating wouldn't help the situation.

The scrub shifted. She heard a cough. Gurgly, she thought, and kept her gun angled skyward.

"I don't think he's baiting us," she whispered. "He has fluid in his lungs."

With the tip of his rifle, McVey parted the bushes. She spied a gleam of metal before he blocked her from sight with his body.

"Drop it, Westor," he warned, "or you're a dead man."

Propped against the base of a chestnut tree, Westor let out a wet laugh and lowered his arms.

"Not a problem, old friend." Blood glistened on his teeth when he smiled. "I'm a dead man already."

Chapter Thirteen

"I need my medical bag."

But even as Amara started to stand, McVey slung the rifle over his shoulder and prevented her from leaving. "It's too late."

Helplessness clawed at her. "There must be something we can do." She tore at the bloody front of Westor's shirt—and knew the moment she saw the wound that McVey was right. The hole, less than an inch below the man's heart, oozed blood every time he coughed.

McVey stopped his head from lolling. "Talk to me, Westor." A firm shake kept him from slipping under. "Come on, old friend, don't let whoever did this to you get away with it."

Westor's eyes rolled. "The alley...it was... Oh, man. Hurts like a bitch. Hot knives, you know?" He clutched McVey's arm. "Bury me with mine," he said clearly.

"Try not to move," Amara told him gently. He slumped back, smiled again and set his half-open eyes on her face. "Never be a witness..." The words slurred and overlapped. He trailed off, still smiling.

"He's dead." Amara double-checked the pulse in his neck. "I'm sorry, McVey."

"I imagine he is, too."

"He mentioned an alley. If he meant the alley behind

or beside the Red Eye, it would have taken him hours to get here from there. I mean, he obviously did it, but…"

"Yeah. But." McVey closed Westor's eyes. "Do you have a signal on your cell?"

She checked. "No."

"We'll have to leave him. I'll contact the sheriff from my truck, tell him to bring extra men. The Hardens are on duty in the Hollow today. Dean, my junior deputy, can handle the Cove."

Amara stood. "Do you think this is Willy Sparks's or our mysterious other killer's doing?"

"I'm leaning toward the mysterious other myself."

"He's starting to terrify me more than Willy." She stared down at Westor. "How is that possible?"

McVey set a hand on the back of her neck and gave her a reassuring squeeze. "There's a reason for everything that's happening, Amara. It's a matter of connecting one dot to the next and seeing if we're looking at a single large picture or two smaller ones."

Amara said nothing, just watched in thoughtful silence as a raven swooped down to perch on a broken branch.

In Raven's Cove, three raven's feathers placed on a door meant the person to whom the door belonged was destined to die. She didn't know what a staring raven might mean. She only knew this was the second time she'd noticed one watching her.

And her Blume blood recognized the potential significance of this one doing so from a point directly above a dead man's head.

LESS THAN AN hour later McVey was wading through the scorched debris that had once been the Red Eye. Little remained of the bar except the walls, and the chief inspector had declared them to be highly unstable. No one would be allowed near the burn area.

Businesses on both sides had suffered major smoke and water damage. That meant there'd be no barber service or Chinese takeout in the foreseeable future.

After a long chat with the inspector, McVey posted guards in shifts and went in search of Amara at the clinic. She'd gone there when seven-months-pregnant Megan Bellam—undoubtedly a cousin—had asked her for more detailed medical advice than the midwife could supply.

Amara was drying her hands on a towel as he came in. "If you've got a crappy mood going, McVey, listen to a baby's heartbeat and all's well with the world. Megan's having a girl."

"Nola's line or Sarah's?"

"Nola's. In an ode to Edgar Allan, plus the fact that her daddy's got Blume blood, they're going to call her Lenore."

"Excellent news on all fronts. Now, at the risk of bursting your baby-heartbeat bubble, it's time for us to gear up and head out."

"From death to life to death." She hoisted her medical bag onto her shoulder. "Will we be spending the night on Bellam Mountain?"

He let her precede him through the clinic door and into the brilliant May sunshine. "Depends how the investigation unfolds. If it's down to you and me, we can stay at Hannah's. There are some fairly cool rooms in her wing."

"I'm told she was a fairly cool woman. Sort of Katherine Hepburn-esque in her prime."

"More Mother Goose-ish in her later years."

"I think the Mother Goose comparison came from the fact that she made up kiddie rhymes about the local legends. I only remember one—

'Red eyes, black feathers. Once a man,

But now a raven. Evil can
No longer feed on wretched soul,
And yet shall ever take its toll
On Hezekiah Blume. And all
Who share his blood, will share his fall....'"

"I wouldn't call that especially kiddie-like."

"It is if you live in the Cove or the Hollow. Did you talk to the sheriff about Westor?"

McVey nodded. "He's sending some people to retrieve the body. We didn't kill him, Amara. Remember that. And whoever did will pay." When his phone beeped, he reached into his jeans, pulled it out and hit Speaker. "What is it, Jake?"

"It's a pair of frigging feet's what it is. I was moving a nosy Parker along and he tripped. Fell on some trash bags. He started flailing because they smelled bad. When he got clear's when I saw the feet." Jake's voice tightened. "They ain't moving, McVey, and they ain't the right color, either. I'm thinking we got us a corpse."

SHE'D BEEN UP since 6:00 a.m., Amara reflected. Barely four hours. And already two people were dead.

She spotted Jake squatting in a sea of green trash bags and carefully made her way with McVey into the side alley.

"Report, Deputy," McVey said as they got closer.

Her cousin looked up. "She's dead."

Amara skirted him, hoping for a clearer view.

"Her face is familiar." Jake screwed his own up. "I just can't place it."

"Mina." Amara knelt beside the body. "That's her name. Mina Shell. She was in the pharmacy the day Westor grabbed me. He grabbed her, too...." She bent closer. "What's that in her hand?"

McVey shifted the green bag that partially covered the

woman's right arm. "A rag stuffed in a bottle. It's a Molotov cocktail. The one that started the fire was tossed through the window at the street end of the alley."

Puffing hard, the sheriff, a short, potbellied man, joined them. "Is this the firebomber, then?"

Because she was closest, Amara sniffed the rag. Over the odor of rotting trash, she caught the distinct smell of gasoline. "I am so lost." She sighed. "Mina said she came here for the Night of the Raven, but what she really intended to do was blow up the Red Eye? Why?"

"Gonna have to leave that one for now, Red." McVey moved more of the bags. "She's wearing a watch on her right wrist. And her left thumbnail's shorter than the right, possibly for texting purposes. She could be left-handed."

"What difference does that make?" Jake frowned when McVey didn't answer. "Does it make a difference?"

Amara sat back. "She's holding the bottle in her right hand, Jake. If she planned to throw it, shouldn't it be in her left?"

"You saying it was put there after she was dead?" Jake's frown deepened. "By who?"

"Whoever firebombed the Red Eye." McVey shrugged. "Theoretically."

Amara thought back to the pharmacy. "I think—I'm not sure, but I think—Mina reached for the lipstick with her left hand. Having said that, of course, she might have been holding the bomb in one hand with the intention of switching it to and throwing it with the other."

McVey ran his gaze over the body. "I only see one entry wound. One shot, middle of her throat. Someone knows how to kill quickly and efficiently."

"Someone like Willy Sparks." Amara assumed. She rubbed a sudden chill from her arms. "Westor said, 'Never be a witness.' He must have seen this happen, or certainly something that happened here last night."

Jake slashed a hand in front of him. "Wait a minute. Are we saying this woman did or didn't throw the first Molotov cocktail through the window?"

"We're saying we don't know who did what to whom, when or in what order. Yet." McVey regarded the portly sheriff. "It's your call, Walt. Do you want to stay here with this or make the trip up to Bellam Manor?"

"Best if I stay and you take the teams up. I'm a damn sight better at solving murders than I am at navigating shaky bridges."

While they talked, Amara regarded Mina's lifeless body. Three people were dead, and only one of those deaths made any kind of sense to her.

Like Hannah's, Mina's glassy eyes looked up at nothing. Her mouth hung open and there was a smear of pink lipstick on her upper teeth.

Had she and Westor simply been in the wrong place at the wrong time? Had they been in that place separately or together? Stranger things had happened, and for all his leers and lewd remarks, Westor had been a hot-looking man. Maybe Mina had slept with him— And where the hell, Amara wondered, was she going with that idea?

Not a cop, she reminded herself.

She tuned back in when McVey came up behind her.

"Time to roll, Red. The sheriff's got this one. We're down a few people on each team, but we'll manage. Hannah's death needs investigating as much as Mina's."

"And Westor's."

"His, too." McVey held her gaze. "I don't want anyone else winding up in the morgue."

Amara nodded. She needed quite badly to believe that no one else would die. But in her mind, she saw the raven watching her from a branch above Westor's body while a dead man's last words echoed eerily in her head.

Never be a witness....

THE DRIVE UP Bellam Mountain was nothing next to the step-and-cling crossing of Bellam Bridge. McVey took the less-encumbered team members up the steep stone path. Amara and the others made the longer trek to the manor via the twisty access road.

The unseasonably hot day had turned out muggier than expected. McVey hadn't moved Hannah's body, and the central kitchen's windows faced north. It would have received a strong dose of morning sun.

A note from Brigham on the door told him the big raven tamer had been watching the manor. No one had come near the place or attempted to disturb the body, making it unlikely in McVey's opinion that they'd find a murder weapon. Still, procedure dictated that a full-scale search be undertaken.

Amara arrived twenty minutes later. She wore his Dodgers baseball cap, oversize sunglasses and had her jacket tied around her waist. His blood did a lot more than stir when she herded her group into the manor and he caught the subtle scent of her perfume.

This was death and a decomposing body. He had no business thinking about Amara's soft skin, her silky hair or how her mouth would taste. And it seemed just plain weird to wonder what it would feel like to make love to her in the grass next to the pond they'd passed the other night on the way to the raven tamers' camp.

Thankfully, his iPhone beeped as the last few team members passed between them. He kept his eyes on Amara's face when he answered on speaker. "More problems, Jake?"

"We can't find her purse."

McVey had to kick-start his brain. *Her* could only be Mina Shell. "How large an area have you searched?"

"Most of the alley. Sheriff made me call up to Blume House. She's not registered there."

"She could have been camping."

"Maybe, but not at the Ravenspell campsite."

"Run her name through the DMV, see what comes up. Has Westor's body been recovered yet?"

"Just." The deputy grunted. "Think I might know where he was flopping. There's an empty apartment in Yolanda's building. Turns out maybe she wasn't harboring a fugitive after all. The lock on the empty place was jimmied, and the Hardens found stuff on the floor. Food wrappers, wine bottles, sleeping bags, a .30-30 rifle, a couple boxes of bullets."

"Dust for prints and keep me informed about the woman." McVey signed off. "What?" he asked when he saw Amara drawing an air picture.

"I'm thinking back." Her brows came together. "She didn't have paper or a pen. I tore off a sheet of paper and gave it to her. That's when Westor grabbed me—us."

"And translated that means?"

"I told you earlier, Mina found the lipstick she wanted behind the cosmetics counter in the pharmacy. She picked it up with her left hand, but even more significant, she took the pen I gave her with the same hand. That still doesn't prove she wasn't simply holding the bomb bottle in her right hand, though, does it? Ah, except…" She swung around. "That's not the point. The point is, why would Mina want to set fire to the Red Eye in the first place? We're saying the bottle might have been planted on her to deflect suspicion from the real firebomber."

"Head of the class, Red."

"With a detour you apparently didn't take." Smiling, she strolled up to him and tapped a finger to his chest. "Guess that's why you wear the badge."

"Lucky me."

"The day's young. We'll see." She kissed him so thoroughly that bullets of lust shot off in multiple directions. He started thinking perfume, skin, sex and, oh, yeah, pond all over again.

Unfortunately she stepped away before he could pursue any of those thoughts. "Back in the real world, what's happening with Hannah?"

A picture of the older woman's body flashed in McVey's head. No question, there were times when a grisly visual was far more effective than a cold shower. "Let's say she's looking a little less healthy than the last time you saw her."

"He means she's gone gray and putrid."

Brigham approached from the side. His arrival wouldn't have surprised him, McVey reflected, if he hadn't let the idea of sex with Amara tie his senses in knots.

"We're heading down to the Hollow." The big man jerked a thumb. "Taking our ravens and our bits and pieces for the street show/parade with us. You figure on spending the night up here?"

McVey glanced at his phone. "It's almost two o'clock. I'd say there's a fair chance."

"Everyone or just you and Amara?"

"Just us. The teams know the way back."

"Uncle Lazarus asked me to pick up a number of Hannah's personal effects and bring them down," Amara said. "Mostly small items. Some of them might be tricky to find."

"Yeah, well, just so you know, the rain's coming back."

She held her smile at Brigham's dire prediction. "Of course it is. Because legends rule here, and according to one of them, it always rains at night up on Bellam Mountain. Has to be Sarah's doing. What else would a mad witch jailed in an attic room do but put nasty spells on everything she could think of?"

Brigham gave her a deliberate once-over. "You being her offspring, so to speak, and common to us tamers now, maybe you could spend a few minutes working out how to stop the wet. One more mudslide and we'll have to move our camp."

Which they probably did every few years in any case. But right then McVey had weightier problems to handle in the form of three murders, no solid leads and still way too much sex on the brain.

He used the familiar routine of police work to combat the latter. But four frustrating hours into it, they still hadn't turned up a single piece of evidence in or around the murder scene.

"She died where she fell." The head of the forensic team wiped a grimy arm across his face. "Blood loss tells us that much even without a weapon. Seeing that leg of hers, though, I can't imagine why she came to this derelict part of the manor. It's a head-scratcher, McVey, and that's a fact."

Another fact, McVey noticed when he took a moment to look outside, was that Brigham's forecast had been dead-on. Black clouds were massing over the water, and they appeared to be creeping inland.

It took the better part of another hour to stretcher and bind Hannah's body, then pack the equipment for the return trip. Once the teams were ready, McVey secured the central core, separated Amara from her new physician friends and pulled her toward the more livable west wing.

Digging in, she glanced behind them. "There must be more we can do here, McVey."

He kept a firm hold on her hand and a close eye on the clouds. "There's more, Amara. It just can't be done in the dark or by us alone. Brigham left some wine, you want to go through Hannah's things, and I want a shower before whatever's blowing in with those clouds knocks the power out for the better part of the night...." Mild impatience brought his brows together. "Why are you dragging your feet?"

"Because I'm superstitious enough not to like what's sitting on the lamppost outside Hannah's door."

"You're half Blume and you don't like ravens?"

"One raven's not a problem. Two, I can deal. Three starts to freak me out." She continued to resist his pull. "Is it staring at me?"

"If it is, and it's a boy bird, it has excellent taste. If what you really want is for me to shoot it, tell me so we can get inside the damn house."

She twisted her hand free. "You don't shoot a raven, McVey, or anything, for staring." Her declaration ended on a shiver. "I knew this would happen. I'm letting the legends get to me. It's the curse of being a Bellam-Blume. You get swept up."

"There's a thought," he said, and, sweeping her into his arms, carried her past the watchful bird. "What do you know?" He deposited her on the porch. "You're still alive."

"And kicking," she said, but left it at a cool verbal threat rather than a physical demonstration. "First shower's mine. You'll want to batten down the hatches. And the shutters." When he narrowed his gaze, a smile blossomed. "Add my warning to Brigham's and heed it. With the thunder will come strong winds." Stepping closer, she stroked a deliberate finger from his cheekbone to the corner of his mouth. "Trust me, McVey, however many storms you've experienced since you arrived in the Cove, this one will top them all."

His eyes glinted in the shadowy half light. "Are you trying to convince me that you're a witch or frighten me with your ominous prediction?"

Letting her hand fall, she hooked his waistband and tugged him forward. "I'm not a witch, McVey, I'm a woman." She turned her face up to his. "And right now I want."

He thought he detected a rumble of thunder and maybe a warning burst of wind. But all he really heard was the rush of blood in his head and the roar of it in his ears. He felt it pulsing in his groin as her mouth fused itself to his and hurled him—hurled them—into a far more frightening fire than the one they'd taken on last night.

Chapter Fourteen

Amara intended to get what she wanted—hot, steamy sex, with a hot, sexy cop. She didn't care where it took place. Outside, inside, on the floor, on a bed, on the table. She wanted McVey's mouth on her mouth, his body pressed against hers and his hands anywhere at all.

Desire curled inside as he took her by the hips and brought her up to him. More than heat pumped from his body. She felt need as well, raw and unbridled, with an edge as keen and urgent as her own.

Her back bumped the door. Then that door was gone and a cloud of warmth engulfed her. But the real burn was in her belly, in her blood, in the hands that glided with abandon down his chest to the front of his jeans.

"This isn't how I thought it would be." Her breath unsteady, she obliged him by letting her head fall back and exposing her throat to his lips.

"If slow was the goal, Red, we started off all wrong." He eased away just far enough to fix his dark eyes on hers. "Jumping you that first night planted a seed inside me I haven't been able to exorcise."

She teased him with a smile. Her hand slid to his lower belly. "I'm sure you can imagine. I'm all about exorcism. Or possession, depending on how you look at it."

"Right now I'm looking at you."

Her hand tightened on the front of his jeans. "Excellent response, McVey."

The shifting shadows played across his features. His eyes grew darker in the changeable light. He ran his hands under her tank top, brushed callused palms over her bare skin. When his thumbs grazed her lace-covered nipples, Amara hissed in a breath of pure pleasure. And laughed it out when he took hold of her hips and this time lifted her right off her feet.

She wrapped her legs around him in a move that was as much reflex as desire.

Excitement leaped inside her. The pulse at the base of her throat throbbed. He pressed his lips to the delicate hollow and she bowed her body toward him, determined to absorb as many sensations as possible.

"Are we moving, or have my head and body separated?" With her eyes firmly shut, she summoned a feline smile. "More to the point, am I talking or dreaming?"

"Talking." McVey explored every part of her mouth. "I like it. I like your voice. It haunts me. I hear it in my sleep."

"You hear…" Her lashes flew up. Her heart continued to pound and her breathing was far from steady, but she couldn't let that pass. "I'm not her, McVey. Not the woman from your dream."

"Nightmare." He corrected and then kissed her so thoroughly she almost lost the thread of her objection. Did lose it for a blissful moment. "It's your voice I hear, Amara. I never wanted her."

Need gathered in a fiery ball in her belly. When he brought her up higher, it speared outward to her limbs and took most of the air in her lungs with it.

Darkness and light collided. Wind whipped the turbulent clouds into a frenzy. Stairs groaned; the floor creaked. Amara kept McVey's mouth busy and at the same time used her hands to touch and savor and hold. To push him to the limit and that one step beyond.

He laid her on something soft—a mattress?—and, freeing his mouth, stared down at her.

"Gotta get you naked, Red, while I can still form a thought."

If he could form thoughts, he was far ahead of her.

Her lips curved and she willed her hazy eyes to focus. Bed, walls, window, storm. McVey undressing her while her own fingers worked feverishly on the fly of his jeans. She tugged and dragged and tossed. She felt air; the hot, muggy weight of it on her skin as he pulled the white tank top over her head and cupped her breasts.

"Beautiful," he murmured.

Leaving her lace bra in place, he lowered his mouth to her nipple. She arched her back in reaction, heard the purr of approval that came from deep in her own throat.

Her fingernails bit into his shoulders, raked along his upper arms. She was lost and not looking to find herself any time soon. The torture of foreplay was too delicious to rush, the need for more exquisitely painful.

Heat and hunger throbbed in her veins. The combination threatened to consume her. The fire at the Red Eye had nothing on what burned inside her right now.

She fed on McVey's mouth as he slid his hand lower over her belly. He swallowed the gasp she couldn't contain when he slipped that hand between her legs and began to stroke her.

In a move as swift as the first streak of lightning, Amara took the full, hard length of him in her fingers and brought him with her to the slippery rim.

She felt his jerk of reaction. "You don't play fair, do you, Red?"

Her entire system jittered. "Fair's not in my genes." To

prove it, she gripped him tighter. And through her lashes had the satisfaction of seeing his eyes darken to near black.

The image lingered long after her vision wavered, until all that remained was a wash of color as she streaked toward that lovely peak.

When she brought him inside her, when he filled her, she clenched around him and held fast.

"Now, McVey. Right now!" She gasped the words, might have shouted them, because, for a moment, every part of her seemed to fly, to race through the night like the approaching thunderbolts.

In her mind she found the source of the lightning and grabbed it. Rode on its wild, electric back through the sky. Then it vanished. Her muscles went limp, her arms fell away and she tumbled slowly back into herself.

Now, that, her dazed and bleary mind managed to reflect, was what she called a wicked light show. And now she drifted on a sea of black raven's feathers.

She had the ancestry for it. Ravens didn't necessarily foreshadow death in the Bellam world. On that side of her family tree, the birds were often harbingers of hope. And to some degree, she supposed, love.

"Did you say something?"

McVey sounded the way Amara felt—spent, dazed and thoroughly sated. He lay facedown on the bed with his face buried in the pillow and her hair. The arm he'd slung over her held her firmly in place, or would have if she'd had the energy to move even one muscle.

"Not sure I'm up to talking yet." The illusion of drifting resumed when she closed her eyes. "Is my body vibrating or is the house shaking?"

He raised his head to glance at the window before propping up on his elbows. "Likely some of both. The sky's a light show."

"So's my mind. That was—amazing. I swear I saw stars."

"I think I blacked out."

She laughed. "Before, during or after?"

"Take your pick." A smile tugged on his mouth and, lowering his head, he took hers again.

Her heart, not yet back to its normal rhythm, threatened to hammer out of her chest. She hooked a leg over his hips and moved against him in sly, suggestive circles.

Sliding his lips over her cheek, he chuckled. "Need a minute here, Red. I'm still working my way down."

"I know it." This time she ravaged his mouth. When she was done, her eyes glittered. "What do you say to a change of pace? Not that I don't love fast and furious, but building from slow and easy might be nice."

"Might be," he agreed. "But I think..." Catching her waist, he rolled her on top of him so her legs straddled his lower belly. "I want to see you with lightning flashing around your head, then streaming down over your body."

The slyness spread to Amara's eyes. Leaning closer, she whispered a teasing, "In that case, McVey, I hope you're well-grounded. Because the storm out there is a spring shower compared to what's in store for you in here."

THE WORLD AS McVey knew it gave a mighty quake. His eyes snapped open to shadows. The floor beneath him threatened to buckle and the air was rich with the mingled smells of smoke and storm.

A fire, tinged with green, flamed high in an impossibly tiny hearth. A small black pot hung over the flames. Three others stood smoking on a heavy table.

A woman in a cloak moved from pot to pot. She mumbled and chanted and sprinkled powders that made the contents boil over the sides. "Betray me and suffer the consequences," she vowed. "What was love has transformed into hate. I pit brother against brother and seek destruction for both. At night's end, all that the first one possesses shall pass to me and mine."

"Go!" Whirling, she held her hands out, palms up. As they rose, so did the flames in the hearth. Her voice dropped to a malevolent whisper. "Never forget, Hezekiah. It was your own brother who killed your wife—your wife, who was my sister. He raped her and then he killed her. He betrayed us both, for I loved him, and I foolishly believed he loved me."

Fury smoldered in the air. Vicious streaks of lightning revealed more than a desire for revenge in her eyes. From the floor where he lay, unmoving and with his own eyelids barely cracked, McVey saw the madness that simmered inside her.

"All will be mine," the woman promised again. "Before this night is done, there will be death many times over, and the perpetrator shall be deemed to be evil...."

Her words echoed in McVey's head. Echoed and expanded. In his mind he saw a man. There was blood, and suddenly the man was alone with bodies scattered across the forest floor. His brother lay dead at his feet. His breath heaved in and out, and tears ran down his cheeks as he cried a woman's name.

"Nola...!"

The smoke in the attic thickened. The storm beyond it grew wilder still. But in the forest of his mind, McVey glimpsed a raven. It swooped down and landed in front of the sobbing man. It spread its silky black wings and grew to full human size.

When it spoke to him, it did so in a woman's soft voice. "I can do but a small spell, my love, yet I shall do all that is possible to save what remains of your soul. You must embrace the raven, Hezekiah. You must embrace and become the raven....

The image in McVey's head fractured. He saw fire and blood and the dripping black mass that the cloaked woman had given to the damned man.

But it was fragments now; frozen images caught in time-lapse photography.

He had to get out, McVey thought. He had to do something. Find someone. No, protect someone. Protect Amara from the person who wanted her dead.

Without warning, the woman's strong fingers gripped his wrists and hauled him to his feet. "I knew you were awake, Annalee. I know what you have seen and heard. I know what you think."

McVey seriously doubted that. How could a mad witch know the thoughts of a man who was, however briefly and for whatever reason, trapped inside the body of her sister Nola's daughter?

"McVEY, WAKE UP!" He felt himself being shaken—not by the wrists, but by the shoulders. "McVey!"

The female voice, muted at first, came clearer. She shook him again, then committed the cardinal sin of wrapping her fingers around his wrist.

"McVey!"

Hell with that, he thought and, yanking free, took a hard swing.

"Not tonight, slugger."

His fist punched air. The momentum of it landed him facedown on a dusty floor.

Weight descended on the small of his back. Firm bands cinched his ribs on either side. A hand grabbed his hair and pulled.

"Wake up!" a familiar voice said in his ear.

Reality trickled in, slowly at first, then like a bucket of ice water dumped over his head.

He came back swearing and reaching for his gun. When he surged up, the weight vanished. He made it to his hands and knees, looked around—and saw Amara sprawled on the floor.

Concern struck first, a brutal kick to the gut. "Are you hurt? What are you doing?" He shoved himself upright, swayed. "What am I doing?" His mind began to clear and he frowned. "Where the hell are we?"

"All good questions." She pushed to a crouch to study his face in the shadowy light. "Are you *you?*"

The dream—hell, nightmare—slithered back in. So did a truckload of confusion. "I don't know who I am, or was. Is this an attic?"

She continued to inspect his face. "Yes. We're in the central part of the manor. I woke up when you got out of bed and pulled on your jeans. No big deal, I thought. Until the lightning flickered and I saw your eyes. They looked wrong. Trancelike. I called your name, but you didn't answer. When I touched you, you shoved me onto the bed."

"I shoved…?" Revulsion swept through him. "Jesus, Amara, did I hurt you?"

"Onto the bed, McVey. No. I tried to follow you, but you're very fast, and when I realized you were heading outside, I had to run back for my boots."

And his T-shirt, he noted. "Your hair's wet."

"It's raining. And blowing. Hard. I don't know how I knew you'd gone to the main part of the house. Maybe I sensed you. Or maybe it just made some kind of weird sense to me that you'd come here, but I ran upstairs when I heard the attic door slam."

"I hope it was me who made that happen and not the house."

She smiled. In relief, he imagined.

"I don't think the manor's possessed, McVey, but the central attic is believed to be where Sarah Bellam was confined after she was pronounced insane."

"Insane and pregnant."

The smile spread to Amara's eyes. She held her hands out to her sides. "Tah-dah."

"With Ezekiel Blume's child."

"Thus the sparsely populated branch that binds our family trees."

McVey lowered his gaze to his forearms. "She grabbed me, dragged me to my knees and threatened me. With amnesia in the original dream. Possibly with something worse tonight."

Amara skimmed a speculative finger over his wrist. "You were breathing strangely when I found you. I tried to take your pulse. You tried to punch me."

His eyes shot up. "What?"

She grinned. "I saw it coming, of course, so you missed. You hit the floor. I jumped on your back. McVey, Sarah was a small woman, no more than five foot three or four, and according to all the historical records, very slender."

"So how could she drag me to my knees?" He let his mind crawl back into the nightmare. "Annalee," he murmured, and heard Amara's comprehending "Ah."

"I was a girl in the dream," he went on. "Seven, maybe eight years old. I was hiding in the attic. Sarah pulled a dripping black blob out of a boiling pot and handed it to a man."

"Did the man have long black hair and the face of a demigod?"

Amusement stirred. "From the perspective of both man and child, Amara, he was just a guy in a cloak."

"Some people say... Uh, okay, are we leaving?"

As lightning raced through the sky, McVey stood, flexed a sore left shoulder—he probably didn't want to know the source of that injury—and extended a hand. "I'm in the mood for some raven's blood wine. If you have theories, and I'll lay odds you do, we can talk about them downstairs."

Instead of appearing rattled, she trailed a suggestive finger over his collarbone. "The wine part's an excellent idea, and the prospect of talk's intriguing, but I think I'd like something more stimulating between the first and second things."

He allowed himself a brief smile when her hand clamped his half-zipped fly, and he felt his body's instinctive reaction. "Having been trapped inside a girl's body a few minutes ago, I'm more than happy to find myself back on form." He ran his gaze over her face as the heat in his groin ramped up to painful proportions. "In fact..."

Eyes glittering, he lifted her off the floor by her hips. Her long legs twined automatically around him. With his mouth already locked on hers and need raging like thunder inside him, he found the nearest wall, pressed her to it and tossed the last of his nightmare into the storm where it belonged.

"LET ME GET this straight." Inside Hannah's cozy west wing living room, with a wood fire glowing in the hearth, Amara endeavored to sort through all that McVey had related. "In your dream—okay, nightmare—your name is Annalee. As Annalee, you saw Sarah give Hezekiah something black and icky, probably a magical root. After Hezekiah left, you heard her claim that brother was going to destroy brother. Meaning Hezekiah was going to destroy Ezekiel for raping and murdering Hezekiah's wife, Nola. You're saying it really was Sarah who gave Hezekiah the power to be...well, evil."

"Sarah knew Ezekiel had betrayed her love. She knew he wanted Nola for himself."

"That part's in the original legend, the one written by the Blumes. But years ago a Bellam suggested the very thing you're telling me now. That Sarah was actually the 'evil' spirit. That she caused Hezekiah to go on a killing spree. Except Nola wasn't dead, only in a state of limbo. When Hezekiah's spree ended, it was Nola who came to him as a 'good' spirit."

McVey took a long drink of wine. "A good spirit in the form of a raven."

"Raven Nola told human Hezekiah that the best she could do was transform him into a raven as well, a condition in which he would remain until someone who was fated to die succeeded in cheating death."

"Told you it was a nightmare."

"But with a slightly different twist tonight, one you sleepwalked through."

His gaze swept across the high ceiling. "Could be the surroundings. Proximity to the place where the original nightmare unfolded."

Thoughtful now, she poured him another glass of wine. "Still, McVey, everything you've said is just background information to the really fascinating part."

"That I was a girl in a former life?"

"That you were Nola's daughter in a former life. I had a dream, too, the night we stayed in the raven tamers' camp. The name Annalee came up. I was sure I'd heard it before, and it turns out I had. Annalee was Nola's daughter, born before she met Hezekiah. You were Annalee."

"Only if you believe in reincarnation, Red. Which I don't."

"Which you don't want to." She curled her legs under

his black T-shirt, then, unable to resist, leaned in to whisper an amused, "Makes you a Bellam, you know."

He poured more of the wine into her glass. "I guess it also makes us kissing cousins."

"Fifty or sixty times removed. Tell me, have you ever had the urge to cast a spell?"

"Or ride a broomstick?"

"No male Bellam ever rode a broomstick, McVey. I doubt if any of them even knew what one looked like."

"Apparently, I'm more enlightened. I swept the floors in my father's antiques shop as a kid."

"I love antiques—" Her head came up as something slammed against the side of the house. "Well, wow. If that whatever-it-was was wind driven, Bellam Bridge might not even be in the state of Maine tomorrow. Which could be good or bad, depending on Willy Sparks's present location—and why on earth did I bring that up?"

McVey shifted so they were both facing the fire. Resting an arm across her shoulders, he played with her hair. "Talk more about Sarah."

"What? Oh." She pushed fear aside and gave his leg a smiling pat. "That's your story. You said Sarah said she wanted both Hezekiah and Ezekiel destroyed so she and her unborn child—Ezekiel's child, obviously—could inherit Hezekiah's vast estate. Money, land, homes, et cetera."

He grinned. "Give the woman credit, it was an ambitious plan."

"Yes, and only two Blumes and a Bellam had to die for her to achieve it. Oh, and I forgot, all the townspeople who followed Ezekiel into the woods and helped him 'murder' Nola."

"Ambition isn't always pretty, Red."

"Jimmy Sparks is an ambitious man."

"So was I once, in what I thought at the time was a more positive way." McVey took a drink of the bloodred wine. "Life can screw you. Lines are irrelevant. Good, bad, pick a side, stand back and watch the mighty fall."

She regarded his profile. "I'd call that an extremely cryptic remark. I hope you're going to elaborate and not force me to draw my own conclusions."

He linked the fingers of his left hand with her right. "Let's just say my last bust as a city cop proved to me that once in a while the so-called good guys go bad. Unfortunately, if their connections within the department are important enough and reach high enough, Internal Affairs will turn a blind eye and the dirty deeds will get shunted to the investigative morgue."

"Causing at least one good cop to go looking for something better. Somewhere better. In this case, a spooky little town on the coast of Maine."

McVey examined the wine bottle. "We're down to the dregs, Red, and I'm not feeling a single adverse effect. You?"

"No, but then I hit my head when we made love in the shower, so I can attribute any dizziness I might be experiencing to that."

"I'm the one who got whacked by the showerhead." When Amara laughed, he set the bottle aside and pulled her onto his lap. "If you're dizzy, what you need is exercise."

"From a medical standpoint, I have to tell you, that's really bad advice. However…" Eyes dancing, she hooked her arms around his neck and wriggled until he went hard. "Seeing as I know what you're doing and what you want, all I can say is—"

The rest of the sentence stuck in her throat as lightning

flickered and her eyes, now facing the living room window, picked up a movement. For a split second she saw someone in the driveway.

Someone wearing rain gear and carrying a rifle.

Chapter Fifteen

"You coulda shouted, McVey." Clearly annoyed, Brigham stripped off his muddy raincoat and dumped it on the porch. "Come at me like a battering ram and I'm gonna batter right back."

McVey took the bag of frozen garden peas Amara handed him and pressed it to the side of the knee Brigham had injured during their brief skirmish. She plunked a similar bag of lima beans on Brigham's head and told herself this ridiculous comedy of errors wasn't funny. It could have been Willy Sparks or even Hannah's killer sneaking around the perimeter of the manor instead of her raven tamer cousin.

"You helped Rune," Brigham grumbled, "so I figured I'd help you."

"Next time, mention it," McVey said through his teeth. "I'm too young to be thinking about having reconstructive surgery on my knee."

As she rooted through the cupboards, Amara shook her head. "You're never too young, McVey. I've reconstructed feet, ankles, knees, hips—the list goes on and up—for people a lot younger than you." She located a bottle of amber liquid and held it up for Brigham to see. "Is this raven tamer whiskey?"

"I don't know. My head hurts worse when I open my eyes. If there's no label, it's ours, and gimme."

She placed it in the middle of the kitchen table within easy reach of both men. "You can share the bottle or wait until I wash some of the glasses Hannah left piled in the sink. I'll go out on a limb here and speculate that dish washing wasn't one of her favorite chores."

Brigham shot McVey a glare. "I can handle a dirty glass."

"As a medical practitioner, I'm forced to say, yuck."

McVey worked up a faint smile. "Is that doctor talk for 'it's an unhealthy practice'?"

"No, it's woman talk for 'it's gross.' There's black gunk hardened on the bottom of every mug, it'll take a week's worth of soaking to soften whatever she burned onto this casserole dish and the red stains in the wineglasses are probably permanent by now.... Why didn't you tell us you planned to stick around, Brigham?"

The big man shrugged. "Didn't know it myself until we started moving out. Then it came to me. Too many people are dead who shouldn't be. Would a hit man leave a trail of bodies like this?"

McVey reached for the bottle, took a long drink and shot it across the table. "Depends on the hit man. In Willy Sparks's case, I'd say it's unlikely."

The lights, which had held to this point, began to wink out as Amara filled the sink with hot water. "I still can't think why anyone would want Hannah dead. We assume Westor witnessed something in the alley at the Red Eye. Possibly ditto for Mina, but..."

"Is she the tourist I heard about?" Brigham asked.

McVey shifted the frozen peas to the other side of his knee. "One more piece of our ever-expanding puzzle."

Amara glanced up as the lights fluttered again. "It

crossed my mind that Mina and Westor were…you know, together."

McVey nodded. "You could be right. Jake said he found sleeping bags—plural—in an empty apartment in Yolanda's building. I'll check it out when we get back."

"If we get back." Twitching off a chill, Amara plunged her hands into the hot, soapy water.

Westor's and Mina's deaths disturbed her, but Hannah's completely baffled her. She'd been a harmless eccentric—a hermit with a bad leg and really nothing a thief might want.

Amara wondered if her mental state had been deteriorating without anyone realizing it. She could have had too much to drink, wandered into the manor's central core and bumped into a homicidal hobo.

"Right," she said under her breath. "A hobo who took the murder weapon with him when he left, because…" Like the question, her theory sputtered out.

Behind her, McVey and Brigham continued to bait each other while the overhead lights surged and faded. They winked off completely, but popped on again as she put the last glass in the drain rack.

Still wearing his frozen vegetable hat, Brigham took a swig of whiskey and fished an iPod out of his shirt pocket. "I'll take first watch, Amara, if you and McVey have something you'd rather be doing upstairs."

She regarded him through mistrustful eyes. "You weren't spying on us earlier, were you?"

"Only in my lurid imagination." He made a sideways motion. "I'll camp out in the living room."

She watched him lumber away, grunting out an old Johnny Cash song.

McVey went to take stock of the yard through the kitchen window. "I don't see Sparks braving a storm like this on the off chance he might be able to get to you. Not sure about our mysterious other."

From spectacular sex to abject terror—she'd run the gamut tonight, Amara decided. And dawn was still several hours away.

"You missed a spot, Red." McVey surprised her by coming up from behind and tugging on her hair. "Don't get tangled up in all the loose threads. You'll only freak yourself out."

She rubbed at a smear on the rim of a wineglass. "I've been freaked out since I walked onto a hotel balcony in the Vieux Carré and watched Jimmy Sparks put a bullet in a woman's chest. She took one step, McVey, and dropped like a stone. It happened in a back alley on a night almost exactly like this. Sparks didn't check to see if there might be witnesses. He just stormed into the alley and shot her."

"Jimmy Sparks is famous for his volatile temper."

"His lawyers claimed it was a drug-induced homicide. He takes a number of meds, all of which are strong, but none of which, even in combination, would drive a rational man to commit murder. The victim was a call girl. She tried to roll him. He took exception. That's not good when the John in question is known to fly into violent rages without warning."

"What were you doing on a hotel balcony in the Vieux Carré?"

"I was visiting a patient, doing a follow-up to a surgery I'd performed. She wasn't a friend exactly, but I liked her and I wanted to make sure she was happy with the results."

"She being Georgia Arnault, former registered nurse and mother of six. Lives in a small town in the bayou. Her cousin works at the same hospital as you."

"You've done your homework." Amara arched a brow. "Should I be impressed or flattered?"

"Fact-finding's easy when you're a cop. In this case, the deeper I dug, the more I learned."

"And didn't like."

"It's hard to like a police officer who'd abuse his badge the way your patient's boyfriend did over—what was it?—a ten-year period."

"Twelve. Every cop on the force in the town where they lived knew he was beating her. That's five men who refused to see or act. Georgia said it was a solidarity thing, good old boys sticking together. I say all of them, and her so-called boyfriend most especially, should be subject to the removal of certain body parts."

"I wouldn't argue with that." McVey tucked a strand of hair behind her ear. "You reconstructed Georgia's face—nose, cheekbones, chin—and erased as much of the damage as you could."

"She'd been working on the emotional side of things, seeing a psychologist in New Orleans, which was why she was in a hotel the night of the murder. We were both on the balcony at one point. But Georgia's afraid of thunderstorms, and the storm that night was wild.... What are you doing?" Amusement swam up into her eyes when he scooped her off her feet. "I saw that knee of yours, McVey. You can't possibly carry me all the way upstairs and down the hall without experiencing tremendous pain."

Hiking her higher, he caught her mouth for a mind-numbing kiss that stripped away her breath and her mild protest. "I won't be experiencing any pain, Amara. Not until tomorrow anyway."

She repositioned herself in his arms and used her teeth on his earlobe. When his eyes glazed, she whispered a teasing, "Wanna bet?"

OWING TO THE fact that Bellam Bridge appeared to be standing more out of stubbornness than any true structural support, Brigham reluctantly showed them an alternate route off the mountain.

"Mention this to anyone," he warned, "and not only will you be 'uncommon' faster than you can blink, but you'll also find yourselves being watched by ravens every night."

Clinging to the base of a sapling and preparing to jump off a six-foot ledge into a puddle of mud, Amara didn't ask the obvious question. She merely reminded herself that he was on her side and not trying to help Willy Sparks achieve his murderous goal.

It took them more than ninety minutes to access the main road. They backtracked for another twenty to McVey's truck, then squeezed into the cab for the remainder of the bumpy trip.

Fanning her face with a clipboard from the dash, she pushed on her cousin's massive leg. "I'm not six inches wide, Brigham."

"You want me to ride in the back like a dog?"

"No, I want you to tell me what the deal is with staring ravens."

He grinned at her cross tone. "Hell, that's Legend 101, Amara. Feathers delivered to doorsteps by a raven mean death. Ravens that sit and watch are doing it on someone else's behalf."

"Someone good or someone evil?"

He bared his teeth in a menacing smile. "That's for you to figure out."

She frowned up at him. "Are you trying to scare me because I landed on your foot when I jumped from that big boulder earlier?"

McVey, who'd remained silent until now, chuckled. "More likely he's cranky because he's hungover and Hannah's coffee tasted like crap. Ravens fly, land and occasionally stare, Amara. So do crows and no one thinks twice about it."

Brigham snorted out a laugh. "Unless the people those crows are staring at live in Bodega Bay and they've watched *The Birds* one too many times." At Amara's exasperated look, he shrugged a beefy shoulder. "Just saying."

"You know as well as I do that ravens have a stigma attached to them. When he was a raven, Hezekiah's action—leaving feathers on doors—portended death, but didn't actively cause it. He was a sort of middleman."

"Middle raven," McVey said.

Because she knew he was trying not to grin, she jabbed an elbow into his ribs before reaching for his ringing phone.

"We're driving, Jake," she said. "On a road that requires skill and concentration. I'm putting you on speaker."

The deputy opened with an irritable, "There's a bunch of raven tamers wandering around the Hollow, McVey. People keep giving them the thumbs-up sign. Can I arrest them on the grounds that they're gonna get half the town tanked tonight on their illegal hooch?"

"It's not hooch," Brigham shouted over Amara. "It's frigging superior whiskey and wine that goes down like honey."

McVey's lips quirked. "Been a while since you've drunk your own wine, I think."

On the other end of the phone, Jake growled out a terse, "Tell me you're not giving a raven tamer a police escort into town, McVey. Some old crone tried to tell me you were tight with them now and I should mind my own if I want to go on being a deputy, but I figured she was drunk on her own stuff and hallucinating."

McVey braked for a deer. "Leave the raven tamers alone,

Jake. Their parade kick-starts the festivities. It's tradition. What's the real problem?"

"I got six positives from the DMV for the name Mina Shell. Two of them might be her. I did background checks. North Carolina Mina has brown hair, not blond, and I can't see her eyes very well. She's twenty-eight and works in a bank. Nashville, Tennessee, Mina is a dental hygienist and looks thinner than corpse Mina, but weight changes and these printouts are lousy anyway."

"Did you run our Mina's fingerprints?"

"Er, yeah. Just."

McVey swore softly. "Get a clear set, Jake. Is the sheriff still there?"

"He left two hours ago. Something about a domestic hostage-taking five blocks from his office."

"Send the victim's fingerprints off to the county lab before I get back. You've got about thirty minutes....Shut up, Brigham," he said in the same uninflected tone after disconnecting. "Deputies are as hard to come by as police chiefs in these parts."

Amara sighed. "It wouldn't matter how good either of them was if I'd gone into hiding in New York instead of here."

"We've been down this road more than once, Red." McVey eased through a deep puddle. "Hannah's not dead because of you."

Inasmuch as she could, Amara folded her arms. "Westor is. And probably Mina."

"Westor came here wanting revenge on me."

Brigham bumped Amara's leg with his. "We in the raven tamer community call a death like his poetic justice."

"What do you call Mina's death?"

"Would you feel better if everyone hereabouts just said

to hell with it and told this Willy Sparks person where to find you?" Brigham demanded.

She worked herself around to glare. Then an idea occurred and her animosity dissolved. "Actually, that could work."

Brigham glanced at McVey, shrugged. "You had to figure. Descended from Sarah Bellam and Ezekiel Blume, the crazy was bound to pop out at some point."

Because any other movement required too much effort, Amara kicked the big man's foot. "I'm talking about setting Willy Sparks up, not running through town with a target painted on my chest. Have you ever done that, McVey? Drawn a murderer out using bait?"

"Twice."

"Did it work?"

"We used a ringer the first time. He got shot in the shoulder and the leg. The second time, circumstances forced us to go with the intended victim. He survived but three officers were hit. One died." A brow went up. "Answer your question?"

Unfortunately, yes. But that didn't mean she had to like it or to close mind completely to the possibility. This was small-town Maine, not Chicago or New York. They might be able to minimize the risks in a more constricted environment.

Or more people might die and Willy Sparks would slip away into the night.

Guilt gnawed at her for the remainder of the drive.

They dropped Brigham off at a service station half a mile from her uncle's motel, which was apparently where the raven tamers would be staying during the Night of the Raven festival. They stayed, they paid. When it came to money, Lazarus Blume seldom missed a trick.

While Brigham leaned in the window of McVey's truck for a final chat, Amara bought coffee and used the station's restroom.

Locked in, she stared at her reflection in the hazy mirror.

She could leave right now, today, and not tell a soul. She only had to let McVey become embroiled, then she could borrow her uncle's truck and disappear. Force Willy Sparks to come after her.

Give Willy Sparks a perfect opportunity to kill her. "Because, face it, Red," she mocked her reflection. "He'll do it before the day runs out. Everyone who's dead will still be dead, and like McVey said, he'll simply fly off to a tropical destination and wait for new orders." She huffed out her frustration. "I hate cop logic."

She saw McVey heading toward the building as she stepped back outside. "I was thinking…" She frowned when he grabbed her hand and pulled. "What is it?"

"Jake called."

She had to trot to keep up. "Obviously with bad news." Her blood turned to ice and she clutched his arm with her free hand. "Please tell me no one else is dead."

"No one else is dead, Amara." He didn't wait for her to climb up, but caught her by the waist and set her in his truck.

"What's going on?" she demanded again. "What did Jake say?"

For the first time since they'd met, McVey turned on the flashing lights and siren. "He tried to take Mina Shell's fingerprints. He couldn't get anything."

She opened her mouth, considered and closed it again. "That's impossible. Everyone has fingerprints. Unless Mina…"

"Yeah." He tossed her a look rich in meaning. "Unless Mina."

Amara stared at her own fingertips. "Are you saying she deliberately removed them? Well, yes, you are. But—ouch."

"Big ouch. Done for a big reason."

"She didn't want to be identified."

"Exactly." A grim smile appeared. "All we have to do is figure out why."

AMARA DISLIKED EXAMINING CORPSES. She actively hated touching them. But she had to see Mina's fingers for herself.

"I'm not a complete moron," Jake called across the back room at the station house. "I know how to take prints. Another hour and it would have been out of our hands. Mina Shell and Westor Hall are scheduled for transfer to the county morgue at 1:00 p.m."

Amara heard him, but only as a curious buzz in the background. "Why do I find this so incredibly creepy?" she wondered aloud.

"No idea." Jake inched cautiously closer. "I find the idea of raven tamers way creepier."

"Only because you're afraid of them."

"Isn't everyone? They're freaking lawbreakers who make themselves seem mysterious by living in the north woods and selling booze local crime labs can't analyze."

"Really?" She laid Mina's hand down but didn't rezip the body bag. "Maybe they incorporate some of Sarah's roots and powders into the mix."

"You're talking, lady, but I'm not hearing… Aw, crap sakes, Amara." Jake jerked back in revulsion when she pulled the flap down farther. "I don't wanna look at a naked dead woman."

"Neither do I, but I saw the photos you showed McVey. She has tattoos."

"A leaf, a splat and a heart with initials inside it. Who cares?"

Amara regarded the red heart over Mina's left breast. "*WS,* Jake." She raised speculative brows. "Willy Sparks, maybe?"

"You mean the guy McVey said is after you? You think she had his initials tattooed on her chest? You think she came here with a hit man?"

The clinic door opened and closed. Amara recognized McVey's long stride, but she didn't remove her gaze from the dead woman.

Jake stabbed a finger. "Amara thinks Mina Shell came to town with that hit man you've been looking for. Is she North Carolina Mina or Tennessee Mina, McVey?"

"Neither."

Amara examined the tattoo on Mina's hip. "That's a spark, isn't it?"

"Be my guess," McVey said.

"And the leaf on her shoulder. Some kind of poisonous plant?"

"Go with hemlock. I'll explain why later."

"Okay, I take it back." Jake stepped away, palms up. "She's as creepy as the raven tamers."

"Mina…" Amara let the name roll off her tongue.

"You're almost there, Red."

Something cold and slippery twisted in her stomach.

"Excuse me, people, but am I missing something?"

"*WS,* Jake." Amara said softly. "I'm willing to bet Mina's full name is Wilhelmina. Meaning Mina Shell is really Willy Sparks."

Chapter Sixteen

"What would you have done, McVey, if Mina Shell, aka Willy Sparks, hadn't brought along a passport in her real name?" Pacing her grandmother's kitchen, Amara shook her still-tingling fingers. "Would you have sent a picture of her corpse to Jimmy and had the prison guards watch to see how he reacted?"

McVey straddled a hard chair. "It's been done before. But thanks to the fact that she stashed her shoulder bag at the bottom of one of the sleeping bags in the apartment Westor was using as a flophouse, not a necessary tactic. You were right, by the way, about Willy and Westor."

"They must have walked into the alley together and at the worst possible moment—for them anyway." She ticked a finger. "But back to Willy. Could you have identified her without her passport?"

"Passport and tattoos aside, Red, Willy Sparks had a scar where her appendix was removed."

"Saw that. It's at least ten years old.... Ah, right. Hospitals keep computer records."

"And more criminals than you might expect use their real names for surgeries. On top of that, at eighteen years of age, most girls aren't thinking they'll become hit men for their uncles after college."

"I don't know, McVey. I had my career path firmly in mind at eighteen."

"Willy's appendectomy was an emergency surgery. No time for fake IDs."

She smiled. "I love a thorough man."

"It never hurts to double-check. As for her picture, I might have sent it to Jimmy Sparks—if my motive had been anything other than pure spite."

"Probably just as well. Lieutenant Michaels said Jimmy's health has been declining steadily since his incarceration. Seeing his niece in a morgue might be too traumatic for him to handle." Amara's brows came together. "Am I feeling sorry for a man who murdered a call girl and three people I knew in cold blood?"

"You're a doctor, you're allowed to be compassionate." A smile touched McVey's lips. He caught her hand in passing. "Makes you better than him."

"Right. Good." She regarded their joined hands. "Why am I still spooked?"

"Because there are significant questions that still need to be answered."

"Like who killed Willy Sparks and Westor Hall? Or did they kill each other?" She considered for a moment. "Maybe Westor saw Willy tossing a Molotov cocktail into the Red Eye. Willy pulled a gun on him, he pulled one on her and they both pulled the trigger."

"It's a tidy theory, Red."

"I'm getting more invalid than tidy. Why?"

"The only weapons Westor ever used were knives—specifically his own—and rifles. Willy was shot with a Luger."

"And Westor?"

"Same weapon."

Frustration swept in. "So what now? With Willy Sparks

out of the picture, am I safe from Uncle Jimmy? Or will he have a contingency plan I should worry about?"

"I doubt if he knows about Willy yet, unless they had some prearranged check-in that she missed."

"Meaning my extended family and I are safe?"

"From Jimmy Sparks, probably, for the moment. From our mysterious other? That depends on his or her motive, which unfortunately we haven't established."

Amara drilled the fingers of her other hand into her temple. "My head feels like a centrifuge. You're telling me Willy and Westor were both shot with a Luger in the alley outside the Red Eye the night the bar was firebombed. Are we assuming the mysterious other who killed Hannah is the firebomber, or are we going with a different person?"

McVey ran his thumb over the back of her hand. "For no reason beyond gut instinct, I'm going with the mysterious other as both Hannah's murderer and the firebomber."

"Two killers, then, and one of them, Willy Sparks, is gone. I swear my brain's going to implode."

Standing, he tipped her chin up and kissed her until the implosion became a fiery blast of heat.

"Well, good on you, Chief," she managed to say when her mouth was her own again. "Our entire conversation flashed briefly before my eyes, then vanished in a puff of smoke." Setting her tongue on her upper lip, she snagged his waistband and backed toward the rear staircase. "Rumor has it the raven tamers will be doing some preparade publicity in and around the Hollow after sunset. You probably shouldn't miss that, given Jake's weirdly obsessive desire to lock them up and toss the key. Having said that, however, sunset is still hours away." She mounted a step, tugged him closer and bit his lip. "You've been pulling double shifts." Both hands fisted in his hair. "And I want sex." She kissed him long and hard. "Right here, right now. With you."

His dark eyes gleamed in the shadowed light of the stairwell. "Got you covered there, Red."

Lifting her off her feet, he spun her back to the wall and took her as she'd hoped right where they stood.

MAKING LOVE WITH Amara was the lone bright spot in an otherwise problem-filled day. Unless he counted the discovery of Willy Sparks's purse, which had contained five hundred dollars in cash, a bank card, her passport, keys to a Jeep—he'd sent one of the Harden twins out to search for that—a pressed powder compact and four tubes of bubble-gum–pink lipstick.

"I bought right into her story." Amara flicked through the lookalike tubes. "Do you think Westor and Willy had already met the day Westor threatened me in the pharmacy?"

"I don't think Westor had been in the Hollow long at that point, and we know Willy was a new arrival, so I'd say probably not. You said he grabbed her, too?"

"By the scruff of the neck."

"Some people find a dangerous meeting sexually stimulating."

She laughed. "No comment." Then she raised a speculative brow. "Westor couldn't have known he was having sex with a hit man, could he?"

"Not a chance. One, Willy wouldn't have told him, and two, he'd have pissed himself if she had. It's not the kind of knowledge a person wants to possess. You know, you die. Westor didn't want to die."

"But he did die."

"Not at the hands of Willy Sparks."

"And the wheels spin in place yet again." She shook it

off. "I'm going to balance my mind and spend a few hours at the clinic."

McVey frowned. "Jake broke a tooth at lunch, Amara. I sent him to Bangor to have it fixed."

"Now, there, you see? Every cloud does have a silver lining."

He slid a hand along her bare arm. "I don't want you at the clinic alone."

She motioned toward the door. "Willy's gone, McVey. She and Westor left four hours ago. Even if corpses could do the zombie thing and arise, she'd have to hitchhike back here to do whatever it was she'd planned to do to me." Side-tracked by her own statement, Amara hesitated. "What do you think she planned to do?"

McVey pushed off from the front desk where he'd paused to perch. "Doesn't matter what she planned. It only matters that she didn't succeed."

Amara released a ragged breath. "I guess I love cop logic after all. Don't ask." She kissed his cheek. "I'll let Brigham play guard dog. He's been doing it since we got to town anyway."

"Being common has its advantages."

"Apparently." She kissed him again. "Catch you at the preparade party, Chief. I've got notes to compare with the local midwife on Megan's pregnancy."

And he had two towns to police. Towns that were filling up fast with a mix of watchers and participants. He had no idea where the majority of them might be staying, although when fully open and occupied, word had it Blume House could accommodate a large number of guests. Directly below the house stood the also-large Ravenspell campsite. And farther afield, serious tenters could choose from a number of north woods clearings.

Satisfied that Amara would be safe—he'd spoken to Brigham earlier—McVey turned his mind to other matters.

Lazarus Blume had texted him an hour ago. He wanted Hannah's personal effects brought to the motel as soon as possible. Tomorrow would have to do. In the meantime, McVey thought, if he could eke out an hour or two, Hannah's Blume's death required a great deal more investigation.

Forensics had discovered a substantial amount of alcohol in her system, but no poisons or painkillers. Factor in the impossible positioning of her body and, any way he approached it, her death read like a homicide.

So. Had Luger-man killed her, or were they dealing with a pair of murderers?

Lieutenant Michaels's captain had contacted him that morning. Michaels had been poisoned with a derivative of the hemlock plant called conium, a toxin usually introduced to its victim through some form of liquid. That probably explained the hemlock-leaf tattoo on Willy Sparks's body. One swallow of whatever she'd poisoned and the lieutenant had been a dead man. Westor and Willy, on the other hand, had died in a far more blatant fashion.

The station phone rang as he was pulling up files on Westor and the Sparks family. He glanced at the computer screen and clamped down an urge to swear.

"Hey there, handsome," a familiar voice cooed.

"No, you can't have a last-minute license to sell liquor in the street, Yolanda."

There was a trace of venom under her petulant response. "Well, that's just mean, isn't it? You know I can't miss the Night. I was telling Uncle Lazarus earlier how easy it would be to do a tent with benches and tables. Like an Oktoberfest. I have stock. The Red Eye's cellar didn't burn."

He was tempted to cave but... "Okay, here's the deal.

Email me a plan that works, and I'll think about issuing a license for tomorrow night."

Her already high-pitched voice rose. "By tomorrow, the raven tamers will have over half the town buying their stuff, and the rest will defect to Two Toes Joe's in the Cove. I can't afford to lose my regulars."

McVey tapped a few computer keys, saw nothing of interest and rocked his head from side to side to ease the building tension. "Look, you didn't hear this from me, but why don't you talk to Brigham about selling raven's blood in your rebuilt Red Eye? Come to an agreement, and the tamers might let you have a barrel or two for your temporary street digs. That should entice your regulars back. Tomorrow."

"I don't like raven tamers, McVey. My brother says a single bottle of their whiskey could blow out the side of Bellam Mountain more effectively than nitro. He figures if the crazy person who firebombed me out of business had been smart, he'd have used it in his Molotov cocktails. Who needs gasoline when you've got raven tamer whiskey?"

"Send me a plan."

"McVey..."

Damn her. The wounded tone struck its mark. Unfortunately he wasn't in the mood to be guilt-tripped. "Really busy here, Yolanda."

"She won't stay, you know. She wouldn't make you happy if she did. And that's a big 'if' considering a baddie like Jimmy Sparks wants her dead." The venom bled back in. "My bar's gone because of her."

"Your bar's gone because someone—not Amara—rigged explosives to blow inside and tossed firebombs through a couple of windows. Talk to Brigham about the raven's blood. Sorry, but I've got work."

He cut her off midprotest, called himself a bastard for his lack of sympathy and turned back to Jimmy Sparks's police file.

He spent forty minutes with the reports, but knew his viewing time was up when the remaining Harden twin stuck his head in the door.

"Got a problem brewing, Chief."

"Blume, Bellam or raven tamer?"

"Yes. And all six of them are boiling mad."

An unanticipated spark ignited in McVey's belly and spread quickly to his eyes. Oh, yeah, here it was. This was why he'd come to Maine. Where else on the globe could a legend about a transformed raven clash with a legend about a mad witch and cause people to come to blows? Only in the place where those legends had been born.

The place where the person he'd been long ago had been born.

AMARA WORKED AT the clinic until Brigham insisted he needed food.

"We've got a caravan, a truck and a couple of jazzed-up wagons parked along Main and in front of the square. Marta's big on sausages, root vegetables and herbs roasted in their own juices. Makes the street smell like heaven." He shrugged. "We mostly do it for the tourists and the show. I planted a garden once, and everything I grew turned black."

"Vegetable gardens do very well everywhere else in the north woods." Amara grinned. "Maybe Sarah cursed the soil on and around Bellam Mountain." Movement at her feet distracted her. "Ground fog. Very cool. Looks like snakes. Did you order this as part of your pre-Night publicity?"

"No, but if you tell Marta you conjured it, could be she'll cut you in on a share of the profits."

"Which I in turn could funnel into the Hollow's so-called medical clinic."

Brigham sniffed the air. "Roasted yams and beef stew. Man, I'm starved. Never thought I'd say that after seeing a man with some kind of foot fungus."

She laughed. "Do you know if McVey's here or in the Cove?"

"He drove to the Cove to check in at his badly neglected office."

"Wonderful. More guilt on me."

The shoulder knock Brigham gave her almost sent her into the side of a painted wagon. "Don't sweat it, Amara. Cove people being mostly Blumes are used to not having a police chief around. Trouble tends to unfold more in the Hollow, where mostly Bellams live."

"At the risk of sounding contentious, you raven tamers—mostly Blumes—currently reside on Bellam Mountain and are planning to line your collective Blume pockets with a substantial amount of Bellam money during the festival."

"Pick, pick, pick." Brigham jerked a thumb. "I'm getting some of my cousin Imogene's stew. Stay where the light's good."

She'd have to go to Bangor to do that, Amara reflected, because neither the Cove nor the Hollow boasted well-lit streets.

The scent of fresh buttermilk biscuits drew her toward a red-and-black caravan with a collection of animated ravens on the top. She was marveling at the combination of artistry and engineering when her phone went off.

Her first thought was McVey. Her second was *Damn*. But she sucked it up and summoned a pleasant "Hi, Uncle Lazarus. Sorry, I got sidetracked. I'll bring Hannah's things to the motel as soon as McVey gets back from the Cove."

Raspy breathing on the other end had her raising wary eyes. "Uncle Lazarus?"

"Amara..." He wheezed out her name. "Not sure... Might be my heart. I...took a pill."

She spotted McVey climbing out of his truck and jogged across the street toward him. "When did you take it, Uncle?"

"Five, ten minutes ago." He sounded painfully short of breath, which might or might not be due to his heart condition.

"Breathe as evenly as you can and try not to move. Where's R.J.?"

"Went to the Cove... Still there."

Amara waved McVey back to his truck.

"Problem?" he asked.

She covered the phone. "It's Uncle Lazarus. He might be having a heart attack."

"Motel?"

She nodded, returned her attention to her uncle. "I need you to stay on the line. Don't exert, just relax and breathe. Are you sitting down?"

"Yes."

"Good. Now stay where you are, no extraneous movement."

"No extran..." He tapered off.

McVey spoke to one of the Hardens. The young deputy nodded and took off running. Tossing her medical bag onto the seat, Amara climbed into the truck. "Uncle Lazarus, do you have R.J.'s cell number?"

Her uncle's voice came back reed thin. "Not memorized... Speed dial."

"Okay. McVey's here. We're on our way. We'll be there in..."

"Fifteen minutes."

McVey flipped on the siren and flashers to clear a path through town. Amara put her uncle on hold and punched 9-1-1.

What had been ground fog in the Hollow thickened and crawled higher as they wound their way toward the motel. Filmy finger clouds stretched across the face of a nearly full moon. If the leaves hadn't been new and green, May could have passed for October—although why she was thinking ridiculous thoughts like that when her uncle might be having a massive coronary, she couldn't imagine.

"He didn't mention pain," she said to herself. "But I can hear he's short of breath." She made a seesaw motion with her head. "Happens. Not all the symptoms all the time." She raised her voice. "What's the usual response for the paramedics, McVey?"

"As much as thirty minutes. If we take the old logging road, we can shave five off our time."

"It would help."

For the life of her Amara had no idea how any vehicle could navigate ruts large enough to swallow a full-grown man. But somehow McVey pulled it off. Several terrifying pitches later she realized that they were only a mile or so from the motel.

"Uncle Lazarus?" she said into her phone.

He didn't respond.

When the skin on her neck prickled, she glanced around. "Something's wrong. Do you feel it?"

"Define *it,* Amara."

"I don't mean Uncle Lazarus. Or not just him. I was examining a woman's breast this afternoon and suddenly my mind wandered off. That never happens. I'm not sure where it was trying to go, but it never got there. Is that stress or is the general weirdness of the area getting to me?"

"You lost me at 'woman's breast.' And I'm still coming to terms with the general weirdness of the area."

"That's not exactly… Oh, good, we're here." She took a moment to regard the collection of wagons and caravans parked every which way around the motel. "Whoa, raven tamers. Go big or go home."

A single light burning in her uncle's room brought her back. Grabbing her medical bag, she hopped out and ran for the door.

She had her hand on the knob. Then suddenly she didn't. The ground under her feet vanished. So did the air in her lungs as she landed on top of McVey in a patch of gravel, dirt and weeds.

She couldn't speak, literally could not get enough breath into her lungs to make a sound. But McVey covered her mouth anyway and rolled them both into a crouch.

"There's someone inside."

The clutch of stars that had erupted in Amara's head faded. Her brain settled sufficiently for her to understand they weren't alone. Not them, and not her uncle.

She twisted on McVey's wrist.

"No sound," he cautioned, releasing her.

She drank in the cool night air. Her knees wanted to buckle and her chest felt as if Brigham's foot was lodged in it, but at least the ground was beginning to steady.

"Did you see Uncle Lazarus?"

"He's slumped over the table." As he spoke, McVey drew his Glock. "Backup's in my left boot. Get it, stay low and stay behind me."

Who was inside? The question echoed in Amara's head. It had to be the person who'd killed Hannah, didn't it?

At the edge of the window, McVey aimed his gun skyward.

They heard it a second later—a protracted creak behind the motel. A creak, followed by a slam, followed by an engine roaring to life.

With his gun still angled up, McVey shouted, "Get inside. Doors locked, shades down. Minimum light." He tossed her his keys. "Use my truck to drive him out if you have to."

"I— Yes, okay." She ran, spun. "Be careful." Already at the door, she shook off her frustration. "Part man, part Merlin."

Naturally the door jammed when she tried the knob. To her relief, one hard shoulder bump and it sprang open.

"Uncle Lazarus?" Shoving the dead bolt in place, Amara yanked the shade down but left the light in the kitchenette burning. She needed something to see by.

She set McVey's gun and her cell phone aside, went to her knees and checked her uncle's neck for a pulse. Thready and rapid, she realized. Too rapid.

With her left hand she unzipped her bag and pulled out her stethoscope. Pushing away a glass of milk, she placed the chest piece over his heart and listened.

His heart was definitely beating too fast, yet there was no sign of ventricular fibrillation. "Hmm." Removing the earpieces, she lifted one of her uncle's eyelids, sat back and thought for a moment.

Her uncle suffered from arrhythmia—an irregular heartbeat—for which he took medication. Yes, his heartbeat was wrong, and he'd sounded extremely short of breath on the phone, but he'd taken a pill to combat the condition.

"Need to see your meds," she declared.

She made a point of switching off the light in the kitchenette before turning on the much stingier one in the bathroom.

"You could be a little less frugal where your own comfort is concerned," she muttered and, knowing exactly what her uncle would say to that, let a faint smile cross her lips.

Her brief amusement lasted until she opened the medicine cabinet. One look inside had a scream leaping into her throat and her vision starting to blur.

Chapter Seventeen

The engine of Lazarus Blume's 1954 Dodge continued to roar long after McVey reached the corner of the motel. Although the ass end of the truck was pointed toward him, he had no sight line through the rear window.

He knew a ruse when he saw one. He also knew movement when he spotted it, and he saw someone dart around the front of the truck into the shadows of the motel. It wouldn't have been a problem if there hadn't been twenty raven tamer vehicles parked at cross purposes directly in front of him.

With Lazarus's truck belching exhaust and tendrils of fog winding around everything in sight, McVey stayed low and eased forward.

He caught sight of the figure thirty feet ahead. Bent slightly at the waist, it crept along the side of a caravan. It seemed to be searching for something.

Or someone, McVey reflected darkly.

Cutting the guy off was easy enough. He slipped between two trucks, skirted a tall wagon and waited until the man tried to sneak past the hitch. When he did, McVey met him gun first with the barrel aimed at his head.

"Hey, R.J.," he said softly. "Why the military stealth?"

Lazarus's nephew froze, raised his hands. "Don't be

getting trigger-happy, McVey. I have no quarrel with you. I just got here myself."

"In your uncle's truck?"

"Hell no, in my own. It's parked out front of cabin ten. I hightailed it back here when I heard Lazarus's old Dodge start up. He's not supposed to drive at night."

"He's not in the cab," McVey told him. He made a quick but thorough sweep of the shadows. "No one is. The truck's a diversion. I thought you were the perp."

"What I am," R.J. countered, "is confused. I saw right away there was no one in the truck, yet all the lights are on and the engine's racing. Lazarus babies that engine. He won't let anyone but him behind the wheel. So like I said—confused. Can I drop my hands now?"

"Be my guest." McVey looked from wagon to truck to caravan. "Have you seen anyone in the past few minutes?"

"Haven't seen anyone at all. That's the problem. But I know this. Trucks don't start themselves, and you wouldn't be sneaking around here with a gun if they did. What the crap's going on?"

"I'll let you know when I find out."

He spotted it a split second too late. By the time the quiet thwack that made R.J.'s eyes widen registered, the cane was less than a foot from his head.

He had no time to prevent or even deflect the blow.

But he glimpsed color and had enough time to curse himself for not twigging to the deception sooner. Raven tamer whiskey got people drunk quickly, and it could do a lot more than burn holes in stomach linings. A hell of a lot more.

As pain shot through his skull, however, it wasn't whiskey McVey thought about—it was Amara. She was inside her uncle's motel room. Safe from Willy Sparks, but not from a much closer killer. A killer whose motives and methods mimicked those of a long-dead, frighteningly mad witch.

"UNCLE LAZARUS!" AMARA gave him a desperate shake. Her eyes darted around the room. "Wake up! Please, I need you to wake up so we can get out of— Damn! Damn, damn!"

She jerked upright, her gaze glued to the floor.

"Uncle Laz…" This time she choked his name off.

A reflection in the framed print on the opposite wall revealed a movement outside, nothing more than a glimmer of motion. Amara ducked as a bullet blasted through the window and embedded itself in the wall next to the print.

She took off like a runner from her mark. With her stomach churning and her fingers stiff, she reached for the bathroom door, yanked it shut. Her action blocked the light, but didn't, probably couldn't, contain anything else.

Knowing she'd be visible as a silhouette, she used the threadbare sleeper sofa for cover. She was both relieved and horrified when a second bullet whizzed past her. Her uncle wasn't the target.

On the other hand, obviously she was.

Casting a fearful look into the darkness, she fought for calm. Options. There had to be at least one other means of escape besides the front door.

She swung her head around. Yes, there! The kitchenette had a window. If she could open it, she could get outside.

Hugging every available dark patch, Amara worked her way over to the window. She pulled and tugged on the latch until the slider stuttered sideways.

A quick look revealed nothing except fog and a swarm of raven tamer vehicles. Two more bullets burst through the front window as she climbed over the sill and hopped down between the cabins.

She wanted to scream, longed to run and hide until the danger and the terror passed. But she maintained her crouch and ordered herself not to make a sound. She only remembered to exhale when everything around her started to spin.

Chills scraped like claws along her spine, over her skin, through her head.

Shut the fear out, she told herself. *Think about McVey.*

She could see the back of his truck from her current position. If she could reach it, she could—what? Not leave. Never leave. Because somewhere in her jumbled head she felt certain she had the answer.

This was about revenge—it had to be—for something she'd done as a child.

She and Yolanda had traded barbs her first night back in the Hollow. So had she and Jake.

Spiders, Amara recalled. Years ago, Yolanda had wanted to terrorize her. For reasons of their own, Jake and Yolanda's brother, Larry, had collected a jarful of the horrible creatures, then put the jar in her bed. Jake in particular had enjoyed the so-called prank.

Had Jake and Yolanda been friends as children? Had Jake and Larry? Amara didn't think so. Why, then, had Jake been so eager to participate in Yolanda's scheme? Because of his younger brother, Jimbo?

From Jake's perspective, it made sense.

But would Jake want Hannah dead? Would he blow up the Red Eye? He certainly could have left the bar without anyone noticing. But why destroy a place he liked?

Unless his plan had been to murder her and cloud her death by killing innocent people with her. Would Jake go that far out of spite? Would anyone?

There had to be more.

The "something" she'd mentioned to McVey tapped

a sly finger on the shoulder of her memory. It almost scratched its way through. But as before, "almost" faded to black, leaving her frustrated and frightened.

Where was McVey? And the paramedics. Surely thirty minutes had passed. Why hadn't they arrived?

Why had she left McVey's backup gun and her cell phone on the table in her uncle's room?

Okay, enough, Amara decided. There was a plus side here. She had McVey's keys in her jacket pocket, and there was a police radio in his truck. She could call the Harden twins for help.

She waited until long wisps of cloud passed across the moon; then she slammed the lid on her terror and ran. She reached the driver's door without incident. Yanking it open, she climbed onto the running board.

And spied a dozen spiders crawling across the seat.

She jerked back as if electrocuted.

Spiders in McVey's truck. Spiders in her uncle's medicine cabinet. Jake would not do this. He'd always been bitter and spiteful, downright hostile toward her, in fact. But torment wasn't his way. He was a hothead, and hotheads tended to want the job done.

The elusive "something" she'd been struggling to identify all day struck her as she backed across the parking lot. Maybe it was the cotton-candy streaks on one of the raven tamers' wagons, but suddenly there it was, front and center in her head. A smear of pink lipstick on the rim of a wineglass in Hannah's kitchen sink. Bright pink. Like the lipstick worn by Willy Sparks and…

"One more step, Amara, and you're a dead woman."

The voice grated along her nerve ends. But Amara halted because she knew. This was no idle threat. Not with three people dead and a bar in smoldering ruins.

Footsteps crunched on the gravel. She saw the gun first,

then the arm, and finally the hatred that spewed like poisoned darts from her cousin Yolanda's glittering blue eyes.

McVey STRUGGLED TO RESURFACE. Unfortunately, to push through, he had to battle distorted visions of smoking pots, dripping black blobs and the terror of a young girl as she broke free from the woman holding her. As she ran from the attic at Bellam Manor.

Through the child's eyes, he took in stairwells—long, narrow sets of them—and the jagged bolts of lightning that split the sky above the manor.

The high cliffs beckoned, but he ran from them, over rock and rough ground toward the bridge.

He didn't know why he'd chosen that direction until he looked up and saw a raven flying overhead. It seemed to be leading him. To his death or away from it? Too confused to think, he followed the bird on faith and hoped like hell it would take him someplace far away from the madwoman behind him.

"You must cross Bellam Bridge, Annalee." The raven's voice floated down. Could ravens talk, or had he gone mad, too? "You must cross what she cannot."

The child McVey had been knew the structure had been damaged by a series of recent storms. No one crossed Bellam Bridge these days.

"Run, Annalee," the raven urged. It landed on a damaged support, appeared to gesture with its wings. "You must cross the bridge now!"

McVey glanced back and saw her coming. Sarah, enraged, her arms outstretched, her eyes glowing with madness.

Going now, he decided, plunging onto the bridge.

It pitched and rocked and made dreadful screeching noises that rose above the wild thunder. But it didn't buckle, not even when he tripped and went down hard on his hands and knees.

"Run, Annalee," the raven repeated. "I will not allow her to leave this mountain. Here she has built herself a cage, and here will she remain."

McVey almost lost his footing a second time, but he managed to clutch a thick post and prevent the fall. Too winded to look back, he jumped over a broken plank and landed on all fours on the other side.

Sarah screamed into the howling wind, "It's mine, all of it, by right. Do you hear me? It's mine."

Whatever "it" was, McVey wanted no part of it. But Sarah obviously did.

"You have nothing more to fear," the raven told him calmly. "Be still, and know that she who would see you—who would see all of us—worse than dead will herself never see anything beyond the world she has created in her attic room again."

McVey wasn't quite as certain as the raven appeared to be. He watched until he saw double. Stared unmoving as Sarah stepped onto the bridge.

Stared in shock as, three steps later, she fell through, ranting and cursing, yet somehow able to catch hold of a truss.

Her shrieks joined with the thunder. Together, the sounds wrenched McVey out of his dream.

Amara!

Her name was a thunderbolt in his head. Gaining his feet like a man after a three-day drunk, he brought the motel into focus.

On the ground beside him, R.J. groaned and rolled over. McVey saw blood on his shoulder and hoped the wound wouldn't kill him. Because at the same time he spied R.J., he also spied Lazarus's truck fishtailing toward the old highway.

"Go, McVey." Panting, R.J. rolled onto his elbow. "I can manage. Find whatever bastard did this and put a bullet in him for me."

McVey wiped blood from his cheek, spit it from his mouth. "Not him. Her. Check on your uncle if you can. I'm going for Amara." His features hardened because, damn it, he should have seen this sooner. "And Yolanda."

Chapter Eighteen

Woods and hills shrouded in fog flew by in an eerie blur. Despite her terror—which had peaked when Yolanda and her Luger had stepped from the shadows of a raven tamer wagon—Amara knew where they were headed. Bellam Mountain.

With her hands cuffed behind her and her ankles bound by a rough hemp rope, she could only give her body an angry twist. "What did you do to Uncle Lazarus?" she demanded.

Yolanda snickered. "I slipped a mickey into his milk, of course. Right after R.J. left for a night at Two Toes Joe's bar. Traitor likes it there."

"You call R.J. a traitor?" Amara gave another angry twist.

"I call it as I see it." Her cousin smirked. "Fight all you like, Amara. I stole those handcuffs from Jake. You won't be getting out of them any time soon."

"Yolanda, this is crazy. Why are you—?"

"Shut up," her cousin snapped. She beamed a smile across the cab when Amara wisely broke off. "I love it when I give an order and someone obeys. Especially when that someone is you. Now spill. Did you think it was me, Jake or Larry who put the spiders in Uncle Lazarus's bathroom? Go ahead, you can say. Me, Jake or Larry?"

"Jake."

"Seriously?" She wrinkled her nose. "Why?"

"Revenge. I freaked his brother, Jimbo, out when we were kids. I didn't think you'd go that far, and Larry's got his own quirks and hang-ups to deal with."

"So my brother sleepwalks naked. What does that prove?"

"That he has his own quirks and hang-ups to deal with, and while he might be willing to do you a favor, he's not really a vindictive person. Plus, even though he's a Bellam himself, I always thought Larry was nervous about the whole witch thing. He never possessed any power, but I'm pretty sure he believed we did."

"You think Larry believed, but Jake didn't?"

"Jake's too sexist to believe any female could harm him."

"Bull. What it really boils down to, why you really thought Jake put the spiders in Uncle's bathroom and not me, is because Jake's a guy and I'm not." Yolanda gave the steering wheel a petulant thump. "Why do people think only men can kill with guns? Poison, that's a woman's weapon. Fine, maybe I didn't shoot her, but I got Hannah with the butt end of my Luger. One whack and down she went. Not that it took much muscle on my part. She was pretty hammered by the time I coaxed her over to the main part of the manor."

"You got Hannah to walk all that way on a bad leg?"

"She didn't walk, she limped. Stumbled. Laughed like a loon. But come on, Ammie, we're talking raven tamer whiskey here. A few swigs of that stuff and who even knows you have legs?"

"You got an old woman drunk so you could kill her."

"The old woman was a lush. She dumped three fingers of whiskey into her coffee without a word of encouragement from me. I'll cop to adding more while she was pouring me a glass of that gut-rot raven's blood wine, but honestly? It was superfluous at that point."

Working herself around so she could lean against the door, Amara regarded her cousin's profile. "Call me dense, Yolanda, but I'm still not getting this."

"You're dense." Only Yolanda's eyes slid sideways. "You're also stupid, stupid, stupid." Grinning, she did a little butt dance. "Knowing that makes all the trouble worthwhile."

"*Trouble.* Is that your euphemism for *murder?*" Amara tugged experimentally on her wrists, but, as predicted, the cuffs held. "When did you go insane?"

Her cousin sneered. "You're such a weenie. People die every day. Some do it naturally. Others are helped along. I subscribe to the second way of thinking. And in support of my earlier remark about women and guns, Hannah wasn't the only person I 'helped along.' I also offed the cute jerk with the knife who wanted the bimbo with the overbite instead of me. I admit that night's a bit fuzzy, but I think I put a bullet in her before I did him. Would you believe the bitch pulled a gun on me at exactly the same time I pulled one on her? I mean, talk about your bizarre coincidences."

She didn't know. Yolanda had no idea who she'd murdered in that alley. Growing desperate, Amara worked on freeing her ankles rather than her wrists.

The foggy landscape rushed past as her cousin pounded through ruts and potholes, mindless of the damage she might be inflicting on the truck's undercarriage.

"Yolanda... Ouch. Damn."

"Almost bite your tongue off there, cuz? Not to worry. You'll be dead soon. Won't matter."

"Yeah, I got that part. What I still don't get is why? I know you hate me...."

"Loathe, despise, put a thousand curses on you that unfortunately never took." Yolanda shrugged. "No point understating things."

"We'll agree we're not friends. I never liked Jake's brother, but I think murdering him would have been a little extreme. So I'm guessing there's a reason other than loathing behind what you've done."

"Well, duh." Yolanda swung the truck with reckless abandon around the remains of a fallen tree. She did her second butt dance to an old Abba song. "Money, money, money. I want it, honey. When the rich man croaks."

Astonishment momentarily blotted out every other emotion. "That's what this is about? Money?"

"Rich man's money. Richest man in the Hollow and the Cove combined's money."

The missing puzzle piece fell into place at last. All the way into place as Amara recalled the contents of their uncle Lazarus's medicine cabinet.

"Oh, my God," she exclaimed softly. "Sunitinib. And everolimus. The first drug was farther back on the shelf. It would have been older."

"Is that doctor talk for 'oh, what a dumb ass I've been'? Which you totally are, and I'd be the last person to argue the point. But bottom line? Uncle Dearest's life is winding down like an eight-day clock ticking through the last few minutes of its final hour."

Amara only half heard her. She'd been blind. She'd seen the drugs the night she'd gone looking for antacid. Seen but hadn't absorbed.

"Saw the trees just fine." She sighed. "Missed the forest completely."

Yolanda ticked a finger. "More doctor talk, I assume, meaning your teeny, tiny mind overlooked what would have been a no-brainer for most first-year med students."

Ignoring her, Amara let her head fall back against the window. "Those drugs are used to treat renal cancer, the newer usually after a failure with the older. But even the new drug didn't have a recent date on it." Her terror momentarily suspended, she regarded her cousin. "Uncle Lazarus has kidney cancer."

"Yes, he does. It's also in his bladder and, fingers crossed, his liver. And how do I know this, you ask, when in all probability he hasn't told a soul?"

"You went through his desk?"

"Nope. One day, R.J. got sick and Uncle had to go to Bangor for a check-up. I offered to drive him. I mean, a girl's gotta suck up, right? We drove, I made a show of leaving the doctor's office, and on a lovely spring day, I stood under an open window in an alley very much like the one where I shot the jerk and the bimbo and I listened to Uncle's doctor tell him he needed tests. Of course, Uncle Lazarus always does what's needed, including getting himself to a lab at some point. The next part was a guess, but a good one, I think."

"He wanted to see the test results," Amara said. "All of them, personally, so he had copies delivered by express mail as soon as they were available."

"Exactly. I retract one 'stupid.' The results arrived. Uncle got uncharacteristically drunk and punched the courier—or you could say messenger—down at Two Toes Joe's bar."

Amara was so far beyond shock, her mind simply went numb. "Did you see the results or just go with your guess?"

"Uncle's drunken punch spoke for itself. It validated my guess well enough."

"So all this death, all these murders, are about money."

"Whacks of money, Amara."

"Did you kill Uncle Lazarus's sister, too?"

"Aunt Maureen? Didn't have to. The old girl smoked herself to death. Thank you very much, Auntie Mo. But I will admit, it was her death that planted the seed in my head. As the seed grew, I said to myself, 'Wait a minute, Yolanda, the old guy must have a will.' So I skulked and I lurked and eventually I said to hell with it. One afternoon, when I knew he and R.J. would be in Bangor, I did what you said and searched Uncle's office. Jackpot."

They clattered over a broken-up section of the road. Amara stole a glance behind them. There were no headlights. Did that mean Yolanda had seen McVey tonight? Seen and... No, not going there, she decided. "Obviously you're named in the will," she said instead.

"Number four on the list," her cousin confirmed. "Good old Uncle thinks I'll be thrilled to inherit the Red Eye. Woo-hoo. You, on the other hand, as number-two heir, were initially in line for Bellam Manor and an offensive amount of cash. I don't remember Hannah's bequest—she was number three—but I do know Aunt Maureen was slated to receive the lion's share of his estate. Here's the best part, though, and the reason I did what I did. According to the terms of Uncle Lazarus's will, if one heir predeceases the others, whatever bequest he or she would have received goes to the next person in line. How cool is that?"

"Too cool." Amara closed her eyes. "So after Aunt Maureen died, I became number one. If I'd died, everything would have gone to Hannah."

"'Would have' being the operative phrase."

"And with Hannah and me both gone, you're the big winner."

"Bigger than big, Amara. Oh, I'll share some of my winnings with my brother, but for the most part Larry's perfectly happy setting off controlled avalanches in the Rockies during the winter and hanging out with his too-

cool-for-school sister—who happens to be a Bellam female and a teeny bit scary when she doesn't get her own
way—in the spring and summer."

"For the record," Amara remarked, "in the bitch-witch
pecking order, you're miles ahead of me."

"Why, thank you, cousin."

"It wasn't a compliment."

"No? Huh. Guess I'll have to make your death doubly
painful. Should anyway." She huffed out a breath. "I'm
pretty sure McVey'll have to go once I do you."

Relief coursed through her. McVey was alive. Thank
God, he was alive. "You're not a witch, Yolanda," she
snapped. "You're a demon from hell."

"Maybe, but I'm a smart one." Her cousin buffed hot
pink fingernails on her jacket. "Wanna know how I way-
laid McVey?"

Amara shot her a look, but Yolanda merely snickered
and sailed on.

"I smucked him with the spare cane Uncle keeps in this
very truck. Had to shoot R.J. first, of course. Not fatally,
mind you, just enough to knock him off his feet. I know,
I know, I should have shot McVey as well, but I've been
trying really hard to think of a way to finish this without
offing him. I mean, it kills me—pun intended—to think
of the waste. The man's smoking hot. Unfortunately, I
can't get around the fact that he's also a freaking great
cop. Too great."

"Meaning you're not an equally great murderer?"

"I'm getting the hang of it—but, no, I'm not a major
league player quite yet."

"Is that your goal, Yolanda? To make the big league?"

"Only in the money column, cousin. Once the killing's
done, it's done. If R.J. can't identify me, he can live. He's
in the will, but lower on the list than me." She widened

her eyes. "I don't need absolutely everything. Just most of it will do."

All Amara could think right then was that Yolanda hadn't killed McVey. She'd knocked him out, but he was alive.

And they were getting very close to Bellam Bridge.

She tried not to notice the baleful looks Yolanda cast her. Fear was an endless slither in her stomach. Her cousin wouldn't be talked out of her plan, and Jake's handcuffs were holding fast.

"I watched you the morning after you got here," Yolanda said at length. "Took some binoculars and Larry's old .30-30 and climbed a tree outside Nana's house. There was a moment when I was tempted to shoot all of you—Uncle Lazarus, McVey and you—when you were together in the kitchen. But it crossed my mind that if I missed, especially if I missed McVey, I'd be screwed. And, well, hey—superhot cop."

"I'll have to remember to thank him for the reprieve."

"You won't be thanking anyone, Amara. My tiny lapse of confidence and lust only gave you a few more days to be scared out of your wits." She waited a beat before asking, "So tell me—because I can't help being curious—was the cute creep with the knife one of Jimmy Sparks's people?"

"No, he was an old enemy of McVey's people."

"I'd say tell McVey he's welcome from me. Unfortunately... yada yada." She jumped on the brake pedal with both feet and almost flung Amara through the windshield.

Grinning, she set the brake. "Road ends here, Ammie." Plucking the Luger from her lap, she straight-armed it so the tip was less than an inch from Amara's forehead. "Now we walk."

Amara forced her lips into a humorless smile. "Or in my case, hop."

Yolanda matched her smile. "If you piss me off, yes. You might actually prefer to hop when you discover where we're going."

"Not Bellam Manor?"

"That would be too cliché, cousin. No, word's out on the sorry state of Bellam Bridge. Why on earth you tried to cross it, no one in either town will ever understand, but you did—or soon will. Tragically, you fell through and died." Eyes gleaming, Yolanda leaned forward to stage-whisper, "Or soon will."

McVEY DIDN'T ASK Brigham how he'd gotten to the motel or why he'd come. He only knew, if it was the last thing he did, he was going to get Amara back before Yolanda harmed her.

Sweeping a dozen large spiders from McVey's truck, the raven tamer tossed a bulky pack onto the floor and plunked his own bulk in the passenger seat. "Go," he said, and pointed. "That way."

McVey wanted to ignore him, but the big man gripped the steering wheel and matched him stare for stare.

"She's common, McVey. And I know that mountain better than anyone alive."

McVey's curse promised more than pain if Brigham was wrong. He gave it another second, then shoved the truck in gear and spun the wheel—in the opposite direction to the one Yolanda had taken.

YOLANDA DIDN'T FORCE her to hop, but after untying Amara's ankles, she knotted the rope to the handcuffs binding her cousin's wrists and wound the other end around her own hand.

"On the very likely chance you decide to make a break

for it," she said, giving the rope a tug that sent pain singing along Amara's arms.

She wouldn't panic, Amara promised herself. Her cousin was clearly crazy. She was also overconfident. And crazy, overconfident people made mistakes.

She hoped.

The wind whipped up as they closed in on the bridge. Not enough to disperse the fog, but enough to stir it around and create patches of white that tended to envelop without warning and vanish the same way.

"I wouldn't waste my energy screaming," Yolanda advised. "I whacked McVey plenty hard with Uncle's cane."

Amara watched for the bridge. "Are you trying to convince me or yourself, Yolanda?"

"Got my gun. Got you. If McVey shows, I'll get him, too. That'll leave Jake in charge until Ty gets back from his honeymoon, and by then... Evidence? What evidence? I might have to lower myself and convince Jake that I've really been hot for him all these years—eww—but needs must in a situation like this, don't you agree?"

"I wouldn't know, having never been in a situation like this."

"Bitch." Yolanda gave the rope a vicious jerk. "Ah, excellent. Bellam Bridge." She reeled Amara in as she might a fish on a line. "What a wreck."

Amara jerked away from the finger Yolanda stroked between her shoulder blades.

"I'm betting you won't make ten steps without falling through." Her cousin looked up. "Oh, nuts, the moon's gone out. But no worries, I have a flashlight. Couldn't risk missing the grand finale, could I? Although technically, McVey will be the finale—still pissed about that one—and R.J. if necessary."

Unable to wrest her eyes from the bridge, Amara asked,

"Were you born with no conscience, or did it die the day you killed Hannah?"

"I killed Hannah at night." Yolanda poked Amara's shoulder. "Walk."

"You want me to die in handcuffs? Won't that look suspicious, even to someone with Jake's limited policing skills?"

"I am so going to enjoy watching you fall," her cousin snarled. "It'll be Christmas in May." Visibly annoyed now, she used her left hand to shove the gun into Amara's back while her right pulled out and inserted a small key in the lock.

The handcuffs fell away. The gun dug deeper.

"Have a nice trip, Ammie."

Her push sent Amara to her knees on the rocky roadbed.

Without making a sound, a raven swished out of the fog. Its talons grazed the top of Yolanda's head. When her cousin swore and waved her arms, Amara took advantage and rolled quickly sideways.

The raven swooped again, but this time Yolanda struck its body with her gun. The bird gave a raucous caw, spread its wings—and began to spark. It fell, beak open and smoking, to the ground.

Furious, Yolanda whipped her gun around while she scoured the trees. Amara sucked in a bolstering breath. *Go big or go home,* she reflected and, using her shoulder, went for her cousin's knees.

If the bridge had been susceptible to sound vibrations, Yolanda's shriek would have brought it down. She fell sideways but kicked out hard and caught Amara in the hip with the heel of her boot.

Wind swirled a thick patch of fog between them. Unfortunately that left only one direction for Amara to take. If she wanted to escape, she'd have to cross Bellam Bridge.

She knew there must be a raven tamer in the vicinity. There often was, and they hadn't all gone down to the Hollow for the parade. If this one was smart, however, he or she would stay out of sight.

Behind her, Yolanda fired several bullets.

"Where are you?" she demanded. Her voice echoed into and back out of the chasm below. She fired again and again. "I've got tons of ammo, cousin. Come out where I can see you or I'll keep shooting into the fog."

Amara crouched behind one of the damaged supports. Her heart had long ago made a home for itself in her throat. Should she attempt to cross the bridge or go wide and circle?

She dipped as a bullet zinged off the support and whizzed past her ear. The near hit made the choice for her. She'd go with the bridge, where the fog was thickest and Yolanda might not think to look.

Uttering every prayer she knew, Amara started across on trembling hands and knees.

A hoarse caw tore through the damp air. Glancing up, she thought she saw a raven go into a nosedive. Several yards back, Yolanda screamed.

Grateful for the distraction, Amara crawled on.

The planks sagged and made dreadful noises, but thankfully none of them broke all the way through.

Her teeth were chattering, she realized. She had splinters in her palms and at least one nail had spiked her knee.

More caws reached her and too many shrieks to count. Then suddenly she heard a thud, like boot heels on wood.

Her eyes closed and her heart plunged into her stomach. Yolanda was on the bridge.

She needed to move faster. No time now to test her weight on the planks.

Squinting through a gap in the fog, she spied a support

post. A raven sat unmoving on one of the pegs that jutted out of it. Unlike its predecessors, however, this bird didn't dive. It simply sat and stared.

A watcher, she thought, and recalled Brigham's words about emissary ravens. Breathing carefully, she offered a heartfelt "I hope you're watching for someone good."

"Its talons are caught in my hair!" Yolanda screeched. "Where are these stupid birds coming from? They're in my freaking hair!"

She was close, Amara realized. Fear spiked—then shot off the scale as Yolanda's frantic fingers trapped her ankle.

But only for a moment. Amara was tugging on her foot when one of the planks gave a long, low groan—and snapped.

Yolanda warbled out a sound between a scream and a sob and fought to grab the broken wood. One moment her fingers were clawing at the splintered end; the next they were gone and only slithering coils of fog remained.

Amara stared at the empty space for several shocked seconds, unable to move or to think. Stared until the raven watching her released a startled caw.

Her head shot up. The wood beneath her protested. It didn't snap as it had for Yolanda. Instead it pulled away from the side of the bridge.

Her scrabbling fingers found a rusted metal bar. But the bar was pulling away as well, and it was too narrow for her to hold in any case.

Overhead, the raven cawed again. And again and again. When it stopped, a strong hand grasped her wrist.

"I've got you, Red." McVey's voice reached her from the girder above. "Just hold on tight and don't look down."

A dozen emotions swamped her, but the one that stood out, that caused her breath to hitch, was that Yolanda hadn't lied. McVey was alive!

Half a lifetime passed in Amara's tortured mind before her knees touched solid wood again. Although solid was a questionable description for the worn plank that currently held not only her weight but also McVey's. Risking it, she threw her arms around his neck and crushed her mouth to his.

"You came," she said between kisses. "How did you know where to come?"

Taking her face in his hands, he looked into her eyes. "Once I figured out who the killer had to be, only the manor made sense. We took a roundabout route."

"We?"

"Brigham's here."

A sigh rushed out. "He brought his ravens, didn't— Oh, my God, Yolanda!"

She pivoted, heard the plank beneath them groan.

Catching her arms, McVey stilled her. "Don't bounce too much, Red. Even raven tamer ingenuity has its limits where ancient bridges are concerned."

"So we lead you to believe." Brigham's growl came from a cloud of fog. "Yolanda's right here. The rope she was holding tangled on one of the supports. I've got her now. Do you want me to haul the murdering witch up or develop butterfingers and end the problem tonight?"

McVey raised a brow. "Your call, Amara."

Now that the worst of her terror had subsided, Amara could hear Yolanda's combination of girlish squeals and vicious threats. "Well, damn." Sighing, she glanced up at him. "You know, I'd love to be lofty about this and prove how much better I am than her, but I guess I'm only human in the end. Haul her up, Brigham," she said. "She's insane, and one day I might actually pity her for that. But for now? I want the witch to burn."

Chapter Nineteen

The way McVey saw it, where there was crime there should be punishment. It didn't always work that way, but when it did, there wasn't a whole lot that made him feel better. Unless you switched gears and started talking sex. Specifically, sex with Amara, which he hoped would cap off one of the most gut-wrenching, yet strangely satisfying nights of his life.

Five long hours after he'd pulled her up onto Bellam Bridge, Amara pulled him to a stop on the main street of the Hollow. "How on earth can you call anything about this night satisfying, McVey? Uncle Lazarus is in a hospital in Bangor...."

"Resting comfortably, Red." He held up two fingers at the raven tamer who was manning the street-side bar, which, in strict legal terms, didn't exist. "You talked to his doctor. Your uncle's day-to-day. Has been for quite some time."

"A fact you apparently knew and I didn't."

"He told me the morning after I arrested him for punching the courier. He asked me not to tell anyone. You're part of anyone."

"I'm his niece, McVey. I'm also a physician. I could have..."

"What? Said, 'There, there,' and prescribed morphine

for the pain? He didn't want that. Private and proud's the way he's built."

She blew out a breath. "Damn…him for keeping a secret like that and you for being right. Damn Yolanda, too, for being…well, Yolanda, and wanting everything for herself."

Accepting two glasses of raven's blood from the grinning tamer, McVey handed her one. "You know her lawyer's going to plead insanity."

"He doesn't have to claim what's perfectly obvious." She watched animated ravens swoop and soar around a still-lively Main Street. "I'm not sure I think she was completely sane as a kid. And I've always thought her brother, Larry, was borderline."

"A man who handles explosives is only borderline sane?" Draping an arm across her shoulders, McVey summoned a lazy smile. "That idea might shake some people's faith a bit. Fortunately, any faith I ever had was shaken apart when I worked in Homicide. There are no absolutes, Amara. In the end, all anyone can do is his or her best."

"Thank you, Mike Brady. But back in this world, I still have questions."

"Will there be sex after they're answered?"

She laughed, and the sound of it made him want to drag her off the street and into the station house.

"Looks like I was right way back when, Chief McVey. You have definite animal—specifically wolf—instincts and appetites." She ran teasing fingers through the ends of his hair. "In this life anyway."

His eyes narrowed. "I knew we'd get here at some point. You're going to remind me I have Bellam blood in my background, aren't you?"

"You know you do. I don't have to remind you. When Nola Bellam married Hezekiah Blume, she already had a child, a daughter. According to one version of the Bellam legend—not to mention your recurring nightmare—it was Nola's daughter, Annalee, who brought about Sarah's confinement in the attic at Bellam Manor. In your dream, Sarah fell through a broken plank, but like Yolanda, she didn't plunge into the chasm below."

"Was Annalee a witch?"

"No one knows. With a little feathered help, though, she took mad Sarah out of the local picture." Amara angled her head. "Kind of the way you did with Yolanda tonight. Spooky, isn't it?"

"Very. But it was me and Brigham, not me alone on the bridge."

"I'd speculate that Annalee has more than one descendant, McVey. And every raven tamer has two parents."

"Pretty sure Brigham won't appreciate that particular speculation."

"He should. The mix of bloodlines is probably why he's so adept—one, at taming live ravens and, two, at creating animated ones. Which brings me to my really big question."

"How did we find you?"

"I already know that. You had to figure Yolanda would want to kill me in or around Bellam Manor, and what better way to do it than by using the bridge as her murder weapon? No, my big question is why did the bridge suddenly become crossable after Yolanda and I both fell through?"

"You and Yolanda didn't know where to walk. Brigham did. The raven tamers dislike intrusions into their privacy. They rigged the bridge to work safely for them and only them. For the rest of us, each crossing was a roll of the dice."

"Why does that sound illegal?"

"Call it marginally unethical, and think of it this way.

The land on both sides of that bridge belongs to your uncle Lazarus. He's the only person legally entitled to file a lawsuit against them."

"Which he won't do because he's enjoying the fact that the person who killed Hannah was caught by one."

"The person who killed Hannah and tried on more than one occasion to kill you." McVey tapped his wineglass to hers. "She might have been in your uncle's will, but Yolanda was never your uncle's favorite niece. He mentioned something tonight about liking her mother and cutting Yolanda a break strictly for that reason."

"Yolanda's mother died in a car accident while I was in med school." Amara paused to watch a meticulously choreographed flock of ravens wing through the sky overhead. "Brigham's distraction helped. One of his animated ravens got its talons stuck in Yolanda's hair. She panicked. If I hadn't been so terrified, I'd have enjoyed watching her freak. She's lucky Brigham was there to pull her up."

"She's lucky that rope she had wrapped around her wrist caught on one of the supports."

Amara smiled. "I'm not thinking she'll see it that way." She paused then said, "It was the pink lipstick that gave it to me. Pink lipstick on a wineglass in Hannah's kitchen sink. Suddenly, I realized. We went through Hannah's things. She didn't wear makeup."

"And Willy Sparks had no reason to want Hannah dead."

"So Yolanda it was. Had to be. What about you? What gave it to you?"

"Her brother works with explosives. She'd have known how to set charges, and anyone can make a Molotov cocktail."

Amara frowned. "Do we know why she blew up the bar? Other than trying to kill me, of course, which would have been her primary motive. But I mean, destroy her own workplace?"

McVey shrugged. "I imagine she was making a statement of some sort."

"I suppose it makes sense from Yolanda's point of view. Uncle Lazarus left the Red Eye to her in his will. She was…unimpressed to say the least."

"I also saw the pink lipstick a split second before she whacked me with your uncle's cane," McVey said. "Then everything went from pink to black."

Tipping her head to the side, Amara rested it on his shoulder. "You have to admit, it's been a hugely eventful day."

"More than you probably know. I got word from Lieutenant Michaels's captain. Jimmy Sparks is dying."

"There seems to be a lot of that going around."

"His position within the family has been taken over by his sister. Rumor has it she's much less vindictive than her brother."

"I really, seriously, hope that's true." When a raven glided in for a landing on one of the wagons, Amara waved her glass at it. "That bird's been popping up everywhere I go since we got back to town. I recognize it by the small gray streak on its head."

McVey grinned. "At the risk of repeating myself, male ravens around here have damn good taste."

She traced the outline of its sleek black wings and shiny feathered head. "I wonder if he's the same raven I saw on the bridge."

"You saw a raven on the bridge?"

She batted his stomach. "Yes, I did, and so did you. You must have. It was sitting right above your head."

"Are you sure it was real?"

"Positive. The tamers are good, but no one's that good.

That raven, like this one, was staring at me. Turning back to the legend, it's possible he was staring on behalf of someone who sent him."

"And that would be?"

"Not Yolanda's brother. And not Jake. I'd say Uncle Lazarus, except he doesn't believe."

"That you know of."

Amara chuckled. "My uncle's a practical man, McVey. Practical men don't buy into legends."

"Once again—that you know of."

"Right." Laughing, she turned to face him and hook an arm around his neck. "So, ignoring the raven, which isn't as easy as you might think, where does that leave us?"

He slid his fingers through her hair, nudged her head up a notch. "I guess the answer to that depends on you. You're going to be a very rich woman in a very short time. You'll be able to come and go as you please. Or stay if you'd prefer."

She regarded him through her lashes. "While I'm torn, I have to admit I'm leaning."

The raven gave an irritated caw and, even to McVey's eyes, appeared to glare at them.

Glancing over, Amara frowned. "Okay, now I'm the one who's spooked. That raven looks scarily like Uncle Lazarus in disapproval mode. Which makes me think I'm starting to buy in to the local legends, and I mean all the way in, because, if you think about it, what did Sarah Bellam ultimately want?"

"Hezekiah's fortune," McVey said without hesitation.

"Exactly. And her solution to the problem of attaining it, once she discovered she was pregnant with Ezekiel's child, was to eliminate anyone and everyone who might also lay claim to it. Add in the fact that she was a vindictive witch whose lover wanted her sister more than he wanted her, and you have the perfect recipe for murder. Two Blumes and a Bellam in Sarah's case."

"If she'd succeeded, and allowing for the fact that Lazarus's sister died without anyone's help, Yolanda had an eerily similar plan." McVey ran a thumb across her lower lip. "Kill you—a Bellam. Hannah—a Blume. And wait for Lazarus—also a Blume—to succumb."

"Two Blumes and a Bellam," Amara said. "And you thwarted their plans in both lifetimes. That's an impressive score, Annalee."

A smile touched McVey's mouth as the raven flapped impatient wings. "No comment."

Amara finished her wine. "A little bird—not him—told me Ty and Molly have decided to relocate to Florida. He also mentioned that late this very afternoon you were offered Ty's job here in the Hollow. One chief, two towns and the saddest excuse for a medical clinic I've ever seen… Am I avoiding the real question here?"

"If the question is where should we have sex, I'll be happy to supply the answer."

She teased him with her eyes. "Answer this instead. Do you want me to stay?"

He held her gaze. "Yes."

"Then I'll stay."

"Good answer, Red."

As he lowered his head, McVey saw the raven spread its wings. It stared a moment longer, then flew off as silently as it had arrived.

If there was anything at all to the local legends, he hoped Lazarus Blume would fall asleep smiling tonight.

* * * * *